HELLER

DYLAN DEGRAVE

For Chelsea, my light in the darkness.

1

DELSON

THE BIRD AND THE WORM

I SOMETIMES WONDER if it's the people who curse Heller County, or the county that cursed the people. Sometimes I wonder if I believe in curses.

"ROBBERY AT HELLER MUSEUM!" is the top story in *Blackroot News Daily*.

Hardly a mention of the security guard who was killed.

I light a smoke, inhaling a hodgepodge of toxic vapor and icy morning air as I fold the newspaper into a floppy airplane. I send it, but it only makes it as far as the front yard.

The shingles of the roof beneath me are slick with a thin, decomposing layer of frost. The sky is a cold, pale blue, streaked with highlights of orange that bleed overhead like outstretched fingers clawing through the clouds. I lift my camera—an old DSLR—from the strap around my neck and peer through the viewfinder.

I zoom in on the horizon: the dark ocean in the distance. Lazy fingers adjust the focusing ring, blurring the trees in the foreground. The photo doesn't quite capture what I hoped it would, but like everything else, it's close enough.

Most things in Heller County are just that—close enough. Almost beautiful. Almost happy. Almost true. Almost living.

There's nothing particularly special about this place. In fact, some might say we take boredom very seriously here. *Bring your kids to Heller County. They'll get bored to death.*

From the outside—from an untrained eye—Blackroot looks just like you'd expect. Like any other small town in the Northwest, somewhere between safe and not safe enough.

Heller is decent, dull, even beautiful if you know where to look. But when you take a look behind the redwood curtain, when you peel back the layers of Pan-Am smiles and forced civility—the mask lifts. You may not like what you see.

The front door squeaks below. I take another drag and exhale a tendril of smoke. Couldn't be Rachel—she won't wake from her coma-like junkie slumber until late afternoon, if even then.

"Delson, what the hell you doin' up there?" Rick huffs from the front yard below.

Rachel's latest conquest in a long line of hopeless, romantic, drug-addicted man-children. At least Rick is just a drinker—doesn't seem to be hooked on much else.

He retrieves the half-crumpled pack of Lucky Strikes— his brand—from the breast pocket of his flannel and flicks a cigarette to his lips. He lights it, inhaling deep.

"Huh?" he probes, thick smoke billowing from his nostrils.

"The hell's it look like I'm doing?" I call back.

He smiles, dragging slow. His dark eyes peer up at me from behind a foggy sigh. He's a bear of a man—hair matches his eyes, salt-and-pepper beard, a shadow clinging to his square jaw.

"You even crash?" he asks. "Or you been up there all night?"

"I slept," I say, pulling the cigarette from my lips. The smoke fades into the mist.

"Early bird gets the worm," he says lightly.

"It's funny, I feel like the worm."

His eyes drop to the ground. "You're eighteen, right?"

"In ten months."

"Shouldn't be smoking." He grimaces. "Look, it's still early. How about we go grab some breakfast before school? You still go to school, right?"

I chuckle and turn back to the bay. Golden light dances on the black water, a warped reflection of the sky.

"I'll pass... Go wake Sleeping Beauty. I'm sure she'd be thrilled." I take another drag. "If she doesn't wake up, number for the ambulance is on the fridge."

Rick drops his halfie and crushes it under his boot. The tendons bulge in his neck, his version of disapproval. I've come to recognize the signs. The roof shakes slightly when he slams the door.

I climb back through my bedroom window, grab my bag, and tuck the small silver heart-shaped locket into the inside pocket of my coat.

Uneven, creaky steps tell the story of a lost boy descending toward the kitchen. The air bites at my nostrils. The sink is piled high with dishes, mold thriving and festering. Empty liquor bottles, cans, and fast-food wrappers claim the counters and floors. I have to remind myself not everyone lives like this. Not that I'm complaining. The seasons change, you adapt. Even the strange shape of Rachel on the couch, cigarette burnt down to the filter—still stuck between her fingers—nose, red and raw, cheeks sunken, dark bags for eyes... not even this fazes me anymore. I stop there in the living room beside the woman. I light another smoke, ignoring Rick as he eyes me from the recliner.

It wasn't always like this. Rachel kicked the drugs and booze once before. But even as a child, I didn't get too comfortable with the idea. Rachel's been hard to trust my whole life, and after Kenzie was born, she started using again. It's been almost eight years and I can't even remember the last time the three of us were together as a family.

"Don't look at your mom like that. What's wrong with you?" Rick grumbles. His tone is stern, but not loud.

I fill my lungs with harsh smoke and exhale across the room, where the gray light from between the curtains catches the tendrils.

"Why are you still hanging around, man?" I say, cigarette bouncing between my lips. "We're not a charity. I don't need your help."

"Maybe your mom's the one who needs help." The floorboards groan under his weight as he stands.

We're about the same height, but he's broader, and he's got at least a hundred pounds on me. But I know I'm faster. My fists clench—just in case. Not that it's ever come to that. Not yet.

"Thank God she has you to pick up the pieces," I sneer, wishing my sarcasm stung more than it seems to. I grab

Rachel's purse off the coffee table and fish out a wad of twenties from her wallet.

"Really? Wonder what your dad would think."

"Yeah, me too," I say, stuffing the bills into my breast pocket. "She wouldn't be collecting a welfare check if it weren't for me. This is, like, my cut. Right?"

I leave before we really get into it, slamming the door for good measure.

HARDENED FEELINGS WORSEN. Intensify. When tears cease to flow, the steel-colored clouds roll in. The silver lining's just a winter mirage. A manifestation of innocence, robbed and manipulated by evil. It embeds itself in wood and stone. It lingers.

Fall is upon us again, and with it, the seasonal invasion of townies crowding The Serpent And The Rainbow. Voices chatter from a line that stretches from register to door, gossiping about the museum break-in. We can't seem to go a year without blood being spilled.

Adele Medot—the owner—waves me forward from behind the counter. I slip past the line. The smell of fresh coffee and bagels cuts through the morning breath and cheap perfume.

"Usual, kiddo?" she asks, tying her wild dark hair back.

"Please and thank you," I smile, avoiding eye contact with the vultures staring me down.

The voodoo atmosphere of the interior this time of year is alluring. It holds a certain... Je *ne sais quoi*.

Adele puts on her busy-shop-smile, setting my usual—a

small black coffee and garlic bagel—on the counter. I reach for my cash.

"No charge. It's sweater season," she says with a wink. Her light brown skin shimmers with small beads of sweat.

"I can stay if you need a hand," I offer.

"Not a chance. Get your ass to school."

I salute half-heartedly, dodging dirty looks, soccer moms and other PTA parents. On the way out I flash my camera behind me. *Click.* If I had to title it, I'd call it *Holier Than Thou.*

A deadpan stare from a static figure turns my ankles into anchors. The tall raven-haired woman across the street looks like a living statue, apart from her glassy eyes that follow my every move. I meet her gaze.

"Is there something I can help you with?" I ask. She doesn't move. She doesn't answer. "Hey, lady..." I fish for a response. Her eyes linger, locked on mine. Lips part, though no words come. I lift my camera and focus on the petrified woman. With a click and whir, I snap the photo.

"Come, boy!" A shrill, throaty voice.

My heart slams into my ribs as a massive black dog appears at my side, like a hellhound conjured from the fog. The woman breaks eye contact and walks away.

The junkies in this town have evolved. Learned to blend in. It's the eyes that give them away, though. Something missing. Or something's sort of... *off,* but that *thing,* you can't quite put your finger on. In my experience, trust your gut; when you feel that dull tug in your stomach, *listen* to it.

The brick clock tower looms in the distance, a rust-colored spire leering over the rooftops of Old Town. As I approach Blackroot High School, a chill tumbles down my spine. The school is like any other building around, like the clock tower, an old ugly skeleton with fresh paint and other things like lawn gnomes or rose bushes. Never mind the tragedy of 1982 when the theater building burned down during the school's rendition of Arthur Miller's The Crucible, killing nearly everyone inside. Fourteen-year-old Allen Ross set the blaze. When asked why, he said, *Why not?* When told why not, he laughed. Didn't stop laughing—not until they found the bodies of his family buried beneath the floorboards. Neighbors complained of a smell.

Never mind that the campus itself, where the school sits so innocently, was the place of a cruel raid on the Natives who owned this land. The perpetrators slaughtered many and forced the survivors onto Bellflower island. That arrangement didn't last long.

This place breeds sickness. Everyone in Blackroot wears masks, and school is no different. I sit by myself in the court-yard, watching as my peers rush around like chickens missing their heads. You can determine with just a quick observation that all they know as truth is right in front of them. They think everything is fine. It's all quite simple for them. Right now, high school is their world. It's like every one of them thinks they're the star of their very own show— certified Fresh on Rotten Tomatoes—and the main character always makes it out in the end. But even I have to admit, not everything here is awful.

Rose Bailey—the White Rose of Blackroot, the town's girl-next-door—approaches. Textbooks clutched to her chest. Her silvery hair floats just above her shoulders in loose curls, held back by a black headband. Her eyes gleam, her smile radiates kindness. She's a light in the dark.

"Delson, I was hoping to catch you before class." Her voice melts the ice on my shoulder.

I say her name, savoring the mild sort of high it gives me.

"I read your editorial," she continues. "Honestly, it really touched me. I see the vision."

"Really?" I try to sound casual.

"Absolutely." She sits beside me. "A town built on blood and lies, hiding behind masks and pretense." She mimics my voice.

"I don't sound like that."

"But you do." She laughs.

"Kind of bleak, don't you think?"

"No, it's more beautiful," she says.

Intrigued by her, I lean in. "Beautiful," I repeat, thinking more of her than my work.

"The way it's presented, it's more so a call to action. It's like, this is what we are, this is what we have and what we are working with. This is what we've done. Let's own it. Do something about it. Don't be afraid to admit to your faults, but you must join the battle for betterment. You know?"

"I, uh, like your thought process." I chuckle. "But yeah, you're picking up some pieces."

Her cheeks pinken with a smile. "Anyway, got plans for lunch?"

"Lunch. Well, actually, I have to speak with Principal Myers during lunch."

"Well, how about after school?"

I hesitate, finding myself questioning her interest in *me*. Her true intent. She has a guy like Sam Lewis begging for her to take him back. And I'm just me.

"I'd like to, but I can't. I'm a little busy this afternoon."

Her brows pinch, surprised. She's not used to hearing no.

"I promised Kenzie I'd take her for ice cream," I say. "You're welcome to join us. Around four. At The Serpent?"

Her smile returns. "I'd love to meet her." She rises, books back to her chest. "It's a date."

"Assuming either of us lives that long," I mutter as she walks away.

"I wouldn't bet against *me*, Delson Heller."

She sounds half-serious.

IT'S like watching a zombie movie. Not the kind where the zombies drag ass, limp around groaning—more like the kind where they're rabid, can sprint marathons and pole-vault. Well, maybe not *that* extreme. But close. My peers shove and jostle through the corridors. The halls, chaotic and wild. Shouting erupts from farther down. Even my heart races. This is a busy week for Blackroot. First the museum gets robbed, then...I hear what sounds like cop chatter over radios. I only catch fragments.

"Cops," someone says amid the clamor of voices.

"In his locker," another blurts out.

"They found a bunch of drugs—he's screwed!" gasps someone nearby.

My heart skips a beat. I left Trueheart's stash in *my* locker. The money, the drugs, everything. I scan the hall, searching for a way out, ready to bolt—until I see the cops. They're cuffing Sam Lewis.

That's not good. Well, not for Sam, at least. The weight lifts from my chest. His eyes meet mine as the officers guide him past the rest of us. He looks embarrassed, mostly angry. And yeah, maybe it's poor taste, but I raise my camera and snap a photo.

For just a moment, some insignificant sign of our shadow has emerged. Inconsequential in the grand scheme. Though this will be a full-blown tragedy to some. Sam was on his way up. Football could've taken him to college, shit, maybe even the pros. But in one blink, it's gone. Future, scholarship, career, all snuffed out. The curse of the quarterback strikes again.

Still, it could be worse. The school will recover. The community will rally. The team will rebuild. This isn't like last time. Ian Bloom's murder *shattered* this school. It's hard not to think of Ian most days, especially with the shrine still standing—his awards, photos, and old headlines sealed behind wood and glass near the front office. The school even printed those huge memorial banners and hung them in the gym. They're still up there. The school, hell, even the town seemed to pause in time for a while. Like everything else though, the dirty details, sobs and outcry sank down into the murky bog, left forgotten. Just took longer than usual.

In any case, I haven't forgotten.

And neither has Edward.

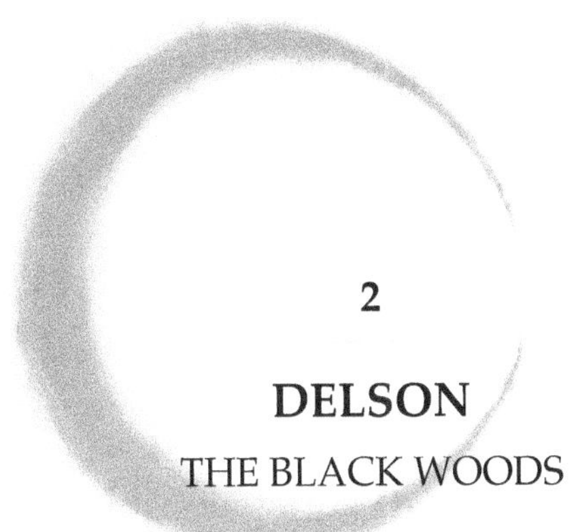

2

DELSON

THE BLACK WOODS

I'M LATE. On my way to the office, I squeeze past stragglers drifting toward the cafeteria in small clusters.

The office is too warm. Mrs. Duncan sits behind her desk, wiping the sweat from her forehead. In slight frustration, she pushes her bright orange hair from her face—plastered there by the heat—and looks up from her computer monitor.

"What can I do for you?" she asks.

My fingertips tap rhythmically on the counter while I explain my planned meeting with Mr. Myers. She turns her head toward his office, but before she can speak, the door opens.

"Come in, Delson." His tone, sharper than usual. Almost strident. No doubt because of Sam's arrest.

I give Mrs. Duncan a smile and head into Myers' office. I sit down in the chair across from him. He's a well liked and unique looking guy. He has Vitiligo—a condition that leaves patches of pigment loss—so pale blotches stand out on his otherwise dark complexion. The most visible ones are on his face and hands. He's a private man. His desk is perfectly organized, a shrine to his neat-freak tendencies. Nothing out of place. No family photos. No framed kids' drawings. Nothing personal.

"Mr. Heller," he says, voice tight.

"Whoa—okay. You only call me Mr. Heller when you're pissed," I say, suddenly on edge.

He sighs. "I've gotten some complaints, Delson."

"Complaints?" I echo. "About what?"

"Your work on the paper."

"Oh, come on." My eyes roll instinctively.

"I'm sorry. I am." His tone is both apologetic and firm. "But I have to take you off the paper." He won't meet my eyes.

"You're joking," I say, hoping he is.

He looks away, searching for the right words. I knock on his desk to snap him back to the moment.

"Hey!" I bark. "Would you rather I put my tail between my legs, like the clowns who write for BND? You read that hack-job this morning?"

"I fail to see your point." His forehead wrinkles.

"Did you know someone stole a set of journals from the museum? Along with personal items—an old pocket watch, photos, some jewelry?"

He nods slowly, eyes flicking up like he's holding back a sigh.

"A woman was shot and killed, but no one cares. All anyone talks about are the missing heirlooms. Why?"

"Perhaps the journals belonged to important local historical figures."

"Then why didn't they release any specifics about the

journals? No names, very vague actually. All we know is that they belonged to founders."

His eyes meet mine for only a second. "I'm sorry, there's nothing I can do. I have to remove you from the paper."

"You're serious right now, aren't you?" I ask as the realization washes over me.

"I'm afraid so."

I have nothing to say back to him. If I open my mouth, I'll end up suspended. He leans in, expression softening.

"Delson, you're a great kid. Life gave you a shit hand, I know that. Believe me, I do." He taps his pen against the desk. "You see the madness around you, and instead of pretending it's normal, you speak up. I respect that. But not everyone else does. Your words..." He trails off with another sigh. "They're too loud for fragile ears."

"What the hell does that even mean?" I ask, exasperated.

"It means it's time to be quiet for a while." He clears his throat. "We'll revisit this in a few months, see where things stand."

"Fine," I mutter, gritting my teeth and leave the office.

School is out, and all is right in the world, according to the ravenous zombies that crowd the hallways and funnel out through the exits. They pack the bus stop and shuffle into the parking lot, eyes glued down to their phones. Edward's big black truck catches my eye as he leans against it. Alissa stands across from him, arms crossed tight over her chest. Her long ginger hair flows around her shoulders, and the raw skin under her eyes tells the whole story. She presses her lips flat, holding back tears, then rips off her ring and hurls it in Edward's face. Her puffy eyes meet mine as she storms past—hurt, humiliated.

It was only a matter of time, I guess. I wish I could comfort her like I used to. Just be someone who listens. Someone she could lean on, even if it's just to vent. When did we become strangers? When do friends stop being friends?

Edward tears off his jacket and tosses it in the cab of his truck. He slams the door and grips his hands over the back of his head. A half laugh, half cry rips out from his throat. It's short but I catch it. His hands run down over his face as reality smacks him upside his head. His usual tame, sculpted dark hairdo is left messy. I can't even remember the last time he and I shared a conversation. I approach him with caution, making sure he sees me coming. His cheeks burn red as his eyes track me.

I ask if he's alright, thinking the gesture alone might show I still care. He stares at the gravel beneath his boots.

"Not now," he snaps.

I chuckle, unable to keep the sarcasm out of my voice. It's my default when things get uncomfortable.

"Right. Fuck me for checking in. My bad, buddy." I shake my head and turn to walk away.

"Listen."

His voice is softer now. I stop, only a few steps away, and turn back to face him.

"I'm sorry, Del. I'm just going through some shit right now." He slams his balled-up fist onto the truck's hood.

I join him there, leaning against the metal beside him.

"Breakups suck. Alissa's great—and so are you. You guys'll make it through."

He rolls his eyes. "Nah, man. It's over. For real. And it's not just us. Everything's messed up right now."

"The Sam thing?" I ask.

"That's part of it. Now the team is counting on me. When Ian died—" Another half laugh, half cry escapes. "Shits just been falling apart, man, one thing after another."

"I understand. I'm here, Eddie. You know that," I remind him.

"You've dealt with enough. I understand you have your own issues." He assures me.

"You lost your brother." I pause. "I know that you've been off dealing with everything in your own way, but I'm still here for you."

His jaw tightens. "I know, man. Since day one."

"Since day one." We bump fists and pull into a half-hug.

"You headed home?" he asks. "I'll give you a lift."

"Nah, I'm going to The Serpent."

"You working there now?"

"Oh—no. I'm meeting someone. Interview."

It's a lie, but it slides off easily.

"Well hey, I'm heading there too. A couple of the guys are trying to rizz up the owner," he says, climbing into the truck with a smirk.

"Adele?" I laugh. "Tell them not to waste their time."

"What, she saving herself for you?" he fires back, laughing for real this time.

"Thinking maybe it has a little more to do with that," I say, pointing out two of the guys from the team. One plugs a single nostril and blows a thick wad onto the pavement, showing the results to the other, who seems genuinely impressed. Two monkeys having a shitball fight couldn't be happier.

SOME GUYS from the football team glance over as Edward and I walk through the coffee shop door. Their laughter dies, replaced by suspicious glares. I shrug it off. So does Edward.

"Better get to the girls," I say with a dry chuckle, nudging him toward the testosterone-soaked table.

He smirks. "And you wonder why they want to kick your ass."

"I never said that." I leave him to his teammates, wave to Adele behind the counter, and head toward the back.

Trueheart is slouched in the far corner, half-buried in his oversized pink hoodie. The hood's pulled tight around his face, and a pair of squared-off sunglasses hides his eyes. An unlit cigarette dangles from his lips, bouncing as he mutters to himself while scrolling through his phone way too fast to be reading anything.

A couple years back, our parents started dating. Somehow convinced it was serious. Their junkie romance made both Frankie and me nauseous. So we bonded over mutual disgust, sarcasm, and strategic avoidance. When things got bad at home, he'd take me for long drives. Anything to get my mind on other things. I figured I had become desensitized to it all over the years, but he could tell when things became too much to handle. He is by no means a contributing member of society, but he has a good heart.

"You wanna make out, or you just gonna stand there and picture me naked?" he oozes his usual. "Jesus, Heller, sit down." He smirks. The unlit cigarette still hangs from his lips.

"Trueheart," I greet him as I take a seat.

He pulls his hood back and pops off the sunglasses, revealing deep shadows under pale eyes. His skin is washed-out, all color drained.

"We're friends, right?" he asks, removing the cigarette and twirling it between his fingers.

"'Friend' might be stretching it a little…"

"We've been working together for over a year now. How many times I gotta tell you? It's Frankie. Or Frank, if you prefer." He shrugs and returns the cigarette to his lips.

"You keep calling me Heller, I'll keep calling you True-heart." I smirk.

He grins and rolls up the sleeves of his hoodie, revealing a scattershot mess of tattoos like cheap patches sewn on too fast.

"Alright, Delson. So, how'd you make out?"

I lean forward. "Yesterday wasn't bad. Today? Nothing."

"Nothing?" his brow lifts.

I shake my head. "Too risky. Cops were crawling all over campus. They got Sam Lewis. I didn't even know he was dealing."

Frankie scoffs. "Yeah. You're welcome."

My eyes narrow. "What?"

He shrugs.

"You're kidding." I flinch at the sound of my own voice.

"Anonymous call," he says, giving me a wink.

"You really think he deserved that? You that scared of a little competition?"

"Listen, you little shit. Kids were ending up in the ER. Lucky I stepped in before someone ended up dead."

My jaw slackens. "I didn't know."

"Fentanyl's a helluva drug." He sighs. "Dude deserves

whatever he gets. Shouldn't be pushing poison to kids anyway." The cigarette bobs as he smiles. "Besides, wasn't he sniffin' around your girl?"

"And having a kid push for you—that's fine?"

"You're mature for your age."

I slide my backpack onto the table. He grabs it, pulls it under the table between his legs, then tosses a different one to me—already packed and prepped, no doubt.

He unzips the bag at his feet, glancing inside with a satisfied grin.

"Not bad for just a week." He slides a roll of bills across the table, rubber-banded tight.

I palm it, slip it into my lap, then slide it into my coat pocket with the other hand.

"Five hundred gonna float you?"

I nod. "Should be enough."

He eyes the new bag in front of me. "I threw in a little something extra."

He leans back in his chair like the world's just background noise, and I'm never entirely sure if he knows this is real life or not.

"You know I don't touch this shit," I say.

"Relax. Not like that. You know I only look out for your stupid ass." He grins.

I unzip the bag to investigate. His hand lands over mine.

"Not here." He gives a slight nod.

The door cracks open, letting the cool breeze rush through the shop. Two girls walk in, smiles just settling from laughs. I recognize Alissa. Her eye catches Eddie's table and her smile vanishes. She blocks her sight of him with her wavy red locks. Our eyes meet and she forces a small smile. I give a sort of apologetic one back.

It's hard watching things fall apart. The four of us used to be inseparable—Edward, Alissa, Rose, and me. Now those memories feel like someone else's dream. Or a bad trip.

I don't recognize the girl walking beside her at first. Her skin is a deep bronze, glowing in the cafe's light. Her hair—long, dark, and braided—spills over her shoulders, parts of it tied back with other braids. Her eyes are sharp and feline. Her lips are full and the soft color of faded roses. I'm staring. I know I am.

She glances my way.

"Friend of yours?" Frankie asks.

I turn back. "No."

He laughs, then checks his watch. "I'm out, man. Told Courtney I'd make it quick."

"Courtney Pierce?"

"The one and only."

"Isn't she a little young for you? And what happened to Lacey?"

His eyes widen. "Okay, first off—she's eighteen."

"She's in high sc—"

"She's EIGHTEEN," he repeats, firmly. "I only graduated four years ago. Don't start calling me *Unc* behind my back. And as for Lacey—" he shrugs, "That Tinder match? That was fleeting."

I lean in. "Courtney's one of Rose's best friends. She doesn't need to know about what we do."

"What, smoke crack and worship Satan?" he laughs. "Relax. Don't stress."

He checks his flashy new smartwatch. "I gotta bounce."

"Alright. I'll see you in a few days."

We both stand and sling our bags over our shoulders.

He shakes his head. "No. I have a sale set up for this weekend. Push nothing at school. It's too hot right now, understand?"

I nod, shrugging the strap over my shoulder a bit more.

He smiles, throwing his hood and dark glasses back on. Without warning, he kisses me on the cheek.

"Stay golden, Ponyboy." He whistles as he shuffles out of The Serpent.

A SMALL ORANGE flame flickers in my cupped hand, struggling against the wind. The cigarette bounces from my lips, fighting to catch the spark. Burning tobacco replaces the scent of fresh coffee. Overhead, the sky hangs heavy— smoky gray and brooding. Street gutters clog with dead leaves. Decrepit trees writhe in phantom pain as their naked spine-like branches sway against their will, battered by the lashing winds. I pull my hood up to comfort my numbing cheeks and ears.

It's a twenty-minute walk to Elias' house, a sprawling cream-colored Victorian tucked away from the bustle of Old Town Blackroot. Nose is raw and red by the time I get there. I trudge up the wide steps and knock on the heavy front door. Elias opens it almost immediately. Tall, blond, always dressed like he's headed somewhere important. His hair is tucked neatly behind his ears, his clean-shaven jawline set beneath a welcoming smile.

"Hey, there he is," he says.

Small feet slap the staircase. I smile back—just in time to catch the little monster who leaps into my arms.

"Delson!" Kenzie squeals, wrapping her arms tight around my neck. Her face presses to my chest as I lift her. Her long, straight hair is tied back with a white ribbon.

"Hey, Kenzie-cakes!" I jerk her back and forth in my arms as she giggles. "You're getting so heavy." I set her back down.

"Eight-year-olds are *supposed* to be heavy." She sticks her tongue out.

I repeat the number back to her, like it's some shocking revelation.

"Did you forget?" she slaps my arm. Her dad chuckles.

I bend down to her level, reaching into my coat pocket. "Forget? Never." I smile and pull out the small, heart-shaped locket on a delicate silver chain. "A day early, I know, but the suspense was killing me."

Her ocher eyes light up, smile stretching wide.

"Here." I clasp the chain gently around her neck.

It dangles just over her chest. She clutches it between her fingers, eyes wide, lips curling into a toothy grin.

"What's inside?" she asks.

"Open it." I wait as she fiddles with the tiny clasp. "It's so you know I'll always be around."

Her eyes land on the photo inside—a younger me, holding her as a baby.

"I love it." She hugs me tight.

"You're welcome, Kenzie-cakes." I kiss her forehead.

"Eugh!" She scrubs the spot with her palm.

My laugh masks my realization of how big she's getting.

"Are we getting ice cream?" she asks as she closes the locket and lets it drop back down.

"When have I ever broken a promise?" I say with a wink.

"One hour." Elias' wife, Kimberly, steps down from the long twisting staircase. The mood shifts in the room.

I twist my tongue nervously in my mouth. I keep my eyes off her out of respect. Instead, I focus on the oversized crystal chandelier above us.

"Kim," Elias says gently, "he's her brother." Then to me: "Just be back before dark." He pats my shoulder.

Her eyes flare at the contradiction.

"Grab a sweater, okay?" I tell Kenzie.

She bolts off and returns a moment later in a fluffy white one.

I take her hand and lead her out the door before an argument breaks out. She swings my arm back and forth as we walk down the sidewalk, avoiding all the cracks as we do.

"Don't step on a crack or you'll break your mother's back," she sings.

"We wouldn't want that, would we?" I snicker at the dark fantasy.

"Nope, nope, nope," she says, jumping over each split in the pavement. "Are we going to the creepy place?"

"Is that where you want to go?"

"Heck yes! She makes the *best* milkshakes!"

"I'll let her know." I chuckle.

Edward and his buddies still occupy their table. Adele is brushing off one of the dumb jocks trying to score her number.

"Hey, Mackenzie!" Adele beams over the counter.

Kenzie waves with a closed-eye smile.

"What can I get you two?"

"Tomorrow's this little tyrant's birthday. I promised her ice cream." I ruffle her hair.

She swats my hand away. "Strawberry shake, please!"

"Strawberry shake for the birthday girl, and for you?"

"Uh, same." I drop a twenty on the counter.

She waves her hand at me. "It's on the house. You know that."

I take the twenty back and stuff a hundred in the tip jar as she turns her back to us.

Kenzie tugs at my jacket. "I have to pee..." I glance at Adele.

"Go on back." She smirks.

I wait in the back hall outside the restroom. My mind drifts, vacant, as it always does when I'm idle. A voice—faint, muffled—pulls me back. I glance around. Empty. Then again. Conversation. Coming from the wall at the end of the hall. Thin structure. I realize it's bleed-through from the secondhand shop next door. Old place. Paper walls.

Adele brings the shakes to our table once we settle in. "Happy birthday, Mackenzie," she says, giving my shoulder a squeeze before returning to the register.

Alissa and the new girl approach our table.

"Hi, Kenzie!" Alissa sits next to her, the new girl next to me. "You're getting so big, it's crazy."

"Eight-year-olds *are* supposed to be big. It's not so crazy." She smirks, her nose pointed up.

"Eight already?" she asks. Kenzie nods her head as she sips her shake.

"You're very pretty, Kenzie," the stranger says beside me.

"I like your braids," she blurts as she nods. "What's your name?"

She laughs. "I'm Cordelia, but you can call me Cordy."

Alissa smirks, tugging playfully at Kenzie's ribbon.

"Stop it, Alissa," Kenzie orders through a mouthful of milkshake.

"Sorry." Alissa laughs, then looks at me. "It's good to see you, Delson."

"Likewise," I say, slurping the overly sweet milkshake.

A soft voice behind me says my name—uncertain, delicate.

"Rose. You made it." I turn in my chair.

"Wouldn't miss it." Her cheeks pinken as she smiles. Her eyes drift to Alissa and Cordelia, then back to me.

"We'll give you guys space," Alissa says, standing and patting Kenzie's head. She smirks at Rose before she and Cordy head to another table.

Rose takes the seat across from me, next to my sister. "Hello, Kenzie. I'm Rose." She offers a hand.

Kenzie stares, wide-eyed. "Your flippin' hair is like snow."

Rose laughs. Her crystalline eyes meet mine for a moment.

"You have *so* many girlfriends," Kenzie mutters at me.

I shush her before she can say more. "I don't," I say, smirking at Rose. "Want a shake? I'm getting you a milkshake."

I hustle to the counter.

"So, *The Serpent And The Rainbow*—what's that mean?" she asks as I set her shake down.

"Voodoo theme. Like the old horror film of the same name."

She tilts her head. "Can't say I've seen it."

"I'll let it slide... *this* time." I chuckle.

A gentle laugh escapes her. "So, I'd love to know what you're working on next for the paper."

Great... "Well, actually nothing." I admit. She questions me with her eyes. "I was fired." I force a smile.

Her eyes widen. "Fired, why?" she probes.

"Well, according to principal Myers, I'm—and I quote—too loud for fragile ears... whatever the hell that means."

"Really? That's ridiculous," she derides. "People never like to hear the truth."

"Tell me about it." I sigh.

Rose turns her attention to Kenzie. And after a couple of minutes, it's like I'm not there at all. She's good with her.

By the time on the wall, I realize our hour's up.

Kenzie waits with Adele while I walk Rose to her car.

"What're you doing later?" she asks.

"Thought I'd do some recon." I lift my camera by the strap.

Her face lights up. "Like how?"

I glance around playfully. "Gonna check out the museum. See what they're not telling us."

"Like investigative journalism." She beams.

"Right—minus the journalism part."

"I'll come with you."

"I don't think that's a good idea. We could get arrested. Or worse."

"Or we could uncover buried secrets. Isn't that the point?"

"Hold on, Nancy Drew—"

"No way. If you're going, I'm going," she says, matter-of-factly.

I take Kenzie's cold little hand just as the wind yanks the coffee shop door from my fingers. I spot Alissa and Cordelia parked across the street. They're looking at me. I tell myself it's just paranoia. Still, I catch the glance they share—the little poisonous laugh before they pull away. Just paranoia. Alissa's always been kind. I'm not so sure about Cordy. I grip Kenzie's hand tighter.

The sky is murky, swollen with clouds. The scent of rain lingers in the frigid gusts, numbing my cheeks. A small silver Honda pulls up beside us, screeching as it breaks to a stop. The passenger door swings open as Dane—Sam Lewis' brother—jumps out and starts toward me. Another jerks his way out of the back seat, his chest puffed out like a human-sized penguin—Paul—I recognize him from the football team. Notice another player is in the driver's seat. Must be Eric. I nudge Kenzie behind me and to the side.

"Think you're real smart, huh?" Dane grumbles.

I freeze in my tracks. "Compared to you? I'm fucking Einstein." I can't help myself.

He pushes me. "You got a big mouth, Heller. Time someone shuts it."

I catch myself from falling back, but I bump into Kenzie, and she nearly falls.

"Leave my brother alone!"

I kneel beside her. "Inside. Now." I hand her my camera. "Keep it safe."

She hesitates, fire flashing in her eyes, but then she backs off and runs for the door.

"What the hell's your problem?" I rise, adrenaline buzzing through my veins.

"You snitched on Sam," Dane snaps. "Don't play dumb."

"Jealous he had Rose first?" Paul adds. "So fucking cringe."

"Stupid ass didn't need my help getting caught," I mutter, brushing past the Rose jab.

Dane grabs the front of my coat and yanks hard, tearing the flannel underneath.

"This is serious, Heller."

I slap his hands off me. "And kids overdosing on fentanyl *isn't*?" I spit to the ground. "I hope this ruins his life."

I see it coming before it lands. I brace—jaw clenched—as Dane's fist connects below my right eye. He screams something at me as I tumble backward. I catch myself, hesitate, the blood already buzzing in my cheek.

I lunge at him, knocking him to the ground. Hunching over the top of him, one fist after the other slams down. I get a few good ones in. Blood coats his teeth, dark streaks smear from his nostrils to his cheeks and chin.

He swings from the left and hits me in the same spot as before. I fall to the ground and he claims the advantage. His left hand grips down around my neck, squeezing. Raising his other fist, he cocks it back. He pants through bloody teeth, and throws his fist down, eyes dark and furious.

My eyes close just as his weight shifts and I feel him tumble off me.

I open my eyes.

Edward.

He's straddling Dane now, holding him down.

I scramble to my feet. Paul stands a few feet off, unsure, fists twitching.

"Come on, then!" I call to him, wiping blood from my mouth.

Edward holds Dane down. "Calm down!" he shouts before getting up and stepping next to me. "Everybody fucking *chill*!"

"This isn't your business!" Dane growls, stumbling to his feet.

Edward keeps his hands loose, ready. "Maybe not," he says, then looks at me. "But I doubt this has anything to do with Delson, either."

"Fuck you, Bloom," Dane spits, red flecks staining the sidewalk.

Edward stays calm. "What's the issue?"

"He thinks I snitched on Sam," I say, voice flat. "Like I had time to care."

Edward shakes his head. "Dane, it wasn't a secret. Word was gonna get around. You think the cops don't have ears?"

Dane glares at me. "Watch your back, Heller. I mean it." He spits again, blood this time.

He and Paul storm off to the Honda. Tires screech. They're gone.

Across the street, a black SUV sits quietly. Mayor Lewis—Sam and Dane's dad—sits in the driver's seat. Could be mistaken, could be my visions a bit blurred from the crack to my orbital socket, but I swear he's smiling, maybe even laughing a little. And the Mayor/Father Of The Year Award goes to... he drives away.

Edward sighs, puffing out his cheeks. "Want a ride home?" he offers.

"Could you drop me and Kenzie off at her house?"

"No problem," he huffs.

I have him drop us off a block down from the house. Kenzie stares up at my swollen face as we walk, this time ignoring the cracks in the sidewalk.

"Why did that boy hurt you?" she asks. A small tear in her eye.

"Don't worry, I'm not hurt." I smirk down at her.

"Why was he so mean?"

I kneel. "Sometimes... people like to take their misery out on others. They think it will make them feel better, like bullies. But when they go home, they're just as miserable. Best not to tell your parents."

At the door, I knock. I keep my hood low to shield my face. Elias opens it and waves us inside.

"You have fun, princess?" light from the chandelier glows above us.

"Yes, Daddy. I had a strawberry milkshake. Adele makes them the best." Her sass returns.

He chuckles. "So I've heard." He claps a hand on my shoulder. "Come in. Stay a while."

I keep my head down. "I should probably get going."

Kenzie tugs at my sleeve. "Yes, stay!"

I can't say no to her. She drags me to the couch and plops down, patting the cushion beside her. I sit, carefully.

"Jesus..." Elias squints. "What happened to you? Did Kenzie see?"

I rub my forehead. "No, I'm sorry. Some jerk from school, thought I—it was a misunderstanding. And I sent her inside the instant I thought things might get physical." I peer at him from under my hood. "I'm really sorry."

"Let me look at that." He sits beside me. He lifts my chin as he examines my cheek. "Delson, she can't be around that kind of stuff."

"Listen, I know. I would never do anything to put her in danger. They totally blindsided me. Like I said, it was a complete misunderstanding."

He nods, letting go of my chin.

Kimberly walks in. Her eyes narrow as she sees my face, immediately sharpening.

"Elias. Can I speak to you in the other room? *Please.*" Her words are tight. Controlled.

He sighs and follows her out.

I turn to Kenzie, tuning out their hushed voices in the next room.

"Hey, Kenzie-cakes, got any new paintings to show me?"

She nods. "Go get 'em," I say with a wink. She smiles as she runs for her bedroom.

I could just leave now. Can't stomach another moment of Kim's judging eyes. But before I can make my escape, Kenzie flies back into the living room. A stack of paintings.

"Wow, you did this?" I ask, holding up the small canvas. The forest that she painted, shadows and splintered wood. Deep reds in the sky, bottomless blacks in the trees. Better than I could do without question. She nods.

Kim and Elias walk back in.

"Mackenzie, it's time for dinner." Kim's voice is stern.

"Can Delson stay?" she pleads.

"No. He's got to get home. It's late." Kim doesn't take her eyes off me.

"She's right. I should go." I rise, glancing again at the

painting. "Keep this up, okay? You'll be the most talented person to come out of Heller County."

"You can keep it," she says, wrapping me in a hug.

"Thanks, Kenzie-cakes." I kiss her forehead, even though I know she'll wipe it away.

3

DELSON

MYSTERY OF THE HELLER MUSEUM

ONCE HOME, I rush upstairs, ignoring Rachel wasting away on the couch and Rick clanging dishes in the kitchen. I open my MacBook Pro—courtesy of Frankie. I never asked where he got it. I'm not sure I'd like the answer. I print a few photos from the Heller Museum website, folding them up before slipping them in my pocket. With my camera in hand, I head downstairs.

"Where you goin'?" Rachel questions as I open the front door.

"Out."

"Dels—" Her voice is muffled by the now closed door.

I stop at the end of the driveway to light a smoke, pretending I don't see the person watching me from their car, just a half-block down.

I realize it's Rose and crush the cigarette under my foot on my way toward her car.

"Your eye!" her voice rises in alarm as she jumps out, grabbing my face with both hands.

"My mom's ex hits harder." I smirk as I buckle my seatbelt.

"That's not funny," she says, dead serious.

"Wasn't a joke." I flash her a grin.

She shakes her head. "When did this happen?"

"Right after you left. Some alpha-male douchebag trying to prove his worth." She demands a name like she's ready to hunt him down. "Not important," I say, nodding toward the road.

We pull up to the base of the bluff. A rusted barrier gate blocks the path.

"The park closed at five," Rose says, reading the yellow sign.

"I know," I say. "Circle back and park on the marsh side."

"Flashlights?" she asks, popping the trunk. The red interior light bathes her in a warm, blood-tinged glow.

I shake my head, and the red light disappears.

We move fast and low. The park's been closed for hours, but with the recent break-in, I don't know what kind of security they've got patrolling. We slip past the gate.

The Adventures of Delson and Rose. I can almost imagine the theme song.

"This way." I say, motioning for Rose to follow me up the side of the hill rather than follow the small serpentine road. I continue in a half-whisper, "The road leads right to the parking lot. It's completely open, and if there's security on the perimeter, they'll spot us."

"But other than the old Ingomar lodging house, it's just an open field up there on this side."

"True, but there's no light in the field. The parking lot has four streetlights; all come on at 5:00pm."

"Fair." She agrees and we continue up the side of the hill, drawing our hoods.

Once at the crest of the bluff, we scurry to the picket fence surrounding the garden behind the old Ingomar lodging house. In crouched positions, we move between fences, down the path separating the dirt plots. The back porch creaks under our joined weight as we flatten ourselves against the weathered siding.

We tiptoe across the groaning boards. I reach the window first.

"Careful," Rose whispers. "Security could be—"

"Right, okay." I swallow some air with a dry gulp.

The inside looks empty, motionless. But it's impossible to see past the dust on the glass. I grip the end of my jacket's sleeve and rub some dirt from the window. A bolt of frozen lighting crashes in my chest before spindling down my spine. The distinct shape of a woman watches me from the other side of the window, not six feet from us. I pull myself back beside Rose, clinging to the wall.

"I'm not sure she saw me." I breathe hard from my nose.

Rose frowns. Her brows pull closer when she steps around me, in careful, slow steps. There's a quick moment where our faces almost touch, her arms on either side of me, palms against the house. Her white curls corkscrew out from her hood in bunches. I give her a little room and scoot down until she's beside the window.

"Careful, if she sees us—"

She cuts me off. "Oh yeah," she says, now gazing through the glass. "The jig is up. She's got knitting needles, and she's not afraid to use them." Rose gestures to the window.

A mannequin in an old dress and bonnet, standing

amongst what remains of an old kitchen. Now frozen in time for elementary school kids to come gawk at during field trips.

My cheeks flush with embarrassment. "That was scary." I smile.

"Fear is inevitable. Don't fight it." Her smile is wicked and teasing.

I lead us away from the house, moving through the field. The bluff drops steeply on the west side. The Blackroot Mall, now decaying and half-abandoned, lies across the 101. Cars weave along the highway like silver insects. Some trickle into the mostly empty EV lot.

"We should stay low to—

I'm unable to finish the thought as my feet slide out from beneath me, and I slip down the steep bank over the highway. My fingers dig into moist dirt and rocks before finally clinging to protruding roots.

"Delson!" Rose cries out.

I curse under my breath, not sure if I should be worried or embarrassed.

Rose seems to flatten herself on the bluff above, her white curls dangling over the edge as she reaches out with her right hand.

"Can you reach?" she asks.

I examine the distance between us. "I think so."

My foot finds purchase on a rock jutting out of the bank. I hoist myself up until our hands clasp.

With a grunt, she helps pull me up.

We both spend a moment catching our breath, and when our eyes meet, neither of us can stifle a smile.

We stay crouched in the tree line, racing toward the

museum—a single-story maroon building. Moonlight beads across the grass, soaking my shoes by the time we reach the pine tree near the restrooms. Still no sign of security.

"So how do we get in?" she whispers. "More importantly—how do we not get arrested?"

"Kinda flying by the seat of my pants here," I admit.

She scans our surroundings, the gears in her head moving in secret, intelligent and meticulous configurations.

"I got it." She crouches near the picnic benches, digs something from the ground, then hoists a hunk of broken concrete up onto her shoulder. "Pocket," she says, gesturing with her chin.

I reach into her hoodie pocket and pull out a smooth, dense rock—about palm-sized.

"You any good at throwing?" she asks.

WE TAKE OUR POSITIONS. Rose hides around the far corner of the building. I perch in the branches of a tree just outside the spill of lamplight across the parking lot. Only one car sits out front—probably the guard's.

Rose looks back at me before striding forward. Shoes soles pattering a soft echo against the blacktop, her indomitable spirit ablaze as she brings the concrete chunk down through the rear window. In a spectacular burst, the glass shatters; time slows, and the fragmented window seems to hold its shape as the sound of it smashing fills the cool air. The alarm sings and Rose runs back to her hiding spot, a sobering alertness paints her face.

Within minutes, the guard staggers into the lot, leaving the museum door open.

"Ah, what the fuck!" he shouts. He examines his car, his hands on the back of his head. "Don't get paid enough for this shit, man!" he waves the key fob around, muttering curses until the alarm stops.

I cock my arm back, eye my target, and let the rock fly. The metal trashcan near the restrooms screams like a mountain lion. The security guard shines his light and runs toward the sound, now yelling at imaginary teenagers.

I drop from the branch and bolt to the museum entrance. Rose's hand finds mine, and we slip inside.

"So what are we looking for?" she pants.

"Any exhibits that were hit in the robbery."

"It was the Ingomar room, right?"

"Yeah. This way."

We pass the intricately woven baskets of hazel sticks and spruce roots, tribal garments and the authentic dugout canoe. Yellow tape flutters across the entry to the Ingomar room. Shards of glass litter the floor. Numbered markers, that I assume track the traces of blood left by the victim.

I reach into my pocket and pull out the folded pictures I printed earlier. I unfold them and hold them up, comparing them to the surrounding room.

"That's the journals that were stolen…" I glance at the smashed case, then back to the intact version, safe and sound in the photo. "It's the masks." I say matter-of-factly. I examine the smashed display, comparing it to the demented leather masks staring back from the photo.

"The masks?" Rose questions, but another voice interrupts her.

"Cops are on their way!" The voice yells from the front entrance.

"C'mon." I grab Rose's hand. She doesn't hesitate.

We sprint toward the fire exit. I slam into the crash bar. The door bursts open, siren blaring behind us.

We cut through the trees, circling the building, running the way we came. Through the field. Past the lodging house. Back through the gardens. Down the hill. We slide halfway on the wet grass before slowing near the little road.

Back in her car, we sit in silence, chests heaving.

Finally, Rose speaks. "Why would someone steal those old masks?"

I turn toward her. "Better question: Why would the media cover it up?"

We sit in silence again, finding ourselves lost in the black woods.

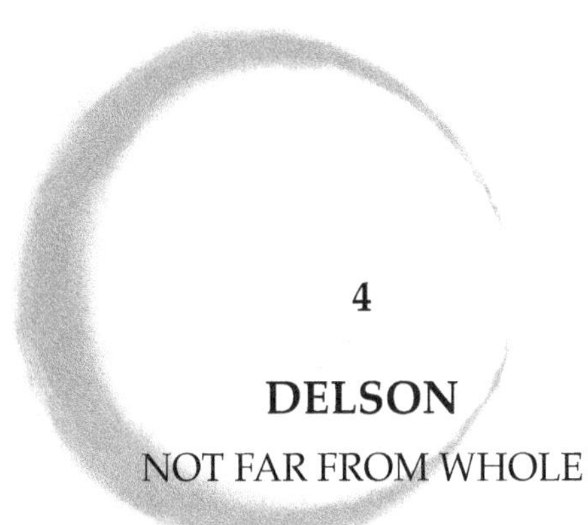

4

DELSON

NOT FAR FROM WHOLE

THE LIGHTS ARE on in the kitchen, and shadows from the TV flicker across the crooked, half-drawn blinds in the living room window. The sharp tang of stale cigarettes and the sweet rot of old booze bottles waft through the gaping front door.

I fish out a cigarette, anything to delay walking inside. The sky above churns—clouds bruised to a deep purple. I snap a photo of the skeletal trees beneath the storm, their silhouettes warped and sorrowful like Kenzie's painting. Tilted slightly, just off-kilter. Ominous. Hollow. Beautiful in the way rot can be. They say a picture's worth a thousand words, and this photo describes Heller county perfectly.

I throw my hood on and enter the house, closing and locking the door behind me. Rachel sits in the living room, cigarette in one hand, a drink in the other. The stench of mold snags at the bridge of my nose. I avoid eye contact, steer clear of Rachel altogether, and head for the kitchen.

Her stare weighs me down like an anchor sinking to the murky bottom of Heller Bay.

My eyes squint at the white light from the kitchen. We never use the fluorescent. I freeze in place when I realize the state of the room, it's *really* clean. Rick stands at the sink, sleeves rolled up, washing the last of what was a comically enormous pile of dishes. I open the refrigerator and stare. Settling on a lonely bottle of zero-sugar Coke, I pop the cap off with the butt of my lighter, making sure he hears the clatter as it hits the floor. His eyes catch mine.

"What are you doing?" I ask, the cold fizz burning down my throat.

"Dishes. What-in-the-shits it look like?" his voice is rough. "And pick that up, will ya? I didn't bust my ass for you to come in and piss on the floor."

I bend slowly, drop the cap in the trash. "Full of surprises, Dick—I mean Rick. My bad." I turn.

"Hold it," he says firmly.

I stop, sighing as I turn back, eyebrows raised.

He glances over his shoulder toward the living room, then back to me. Turns the water on full blast.

"Where'd you get the shiner?"

"Some asshole thought I was someone else."

He repeats my words like they're a joke.

"Something like that, yeah." I grin.

He rubs his jaw, thinking. "How's big man looking?"

"He's looked better." The corner of my mouth draws up.

He leans against the counter, still rubbing his jaw. "Good job." He says, patting my shoulder once.

"Right..." I move my shoulder from his paw. "Hey, just don't tell Rachel, okay?" I understandably ask.

"That's a big 10-9, kid." He frowns.

"You mean 10-4," I say.

"No, I mean 10-9. Y'see, 10-4 means copy, *understood.* 10-9 means I didn't quite catch that, say that again?" he gives a sort of flat smile as he meanders to the living room.

I shuffle up to my room and pop in my ear buds, setting Kenzie's painting and my camera on my bookshelf. I lay back and try to let the music take me away. The textured patterns on my ceiling morph in the darkness. Shadows from the trees outside sway back and forth against the wall.

I wait... it seems we're all waiting for something. Everyone. It can be as simple as a text back from a girl, or waiting for your purpose in life to rescue you from the monotony of yourself. Sometimes it feels like I'm just biding my time before the inevitable dirt nap. A release of all things, good and bad. Nonexistence, if such a thing can be. Or... not be?

I jolt awake as Rachel bursts into my room, flipping the light on.

"What the hell?" I mutter, sitting up, eyes squinting against the glare.

"Delson, what happened?" she snaps.

"Jesus, Rachel—"

"You been fighting?" she barks. "Picking fights at school now?!"

"It's nothing. It's not a big deal."

"Doesn't look like nothing." Her voice wavers under dark-ringed eyes.

"Since when do you care?"

"Delson!"

"It was a misunderstanding. It's over. Let it go."

"Do I need to go down to the school?"

"To do what?" I scoff. "Don't. I mean it."

She sits beside me. "I just want you to be safe."

"I just want to go back to sleep."

"I'm serious."

"You're giving me emotional whiplash, Rachel."

"What does that mean?" she asks. "And stop calling me that. I'm your mother."

I shake my head. "You don't get to have a meth addiction and a Mother-of-the-Year award. That's not how this works. Maybe start with a 24-hour chip, and we'll talk."

Her eyes turn glassy, catching the ceiling light as she gets up and leaves. I slam the door shut, kill the light, and climb out the window to perch on the roof and wait for sunrise.

MY MORNING HOLDS a striking resemblance to the morning before. The Serpent is packed. I shoulder through the crowd and grab my usual, flipping off the red-faced guy who tried to trip me last time. Not today, jackass.

The walk to school is lonely. My reflection in shop windows follows like a bruised ghost. Leaves scatter in flurries along the slick street. The brick clock tower looms above the marina like Blackroot's own Eye of Sauron.

I zone out, footsteps rhythmic. These moments—where my mind goes quiet, autopilot kicks in—I only appreciate them after they're gone. Not asleep. Not awake. Just... weightless.

A shoulder slams into mine as we pass each other. I mutter a thoughtless apology to the man and keep walking. My skin tingles ever so slightly as I pull the air deep in my chest—my senses widen—vision becomes sharp. The smell of morning dew on the grass becomes clear and crisp. A sense of unease rises. Almost anxiety. The man's steps have ceased. Only the sound of my shoes scuff the sidewalk. With a nimble glance, I check over my shoulder. He stares. Still. Blank. My muscles tense and my pace slows. His bloodshot eyes hang on me. He looks in rough shape, like he's peaking on something that's thrown him in a dark place. He looks normal otherwise, though anybody here could be using. Sometimes it's not who you'd expect. Often it's less the 'young delinquent' and more so the 'middle-aged housewife, soccer mom, President-of-the-PTA' type.

"Watch out for cars, man." I suggest not sparing another thought or glance.

Rose stands alone, leaning against the cyclone fence, her eyes set uninterestedly on her phone. She glances up.

I'm not sure who she sees when she looks at me. But I want to be him.

"Walk me to class?" she asks.

I take her hand.

God, I'm sick. Like one of them. I see her face—her smile. Her eyes, ocean-colored and full of something she doesn't let others see. For a second, my worries, my doubts, they melt, and I'm left feeling content. Nor far from whole.

Later, we stop by Kenzie's birthday party. Rose is pulled around the backyard like a celebrity. I trail behind, dodging Kim's dagger stares. We leave after cake, once Kenzie disappears into a game of tag.

A week later, we sit across from each other again at The Serpent. My place—now our place. We've dug and questioned and come up with nothing. No mention of the masks in the papers. When I asked the lady who wrote the article why she left out that detail, she played dumb. Did she really not know? Were they even reported stolen? When I made an anonymous call to the museum inquiring about showings of the Ingomar room, and more specifically the Blackroot Society masks, the man on the other line claimed the masks were temporarily on display with some 'traveling historic showcase' of the Northwest. He hurried me off the phone when I pressed further. Afterward I could find no trace of this little traveling museum online.

"My mom is out of town this weekend," she says, her eyes lost to the table.

"Oh, for sure..." I say.

"It's just me and I-I don't know." She nervously plucks at her lip. "Would you want to come over tonight?" She seems to stop breathing.

I don't want to say something dumb. Don't want to make the wrong decision and risk making a fool of myself. Risk sounding like I'm expecting something more. Guys are always pining for her. I can't be one of them. She deserves to know I see more of her.

"I can't tonight, actually..." Shame coats my tongue.

Her head drops. "Oh, okay. That's fine. Tomorrow?"

"Absolutely." I rush to explain. "Frankie needs help with something tonight. It's important. But tomorrow—yeah."

She smiles. "I'll call you."

"Perfect." My cheeks flush as she leans in and kisses just beneath my bruised eye. The door opens. Cold wind sweeps in. She disappears.

"Smile looks good on you," Adele says, wiping down a table.

"What do you mean?"

"Nothing. Just used to seeing you sulk around like a brooding teenage vampire." She tucks her rag in her back pocket. "It's nice. You look... happy."

Am I that obvious? I laugh. "It's not so bad."

At the door, I hesitate. "Hey, Adele... Can I ask you something?"

She doesn't even turn around. "Boy, you know you should've gone to that girl's house."

I laugh, sheepish. "Next time."

The sun has all but vanished and the lurching shadows in the sky hang overhead with ill intent. Though, the house is worse. There's no sign of Rick and Rachel's passed out in a pool of her own vomit. I check to see if she's still breathing. Her ribs expand and deflate in a steady rhythm. I head to my room and grab my camera and backpack before heading out the door. My phone buzzes. A text from Frankie.

> 1428 Oak Park Road. They're expecting you. I scoped it earlier. Big house party so bring it all. We making a killing tonight fr fr.

K.

I purge my mind of home as I drift through the east side of town, where the old Victorian homes still stand—tall, regal. Most have been remodeled inside and out, restored to polished elegance. But some look like they've clawed their way out of the dirt—sagging and rotted, like corpses too stubborn to stay buried. Leftovers from the early days, when the sickness of Heller County first began to fester and spread, poisoning the ground we built on.

One house sits on a hill, a grand white Victorian. A wrought-iron fence surrounds it, weaved in ivy. A single large oak tree sits in the spacious yard, desperately hanging on to the last leaf. I raise my camera, focus... and snap the photo. I check my viewfinder. It's chilling. Hauntingly beautiful.

I keep on to the destination for another fifteen minutes. Cars line the street on either side leading up to the house. Walls shake and windows rattle. A familiar tune leaps from sociable lips soaked in booze. I hurry to the front of the house, past a handful of college guys lounging on the porch. The air is thick with synthetic mango vape clouds.

"You Trueheart's guy?" one asks. I nod.

Another slides off the porch railing. "Got a name?" he shouts over the music. I don't answer. "Not much of a talker, huh?"

"I didn't come to talk," I mutter.

"Well, let's see what you got," he insists. The others nod.

"Not out here." I glance toward the front door. "Inside."

I follow them through the packed house—shoulder-to-shoulder with sweaty, half-drunk students.

"Party's here!" someone shouts. I keep my hood up and my head down. We go upstairs and I follow them down the long hall that leads to a large empty room. I shut the door behind me. The four of them crowd around as I empty the contents onto the bed. The drugs fall to the comforter and behind them lands a black pistol.

They all share a hyper vigilant look. "Gun's a little sus, my guy."

My eyes widen, mouth agape, I stare down at the firearm. "I—it's for safety." I slowly retrieve the handgun, unsure if it's loaded or not. I smirk, boiling on the inside as I slip the pistol back into my bag.

Their expressions sober, muscles tense. I clear my throat and nod my chin back to the drug-encumbered bed.

"So we have an ounce of some high-quality bud. That's on the house. Twenty capsules of pure Molly. And a half-pound of Skullflower."

"Skullflower? What the hell's that?" one of them asks—definitely not a local.

The blond guy crosses his arms. "Grows here. Only here. It's a type of hallucinogen. Psychedelic flower or something. Pretty sure it causes night terrors, though."

"Depends how you use it. Smoking's safe," I say, picking up the bag. "It's a tryptamine. Skull-shaped petals. Smells like sulfur. No taste. Whether you want to party or meet the Antlered God..." I toss the bag to the blond and smirk. "Tread lightly."

"Antlered God?" he frowns.

"Common hallucination at high doses," I say.

"How much?"

"Twenty-five." I answer.

They shift uneasily, claiming the price seems too steep.

"It's not." I hold out my hand.

They pull out their cash and count it into my palm. I stuff the wad of cash in my backpack as I follow them out of the room. I check the time on my phone. Missed calls from Rose. It's not too late, I could still get over there. My phone buzzes in my hand. The caller ID says 'Trueheart'. Impatient. I sigh and answer.

"Get the fuck out now!"

"I'm headed out. What's wrong?" I probe, now uneasy.

"Cops are about to kick that front door wide the fuck open!"

"Shit." I glance around, trying to stay calm. I retreat into the room. "I'm upstairs! What am I supposed to do?"

"Get out! They're inside! This is not a drill!"

"Where are you?"

"Backyard. Open a window. What room are you in?"

I rush to the window and shove it open. "Okay!" I hear the chaos erupting downstairs—people shouting, furniture crashing.

Frankie's below, phone still to his ear, pool behind him. "Heller, you gotta jump!"

"Easier said than done, asshole!" I shout, tossing my backpack down.

"You will not survive prison! Trust me—you're far too pretty!"

The door bursts open. A stocky officer lumbers in, barking something. I dive for the windowsill, throw myself out onto the roof's edge—and leap.

Water swallows me. The pool drowns the noise, the panic. I surface and gasp. Frankie yanks me up.

We sprint across the yard, over the fence, not looking back. We keep running until we reach the woods.

Frankie grins his big, toothy smile. The bags under his eyes are more prominent.

"We gotta split up, buddy." His hands rest on his hips.

"What the hell happened back there?" I demand.

"Someone ratted us out. Don't know who, but I was listening to the police scanner. Someone called it in. The deal was compromised."

"Goddammit, Frankie."

"Don't come at me. I risked my ass getting you out. I'm on probation."

"Right. I know. I'm not mad." I exhale.

He opens the pack. "How much did we pull?"

"Twenty-five."

He flips through the cash. "Here. Fifteen for you." He scratches his head. "For the trouble."

I take the money and shove it in my pocket. Turn to leave.

"Hey," he calls after me. "I really am sorry, Delson."

"I know," I say. Then make my way through a few more backyards to get to the road.

ONE SMALL DRIP AT A TIME, the rain begins with a soft trickle. It bloats and lashes sideways as the winds pick up. Nearly shoving me off the sidewalk, the wind howls with a vengeance. A pit forms in my stomach. Something feels off. The air feels thick in my lungs. My heart pounds.

My shadow follows beside me, lengthening as a pair of headlights cascade from behind. The car speeds up. I glance back. All I can see are headlights. Blinding headlights. The car then slows... I keep my eyes forward, keep walking. Keep calm.

It speeds up again—then crawls alongside me. My chest tightens. Muscles coil. Fists clench so hard my knuckles throb. The air grows thin.

The doors swing open. Three silhouettes spill out.

Dane.

Followed by Paul. Then Eric.

"You're dead, Heller!" Dane roars, charging straight for me.

I drop my bag and swing. My fist connects with his jaw—sharp, clean—but my hand goes numb from the impact. He stumbles back. His friends rush me, grab my arms.

I wrench one arm free and drive an elbow into one of their faces. I hear a satisfying pop. They restrain my arm again.

"Let me go!" my throat strains.

Dane grabs my jacket with one hand while Eric and Paul keep my arms pinned back.

"You little-" He interrupts himself with the blow to my face, or maybe I just can't hear past the white flash of the hit. My vision fades out for a moment. My head turns back to be met with another fist. "Not so tough now, huh!" he spits, slamming a punch into my gut.

"Coward..." I growl through blood and rain.

"What's that, Winona?" he jeers. "You got something to say?"

"Just you..." I say, snorting blood back as it slides down my throat. "You wanna fight?" My words taste metallic. "Just me and you."

He pauses.

"Sure, can't hurt." He grins. "Let him go."

Paul and Eric hesitate, confused.

"I said let him go!"

As they loosen their hold, Dane sucker-punches me straight in the face.

I hit the ground hard. The breath rips from my lungs. Then the kicks come—heel, sole, toe. Chest. Spine. Head. Mud and rubber. I taste gravel and whatever's embedded in the grooves of their sneakers. My vision collapses into a tunnel. The light at the end dims to a pinprick.

I fight it.

I crawl back from the dark.

Each breath weighing a thousand pounds, I roll over. Paul chuckles, snatching my camera from the sidewalk. He fidgets with the focusing ring on the lens, his smile diabolic. With a small click, the lens detaches from the camera. His arm flings down with a furious motion, and glass, metal and plastic spray out in the rain.

"Let me see!" Eric says with an ugly grin as he grabs the camera from Paul. He holds the lensless camera up, like he's taking a picture, then, as if he just scored a touchdown, he smashes the camera into the street. It bounces back up, almost like a football might, twirling in the rain. Pieces fling from it as it spins.

Dane gives it a final kick, saying something I can't make out over the downpour. They huddle back into the car, splashing me with water as they speed away.

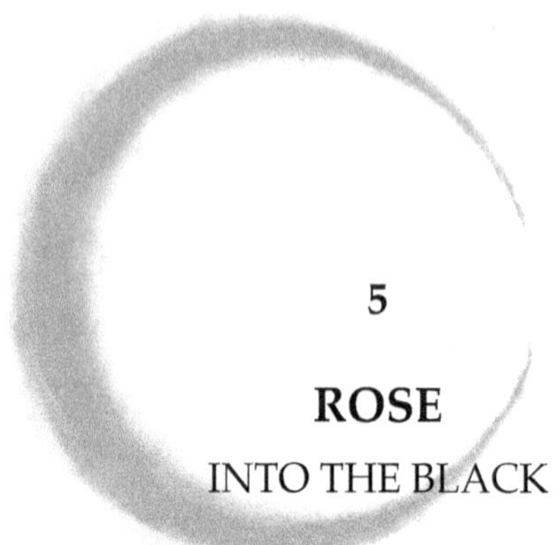

5

ROSE
INTO THE BLACK

I THINK IT'LL RAIN. That scent—palpable and familiar, yet always so tip-of-the-tongue. You can never quite name it, but it never goes unnoticed. As distinct as it is ambiguous. I look for stars but find only clouds—brimming and dark, misunderstood and unloved. Sure, they bring the rain, but they also trap warmth, keep the cold at bay. I'll take rain over the cold, especially those bitter nights when the vast chill of space seems to pour down over Heller Bay, mingling with the coldest parts of the Pacific, blowing its icy breath inland.

The empty trash can scrapes across the driveway as I drag it into the garage. The door groans along its tracks, flexing hollow metal. Fearful of unseen ghouls watching in the dark, I flick the light switch and bolt for the door.

I walk to the front room windows and open them, regretting the last small log I tossed into the fireplace. Wind howls, the house groans, and without Mom, I'm a child again. I close the windows and double check the locks. Steve, my silly little Border Collie, is good company though.

Delson's reaction replays through my head. I shiver at the thought of pushing him away. Did I say something wrong? He's just so hard to read. He's afraid to open up. I just want to be someone he trusts. Maybe he doesn't know how I feel about him. Maybe I need to beat it into that thick skull of his. That perfect, stupid, beautiful skull. I check the other windows and doors, feeling a little ridiculous. Still, I can't help smiling at the thought of him. A fluttery warmth stirs in my chest.

I wander into the kitchen with Steve on my heels. Keeping the lights off, I reach into the cabinet for a glass and crank the faucet. Cold water fills my stomach and calms me. As I set the glass down, something catches my eye—a figure across the street, standing under the streetlight. Still. Watching. I lean over the sink to get a better look, hidden in the kitchen's darkness.

He lifts something.

A camera.

It's Delson.

My heart skips. What is he doing?

He looks at his camera, then turns and walks away.

Confused—and kind of giddy—I rip my phone from my pocket and call him. No answer. I call again. Still nothing. I toss my phone on the counter and run outside to see if I can catch him. I can't get to the sidewalk fast enough. I see no trace of him. I shout his name up the hill, thinking if he's just over, he may hear me. Steve barks at me from the front porch. A single drop of frigid rain runs down my cheek. The rain is colder than usual, the clouds darker. I take a deep breath of the crisp air, wipe the cool streak away, and listen to Steve.

My stomach flutters when my phone rings—until I see it's just Courtney. Probably calling to gossip about Sam.

"Not in a million years," I say, switching to speaker and placing my phone on the vanity. "Even without all the new drama, I wouldn't take Sam back. I never missed him. That means something, you know?"

Courtney agrees immediately. "You don't need to jeopardize your future for that douche," she says, her voice sharp through the speaker. "I can't believe they already released him. That's insane, right?"

"First offense, I guess." I shrug, pulling the clips from my hair.

"I'm sure daddy being the mayor has *nothing* to do with it." She snickers.

"He was only interested in sex, which I never gave him." I laugh. "He said he had a stress disorder."

"You should date an older guy."

I scoff. "Yeah, how is that working out for you?"

"Frankie is different from other guys." Something I've heard at least ten times.

My phone buzzes against the vanity. "Someone's trying to FaceTime me."

"You wanna call me back?"

"No—it's Sam. Ugh, no thanks." I decline the call.

Courtney laughs. "Bet he's trying to relieve some *stress*."

"Yeah, well, he can relieve himself."

"Does he know your mom's out of town?"

"Not like it matters," I sigh.

"You need to ditch his ass for real. I'll see if Frankie has any single friends."

"It's been over. Everyone knows it. And no thanks. I *like* Delson. He's actually amazing. People just don't take the time to get to know him, they just know his family drama."

She scoffs. "Yeah, you guys would have a real John Travolta-Olivia Newton-John-Grease thing goin'." She laughs at herself, as usual. "You know what tomorrow is, right?"

"Uh, Saturday?" I grunt, attempting to banish 'Grease Lightning' from my mind.

"No. I mean, yes, but it's the anniversary of Ian Bloom's murder."

I pause, her statement dripping over me like thick black tar. "It's gone by so quick…"

"Yeah. Crazy right?" She pauses. "You think Edward will snap?" she chuckles.

I grimace. "Don't make light of that. Delson said he's been struggling with it."

"Sad—"

"Hold on," I say as my phone buzzes again. "Sam's calling *again*."

"Just press ignore. He'll get the hint."

I do. "Anyway, maybe we should do something. For Ian. Something meaningful."

"Like what?"

"I don't know… a little get-together. His friends, people who cared about him."

"Like a beach thing?" she suggests. "Get all litty-titty?"

"Edward already has a drinking problem. And Delson doesn't drink."

She sighs. "Lawd. Maybe he *should*."

Another buzz. "He's calling again." I groan. "I'll just call you back."

"For real?"

I answer the video call. The screen is black. There is a slight muffled sound.

"Hello, Sam." I roll my eyes, waiting for his face to appear on the screen.

The image shifts to a bouquet of red roses tied together with a white silk ribbon. His hand grips the bundle of stems, just below the ribbon. He doesn't speak. Bile builds in my stomach.

"Sam, that's very nice, but I don't think we should talk anymore. I've said everything I needed to say."

He still doesn't answer. His hand just squeezes the bouquet.

"Sam?" I call out again. The camera shifts slightly. I recognize his surroundings... my front porch. "Sam, are you literally outside my house right now?" I pause, still no answer. Next, I check my Ring camera notifications. I watch the feed from my phone. "You can't just show up like this. You need to leave." I hang up.

A text buzzes in.

Is Delson Heller there?

A hollow knot tightens in my chest. Did he come here to *fight* Delson? I drop my phone on the vanity. Knocks echo from the front door—sharp and urgent. Steve barks as I snatch my phone and call Courtney.

Her face pops up. "So—"

I cut her off. "Court, he's banging on my front door right now with a bunch of flowers. I told him to get lost, and he's just out there knocking, asking if Delson is with me."

"What a loser." She laughs.

"It's not funny. At this point, he should take the hint," I explain.

"You look way too freaked. You feeling okay?"

"Shut up. I was in the middle of removing my makeup. And yes, this is me freaking out."

"Tell him you're calling the cops. He'll leave."

Another set of knocks pound from the front door downstairs, this time much louder. Steve scrambles at my bedroom door, barking.

"Go down there and kick his ass, Rose!" she eggs me on.

"Right." I roll my eyes, huffing, as I make my way down the hallway to the stairs. I take each step slow. It's quiet now.

"KI KI KI-MA MA MA…" Courtney mimics the sound from those old scary movies, the ones with the machete-wielding hockey player.

"Can you not!" I whisper as I tiptoe to the last step. She laughs. "It's not funny…"

"Just open the door and punch him right in the dick. Can't ignore that," Courtney grumbles.

"Seriously?" My heart drops into my stomach. "Get the hell out of here, Sam!" I shout at the door. Tears well in my eyes. "He must be wasted. I'm calling the police!"

A heavy slam shakes the door. I flinch.

"Do I need to come over?" Courtney asks, suddenly serious.

"Could you?" I whisper.

"On my way. I'll be there in ten."

"Wait. Don't hang up, okay?"

"I won't." I hear her moving, getting in her car. She props her phone on the dash. Her face reappears. "I'm gonna kick his sorry ass!"

Another bang.

"I'm calling the cops!" Courtney shouts through the speaker.

"Court, no! Don't hang up—" But the line goes dead.

And panic floods in.

I get a message from Sam. I open it.

ANSWER THE FUCKING DOOR ROSE!

"Courtney's calling the police!" I scream through the tears now flooding my lashes. "Just leave!" One final, thunderous pound rattles the door. I hush Steve, trying to calm his relentless barking. The house slips into sudden silence. My phone buzzes violently in my hand. I fumble to answer. Courtney's face flickers onto the screen.

"Cops are on the way—and so am I!"

"I think he left." I sniffle.

"Good, maybe they'll see him on their way over. If he's lucky, I won't see him first!" she growls through her teeth.

I squeeze my phone and rush back to my room. I slam my door behind me. Steve still barks downstairs. I crack the door open and call out to him. He keeps barking and growling.

Courtney screams in a panic, followed by the sounds of crumpling metal and shattering glass. The image of her on my screen jerks around and flickers as her cries cut in and out. I call out her name! Pleading for her to answer me. She stops screaming. The incessant boom of a car horn only comes through the speakers of my phone. The call ends and Steve's barking goes silent with a small yelp.

I scramble to my bed, throwing the blankets over myself like a small child hiding from the Boogeyman. I check the Ring camera; the porch is vacant. Steps. I hear them. They're coming for me. Boots step down the hallway toward my bedroom. The doorknob jiggles and twists. The door opens; darkness follows with a click. The steps get closer. My breathing stops. The hot salty streams still pour from my eyes. Something drags across the wall. It squeaks with each stroke. I grasp the blanket . A tall, hooded figure in black glides into view. His hands trace the wall. Then he kneels... and rolls himself beneath my bed. My hands tremble uncontrollably. Sam's gone completely insane. I bite my tongue to choke the scream clawing up my throat. I glance at the wall. Big, red letters drip down in thick, oozing trails:

MOONLIGHT MATTERS!

I fling the blanket off and leap to my feet—just as the bed slams upward and crashes against the door, trapping me. The man in black lunges upright. The hood shrouds his face. Thick black gloves stretch from the baggy sleeves of a black rain poncho. I dive to the side as he slams into the doorframe, tripping over the overturned bed.

I scramble toward the vanity. The window—my only way out.

He charges. A long silver blade flashes.

I kick the wicker bench into his path. He stumbles. I duck—

The knife misses by inches as he crashes into the mirror.

I slip beneath his arm. He bursts up! To his feet as I bolt for the window! My body slams to the floor as he trips me. My shoulder smashes into my nightstand, knocking the crystal lamp to the floor. He lurches over me. I don't think! My hand reaches beside me. I smash the heavy lamp into the side of his head.

Black empty eyes.

He rolls to the door. I struggle to my feet, rush to the window! The backyard waits two stories below. No time. I lift myself up onto the windowsill and drop.

The fall takes longer than I thought, but still I have no time to brace myself. I can't breathe! I pull myself to my feet, promptly falling as my ankle pops. The rain soaks my clothes as it thickens into heavy sheets. I pull myself back up. I squeeze my fists and gasp as my ankle cracks, burns. With each agonizing step, a shock wave radiates up my leg and to my teeth.

The neighbor's lights are on! I just need to get over the fence. The sliding-glass door opens and the man in black appears before me. He grabs me by my shoulders and throws me through the glass, back into the dark living room. Horrific silence fills the room until his boots crunch glass shards into the carpet as he moves to the light switch. The room fills with light as the ceiling fan whirls.

Steve is twisted and bloody, black and white fur, lifeless plopped on the table not six feet from me. I scream! His guts twist and intertwine in the blades of the fan as it spins, wringing fluids out from the tissue. The harsh white lightbulbs drip with blood, coating them in crimson. The room turns red.

I gag, turning my face away, mouth filling with hot saliva. Sam is lifeless on the floor near the front door. Oh God, who is this? I feel sharp stabbing pains in my back as I roll over the glass. He stands over me. I slam my heel into his crotch. He falls to his knees! I scramble to get up and stumble my way back into the yard, racing for the iron fence. My ankle burns and I can feel the stinging in my back. I grip the wet iron rods of the fence and pull myself up! Ignoring the pinch of the sharp wrought-iron rods, I swing one leg over. His powerful hands grasp my leg. His gloves squelch with blood as he squeezes my leg and rips at my shirt.

"HELP ME!" I scream! "PLEASE SOMEBODY HELP!"

He rips me off the fence and slams me to the soggy ground. He stands over me and flashes the instrument of my demise; the long silvery blade, at least a foot in length, handle wrapped in black leather. His black vinyl poncho snaps and slaps around his legs just at the knee as the wind lashes. The hood shifts and his face appears. He stares, tilting his head as if to question my wailing. The mask is the thing of nightmares, a darkly stained, fleshy brown-ish leather. Almost bony, light casts to the forehead, cheekbones, chin and nose. Two black misshapen asymmetrical craters for eyes. Dark stains like bags underneath stretch down, blending into the shadowy concave of sunken cheeks. The jaw comes to a sharp chin. Its nose flattened and just barely twisted to one side. Crude stitches line the seams. Lips frozen apart, stained black—sculpted leather—jut out as if to shush my cries. I can't help but to remember the first time I ever saw this mask, on a field trip in fourth grade.

With a heavy motion, he slams the blade into my gut! It burns and aches and pinches as he twists it and wrenches it back out! With an animalistic grunt, the blade plunges back inside me. I try to scream, but nothing more than a whine escapes my lips.

"P-please..." I beg, whimpering as acid and iron slither up my throat. "I don't want to die." The tears stream down my face. He draws the weapon back over his head, his knees on either side of me. He hesitates. A burst of energy, or desire to live! I claw out from under him, pull myself through the mud.

"I'm not ready. Not ready to die!"

Fingers twist through my hair, snapping my head back. Body pulled over itself until I'm on my back again. The blade glistens red.

"**Death is inevitable.**" His voice, more than one, intertwines and overlaps. "Don't fight it," Delson says.

The knife hacks into me again. He twists it, seeming to savor my anguish. My vision fades as he drags me along the soggy yard. Delson, no, that can't be. The world spins as I sink into a numb cold. I feel myself floating... Delson, holding me in his arms. No, the man in black lifts me up. The cold, hard fence slams into my back as he holds me against the iron rods. He pulls a bundle of skinny rope from his pocket and cinches it around one of my wrists, then the other. My head hangs as my arms stretch out above me. I feel the rope wrapping around my neck. He pulls it tight until it burns. I try to speak—I can't.

I've felt lonely before. But not like this.

Nothing can prepare you for the loneliness you feel at death.

True aloneness.

There's no light. No tunnel.

No voices. No angels. No fire and brimstone.

None of that.

Just the weight of everything I never said.

Every regret, all at once.

And it all meant nothing.

6

EDWARD
THE MESSAGE

THE GUYS'LL BE PISSED I ditched practice—especially now. But Sam's the fuck up, so why's it feel like I'm catching all the shit from the team and Coach? I used to like the guy. Coach Dean has been my dad's best friend since childhood. Over summer break, it was a pretty normal sight seeing the two of them sipping on beers by the barbecue in the backyard. They never shut up about playing for the Jackals during their high school heyday. But I don't need the pressure or the expectations today. Not today.

All that attention from Coach Dean felt like something— like maybe he saw potential. Maybe he was grooming me to take over as captain. But looking back, I was just Plan B. A placeholder if Sam imploded. I don't even know if I wanted it. Not really. Not when it started to feel more like a sentence than an honor.

As I drive to the motel—watching the fog devour Blackroot in the rearview mirror—I wonder, when will I see that for the last time? But soon those thoughts are replaced by her body against mine. The reddening of our shoulders beneath the blistering stream. The rank scent of the bay demolished by the cheap chalky motel bar-soap. Even stronger, the smell of her perfume, not like girls from school —not even like Alissa—more matured woman than girl.

I step out of the shower before her. The cheap motel towel is rough and thin. I grab my pants as she presses a towel to her face. She's quiet. Is she left unsatisfied? I wanna bury that thought, replace a truth I'm afraid to face with an excuse. After all, shower sex always sounds good in the moment. Shit, just doesn't usually work out the greatest. Movies make it seem passionate, hot, and completely comfortable. Maybe it has to be a bigger shower. Or is it because I can't get Alissa's face out of my mind? It felt weird last night too and I don't have the steam to blame then. Why now—now that she sees what I really am—is it her I want most? What kind of bastard does that make me?

I walk to the mini-fridge, grab a beer, pop the top. The bitterness hits my tongue. My stomach growls when it hits bottom.

"Hey, Bridge?" I call toward the bathroom. "Bridget?" Louder this time—fighting with the hair dryer.

"Yeah?" she calls back.

"I'm grabbing something from the vending machine. You want anything?"

"I'm okay—just be quick."

"'Kay." I grab my phone and sneak out the door.

The sun sets and the icy wind turns my skin to goose-flesh. The hairs on my arms stand up. I walk down the stone pathway toward the vending machines. The stones beneath my bare feet, frigid and uneven. I turn my phone on and wait for the lock screen to appear. Facial recognition takes a moment too long, with my hood hiding half my face. One post after another, my timelines going wild.

> REST IN PEACE. 🙏
> R.I.P. YOU'LL BE MISSED!
> I'LL NEVER FORGET THE TIME WE—
> GONE TOO SOON.
> OMG. I'M LITERALLY CRYING RN! 😭

All from kids at school. Who died? I tense. I know this feeling. This is exactly how it played out with Ian. Social media vultures pretending they were closer than they were. Competing for grief clout. Mourning as performance.

Who...?

I scroll faster.

> SAM LEWIS, GONE BUT NEVER FORGOTTEN...

Photos of him with the team.

> ROSE BAILEY, YOU DESERVED SO MUCH
> MORE. REST IN PARADISE... 🤍

Rose's face stares up at me. Smiling. Unaware.

No...

Bridget.

I sprint back to the motel, slam the door open.

"Bridget!" I shout, louder than I mean to.

She rushes out of the bathroom wrapped in her towel. "What?" panic strikes. "What is it? What's wrong!"

I freeze. I don't know what to say. "I—" My throat aches. Can't speak. "Sam and—" I pause. "Rose..."

Her eyes widen. "What, what about Rose?" She stumbles, pulling her clothes on. "Is she outside or something? Did she see you?" I can't say it. I don't even know how to start. "Edward?" she demands.

"Turn on your phone..." I murmur.

She slows. Eyes narrow. She grabs her phone off the desk. "You're scaring me." She powers it on. "I have, like, thirty missed calls?"

I begin to tear up. A cry whispers from my breath. "Rose... she's..."

Bridget places her ear to her phone, listening to a voicemail. Slowly her face shifts into shock, fear. It contorts into agony. She stumbles back, her phone falling to the carpet.

"No, no, my baby..." The tears pour down her face. Her eyes widen with panic, disbelief. Frozen in a single thought. She doesn't breathe. "No!" she screams! Then collapses into her grief on the floor.

I fall down beside her and wrap my arms around her, pulling her into my chest. I have no words.

"I h-have to go." She pulls on her clothes, hyperventilating.

"Bridget—"

"No!" she screams. "I HAVE TO GO!" she pulls on her jeans and a sweatshirt, then bolts to the car. I chase her, but she locks the doors.

"Bridget!" I pound on the window. "Stop, let me in!"

She says something, but I can't make it out. She's sobbing as she slams the car into reverse and speeds off.

I run back inside, ignoring the stares from the regulars. I grab the keys to my truck and slide on my shoes. The sweatshirt squeezes over my head as I swing open the door. I peel out of the parking lot after her.

"Come on!" I scream to myself as I bomb down the street. The road is wet, and the wind is serious. My headlights light the slick pavement as the sky darkens. I push a hundred on the highway back to Blackroot. I press the command button on my steering wheel.

"Call Bridget!" I yell at my dashboard.

CALLING BRIDGET

Rings. No answer.

"Shit!" I slam the phone down. The wind howls around me. The wheel jerks. The road winds and the tires of my truck screech. Sliding sideways, the truck's back end comes out. I slam the steering wheel in the other direction and I spin out. My heart pounds as I smash on the brake and come to a stop stretched across both lanes. My heart bashes my ribs and my vision blurs with every thud.

Black leather hands reach out from behind me. I flinch, but the rope is already around my neck, slamming the back of my head to the seat. I gurgle as I try to catch my breath. I try to speak. It's impossible when your windpipe is being crushed.

"**Do not scream,**" the chilling voice speaks from behind, raspy and unnatural. Like some demon-possessed woman, more than one voice speaks the words. The rope loosens as a silvery glint flashes. The big ass blade presses to my throat.

I slowly catch my breath. "W-who are you?" I ask. The knife presses down harder in response. "What do you want from me?" I ask.

There is only silence for a moment, then the voices

return. "**I want you to deliver a message.**" Dozens of voices in one. Male. Female. Human. Not.

"W-what message?"

"**Tell her death is coming...**" the voice growls, thick with something unholy. "**Only a river of blood will set them free.**"

I glance at the mirror.

The thing behind me stares.

A twisted, stitched face—part hag, part ghoul. All nightmare.

Its eyes—black, sunken—watch me with something worse than hunger.

Absence.

"Why me?" I ask.

"**Tell anybody other than Bridget Bailey about this encounter and Delson Heller dies next.**" The door opens. I hear the quick steps of his boots as he vanishes into the fog rolling from over the bay.

***

HOURS LATER, I find myself parked outside Bridget's house. I found her at the police station first, then followed her to the coroner's office. She sat in her car, unmoving, eyes peeled back like she was trying to force herself awake. From frozen statue to sobbing, screaming wreck—back and forth for hours. I stayed back. I don't even think she saw my truck. Now I'm sitting here, afraid to go in.

Her car's still in the driveway. Loose yellow caution tape flaps from the porch where she shoved her way through the front door. She's inside. Alone. Goddamn it—how did this happen? My fist slams into the steering wheel. The mirror shakes. My eyes catch on the memory of that mask—tight, leathery, impossible. That face still clings to my nerves like rot. Why do I know it?

The living room light flickers on. A reddish hue emanating out through the windows. I hear a scream. I rush from the truck and barge into the house. Bridget lays in the middle of the floor. A crime scene, that's all it is now. I don't even think she's supposed to be here. They left her house just as they found it, and she has nobody. I fall to her side, pulling her in close. She groans and cries into my chest.

She begs and screams. "Who did this?" Her face peels back with agony. She calls out again to God, begging for an answer, or to wake up.

"Death is coming..." I murmur.

Her sobs break as she glares at me through tortured eyes. "What?"

"I saw him, the man who did this." I hesitate as her breath slows.

"Who?"

"He wore a mask. Looked like it was made of leather... or skin." I pause. "That's what he said. Death is coming. Only a river of blood will set them free."

Her expression shifts—fear creeping in beneath the grief. Something darker. She doesn't respond.

I try to get her to leave. Beg her to come with me, to get a hotel room, just—anywhere but here. At first, she won't move. But eventually, I help her to her room.

She stops crying.

Now, she just stares out the window. Her body is still here, but her mind's somewhere else entirely.

Her breath is soft, almost nothing. "Will you stay with me?"

It's barely a whisper.

"...okay."

I hold her tighter, swallowing back bile as the weight of it all sinks to the bottom of my stomach and stays there.

7

DELSON

SAVAGE GARDEN

GROGGY AND SORE, I roll out of bed. My ribs ache and face stings. I chug the bottle of water on my dresser, soaking my dry cracked lips and soothing my sandpaper throat. The cool liquid hits my gut like a tidal wave, clearing the fog in my head and bringing life to my organs. I gasp for air as I plop the bottle back down. I stagger to the bathroom to claim the hot shower, shielding my face from the potential glares of Rachel or Rick. The steam from the shower knocks loose the clotted blood from my nose. I tilt my head back and revel in the scalding streams as they beat down on my muscles, slowly smoothing out the knots as my skin becomes numb to the heat.

The first cigarette of the day goes down like bear mace. I bark a shallow wheezing cough and drop the halfie to the ground, grind it beneath my shoe.

My phone buzzes in my pocket. I smirk, expecting a call from Rose. It's a text from a blocked number. I swipe, curious—

"Delson!" Rick's voice explodes from inside.

I flinch. There's something in his tone—fear. Genuine fear. And that sounds the same in everyone. I shove my phone back in my pocket and throw the front door open. Rick's hunched over Rachel on the living room floor, cradling her limp body.

"Delson!" he yells again. "She's not breathin'! I think she OD'd!"

I claw my hands into my hair. "You've gotta be fucking kidding me."

"Call an ambulance!" he shouts.

My hands shake as I fumble for my phone. I call. My brain blanks. "She's not breathing! She's turning blue!" I scream to the dispatcher on the other end.

———

FLUTTERING LIGHTS WASH across the living room walls as the EMTs rush inside. They lift Rachel onto the gurney, moving fast. I follow, ready to climb into the back of the ambulance.

One medic blocks me with a hand. "Sorry. You can't ride with her."

"She's my mother!" I growl, stepping in.

"I understand, sir—"

"Come on." Rick hollers from his truck. The door's open. Engine running. He's already behind the wheel.

We tail the ambulance, blowing through lights. I gnaw at my nails, eyes locked on the flashing vehicle ahead.

"She'll be okay, Delson," Rick says, too calm. Too sure.

"What happened?" I snap. "What the hell was that?"

His jaw flexes. "She said one more time, and she'd be done with it. I shouldn't have—"

"Really?" I hiss. "If she dies, I swear—"

"She ain't gonna die, goddammit!" he yells back at me.

I feel my face twitch. I glare at him. "You better hope she doesn't." My words still drip with venom.

Snot-nosed, flu-ridden brats cough and moan behind thin paper masks in the crowded, stuffy waiting room. No place to sit. I couldn't sit down even if I wanted to. No, my legs couldn't break my pacing.

I catch a few side-eyes and even some full-blown stares, like I'm some kind of animal or criminal. A couple of nervous mothers watch me the closest. My face throbs, reminding me of how I must look.

"Heller," a voice calls from behind the counter.

I rush to the woman. "Yes!"

"You can see her now."

I shove past the nurse. "Where is she?"

"This way." She leads me down the hall.

"How is she?"

"She's stable..." The nurse pauses at the doorway. "She stopped breathing for a while. She may have suffered some brain damage."

I push past her into the room.

Rachel lies still. Her eyes drift toward me, barely tracking. "...your face..." she says, voice thin and crackling.

"I fell. How do you feel?" I sit beside her.

"...felt b-better..." she whispers.

I shake my head, jaw locked. "You almost died." I stare down at her, holding back the burn behind my eyes.

"Oh, baby..." Her voice wavers. "I'm not going anywhere."

"That's not a promise you get to make, Rachel." I wipe my face. "Not after everything you've put me through." Rage claws up my chest. "Mom!" I shout. "Sometimes I wish you were dead, just so I could stop worrying about when it's going to happen."

"I'll stop... I swear it." She reaches for my cheek. "I promise. I'm through with this shit."

I stand, out of reach. "Just give me the courtesy of a good goodbye next time. Don't make it like that." I pause. "I gotta go." I grab Rick's keys on the way out.

Putting faith in a junkie's promise is like building a house on sand.

I park on the dunes and walk to the shore. The sky is a blackened bruise, rain falling cold and sharp. Smoke from my lungs disappears in bursts on the wind.

I unlock my phone, tempted to call Rose. But the message from this morning still lingers. That blocked number. That link. I open it.

It's a video.

The house seems familiar. I know that—

Sam Lewis.

He walks toward a porch with a bouquet in one hand, phone in the other. He's calling someone. He doesn't knock. He just stands there.

Whoever's filming stays low—moving through bushes, ducking behind trees. Watching him. Hunting him.

Is this Frankie? Trying to rattle him more? He already got him arrested, expelled... What more?

The camera creeps closer. A gloved hand reaches out. A long syringe. It jabs into Sam's neck. The plunger slams down.

Sam jerks.

Too fast for him to scream.

My gut flips. This isn't some prank.

The gloved hand lifts Sam's phone. A voice answers.

"Hello, Sam." It's Rose. I'd know her voice anywhere. And for the first time, I'm terrified at where this video is going.

The camera tilts to show the roses in Sam's hand.

Rose speaks through the phone screen. "Sam, that's... very nice, but I don't think we should talk anymore. I've said what I needed to say." She looks annoyed. "Sam?"

The camera turns back to Sam. He doesn't speak. He doesn't move.

Rose's voice cracks through the phone again. "Sam, are you outside my house right now?" She waits. "You can't just show up unannounced. You need to leave." She hangs up the phone.

The dark hand bangs on the front door as Sam stands still, clutching the roses. Knocks again. This time much harder. The hand drops from the door. It comes back into the camera, a large knife gripped tight. I take a screenshot. My heart clenches into a meaty fist. But I continue to watch. The hand bangs on the door again, this time with the butt of the knife.

"Get the hell out of here, Sam!" Rose's muffled yell beats back from the other side of the door with her dog's barks and growls.

The gloved hand holding Sam's phone begins texting. I can't make out what it says.

"Courtney is calling the cops!" Rose screams. "Leave!" Her sobs punch through the speaker.

The gloved hands vanish. When they return, they're holding tools. Picking the lock. Quick. Efficient.

The door unlatches.

The knife reappears, zipping across sam's throat in a blur.

He staggers forward. Blood gushes down his front as he stumbles through the doorway. I can't pull my eyes away. I watch every second of the video. And with each passing moment, the certainty of a life where Rose doesn't exist becomes more... *real*. An elaborate prank? It has to be!

I close the video and go online. I check BND. The first article I see sets it in stone. It's real. No. I can't fight back the bile from my stomach and vomit into the sand. I cough as my throat tightens and the blood vessels in my eyes burst. The throbbing in my head pushes my vision into the shadows.

The white Rose of Blackroot has been ripped from the savage garden. And just like that, the darkness preys on the people of Heller once more. It hid. It slithered at our feet for a year. Coiling around us... waiting for its moment to strike.

8

DELSON
ONE MORE LIGHT

THE NIGHT BURNS on like a fever dream—drifting in and out —I lie here on the hardwood of my bedroom floor, sobbing only when the knotted cord in my throat tightens again. Visions of unthinkable things haunt me, and when I still can't lose sight of her—even with closed eyes—I beg, and I scream. Yet somehow, barely treading the dark, suffocating waters of grief, I sleep. Even in this half-dead state, I can't escape her. Rose.

The vacancy of the house disturbers me more so than the thought of school, of another day. The world continues without her. Life goes on and she isn't here. Something so simple never made any less sense.

The shock of reality still firmly grips my heart as I sleep-walk through my habitual morning routine. I pass by The Serpent And The Rainbow without slowing my pace, even as Adele's eyes meet mine through the windows. She doesn't need to see me like this, right back in my head, in the shadows.

"Delson!" her worried voice shouts from behind.

My feet slow to a dragging stop. I pull the cigarette from my lips, the smoke drifts up, stinging my sore eyes. I turn to face her, silent. Her arms clamp around me.

"I'm here," she whispers.

I swallow back the aching knot in my throat.

She pushes back to see my face. "I'm sorry," she squeaks as drops tumble from her lashes and her arms constrict me again, pulling me in for too long.

The school moves in slow motion. Students drift in small, silent clusters. Many dressed in black hooded rain ponchos, the same vinyl ones the school provides during rainy football games. Whispers swell behind cupped hands. Suppressed sobs leak out in hiccuping bursts. And the eyes —they're all on me. Like they expect me to say something, to explain something. A year ago, someone murdered Ian. Now, it's the same thing again. The same expressions. The same murmured heartbreak. Whoever killed Ian killed Rose and Sam. I'm sure of it. But why wait a year to strike again?

The classroom is just as heavy as the courtyard. A fog settles over everyone. Every face pale and dazed. Wide-eyed. Silent. And today, they're innocent. Death does that. It absolves.

Mrs. Thompson stands at the front, leaning against her desk. Her bloodshot eyes scan us with visible heartbreak.

"It's... it's a tragedy, what happened to Rose and Sam." She tries to hide the watery clutch that sorrow has on her voice. "They'll be deeply missed. There will be a candlelight vigil held for the both of them here tonight, down in the stadium." She wipes the tear from her cheek. "I'd like us to share a moment of silence. Then we can all go around the room and share a positive memory we have of either of them." She curls her lips down to intercept her cries. She exhales.

The room goes quiet. Some drop their heads. Others stare at their desks in unfaltering disbelief. I feel so empty. I clench my fists at the sting of the gaping hole in my chest, but it only makes it worse. It's nearly silent—

It starts with muffled vibrations. A sudden burst of electronic melodies jingle over each other as every phone chimes in unison. Mrs. Thompson looks up, almost angry at first, until her phone buzzes with the rest of ours.

Gasps and cries slug the air.

"OH MY GOD!" one girl screams.

I reach for my phone, its vibrational taunt mocking me from my front pocket. My mind drowns out the cries that whirl around me. I unlock the screen, open the message.

Rose clings to the wrought-iron fence, her arms strung up to the rods. Her stomach is hard to look at, layers of flesh carved and peeled back. A gaping, bloody hole. Her insides piled at her feet. My stomach clenches, and vomit rises in my throat. I choke it back, dropping my phone to the desk. The room spins. Head buzzes. Mrs. Thompson yells, her voice just a warbling thread in the madness. Another image appears. Mrs. Thompson's hand slams over her mouth as her phone falls to the floor. The screen is dark, aside from the ghoulish mask.

THE PATRONS of The Serpent talk too loudly about morbid things. Rumors, robberies, drugs, and petty crimes are the usual. But today it's conspiracies, murders, and that text message—the one the whole town received. Everyone's wondering the same thing: what's next? But now I wonder—was I the only one who got the video?

Edward's different. Quieter than usual. Not withdrawn, just... tense. Like he's bracing for something. But I guess we all are. Adele sets my coffee and his protein shake down before gently squeezing my shoulder. I glance across the table.

"Eddie, you okay?"

His eyes lift to mine. He clasps his hands together, resting against his chin and lower lip, elbows set on the table. "Are *you* okay?"

I hesitate, thinking again of the video from the unknown messenger. "That's not the first text I got from...whoever this is." I glance down at the black coffee. "I got—"

"A video?" he interjects.

Our eyes lock. A hair-raising chill skitters down my spine, and by the look on his face, I'd say he feels the same.

"I got one too," he says. "This morning, before school."

My heart doesn't race, it bounds, sluggish and hard. Throbbing in my neck. "Did you tell the police?"

"No. Did you?" his hands fall to the table.

"I haven't said a word." I picture Rose again, try to quantify the idea of her being nonexistent. "When I try to reopen the link, it errors out."

"Same."

The wooden legs of a chair screech against the floor as Luca Reyes slides in beside us. Tall. Lanky. Faster than Edward on the field. He leans forward, shooting us both a look. His thick dark hair hangs around his chestnut eyes.

"I told the PoPo," he says, tapping the table. The tendons in his hands shift under his light brown skin.

"You don't even know what we're talking about," Edward mutters through clenched teeth.

"I got the video too. No cap." Luca sighs, puffing out his cheeks. "Shit's scary."

"What'd the cops say?" I ask.

"Not much. Took my phone though."

"I wonder who else got it," Edward says.

Alissa and Cordelia walk in together, all eyes on them as they quietly approach our table.

"Take a wild guess," Luca says under his breath. "Speak of the she-devils." He pops a stick of gum into his mouth.

"You two get the video?" I ask.

They both nod.

"You did too?" Alissa asks, her eyes wide.

"We all did," Edward says.

They grab chairs and sit. The tension between Alissa and Edward is thick, but neither of them mentions it.

Alissa shakes her head. "What does it mean? Why us?"

"Why do serial killers do anything?" Cordelia retorts.

"Yeah right," Luca scoffs. "A serial killer in Blackroot?" he squints and wrinkles his nose. "C'mon." His tone is offensive, though he doesn't mean it that way.

Cordelia rolls her eyes. "Really?" she probes. "And it's just *normal* for the entire town to get a mass text with a picture of—" She stops herself. "And that *mask*?" she asks. "Because that doesn't scream *serial killer*."

Edward flinches.

Luca leans back in his chair and pops a gum bubble. "You got me there."

"Statistically speaking, it's pretty uncommon for a serial killer to wear a mask."

"Point being?" Cordelia's eyes widen in sarcastic suspense.

"If he simply wanted to hide his identity, a ski mask would suffice. Why go through all that trouble for a mask? It stands for something and he *wants* us to know it," I say. "It's not just a mask, it's a message."

Luca pops another gum bubble. "So then, what's it mean? Because doesn't it kind of remind you of the—"

"It is," I interject. "They omitted it from the report, but someone stole the Ingomar masks during the museum robbery."

Alissa stares vacantly at the table. "The Blackroot Society."

"What the hell is that?" Cordelia asks.

"They were a cult," I say. "Back when the land was first being settled, there was a man—one of the founders—a Civil War general named Victor Ingomar."

"Ingomonster," Luca adds. "That's what we called him growing up."

I continue. "He was a powerful man, whose hands were in all sorts of budding businesses. Most of the mills were his, a few of the fishing boats. He launched ruthless raids against local tribes, forcing the surviving natives to Bellflower Island. When he suffered injuries in the war, he returned horribly disfigured. The burns were so bad they took his eyelids, supposedly preventing him from going out during the day. The most unrelenting man in Heller County was now seen as vulnerable. It drove him mad." I pause. "You know those World War I post-op portrait masks they made for injured soldiers? Well, he thought of it first. But he didn't want to go back to looking passable. No, he hired a local Leatherworker and doctor to craft him a custom mask. Something that would strike terror in his enemies and turn the locals pity into fear. He started the Blackroot Society as a sort of gentleman's club, but it was just a cover."

"He held extravagant parties, had the whole town fooled. But word got out that they were performing secret rituals, supposedly involving human sacrifice. The cult took canoes across the marina to Bellflower Island in the dead of night. To avoid waking the townsfolk, they left their guns behind. They nearly killed every member of the tribe, using clubs and rocks and knives. The cult started hunting people in the town, those they deemed as sinners, impure. Envisioning their perfect society, they decided who should live there. They would stalk the streets in black cloaks, their faces concealed under leather masks to hide their identities. Allegedly, many of the members were powerful people in the county. Lawmen, mayors, doctors. Protected by their status."

Cordelia's jaw hangs open.

My phone buzzes. Frankie.

I stand. "Eddie, I'll see you at the vigil. I gotta check on my mom."

I step outside, grateful for the air, the moment alone. I answer as I leave The Serpent. "Frankie, we need to talk."

"Meet me in the alley," he says—and hangs up.

I round the corner and walk into the alley. Frankie steps out from behind a dumpster. "Sup, dork." He smirks, lighting a cigarette. "You look how I feel." He grimaces at my bruised face.

"Then you must feel pretty damn good."

He chuckles. "Was, uh, Courtney at school today, by any chance?" he asks.

"Didn't see her," I say.

"She was supposed to head over Saturday night. She never showed." He takes a long drag. "I've tried calling her a thousand goddamn times. At this point I'm like, fuck it."

"Rose was her best friend. I'm sure she's mourning."

He nods, taking a drag. "Yeah, maybe. I just wanted to say sorry. Like, really."

"Fuck you."

"Fuck you, too."

"No. I'm done, Frankie. For real."

"Shut up." He tries to grin.

"I mean it. I'm not selling for you anymore."

"That last time was just a hiccup."

"That last time was a *disaster*." I shove him. "I'm serious."

He holds his hands up, cigarette bouncing on his lips. "Don't push me."

"Cops? A gun?!" I shove him again.

His smirk falters. "Don't push me, Heller."

"I don't care if you're on probation. Get somebody else to sell for you. I'm done. Coward." I push him again.

His fist swings from the side and plows into my already bruised cheek. I stumble back, holding the burning spot.

"Shit!" he blurts. "I'm sorry!" he holds out his hands. "I told you not to push me."

I drop my backpack and unzip it, retrieving the gun and pointing it at him. My hand shakes.

"Whoa!" he holds his hands up. "Jeez Christ!" cigarette still in his lips.

"Did you kill Rose and Sam?" I ask.

"No, what the fuck!" His cigarette drops. "You think I'd kill somebody?"

"Ian Bloom?" I grit my teeth.

"Delly-belly, think about who you're talking to. You *know* me."

"Do I?"

"I'm a lotta things, but I'm not a killer." His signature smirk is still there, but it's holding back tears.

I let the gun hangs loose in my fingers at my side.

He bumbles his lips as he lets out an enormous sigh. "Okay, giving you the gun was a mistake, I admit. I'll take it back now."

I ignore his request. I needed this reaction to know for sure. But I can't go shoving a gun in everybody's face until I'm confident of a suspect.

"Del—I—just gimme the fuckin' gun." I hand it to him. "Thank you." he stuffs it in his waistband. "Holy fuck..."

"You and I are done." I turn my back on him.

"Wait—" he pauses. "Delson... I—uh—I need you, man."

I turn, face him one last time. "Find another lackey."

He shakes his head. "Nah, Del. It's not like that. You—you're like my only real friend, man." He lights another cigarette. "I know. Pathetic right?" he pauses. "I'm sorry. I didn't mean to fuck things up so bad." Salty streams break through his lashes like the unforgiving ocean smashing through failed levees.

THE SUN CREEPS behind rooftops and chain-link as townies gather on the football field. One candle lights another, until a few hundred glowing faces flicker behind tiny flames. I hold my unlit candle close, watching as people take the stage one by one. They share memories of Rose and Sam—voices heavy with grief, eyes weighed down by something darker. Fear.

"So... what happened to them?" Cordy asks me.

"Who?"

"The cult..."

Right. I forgot I never finished the story. "Eventually the founding families had enough. Someone torched the Society's temple during a ritual. Most died inside. The ones who made it out were gunned down in the street. They called it The Founders' Fire. The day Heller County rid itself of evil. We celebrate it every year," I pause. "It's almost the anniversary."

Rose's mother, Bridget, steps up to the mic. Her swollen eyes and chapped lips speak before she does.

"My daughter..." Her voice wavers, echoing through the PA. "My Rose. My baby—" She breaks, trembling. "I'm not surprised so many came to celebrate her. She changed people, and never realized it. She was a light in this dark place..." A quick sob slips out, but she catches it. Her eyes fix on the lake of flickering candles. "Sooner or later, we'll all have to answer for what we've done." Her jaw sets, her voice steadies. "You know it as well as I do. You know who you are. It's not over. And you *know* it." She slams her fist against the podium. "Moonlight matters!"

The crowd freezes in stunned silence—then erupts into a

confused, rising murmur. The sheriff moves in, escorting Bridget from the stage.

Mayor Lewis takes her place behind the wooden podium. "I apologize, everyone." His voice is a low, conciliatory tone that sounds forced. "I'm sure you can all understand and appreciate what Ms. Bailey is going through." He wipes a tear from his eye. "I know I do." His voice is calm. Confident. And somehow, even now, he sounds smug.

Edward races off toward Rose's mom, tailing her up and out of the stadium.

Alissa grimaces, catching my eyes for a moment, and looks back to Mayor Lewis.

"This weekend I lost my child. My son lost his brother." His lips tighten as he pauses. A contemplative gaze into the crowd.

Sheriff Lancaster steps to the microphone. "We're enforcin' a 9:00 curfew starting tonight. We just want you all to be safe. And please, kids, don't walk home alone. Stay in groups. We have this under control."

Alissa and Cordelia leave early with their parents'. I light a cigarette, dragging my feet through the wet field, feeling the cold dew seep into my shoes. Bridget Bailey knows something, and she's not the only one. Who was she talking to specifically? And why does *moonlight* matter? My shoulder juts back as I'm thrown off balance from a passing shape in the dark.

"Watch it dick," I mutter as I turn away.

"What's that, Heller?" Dane's voice grunts from behind me.

Shit. I face him fully. "Not in the mood, princess. Go flirt with someone else." I flip him off.

"It's never enough for you, is it?" He closes the distance.

My cigarette sparks across his chest as he slaps it from my fingers. His palms hit my chest and I stumble backward. A smile creeps across my face. Part of me wants this. Wants the excuse.

"That's enough!" Mayor Lewis snaps, grabbing Dane by the collar and yanking him away from the crowd. He hauls him into the parking lot, dragging him toward the old gym.

I glance down. My cigarette still glows between the grass blades. I pick it up, take one last drag. It doesn't help. I crush it and move toward the lot. Then I hear it—grunting. A muffled cry.

Rounding the corner, I catch it: Mayor Lewis slamming a fist into Dane's stomach.

"I will *not* have you embarrass me in front of the whole town!" His voice shakes with rage. One hand clutches Dane's shoulder. The other curls into another fist.

Before I can fully grasp the situation, I yank Dane from his father's clutches. "What the hell are you doing?"

Mayor Lewis looks stunned at first, surprised he got caught, then relieved it was only by me. "Between me and my son. Get out of here, boy."

I hold Dane up. He's embarrassed and afraid. I look back at Mayor Lewis. "You can't treat him like that. This is your kid, man." I can't help but wonder how he treated Sam after his arrest and expulsion.

"What's going on here?"

I turn to see a woman—late twenties, maybe early thirties. Blond ponytail down her back. Leather jacket clinging to her athletic build.

"None of your concern, ma'am. Just guy stuff," Lewis says, forcing a grin.

"Consider me concerned," she replies, expression flat, unshaken.

His smile fades. "Wait... I know you. You're that P.I. the Blooms hired." No response. "Go do your job."

"I am," she says, crossing her arms.

He scoffs. "Do you *know* who you're talking to?" he asks with a mirthless smile.

"A two hundred pound man-child failing at fatherhood and wondering if hitting a woman he's not married to is worth the hassle." Her voice holds steady. "Keep this up. It'll be you and I in this parking lot, understand?"

"Is that a threat? I'll have you arrested."

"I think once the police see the security footage, it's you they'll be arresting." She smirks, nodding to the camera perched on the corner of the building.

Mayor Lewis eyes the camera. His teeth grit and he curses under his breath. He grabs Dane by the arm, but he yanks himself away. His eyes flicker between his father and us before he runs back toward the football field.

"Dane!" he screams for his son.

"I'm sure he has some reflecting to do." She pauses. "Maybe you do too?" Her eyes narrow.

Mayor Lewis storms to his SUV and peels off into the night.

"Thanks for that," I say.

She smiles at me. "No problem... Delson, right?"

I pause, scrutinizing her before I nod. "You're a private investigator?"

She extends her hand. "Jenna Darkly. Private Eye."

I shake it. "Eddie never mentioned his parents hiring a P.I."

She glances down. "You didn't light your candle."

I look at the pale, untouched wax in my hand.

She flicks open a silver lighter. A small flame blooms. "Sometimes the things we keep buried inside, things we're afraid to face, hurt us more than what's outside."

I stare at the flame, then glance back toward the field—hundreds of candles flickering.

"I think theirs should suffice."

"One more light couldn't hurt," she says softly.

I stare again at the flame.

9

EDWARD
RED HANDED

BRIDGET SLAMS her palm against the dashboard again, crying out in fury. "That bastard!"

I just sit there. I wouldn't know what to say if I tried.

"He's a monster!" she chokes. "He doesn't even care—" Her voice cracks as fresh sobs wrack her chest.

I don't even know who she's talking about, and I'm afraid to ask.

"How can Will live with himself? How can he look in the mirror?"

"Who are you talking about?" I ask, my voice small. My stomach knots.

"Mayor Lewis!" Her face is flushed, eyes wild.

The nerves in my gut churn. For the first time, I feel the scope of our age gap. She's lived an entire life—has entire wars behind her—long before I existed. Suddenly, her pain feels too big for me to hold.

"His own daughter." The words slip from her like poison, low and sour.

"Bridge…" Looking at her is harder than head butting a brick wall.

"Will is Rose's father." She forces out. "He's paid me for years to keep it quiet. He never even held her once. And now my baby is gone and he couldn't care less!"

I struggle to grasp her words. It's hard to comprehend THAT when my biggest problem is winning a high school football game.

"He thinks his life is so perfect! He thinks he's better than the rest of us. He only cares about his delinquent sons!"

A new realization plows into me. "Sam and Rose were—" I mutter as the ugly puzzle pieces together.

"I forbade her from seeing Sam, but it was no use. I couldn't tell her the truth. Will said he'd take care of it." Something in her snaps. The sobs vanish and a sort of smile takes its place. "They'll come for him too. It's not over." Her eyes seem dark. "He was right." A raspy chuckle pops from her throat. A short whine. "Jason was right."

"Jason who?" I ask. "Right about what?"

"Jason Heller," she answers, her voice cold. "I think you should leave now." Each word comes out flat and hopeless, like she's already dying.

"What? No. I'm not going anywhere."

"Get. Out." Her tone is dead. I stay frozen. "Now!" she screams, leaning over and flinging the passenger door open. "Now, Edward!"

Gritting my teeth, I step out of the car. My fists burn with frustration as her tires squeal and kick gravel, disappearing into the night.

Pacing back and forth—biting the inside of my cheek—I wonder where Bridget went. If she's okay. If she's even thinking straight. My parents already snuck off to their room, dead to the world, thanks to their sleeping pills and three bottles of wine.

I take a swig from the warm bottle of rum. It coats my throat, sending saliva surging as I stumble down the hall. I stop at Ian's door. I can still feel the damn football bouncing off my head. Every time I barged in without knocking, he'd get me. I'm a pretty good catch now. But that habit—*knocking*—still hasn't stuck.

It's always the same memories, playing on a loop. Hide-and-seek with the neighborhood kids. Ian daring me to climb the fence between our yard and the neighbor's. It felt impossibly tall at seven. But once I made it over, I felt invincible. My first day of kindergarten—his first in second grade—he held my hand all the way to class. He knew I was scared. But he made it seem easy. "Act confident and you will be," he used to say.

When he found football, it was like he found purpose, and the way dad looked at him, I wanted that. He was so excited to show me how to play. We'd throw that ball back and forth for hours. Didn't need dinner. Mom would have to pull us in by our ears.

It's like I can feel him on the other side of the door as my fingertips grasp the knob. I twist the cold metal and the door squeals into the darkness of the room. Into the emptiness. His collection of trophies line the headboard above his bed. Pictures of him, his friends, and us as kids frame the large mirror on his dresser. I can pretty much pretend he's still here, if it wasn't for the bed being kept so neat, or untouched, I guess. I sit down. Another spicy gulp of rum rolls over my heart.

I wasn't drunk, maybe buzzed. I left the party, Alissa and I were fighting. I didn't take my truck, didn't want to risk it. I was angry. I remember that. It was dark, but the rain had let up a bit. I made my way home on foot. It was only three miles. Delson tried to stop me. Then he even offered to walk home with me. He insisted. I agreed, then took off when he went to the bathroom.

The lights were all on when I got there. The front door was cracked open, and I knew something was wrong. That sinking feeling—same one I get just before a sack.

Mom and Dad were out on a date. Ian had stayed home to rest before the game.

The first drops of blood were near the kitchen.

"Ian?" I called. I kept walking. More blood. A small pool in the hallway. "Ian!" I yelled louder. A red handprint smeared across white paint at the end of the hall.

Something darted through the living room—black hoodie. It bolted into the dining room. The black-hooded man disappeared through the sliding-glass door leading out back. I ran after him, leaping over the couch and hurdling through the dining room. Outside was quiet. The yard was empty. I turned back, yelling for Ian again.

I wasn't prepared for what was waiting for me. I followed the thickening trail of red goo. Ian was on the floor, twisted, mangled. A dark ooze pooled around him, soaking into the carpet. His chest... was opened, slit from the neck down. I couldn't scream. I could barely breathe and each attempt brought me closer to the floor. I steadied myself, gripping the wall beside me. His head was bruised, bloody and dented. Eyes stared, lifeless and filmy, at the ceiling, one bulging out of its socket. His jaw was open, too wide, and cranked to one side. An ugly sound wailed in my throat. That's when it got dark... I stumbled forward, dropping to the ground. Beside Ian, devoid of everything that made him... him.

I jolt up from the bed, like ripping myself from some nightmare-hellscape. My hands shake as the fire twists itself into my muscles. I grit my teeth, squeezing the neck of the bottle and stumble from the haunted room. I find my keys on the coffee table in the den. Not sure I locked the door behind me. Sheets of rain roar. White noise. The gutters flood as the drains clog with sopping piles of leaves. Closing myself in the truck, the sound becomes a rapid drumming, like a thousand fingers tapping along the outside of my truck, reaching out from the darkness. I try to mind the stop signs and speed limits, but I struggle. My foot pushes hard on the gas pedal every time I feel a surge of violence bash its way through my veins. I know where I'm going. I'm just not sure why. A smart person would turn back, wouldn't drive at all. A smart person wouldn't park his truck outside the Mayor's house to spy during curfew hours.

I take another drink from the bottle, numb now to the burn. Lights turn off, one after another. The porch light is the only one left on. I don't know what to do. But I know I need answers. Bridget said they'd come for him too.

Two hard knocks slam against the window, and my sack leaps into my stomach.

A flashlight blinds me.

"Step out of the vehicle." His voice is cold and firm.

Shit. I get out slowly.

He spins me around, presses me against the truck. "Any weapons on you? Anything I should know?"

"No, officer," I say, flat.

He pats me down, then turns me to face him. Slams me back into the side panel. "You know curfew's nine p.m., right?" The light stays in my eyes.

"Yes..."

He sniffs. "You been drinking?"

I lie. "No."

"Bullshit." He grabs my wrists and snaps the cuffs around them. "What the hell are you doing out here, anyway?"

"Nothing, I swear."

He sneers. "Come on." He pulls me to his cruiser and shoves me in the back. He mutters something into the radio on his shoulder.

It takes three hours before they start berating me with questions. The same ones over and over again. My parents get really pissed when they question me about Sam and Rose.

"Our son isn't capable of something like that." My father says. My mother nods her head hurriedly as she wraps her arms around me.

"Now, we aren't necessarily saying that, but given our current situation—"

"Listen, Sheriff," my mother barks, "We've been through this. It's been a year and you still haven't caught the man who killed Ian, now Mayor Lewis's son? And the Bailey girl?" she leans forward. "And you have the *nerve* to even suggest—"

"Mrs. Bloom, I'm not suggesting anything." He adjusts in his seat.

Dad huffs. "These kids' blood is on your hands, Emmet. If you just did your job the first time—"

"Dammit, nothing suggests that these murders are connected. Now you just watch how you speak to me in *my* station!"

"Come on, Edward." My mother pulls me up by my arm. Dad follows behind.

"David, hold on," the sheriff urges.

Dad stays as my mom tries to pull me away. "Wait," I tell her. "I'm waiting for Dad."

"Now, Edward," she snaps.

"I said *wait.*"

She storms off.

The office door clicks shut. I press my ear against the glass. Just enough space to hear. Enough of a gap in the blinds to see.

"Listen, and listen good," Sheriff Emmet growls.

"Save it," Dad says. "You need to take responsibility. Get this thing under control. Contain it. Before it spreads."

"Responsibility?" he snaps. "This blood's on *all* our hands. Don't act like you're the goddamn saint."

A beat.

"What if he's back?" Dad whispers.

"It's been twenty-five years, David. He's dead."

"What if he *wasn't* the last?"

"There *is* no 'them,'" Sheriff Emmet insists. "He was a lunatic. And he's gone. There was no one else... but us."

The doorknob turns. I scramble back, nearly falling.

"David!" he growls. The doorknob stops. I press my ear

back to the cold glass. Can even catch glances from the small space between a couple of crooked blinds. "Last month there was a break in at a local storage facility."

Dad shrugs his arms out. "You must be swamped."

"My storage unit was the *only* one that got busted open. Completely ransacked," he pauses. "The only thing missing was the DVD."

"What DVD?" Dad asks. Impatient.

"You know."

Silence.

"That footage should've been destroyed years ago."

The door swings open. "Edward." Dad calls as he passes by, slamming through the door. I follow him, more lost now than I was before.

10

DELSON
PHOTOGRAPHS

I CAN NO LONGER SAY I know emptiness. I *knew* it, once—but now, I am far from empty. Dread has crept in. Deep. It's made a home inside my chest. Its fleshy claws cling to my ribcage, its pointed chin pressed to the underside of my sternum. Cloven hooves have burrowed into my gut, churning my insides into sludge.

A string of cloudless days. A conciliatory warmth. Like Blackroot's trying to pull the mask back over its face, hide the rot with a layer of blue sky. A paper apology. A lie wrapped in sunshine for people too afraid to open their eyes. Life *will* return to normal. Minutes crawl like hours, hours like forever. Every day we wait for news of another murder, but just like the year prior, it stops with no news of a lead. Nobody behind bars. Three weeks since the murders and nothing. Elias calls me to ask where I've been, that Kenzie has been asking about me. I see her now only once or twice every other week. I make up some bullshit excuse. Too busy working on a big editorial for the paper. I'm swamped. The truth is, I'm scared. I don't want my toxicity to rub off on her.

Rose's funeral didn't feel real—until it did. Until the coffin lowered into the earth. Until the shovel cracked dirt. Carving her death into the fabric of space and time. That's when it hit, hard and final. Simple, yet, lovely words etched into stone boiled her whole existence down to seventeen years. The crowd stood in black, sobbing softly over the small wound in the ground. Then, one by one, they vanished behind cigarette smoke and grief. I waited until they were all gone before I approached. I wanted her to know I loved her —*if* that's what I felt—AM feeling—is love.

This morning differs from others, though not in its entirety. In fact, I would say it's more like most than it's not. I'm still knocked awake by some cruel dream where I'm with her. I still stare in silence at the ceiling, still weep, until I can't. More of the same. However, at 7:00 this morning my phone chimes, a message from an unknown ID. My heart shudders and a cold ripple peals through my body, like a heavy stone dropped in still water. My fingers shake, opening the message.

Home is where the heart is…

Captioned over a photo of my house.

The trash cans on the sidewalk tell me it was taken *this morning*. The sun had already risen—so the picture had to be only minutes old. I bolt down the stairs, steadying myself against the wall. I throw the front door open and burst into the yard.

No one. Nothing. Just the still morning fog.

It's a warning. I *knew* it. I'm next.

Makes sense enough to me, enough to accept the waves of panic that wage war inside, cramping in my lungs and throat. Selfishly my anxiety lessens when I discover the others received the same text—including photos of their own houses—at 7:00AM.

The courtyard still bustles, students huddle together in cliques, some stay in the cafeteria, others skate up and down the street. All are distracting themselves from the unpitying reality that stares them down. It's a cold thing to ponder. It tugs at your nerves, because surely life couldn't be so cruel. Could it?

Yes. It could.

Cordy leans against the chain-link fence circling the side of the campus. I snap a photo with my new—to me— camera. "So, what? You think us defenseless girls will be safer if we have you big powerful men to protect us?" she pouts with unpleasant sarcasm.

Luca smirks. "If I say yeah, does that make me a misogynist?"

"Just overly confident," Cordy says.

"You can have my bed," he offers.

Cordy's eyes slit. "I'd rather birth a pineapple." She flips him off.

His eyes widen at her response. "You guys hear?" he changes the subject. "They found Courtney Pierce's car in a ravine—off Craven Creek Road."

"That's good news, right?" Cordy says flatly.

I shake my head. "She's been missing this whole time. If she was in there... she's probably bones by now." I stare at the dirt. "We're the only ones the killer's contacted directly.

Why *us*? Why send *us* the murder video?" I don't wait for an answer. "Why the message this morning?"

"They're right," Alissa murmurs, glancing at Cordy. "Ian was alone when he was killed." Then she looks at Edward. "Same with Rose." Finally, her gaze lands on me. "We'll be safer together." She nods her head.

Edward tries to keep his gaze from her as he speaks in agreement.

Luca interjects. "Deadass, that's what we're trying to tell you. Stay together, twenty-four-seven, baby." His grin is toothy.

"What about our parents?" Alissa asks. "Do we take turns at each other's houses, or?"

"We can't go to my house." I blurt. "Trust me, you don't want to." I glance up. "My mom's really on one right now. It's not a good idea."

Edward puts his hand on my shoulder. "It's cool. We'll figure something out."

"My place works," Cordy says. "Mom won't care as long as there's no drinking."

"Riiiight…" Luca winks as he hangs his arms on mine and Edward's shoulders.

Alissa eyes her curiously. "Wait. Your mom would just be okay with all of us crashing?"

"Night, week, month—whatever." Cordy shrugs.

"Sounds good, Cordy. Thanks," Edward says, looking around. We all nod.

After school, we meet in the parking lot. The uncertainty of what happens next weighs on us all, aside from Luca. He grins at whatever prospect he ponders quietly in his own mind. His general lack of maturity or perhaps his inability to attain sincerity when a situation calls for such things is mind-boggling. Could be a self defense mechanism. He has the kind of smile that makes you smile, and he knows it.

We gather around Cordelia's and Luca's cars. Alissa is the first to speak it, but we're all thinking the same thing. We all want to know. "Who is this sick—Who's *doing* this?" she asks with a feeble chill.

"How 'bout a student?" Cordy eyes us.

"No." Luca scoffs. "To do what *that* guy did—I mean dude must be a MONSTER, right?" he glances around at the disapproving faces. "I mean, c'mon…" he shrugs his shoulders up, raising his hands. "You all *saw* the video, too."

"Shut up, man," Edward whispers through his teeth.

"Then who?" Alissa demands.

Luca shrugs. "No clue."

Cordy presses. "Let's say it *is* a student. Who could it be?"

"What about Dane and the dickheads?" Edward turns to me.

"They're assholes, but I don't know that they're capable of murder," I say. I hang on the thought for a moment. "They were out driving around," I confirm. "I had a run-in with them that night in Ingomar Hills."

"Isn't that Rose's neighborhood?" Alissa asks.

"Yeah…" Luca confirms. "I live just a couple blocks down."

"Doesn't make sense. Why would Dane kill his own brother?" I say.

An unintelligible bark from behind. I recognize the sound and turn to face Dane's sidekicks. Paul and Eric stride toward us, puffing their chests.

"Watch your mouth, bitch-boy," Paul growls, his fat cheeks red already.

Eric cracks his knuckles. "For all we know, you freaks did it. Been a year, hasn't it? Who's your next victim?"

Luca laughs. "Oh look. The bullies from every Stephen King movie."

They glare at him, then me. "What about you, Heller?" Paul sneers. "You the leader of this little cult? Too much of a pussy to off yourself, so you killed Sam. Killed Rose."

Edward steps forward, fists clenched. I throw out my arm. "Not worth it, Eddie."

They keep laughing. "You did it," Eric says.

Paul grins. "Like father, like son, huh?"

That old, sharp heat cuts through my spine. Without thinking, I turn my whole body and throw all my weight into my fist.

Paul hits the pavement. Two red streaks spill from his nose, his teeth stained with blood.

The chaos erupts.

Arms grab me. Shouts fly.

"Come on, Del!" Edward yells, yanking me back.

"Get up!" I shout down at Paul.

Luca grunts as he joins in Edward's effort, all the while commending me on the punch. They muscle me into the car, but they're left winded. The girls jump into Cordy's car. Tires screech as we all speed from the lot.

THERE IS a long dirt road tucked between the towering trees on the outside of town. We drive down the bending road until the forest opens to a clearing. The house is three stories tall, with two wrap-around porches, one on the first story, another on the second. The outside of the small mansion is redwood. Tall windows envelop the walls, the house almost more glass than wood. The only neighbors are somewhere on the other side of the encompassing redwood grove.

"Oh. Wow..." Alissa mutters as we step out of the car.

"This is me..." Cordy smiles, leading us up the porch steps.

"Gotta be generational wealth," Luca mutters, not nearly as quietly as he thinks.

"Shut up." Edward elbows him lightly.

Inside, the place smells like lemon Pledge and Windex. It's spotless. The picture frames gleam. No clutter. No forgotten mugs or socks. No fingerprints on glass. Not a single thing out of place. Except me.

"Mom?" Cordy calls into the cavernous, open layout.

"Cordelia?" a voice responds, as her mother rounds the corner.

"These are the friends I told you about," Cordy says, then glances back at us. "Guys, this is my mom. Or Nancy, if you prefer."

Looking at Nancy is like peering into Cordy's future. They could be sisters.

"Nice to meet you. I'm Eddie." He shakes her hand.

Luca states his name with a simple wave and smile.

"Delson," I say.

She eyes me. "Heller?" she questions.

"Good guess." I hold eye contact.

She smiles. "I knew your mother," she says. "Your father too. You look just like him at 17."

"How'd you know them?" I ask.

"Oh, we all went to school together. I moved shortly after graduating."

"Why'd you come back?"

Cordy answers for her. "Because Mommy missed her quaint little hometown and thought it'd be a *great* idea to rip me away from mine."

"I'm sensing a little hostility," Luca teases with a grin.

Cordy rolls her eyes.

"I missed the smell of the redwoods," Nancy says. "You don't realize how good it is until it's gone." She leads us into the den, then pulls Cordy into the other room.

The others get comfortable while I watch. Nancy seems upset, not mad, but worried. And Cordy looks defensive, irritated. I try to focus in, but they walk out of view and earshot.

They return with glasses and a pitcher of iced tea.

I join the others, sitting by the unused fireplace as Nancy pulls out a photo album from the bamboo bookshelf. She sits across from us, placing the large binder on the glass coffee table, flipping through pages of old photos until she suddenly stops.

"There we are. I miss those faces."

I look down—and freeze. My heart skips.

Rose. No—*not* Rose, but damn close. Different enough to tell, but close enough to shake me.

"Is that Bridget Bailey?" I ask, pointing to the faded figure.

"Sure is," Nancy nods. "And that's your mom." She points to the girl standing next to Bridget.

I hardly recognize her. She looks... happy. Alive.

"And that's Jason." Her finger moves to the boy behind my mom.

His hair is dark, messy. His face... he looks like me. Too much like me.

"I—I've never seen a picture of him this young before." I let slip.

"Then I'll make a copy for you. I think I have others as well." She turns the page.

"Wait, a second." Edward reaches for the binder. "You knew my dad too?"

"David Bloom is your dad?" she asks.

"Yes, ma'am."

"Small town," she chuckles.

Luca nearly jumps out of his seat. "That's *my* dad right there, no cap." He points at one guy in the photo.

Nancy sinks into herself.

"Okay, what?" Alissa leans closer. "That's *definitely* my dad." The four of us glance at one another. Eddie stays quiet.

"Is that Mayor Lewis?" Edward points to another guy.

Nancy closes the album with a snap and stands up. "I've got some work to finish. You guys go order food or something, alright?" She walks out without waiting for a reply.

"That *was* the Mayor," Edward says, matter-of-fact.

"That's the part you're focusing on?" Cordy scoffs. "There was a whole *lot* of weirdness in that picture."

"It might be a clue," he says.

Luca sighs. "C'mon."

"Think about it," Alissa cuts in. "What do we all have in common?"

"We're all targets," I say.

"Right. And?"

"Our parents all knew each other?" I offer.

"Does that not seem *weird* to anyone else?" Alissa's voice sharpens.

"There were other people in the picture," Luca says, exaggerating his eye roll. "Could've been a club photo. Year-book shit."

Alissa's not buying it.

"One of them *was* Mayor Lewis, right?" I look at Edward.

"Definitely," he nods.

"He's Dane's dad. So, if this is really connected—"

"Then the killer would come for Dane, too," Alissa finishes.

I glance back at her. "Exactly."

———

I DON'T FEEL tired until 3:00 a.m. Luca is already face-down on the bed, claiming it without hesitation. Edward offers me the other side, but I decline, choosing the floor instead. I slip out to the second-story porch, lungs tight as I drag hot smoke into my chest.

"You good, man?" Edward asks.

I don't answer. Just exhale. A cloud of smoke floats out into the cold air like an unspoken thought.

He joins me at the wooden railing, both of us staring down at the quiet property below and the dark woods beyond. "I think it's the Mayor," he says, voice low.

"The Mayor?" I smirk, then take another drag.

"He's involved somehow."

"Why do you think that?"

"Okay, Del..." He glances behind us, making sure no one's listening. "I'm gonna tell you something."

I meet his eyes, heartbeat ticking faster with every shallow breath.

"He's Rose's father." The words hit like an icy wave.

I must look stunned, because he immediately goes on the defensive. "It's true. Bridget told me. Apparently, he's been paying her hush money for years to keep the affair from his wife." He pauses. "My best guess is he got tired of having to pay her, so he killed Rose."

"But why kill his own son?" I prod holes into the idea.

"Maybe his public image is more important to him than Sam or Dane," he whispers.

I think of Mayor Lewis the night of the vigil. Maybe Edward is on to something.

"Wait, wait, wait. Why did Rose's mom tell you all this?" I demand.

He tells me about him and Bridget Bailey, their secret relationship. I'm shocked, more so that he would cheat on Alissa. He then tells me about his encounter with the killer.

"Why would he let you go?" I question as I shake.

"He needed me to deliver his message."

"Right... 'Death comes. River of blood.' Got it. But—"

"I think he's toying with us," Edward cuts in. "He wanted me to tell Bridget. And when I did..." He trails off.

"What?" I push.

"Something changed in her. Like something clicked. And she was *scared*, Del. She knows more than she's saying. And I'm convinced it all ties back to Mayor Lewis—" he pauses, "—and our parents."

He stares back out into the trees, jaw tight, then tells me what he overheard—his dad and Sheriff Lancaster.

11

DELSON
OUTNUMBERED

GOSSIPY PRATTLE HUMS from gawking mouths across campus. Someone tagged nearly every locker in black spray paint—crude depictions of Ingomar's mask. But not mine. Not Edward's. Same for Alissa, Cordy, and Luca.

"What could this mean?" Alissa asks, our group clustered by her and Cordy's lockers.

"He ran out of paint?" Luca offers.

"Maybe a metaphor," Cordy suggests, frowning.

"He's challenging us," I say. "He knows we're sticking together. This is his way of reminding us—we're still outnumbered."

"Or what if it's a hint—a clue?" Alissa adds.

"Why would he help us?" Edward asks, his brow creased.

"Maybe we can *use* this to our advantage," I say.

They look at me questioningly.

"I'll check Dane's locker. You guys see if any others are unmarked!" I say as I stumble backwards, turning to a sprint.

Running down the hall, I race up the steps to the second floor.

Dane stands at his locker, yawning as he retrieves his backpack. I run to him and slam the locker shut. He flinches back, eyes wide, stifling a shout.

No paint.

"What the *hell*!" he yells.

"Your locker didn't get tagged."

"Yeah, so…" he stiffens. "I DIDN'T DO IT."

"Neither were ours."

"And?" he shoves me and starts for the stairs.

"Dane!" I call. He raises a middle finger without turning. "You got a video too, didn't you?"

He stops dead.

"You're not the only one," I say.

He turns slowly, eyes scanning the hallway. Then he storms back, grabs my coat, and slams me against the wall around the corner.

"How do you know that?" he growls.

STUDENTS SHUFFLE into the gymnasium for an emergency assembly, moving like cattle to slaughter. The faculty lead the herd like seasoned butchers. We take seats at the top of the bleachers—backs to the wall. Dane sits apart, but in our row. Principal Myers drones on about increased campus security, vandalizing school property, the sheer disrespect of our fallen peers and fear/rumor mongering.

"Dane is part of this, then," Eddie says.

"Still think Mayor Lewis is the killer?" I ask.

"Pfft." Luca rolls his eyes. "Why's bro offing his *own kids*? That's a dumbass theory."

"Del saw him hitting Dane after the candlelight vigil," Eddie says.

"So?" Luca shrugs. "My mom kicks my ass all the time."

All eyes hang on him.

"What? It still counts if it's a chancla." He says.

Suddenly, a storm of notifications erupts across the gym. Phones vibrate and chime in chaotic harmony.

"Phones *off*—" Myers begins, but stops.

The five of us exchange a tense look as anxiety floods the room. Cordy groans, dropping her phone. Alissa gasps, hiding her face in her hair. Luca leans over to see mine. Edward's already frozen, staring at his screen.

Her bloody arms hang over the sides of the tub, flesh like dark hamburger meat dangles from the bone. Deep red rivulets and inkblots stain the white porcelain tub where she lies. The bathwater is a coppery-pink in sections, clots of blackish-red in others. Her bare breasts fall to either side of the bloody chasm between them.

"Bridget," Eddie whispers a helpless breath.

The gymnasium doors slam open as a group of cops— lead by Sheriff Emmet Lancaster—barge in. Lancaster grabs the microphone from Myers, who backs away in a stupor.

"Edward Bloom," Lancaster calls into the mic.

Silence.

All eyes fall on Eddie.

"Edward, don't make this difficult."

He stands slowly, stunned. He descends the bleachers like he's walking underwater.

At the bottom, Lancaster grabs his arm. "You're under arrest for the murder of Bridget Bailey."

The gym erupts in a chattering chaos.

"What?" Eddie shouts. "I didn't do anything!"

Lancaster wrenches his arms behind his back, locking the cuffs.

We push through the crowd toward the parking lot. Dane trails just behind.

I'M the first through the doors at the station. The others rush in behind me. Sheriff Lancaster appears from a back hallway.

"Sheriff!" I call, louder than I meant.

He stops, scowling like he just caught a whiff of something foul. "What the hell are you kids doing here?" His eyes narrow on Alissa.

Officers glance up from behind desks, coffee paused at their lips.

"Edward didn't do it," I say.

"He couldn't have," Alissa adds. "Dad, he didn't."

He raises his hands. "That's enough—"

"We were together all day yesterday. Last night, too," I insist.

Lancaster's eyes fix on Alissa. His nose wrinkles. "Edward's prints are all over that house. And that's not even the worst of it. I'm gonna need a lot more than the word of a bunch of kids." He huffs. "Until some evidence comes out working in his favor—"

"We aren't lying," Alissa steadies her words into an unfamiliar severity.

"Got any evidence?" he asks simply. "Because from where I'm standing, I see a troubled kid, prone to aggression and violence, whose fingerprints are all over our crime scene..."

We share hopeless glances, knowing this is a losing battle.

"Well no, but—"

"Then leave." He points to the door. "Alissa, I'll see you at home."

The others drop their heads. They're done. For now.

"Edward and Bridget were sleeping together," I say.

The room falls silent.

"NO WAY!" Luca chokes.

Lancaster blinks, caught off guard.

"That's why his prints are everywhere," I add.

"Can you back that up?" Lancaster asks.

"Check his phone," Alissa says. "His WhatsApp. Instagram. It's all there."

Lancaster sighs. "We'll look into it." He rests his hands on his belt. "Now get outta here. And stay out of trouble."

WE SIT around Cordy's fire pit. The night pushes in around us, shadows deep beyond the backyard. The moon glows behind a curtain of silver-gray clouds. Dane throws back a shot. Luca follows. Then Cordy. Then Alissa.

"Bridget knew," I say, drawing their eyes. "She was afraid. Remember the vigil?" I hang on the thought.

"Her kid just died," Luca shrugs.

"The things she said, like she knew it was coming. Maybe even who's doing it."

"That doesn't do us any good now. Does it, Heller?" Dane pours another shot.

"Her DAD sure didn't seem too broken up though, huh?" Luca stares at Dane.

"What the hells that supposed to mean?" he questions.

Luca grins. Dane can sense the deception as we all nervously glance away.

"No more secrets," Cordy says. "From any of us."

"What?" he asks. "What am I missing?"

"There's something we haven't told you," I say quietly.

Orange fire rings dance in his pupils.

"Your dad is Rose's biological father."

"Shut up." He laughs, but none of us joins him. "What are you talking about?"

Luca blows air through his lips. "Daddy cheated on Mommy. Mommy had a baby. Baby was Rose."

Dane's smile vanishes. He looks around, eyes darting. The fire flickers in his face.

"It's true," I say. "He paid Bridget for years to keep it quiet."

He leans back, restless. "That's why you think it could be my dad?"

"Kind of, yeah." I nod. "If nothing else, he *knows* something."

"Our parents were all in that photo you showed me," he reminds us. "So don't just point fingers at mine."

Alissa leans forward. "But your dad has motive."

Dane scoffs. "Not really. Rose didn't even know. And you

think he killed *Sam*." He grits his teeth. We glance at each other and he takes a drink from the bottle.

I slink away from the group to use the bathroom. Once finished, I find my way to the balcony overlooking the front of the property. Burning tobacco fills my lungs with a dizzying embrace that whispers secrets only known to intoxicated souls. In this ephemeral haze, reality softens and I find myself lost in the delicate embrace of smoke and consciousness.

Lights cascade from behind the trees and a series of vehicles pull off the road and park below. Two cars, an SUV and a truck.

"What the hell?" I peer over the balcony. The door of the SUV opens. "Mayor Lewis?" I question as he straightens his suit jacket by the collar. I rush downstairs, bolting through the house, nearly falling through the back door. "The Mayor is here!"

Dane jumps to his feet. "What?"

Cordy grabs the bottle and shoves it in the cooler with the beer. "He's out *front* right now?" she pulls her braids back into a hair-tie.

"And he came with his whole goddamn *posse*!" I say.

Luca chuckles as he stumbles to his feet. "Absolutely diabolical."

Alissa glances at her phone. "Oh no. My parents have been calling."

We rush to the front of the house. Cordy peeks through the peephole.

Knock. Knock. Knock.

As she reaches for the knob, I stop her. "No matter what,

we keep what we know between us. I don't know who we can trust. But I trust you. All of you. At least... I *hope* I can."

Everyone nods.

Cordy exhales, then opens the door.

Mayor Lewis stands on the porch, eyes hard.

"Party's over," he says through clenched teeth.

12

DELSON

LONG HARD ROAD OUT OF HELL

SOFT BEAMS of moonlight struggle to break through the suffocating clouds. We stand, tense before the Mayor as he paces, his grim eyes locked on Dane. He fidgets, indecisive, before finally planting his hands on his hips. Alissa's mom pulls her aside while Sheriff Lancaster scolds her. Mrs. Lancaster's face is as red as her and Alissa's hair. Luca hangs his head, playing the part of the regretful son—poorly. His smirk bleeds through as his dad drags him aside.

The door to the truck creaks open, and Rick steps out.

"What the hell are you doing here?" I ask.

He sighs.

Mayor Lewis steps forward. "What do you kids think you were doing?" he growls. "Sneaking out. Lying!?"

"You'd know all about lying, huh, Dad?" Dane fires back.

Lewis adjusts his suit jacket. "Watch your tone, boy."

"Why, gonna hit me again?"

Silence.

Lewis chuckles, hollow. "Hit?" he scoffs, glancing at the

other adults. "Don't be dramatic, son." His tone shifts—softer, careful. Nervous. "Even you aren't too old or too tough for a slap on the wrist."

Alissa sniffles. "We're sorry. We're just scared. We feel safer together."

Her mom hugs her. "You have nothing to be afraid of."

Her father places a firm hand on her shoulder. "You're safer at home. With us."

A sharp crack interrupts the moment. Luca's opened a beer, pausing mid-sip as all eyes land on him. "What?" he shrugs.

Mr. Reyes pinches the bridge of his nose.

"You kids been drinking?" Lewis growls.

"I brought this from home," Luca says flatly.

Rick meets my eyes with disappointment. I shake my head. Even he should know I won't touch the stuff.

Nancy steps out, wrapping her robe tighter around her as she yawns. "What's going on out here?"

"Oh, real nice, Nancy," Lewis snaps.

"Excuse me, *Mayor*?" she folds her arms.

"You let our children hide out in your home. Allowing them to drink!" He steps toward her. "What have you been telling them, Nancy?" he finishes his question with a whisper I can't make out.

"Nothing," she scoffs. "I assumed you all knew they were here and as for the drinking, I wasn't aware. I assure you, Cordy and I will have a long conversation."

He laughs. "Ah, a conversation."

"Better than a beating," I mutter.

His eyes snap to mine.

His jaw tenses, then he turns back to Nancy. "How can

you be so naive? Do you remember what it was like being a teenager in this town?"

"Trust me. I remember." She rests a hand on Cordy's shoulder.

———

THE CAB of the truck is cold, reeking of Rolling Rock, Lucky Strikes, and faint grease. Rick holds out his hand. With a sigh, I pull a cigarette from the half-crumpled pack. He brings the wad of cardboard to his lips to retrieve a smoke for himself. The tobacco crackles in the flame. I crack my window, releasing the first chemical puff. The window squeaks as Rick cranks it down fully, smoke slithering from his nostrils in little streams that burst out the window.

"You know, your mother—"

"We really gonna do this?" I flick a stub of ash to the wind.

"Yeah, Delson. We're gonna talk about this." He exhales hard. The truck's weak headlights cut only a few feet into the blackness. "She's going through it right now. She's doing her best."

"I've been dealing with her best for seventeen years." I inhale, let the cigarette burn a little longer. "Do you know what it's like to come home from school not knowing if anyone's even gonna be there? If you're going to have dinner? When or if your mom is even coming home?" I exhale. "To be eight years old and alone for weeks? Getting yourself to school just so you can get fed?"

Still nothing.

"And when she was there, God help me if she brought

some junkie boyfriend around. Because guess who took care of her when she OD'd? Who cleaned the bottles. Pulled the needles from her arm. Made sure she didn't drown in her own puke." I take another drag. "She owes me a childhood. I don't owe her a fucking thing."

Silence.

Rick's grip tightens on the wheel, tendons bulging beneath his skin. He exhales a stream of smoke, then reaches over, pats my shoulder.

"Shit, kid." He pauses. "If I had any advice... get out. Get out of this town. Out of this county. Turn on it and don't look back. It's a long, hard road ahead. Don't stop runnin'."

He sounds sincere.

I hang back as Rick goes inside. Rain drizzles down, soaking my back as I lean against the hood. I'm afraid of what's waiting in that house. I've seen detox. Watched every breakdown. Every fake restart. Even if some piece of my mom survives this, how do I forget? Forgiveness isn't impossible—but forgetting? That's something else entirely.

I walk into the house. It's tidier than usual. The smell of mold is faint. I can hear the shower upstairs. I turn the corner and Rachel sits on the couch, wrapped in a blanket. Sweaty, in pain. The cigarette between her fingers shakes.

"Where have you been?" she asks weakly.

"A friend's." I sit next to her on the couch.

"I missed you, sweetie." She takes a puff of her cigarette. "Will you hand me one of those?" She nods her head toward the table.

"What are these?" I ask, grabbing the bottle of pills.

"They help the withdraws... prescribed. Promise," she murmurs.

I glance her name on the bottle, hand her a pill and the glass of water. Her movement is sluggish as she swallows the pill.

"Mom." The word feels foreign on my tongue. "I need to ask you something."

She looks at me, waiting with melting-makeup face.

"How did you and dad know Mayor Lewis and Bridget Bailey?"

"What are you talking about, sweetie?" she avoids my eyes.

"And Nancy Krueger, David Bloom?" I probe further.

Her eyes widen. "Delson, just because we went to the same school doesn't mean—"

"Bullshit." My voice comes out in a whisper.

She sighs.

"What do you know about the murders?" I ask, tiring of her procrastination. "Whose doing this? Who killed Rose?"

Her breath halts for a moment. Her eyes glaze over. She's shocked at first. Fear wells in her eyes, it drips from her lashes. "W-what—" she stutters. "Why would I know anything about that?"

"Be honest with me, *Rachel*," I hiss. "For once in your life, just tell me the truth."

Her eyes shut tight. The tears come fast. "I'm dying, Delson."

I blink. "Don't be dramatic. You'll be fine."

"No. My liver's failing. I need a transplant... but I don't qualify," she chokes back a sob and lifts a warm beer to her lips.

"Put it down." I rip the bottle from her, as she reverts to something like a shamed animal.

She's pathetic.

I smash it against the floor. "I wish I could say you did your best, but that'd be a lie. You could turn your life around *right now* and maybe, just maybe, it would matter. Because once I'm eighteen... you might never see me again."

She flinches.

"You have no idea what I've lost. What I've had to carry. But that doesn't mean *you* stop trying. You can be better than this. And your *seventeen-year-old son* shouldn't be the one convincing you of that."

She crumbles. "I'm so sorry." Her voice is raw. Her apology isn't much—but it's real. And somehow... that means something.

13

DELSON
THE LAST TWO

THE ODDITIES of the little coffee shop are now unsettling to non-regulars. Its voodoo theme, the atmosphere of the *other*, too out of the norm, leaving The Serpent And The Rainbow all but empty. Though the aroma of homemade bagels and freshly brewed coffee still summons those with weak constitutions. Adele draws her washrag from her belt-loop like a dagger, cleaning already-clean tables. She throws a quick glance at me and The Blooms' private investigator, who sits across from me, hair pulled back into a tight ponytail. The bags under her bloodshot eyes add to her 'don't-mess-with-me' facade, surely masking a mountain of stress. She takes her coffee like mine; black, bitter, and hot.

"Heller? How'd you get a name like that? Considering—"

I cut her off. "My Great-great some-odd Great Grandfather—Thomas Heller—was supposedly the one who found the channel entrance to the bay. Other ships, unable to navigate through the dense fog, crashed into the rocks. He was also a member of the Blackroot Society. He died, of course, as the story goes. Burned to death in their temple with the others."

"Quite the history." Her tongue clicks in her mouth. "How long have you known that Edward Bloom and Bridget Bailey were sleeping together?" she asks after a blistering gulp.

"Ms. Darkly—"

"Call me Jenna." She drops a couple of ice cubes in her coffee.

"How long have *you* known, Jenna?"

She hesitates. "A few months."

"What about Mayor Lewis?"

Her eyes sharpen. "What about him?"

"Just that Rose was his daughter. That he had a secret affair with Bridget. That he paid her for seventeen years to keep it quiet—from his wife, the town, his sons. One of whom, by the way, *dated* Rose. Sam Lewis—the son who was murdered that night."

She stares into her steaming cup. "That's a hell of a claim."

I nod. "So you think he's involved?"

"Even if he is... where's your proof?"

"A simple blood test would be all you'd need."

"Rose Bailey is dead."

"There are ways," I say.

"Say it's true—all that proves is adultery. Not murder."

"What about Courtney Pierce?"

"She's been missing almost a month. They found her car wrecked in a ravine off Craven Creek. Cops are working it. People disappear around here all the time."

"Yeah. *Tourists.* Not locals. Not students."

"I was hired to investigate Ian Bloom's murder. I haven't seen any connection between him and Courtney Pierce."

"She vanished the *same* night as Rose and Sam. Exactly one year after Ian was killed. That's not a coincidence."

She watches me, sips her coffee. "I'll look into it."

"You don't think Edward really did this, do you?" I ask.

"No, I don't, but the police do. He has ties to all the victims. His relationship with Bridget Bailey doesn't clear him, not in the slightest."

"They can't just keep him locked up."

"Nobody's stopping the sheriff. He's bullheaded, and he's convinced the Blooms' that it's in their son's best interest to be kept in holding, for now at least."

"What's it gonna take to prove Eddie's innocence?"

Her eyes flick from her coffee to me. "Another murder."

Silence hangs between us.

"I want to show you something," I finally say.

She leans forward. "Then show me."

I set my phone on the table, open the screen capture, and slide it to her.

She studies it. "What am I looking at?"

"The murder weapon."

"How do you know this is the kind of knife that was used?"

I shake my head. "No. You're not understanding me. This is *the* knife." I pause. "It's a Moorhaus D2 Bowie. Thing is 15 inches long." I clue her in on the video as well, leaving the others out of it.

"I need that link, Delson."

"Sorry. It expires after you open it."

"Any idea why the killer sent it to *you*?"

"I was hoping you might know."

GUILT DRAGS through me like wet sand in my lungs. Eddie locked in a cell. Courtney Pierce—sprawled out in a ditch somewhere—bloated, bruised and lifeless. Blackroot's very own Black Dahlia. I should hope she turns up alive. In a drunken stupor. But I don't believe that.

I drift into the cafeteria, linking up with Alissa, who waits at the table in the far corner.

"Two lockers left, Del," she says.

I hold my hand out for the small piece of paper. "Any idea who they belong to?" I glance the numbers.

"No such luck," she sighs. Light-purple bags droop under her emerald eyes. Her long red hair flows down her back in loose curls.

"Eddie will be okay," I say.

She glances at me. "My dad might hate him, but he can't *prove* Edward did something he's just not capable of," she hesitates. "Then again... he's full of surprises." She catches herself. "I'm sorry, I didn't mean—"

"After Ian died, everything changed. That kind of loss messes you up. But if I know Eddie, he'll use every breath trying to fix what he broke."

"You lost Rose," she says softly. "And you haven't—" Her eyes glaze.

"That's different." I glance away. "We all process grief in our own ways," I pause. "You're one of the kindest people I've ever met. Eddie knows that. He knows how badly he screwed up."

"Thank you." Her hand lands on mine.

I pull away gently. "I-I should get on this."

"Need a second investigator on the case?" she smiles as the others arrive with trays of food.

"No. You guys stay. I don't want them to feel cornered." I try not to think of *The Adventures of Delson and Rose* as I slip away.

I find the first locker. I've never spoken to her before, but I've admired her from afar. Rowan Riley is the most loved girl at our school, while simultaneously claiming the title of most loathed. Tall, long brunette hair. Wealthy. I wouldn't be surprised if she hired out for makeup and wardrobe. If this school were a monarchy, Rowan Riley would be Queen. But she's still human, like the rest of us. Her mom died when we were in fifth grade—an aneurism right there during after-school pickup. I'll never be able to unsee the fear and devastation on her little-girl face.

The owner of the last locker—Nathan Barclay, Rowan's best friend—shares a similar loss. I know little else about him, other than his mom owns 'Barclay Electronics & Repair' and that his dad left him the family gym, 'Body By Barclay'. He was one of Coach Dean's best players, but after his dad died, he up and quit, joining the cheerleading squad the next day.

I sit on the stands above the football field, put out my cigarette and watch for eyes watching me. The scent of the night's rain evaporates with the mild heat of the sun's light squeezing through steel clouds. The cheer squad finishes practice while the football team struggles with strategies that don't involve Sam or Eddie. I flick my cigarette, watch the smoke dissolve. Watch the sky bleed gray.

"Rowan," I call as the girls pass.

She blinks, surprised. We've never spoken.

"Yeah?" she stops.

"Can I talk to you for a second?"

Her pale cheeks pinken. "Okaaay." Her hands fall to her hips. "Whaddup?" the 'p' pops off her lips.

Nathan follows behind, tall and broad shouldered, his complexion smooth and dark. His smile is genuine and kind.

"It's about the graffiti," I say.

"Oh, what of it?" she pops a gum bubble.

"I noticed that out of all the lockers in the school, there were eight that weren't touched, both of you included."

Nathan holds up his hands. "We had nothing to do with that."

"I'm not saying you did." I pause. "Any idea why you'd be left out?" they both shake their heads. "Did either of you receive a link from a blocked number after the murders?" I clench my teeth after the words spill out.

A subtle shift on Rowan's face. Caution? Fear? "You're giving major red flags, Delson."

"Rowan, people's lives could depend on it."

Her jaw clenches. Eyes shimmer.

"Did you get the video?"

A beat.

"We got it," Nathan mutters.

"*Nathan*—" Rowan hisses.

"Girl, I'm scared. He clearly knows something."

"I don't know much," I admit. "But maybe, with your help, we can figure this out."

"Figure what out?" Rowan asks.

I pull up the photo Cordy's mom showed us. Hand my phone to Rowan. "Do you recognize anyone?"

They both study the image. Their silence answers before their words do.

"That's my dad," Nathan says. "What *is* this?"

"Yeah, my mom. So what?" Rowan demands.

"Look again," I say. "That's Ian Bloom's dad. Rose Bailey's mom. Mayor Lewis. Every one of them has a kid who's dead. Or got that video."

Her eyes roll. "Okay, take a seat, Delson."

"My parents are there too," I say. "Every unmarked locker? Belongs to someone whose parent is in this photo. All of us got the video. Eleven of us in total. Three are dead. Eight lockers remain."

Delson
~~Rose~~
Alissa
Cordelia
Edward
~~Ian~~
Dane
~~Sam~~
Luca
Rowan
Nathan

MY SHOULDERS ACHE from walking home with every muscle tight, every nerve strung up.

"Delson!" Frankie's voice cuts through the dusk. "There you are."

I glance around, making sure no one's watching, and keep walking.

He falls in step. "Hey, kid," he tries again. I keep walking. He grabs my shoulder to stop me. "Houston, we got a problem."

"What now?"

"They broke into my place. I got ripped off! All the money, all the drugs. EVERYTHING!"

I scoff. "I don't have time for this shit, Frankie."

"This is *bad*. Like fuck-your-face-with-a-brick bad."

"Then maybe don't pull me into it."

"They took *Courtney*."

I stop cold. "What?"

He chews his nail. "Rival dealers. They warned me when they caught wind of our little business. I didn't listen."

"We didn't start anything. It's *your* business. Your shit. *Your* mess." I jab my finger into his chest.

"Not how they see it. They think you're in on it."

"You idiot." I shove him. "If anything happens to Courtney, it's *your* fault."

His cheeks inflate with a worried sigh as he pinches the bridge of his nose. "You think I don't know that?"

Anxiety squeezes my throat. It's hard to look at him. For all of his good qualities, he always gives me another reason to dislike him. "Damn it, Frankie."

A black van screeches to a halt beside us, slide-door shrieking open. Frankie bolts, but hands seize him and drag him back. Arms wrap around me, pulling me in after. A sack over my head, my limbs bound with what feels like zip-ties. My head slams to the metal floor as the tires wail and the van peels out. They fucking got us.

14

EDWARD

FOUND FOOTAGE

I sɪᴛ at the head of my cot in the cold cell, knees pulled up, arms crossed over. Meanwhile, the killer's out there, plotting his next move. Someone else could already be dead. If Bridget had taken me with her... maybe she'd—

I can't believe she's gone.

Heavy footsteps echo down the corridor, keys jingling with each step. The bars clank and rattle as the cop opens the cell. "Come on, Bloom," he barks.

"What now?" I ask, swinging my legs over the cot.

"Move it." His chubby hand grips my arm and pulls me into the corridor.

He takes me back to the little room and sits me at the small metal table. I cross my arms over the cool surface and lay my head down. It isn't long before Sheriff Lancaster joins, dark rings under his eyes, jaw speckled with graying fuzz. His dark hair is slicked back and oily. He sets a brown grease-soaked paper bag on the table. The smell folds my stomach like an origami swan. He removes his coat and hangs it on the back of the chair across from me.

"You hungry?" he asks as he sits down.

"I normally eat like, six chicken breasts and four pounds of rice daily. Yes, I'm hungry."

He grins. "Dig in, son."

I tear open the bag and devour the food. The burger's barely warm, tomato is mushy, but the pickles are crunchy still. I cram salty fries into my mouth between bites. Two minutes. Gone.

He reaches behind him and tosses me a Dr. Pepper. I crack it open and chug until the hiccups kick in. The carbonation burns my throat and waters my eyes. I burp.

"Let's talk about Bridget Bailey," he says.

I wipe my mouth. "There's nothing left to say."

"How long you two been seein' each other?" He leans forward. "How'd it happen?"

I poke my tongue at the burger meat stuck between my teeth. It comes loose, and I swallow. "Last summer. Me and the boys were running some drills down on the field." I remember how hot it was that day—that whole summer hot as balls. We kept running Ian's plays, but they didn't work. I wasn't as good as he was. "We called it a day, and on my way to see—"

His arms cross over his chest. I sigh.

"I was on my way to see Alissa, and... I saw Bridget walking by herself on the side of the road. She had a flat and left her phone at home. I offered her a ride."

"Then what?" his voice lowers.

I breathe deep. "She invited me in for something to drink. I didn't think—"

"Don't feed me that. You went in because you *wanted* something more than iced tea." He scowls. "You broke my daughter's heart. I'd love to crack you right in the goddamn jaw, you know that?" he leans closer. "What happened next? You drug her?"

"Hey, *she* came onto *me*, okay?" I snap. "I'm not that guy."

He leans back, smirking. "So what kind of guy *are* you, Edward?" I say nothing. "Maybe Bridget had second thoughts. Maybe she knew Rose wouldn't approve. Maybe you thought if Rose were out of the picture, you and Bridget could do whatever the hell you wanted. But then the boyfriend shows up. You kill him. Bridget finds out. You kill her too."

"No!" my voice breaks.

"We found her *heart* in a ziplock bag under your porch." His face turns red.

"I didn't kill anyone!" I choke out. "I'm being framed. This is all a game to him."

My mind flashes to that message: *Home is where the heart is.*

"Then give me somethin'. Anything!" The metal table rings after his fist slams down. "Damn it, boy!"

"It was all pretty normal... for a few months. But I couldn't man up to break things off with Alissa. I was seeing Bridget a couple of times a week, maybe more. We'd sometimes get hotels on the weekends." I hesitate, and then tell him about the afternoon we heard about Rose. I tell him about the masked man in my truck holding the knife to my throat.

"Horse shit."

"He wore a black hooded poncho, like the ones they hand out at the rainy games."

"Everyone in town has one of those, boy."

"He also had a leather mask, the one stolen from the museum, the Ingomonster." Sheriff's eyes go cold. "He wanted me to send a message. *Death is coming. Only a river of blood will set them free.*" I pause as the blood drains from his face. "Sound familiar, Sheriff?"

"You shut your goddamn mouth—"

"What happened?" I cut him off. "You. My father. Bridget. Delson's parents. What did you all do?"

He goes quiet.

"What's on that DVD?"

He bursts from his chair. The collar of my shirt ruffles between his clenched fingers as he pulls it taut. He leans in, teeth gritting. "I'm not sure what you *think* you know, but keep it to yourself. Understand?" The stench of coffee and booze wafts from his mouth.

I want to be a man. I want to be strong. Puff out my chest, spit in his face, tell him to eat shit and die. But my vision blurs, and I'm a kid again.

"Do. You. Understand?" he growls.

"Yes, Sheriff."

"*Yes, Sheriff, what?*"

I steady my lips. "Yes, Sheriff... I understand."

The door bursts open. Nancy Krueger storms in, dressed in a tailored blue suit, long black hair over one shoulder. Her cheeks burn red. Lancaster straightens, swipes his hair back.

"Edward, don't say another word." She turns to Lancaster. "Laying hands on a teenager, Emmet? I expected better."

"Nancy, what the hell are you doing here?"

"You're lucky David still considers you a friend. Otherwise, you'd be facing charges." She points to me. "Get up, Edward. Your parents are waiting."

"Yes, ma'am." I move fast.

"*You* should be ashamed," she says coldly.

"Why'd you come back, Nance? We don't need you interferin'."

"If this is how you've been running things, *someone* needs to."

I wait just outside the door.

"I don't know who's doing this," Nancy says, her voice fading behind me. "But ruining this kid's future won't fix the past."

"What's that supposed to mean?" Lancaster growls.

She turns back into the doorway. "Maybe it's karma for what we let you and Will do to Jason."

Jason Heller?

THE OLD GAMER chair creaks under my weight as I sink into it. My chest tightens with worry—Delson is still MIA. I type his dad's name into a search bar. *Jason Heller.* Not much turns up. Arrested for murdering several children between the ages of five and eighteen. It's strange. For years, most of these children remained missing until Jason led police to the unmarked graves himself. This would have been just before Delson was born. He never admitted to killing them, but the authorities charged him with the crimes. He denied it. It wasn't until a few weeks later that additional evidence came to light, incriminating him. Moonstone Prison has been his home ever since.

A text dings on my laptop. The contact is unknown.

Freedom never felt so good, huh?

Two minutes pass before I reply.

Who is this?

Wouldn't you like to know...

My cheeks burn.

You delivered my message. Good boy.

Fuck you.

We have something for you. A token of our gratitude.

Not interested.

Ah, but you will be...

Tell me who you are.

Silence. Seconds crawl by.

You saw how easy it was to put you away.
We can turn this whole county against you.
So do as we say.

Why are you doing this?

I type, hands shaking.

> No more questions. You want to be a hero?
> Be like Delson? Save your friends? Now's
> your chance.

A new window blips open on my monitor. Alissa. Asleep in her bed. Textbooks scattered around her like debris. She looks exhausted, even in sleep.

My heartbeat slams in my fingertips. I reach for my phone—it rings before I can touch it.

"Don't touch her," I say.

"**You are in no position to make demands.**" The voice is just like I remember it. Whispered, layered. Wrong. "**You care for her?**" it asks.

"Of course. I love her." I rise from my chair.

"**Funny how we treat the ones we love, huh?**"

"Why are you doing this? Please don't hurt her. Please."

"**Perhaps it's all for fun, like a game... that is what you said, correct? That we are playing games with you? Well, we can assure you this is *no* game. However, there are instructions. Simple enough for even you to follow. Get the keys to your truck. Drive. We will send you directions when you are on the road. If you do not comply, we will slit her throat and pull her tongue through the hole.**"

The line goes dead, and Alissa vanishes from my monitor.

The sky's a deep black-blue, stars scattered across its skin. Without cloud cover, the cold sinks in, sharp and cruel. The houses are still. Lights off. Curtains drawn. The only movement—a woman walking down the street, black hair glinting under the moon. A huge dog trots beside her. She watches me from across the street. Neighborhood watch. Always watching.

My truck roars to life. The engine rattles my bones. I pray it doesn't wake Dad. Once I'm around the corner, I pound the passenger seat over and over, screaming until my throat burns. Hot tears drip down my cheeks.

"Come on, asshole!" I yell out, as if he can hear me. "Where am I going?" my knuckles go white over the steering wheel until my phone dings as if to answer. It's directions. He's leading me out of town.

Alissa's promise ring stings in my hand as I squeeze.

Houses become a rare sight as I speed further down Craven Creek Road. I slow up as I roll over the old wooden bridge. It creaks and groans under the weight of my F-150. Craven Creek sparkles like stars below. Tall, dark trees run along the road on both sides, leading me up the mountain. After a good twenty minutes, the road comes to a dead end, my throat aching as I pull over.

My phone buzzes.

"Get out." The voice is different, staticky, distorted. **"Walk up the embankment, through the trees..."**

I step out. The cold bites into me. I climb the wet slope, pushing through moss and ferns. My breath clouds the air as I push into the trees.

Then I see it.

An old house, buried in the woods. Its white paint peels in long, curling strips. The porch sags. Steps rotted through. The roof looks like it could cave under the weight of dead leaves. Windows, what's left of them, are fogged with grime. Off to the side—padlocked cellar doors, chains wound tight.

"What are you waiting for?" the voice coils in my ears.

"Y-your voice…" I whisper.

"Sounds familiar?" A pause. *Ian.* Or… who he used to be.

"You're not Ian," I say. "Ian's dead."

My phone vibrates. A FaceTime notification.

"What's wrong?" he asks. "Afraid of what you might see?"

I ignore the FaceTime.

"Go inside. Your prize is waiting *for you*," he says, a demon instead of a ghost.

All my instincts tell me to book it in the opposite direction, but Alissa… I tread carefully onto the porch, afraid my foot might break through the boards where something waits to grab me and pull me underneath in the dirt and muck. Irrational fear, maybe. But something I'm not gonna risk. The door—barely hanging on by the loose, rusted hinges—screeches open. A dull light soaks the inside of the soggy structure from my phone. The air is difficult to breathe, musty and thick with the stench of sour piss. The rotten drywall and floorboards groan, seeming to shift as I walk. Branches, twigs, and leaves, maybe a couple of bird carcasses. Each step takes me further into the gaping mouth of this place. The wallpaper has all but lifted and curled down in strips and sheets. Cracked and sagging, the ceiling threatens to cave in. Cupboards in the kitchen have fallen from the walls. Somehow, the kitchen smells worse than the living room. But it's almost just as empty aside from the busted wooden chair scattered across the old peeling linoleum tile and the doorless refrigerator that houses a pile of brush and twigs.

I search through drawers and cabinets. Nothing. Standing at the bottom step, I swallow hard at the thought of going upstairs. The walls on either side of the staircase drink the light from my phone. The top step is nearly invisible. Each step rises further into darkness, leading to a sheet of solid black. And each step—uneven and soft—threatens to give. I grip the mossy wooden rail to keep from losing my balance. My breath becomes visible, illuminated by my light. Impenetrable shadows stretch from floor to ceiling in the long hallway.

The first door on my right whines as I nudge it open. Empty. The windows busted out. I creep inside. The boards creak all the way to the closet. I pause before I open it. I'm sure this is where I die—just an empty closet. I keep moving. I find the bathroom. A rusty clawfoot tub—with a small pile of brush inside—gleams a dusty glow. Rust, mold, and rot. The toilet sits crooked in the floor, wood swallowing porcelain. I move my feet, never staying in one spot too long, to avoid being digested by the floor like the poor toilet.

Someone shines a bright light in my eyes. They've caught me! No, it's just my light reflected at me from the mirror. The door at the end of the hall is open. The sheet of darkness fights with the light as I enter the doorway. A small gray rectangular device is sitting in the middle of the floor. I shine the light on the outdated thing. A square, clear plastic case is on top with black letters scrawled across.

PLAY ME

I pop out the disc and reexamine the device on the floor. It opens up like a clamshell. It's an old portable DVD player.

The plastic clacks as I open the disc tray and pop it in. The screen is black at first, then streams of gray static zip across the low-quality screen.

"You gotta bring that camera with you everywhere?" a voice says from the tiny speakers.

"Absolutely." The boy laughs. The picture comes into focus. I can't believe my eyes, but I see my dad. He couldn't be more than eighteen years old here.

The scene changes. A group of kids are partying. It's them—all of them from the photo. A man sits in a large chair. A glass of liquor in hand. He watches, smiling.

"Put it down, babe!" Rachel stumbles toward the screen, laughing. She and Jason kiss.

The screen goes black, then flickers back.

They're outside. Its dark.

"W-we have to do something!" a boy yells.

"Like what, Will?" Jason demands.

Will. Mayor Lewis.

"We kill him."

Jason flinches. "We can't just kill someone!"

"If-if we turn him in, we go down with him," someone argues.

"Then it's settled." Will's voice is hard. "We tell the others tonight. Beckett Reid dies." He stares into the lens. "Turn that damn thing off."

Cut.

A new scene. This house. My heartbeat drums in my ears.

Jason stares into the camera. Looks exactly like Delson.

"If anyone finds this, it means we failed. But something has to be done. Beckett Reid is the one. He did this. We just... can't remember where they're buried. It's all a blur. And it's-it's our fault. If we don't stop him, he'll kill us all."

Another cut.

The woods. A circle of cloaked figures. Leather masks. Fire. The angle is low, like the camera is hidden.

Beckett Reid steps forward. A crown of antlers on his head. Knife in hand.

"Let us join hands. Tonight, the Blackroot Society breathes again!"

His voice is wild. His grin, unhinged.

"She is the fifth sacrifice. A noble, virtuous, worthy sacrifice, and so is the beginning. Too long have the families who threaten our existence gone unpunished. No more!" The fire cracks and laps up toward their heads. Beckett reaches into his cloak and draws out a knife. "The small amount of blood spilled tonight will give way for something far greater."

The haunting masks under the dark robes glance back and forth.

He draws the knife up, setting the blade to his hand. "Death is coming for them... death comes for them all! Only a river of blood will set them free." He slides the knife across his palm. "We share the sins of our brothers and sisters, only separate in body. But in soul... we are conjoined." His fist hangs high over the flames, squeezing as the blood drips into the fire. With a grin, he holds the knife out to the hooded figure beside him.

They take the knife. Hold it to their palm.

"Say it." Beckett's eyes narrow with his command.

"D-death is coming for them. Only a river of blood will set them free..." The girl's voice almost breaks with her words. But she slits her palm and bleeds into the flames. The knife gets passed around the circle. One after another, they all say his words. The final hooded figure to his left takes the knife, holding it in their palm.

"Say it..." Beckett says.

They hesitate. Still holding the knife in their hand.

"SAY IT!" Spit flies from Beckett's lips as he howls.

They all flinch at his booming voice. "Death is coming for them..." the figure glances at Beckett. "Only a river of blood will set them free!" The figure plunges the knife into Beckett's stomach.

Beckett falls to the ground. Their hoods all fly back as they rip off their masks. Emmet Lancaster tries to retrieve the knife that he left in Beckett's stomach. Beckett growls as he dislodges the knife himself. He slashes the knife at Emmet. Beckett stumbles to his feet. Rage curdles in his scream. Jason Heller tackles Beckett to the ground. The knife falls beside them. They roll on the leaf-scattered forest floor, trying to retrieve the knife. The others freeze in place. Jason locks his arms around Beckett's neck from behind as they scramble to their feet. Beckett's robe falling to the ground. My dad grabs the knife and rams it into Beckett's chest as Jason holds him from behind, locking his arms around his neck. Beckett hurdles Jason over his shoulder, smashing him into my father. He rips the knife from his chest and stands over them as they scramble back into the dirt.

"I WILL KILL ALL OF YOUUUU!" he screams over the cries of the girls and the roar of the flames.

The gunshots echo as Beckett stumbles back, white shirt clinging to his torso, saturated in deep red. His eyes widen as his rage dissolves. He drops to his knees. The knife falls from his fingers. Will Lewis steps forward with the gun. My dad grabs the weapon from Will and fires three more shots as Beckett tumbles back into the dirt.

The screen goes black for the last time. I put the disc

back in its case and stuff it in my back pocket. *Delson needs to see this.* Shadows drench the room again. I step down the rotting stairs. A large thud crashes from beneath me. The cellar... somebody is here! I run back to my truck, almost falling through the porch as I burst through the front door, followed by a possum. I rip down the trail until I tumble down the embankment. I start my truck and smash on the gas pedal. I can't get far enough from that damn house!

A text buzzes.

Good boy.

I glance into my back seat, just to be sure.

"Where the hell are you, Delson?" I mutter, voice trembling.

15

DELSON
THEY WATCH

AT LEAST AN HOUR has passed since they cinched our wrists and ankles. Heavy sacks pulled over our heads. I stay quiet. Focus. There's a way out of this. Frankie talks shit the entire drive. I hear them beat him when they grow tired of his mouth.

"Delson!" he shouts. "Are you okay?"

"Don't worry, Frankie." I want to say I'm fine, but I can't lie to myself. I'm terrified. Not of what they might do, but of the finality this could mean. I'm scared I didn't get to say goodbye to my little sister. Terrified that I might not see the son of a bitch burn—the one who took Rose from me.

My body jerks forward as the van skids to a stop—my head pounds from slamming into the wheel hub. The men grab us, shoving us out of the van. A man grunts as he cuts the ties around my ankles. Impossible to tell where we are. Small rocks crunch beneath our shoes as the men lead us— the scent of dirt and gasoline filters through the thick sack. I stumble as the toe of my shoe catches a concrete lip. The sun's heat fades as we enter some kind of structure. Our steps now echo on the hard pavement beneath. The smell of gasoline and grease deepens, accompanied by a rusting metal and char aroma.

"Your problem now," a voice says from behind, and the van grumbles away.

"You wanna play?! I'll fuckin' play!" Frankie yells. "Cut me loose, bitch! Let's do this!" There's a thud, then a grunt.

"Frankie, now's not the time…" I mutter.

"Sit your asses down and shut your mouths!" one yells, slamming me into a chair. Frankie groans after another metallic crack.

"Sit tight, boys," one of them snickers. The voice rings familiar.

"He on his way?" the other asks.

"He'll get here when he gets here."

Cellophane crinkles. A Zippo clicks. Smoke slinks through the sack and hits me like a punch—thick, bitter.

"Can I bum one?" I ask.

"Did I say you could speak? No. I said shut. The. Fuck. UP."

The smoke worms its way through the fabric and into my lungs.

"Then how about a cigarette?" I ask again.

"Whatever. Give the loser a stogy." The other mutters. A stinging gray light blinds me as he rips the sack from my head. A ski mask still covers the smoker's fat face. He holds the butt of a cigarette to my chin. I grip it with my lips.

"Can I get a light?" I mutter past the cigarette. "I'm a little tied up." I hold up my wrists, cinched with a black zip-tie.

He flicks the Zippo's flame to life.

The puff fills my mouth. I blow the first drag out of the corner of my lips. The taste of butane coats my tongue.

"It's hard to breathe in this thing, asshole," Frankie says.

The man rips the heavy black sack from Frankie's head. "That better, princess?"

"Yeah, that too much to ask for?"

The smoker feints a punch. Frankie doesn't flinch.

"Can I get one of those?" he asks.

"Yeah, right." The man drags deep and blows it in Frankie's face.

"If you're gonna kill us, don't I get a last request?"

The man stretches his middle finger in Frankie's face. "Fuck yourself, junkie."

"That's nice," Frankie mutters.

A phone rings. "It's him." The smoker nods to the skinny guy, who looks nervous. "Watch them." He steps outside to take the call.

The skinny one groans and sits on the hood of a junked car. He glances at us. Then at his phone. Scrolls. Scrolls. Gone.

I drag on the cigarette until it's an orange sharp ember. I lean forward, press the tip to the plastic zip tie around my wrists. Long, slow breaths. The sour stink of melting plastic is the scent of hope. I fake a wipe at my chin as the skinny guy glances at me. I lay my cinched hands on my lap, exhaling the rancid smoke. He looks back at his phone.

My pulse thuds in my hands as the veins bulge. I twist my arms... and... *snap!*

I press my wrists back together to hold the severed plastic in place. Frankie grins as he spots my freed wrists. I lean toward him, pursing my lips to hand him the cigarette.

He shakes his head, flicking his eyes to his hands. A small pocketknife cradled in his palms. He jerks the little blade back and forth against the plastic tie, his swollen, red fingers working it.

The sun sets, lathering the warehouse in shadow. Several junk cars surround us. An old metal barrel riddled with gaping rusted holes smells like burnt wood and plastic. Missing chunks and garbage pock the concrete floor. Large metal cords and wires drape over the steel rafters and bars of the exposed ceiling, curling and winding onto the floor in coils and loops. A large engine block hangs overhead, hoisted up by some mechanism. Long boards and rope clutter the rafters. Deep orange shapes stain the concrete near where we sit. The smell of iron is heavy in the air. They're gonna kill us.

"What's the plan, Delson?" Frankie whispers. "Either we die, or they do. Then we'll have to split town. They'll hunt us."

The skinny guy glances up. Then down.

I take a final drag and flick the butt. "Carpe diem, Frankie."

"Carpe-what? I don't speak French!" he growls under his breath.

"Shut up," I mutter.

The smoker returns. "He'll be here soon. Bag 'em."

The skinny one hops off the hood. "Lights out." The sacks return.

I *know* these voices.

"Let us go," Frankie pleads. He knows it's coming. A ditch in the woods. Two more missing in Heller County. It's not even news.

Gravel crunches. Headlights pierce the sack. A door slams. Heavy footsteps echo on concrete—dress shoes.

"Gentlemen."

"Boss," they reply together. Like the bootlickers they are.

"We have guests."

"Yessir," the larger one responds.

"Hmm..." shoes tap, tap, tap as he approaches.

Frankie's breathing is shallow, quick, and shaky. It makes my heart punch my ribs and my stomach feel hollow and cold. Blood burns in my cheeks.

"You thought you could sell Skullflower in Blackroot, in Heller County at all? Who is supplying you?"

"Kill yourself," Frankie mutters.

"Let me take a wild guess—" he says. His voice... "Frankie Trueheart." He rips the sack from Frankie's head.

"Yeah. What of it, bitch?" Frankie blurts. His breathing, rapid.

"But *who* in the world is this?" I know his voice. Calm, confident. Smug.

"Mayor Lewis?" I ask, but I know it's him.

He rips the shroud from my face. His eyes narrow, jaw flexes as he kneels over me.

"Delson Heller." He straightens up. "Shame." He pauses. "You know, I knew your father."

"Yeah." I steel myself. "I know all about that." I meet his gaze. "I know *everything*."

His jaw clenches. "Oh, do you?"

"Killing us won't fix this. I'm not the only one who knows. If I disappear—"

Pain explodes across my jaw as his fist snaps my head sideways. "I'll kill them too. This is *my* town."

Blood fills my mouth. I spit it at his feet, wrists still pressed together.

"I will *bury* you," he hisses. "Like I should've buried your father. Stubborn little shit." He frowns.

"My father's a killer. I'm not him. I'm not *you*."

He chuckles. Adjusts his tie. "Kill them."

"Bring it on, baby," Frankie spits.

I stand, raising my fists to the larger one. The zip tie falls to the floor. Frankie squares off with the other.

Mayor Lewis eyes the broken strips of plastic and smirks.

Frankie lunges, tackling the skinny one to the floor. The other walks toward me. I can make out the shape of his smile beneath the mask. He takes the first swing. Misses. He swings again, wide. I pull my arm up to block it and crack him in the nose with my left. He stumbles back.

Frankie straddles the skinny one, fists bashing his masked face back and forth.

Another wide swing misses me. He's strong but slow. I throw a couple of jabs and back off. His fist whooshes past me again, again, and again. I sway through every would-be knockout. I see an opening and drive my fist into his stomach. As he lurches over, I stomp down, his toes crunching under my heel. Create an opening and fill it. A sharp breath wheezes from his throat. He falls back to the floor. His black ski mask is sticky with blood. Frankie stands victorious beside me.

The skinny one scrambles, pulling a gun and aiming the barrel just inches from Frankie's face.

Frankie lunges forward under his extended arm, wrapping around his compact figure and tackling him to the floor —the gun drops. Frankie lays underneath him, one arm cinched around his neck, the other holding the pocket knife. The man's chest and ribs pop and squelch as Frankie jams his blade in repeatedly.

I dive to the floor to retrieve the gun. Got it! I jump to my feet and point the gun at the other sack of shit before he can draw his weapon. "Drop the gun!" I scream. "Now!" I cock the gun.

He scoots his gun across the floor and stands slowly, his hands up. Frankie pushes the body off the top of him and grabs the other weapon.

The SUV door slams shut as Lewis barges back in. "Do I have to do EVERYTHING myself!" he screams as he pulls a pistol from under his suit jacket.

I point my gun at him. "Don't you fucking move!"

The shot makes my ears ring—a burst of light flashes from the barrel of Frankie's gun. The large one's head snaps back as he collapses to the floor. A pool of blood seeps out around him like a red halo, his leg spasming.

"NO!" Dane screams, stumbling from the SUV. "Dad, you said nobody would get hurt!"

"Get back in the car!" Lewis roars.

Dane doesn't move. Frozen.

I pull off the masks.

Paul. Eric.

"You had *kids* working for you?" I turn the gun back on Lewis.

"Drop it, shit-ass," Frankie pants.

"You don't want to do this, boys," Lewis says, calm.

Frankie sneers. "Ooh, how the tables have turned, asshole."

Dane tries to speak. Lewis slaps him. Hard.

I yell for him to stop.

Lewis drops his jacket. Rolls his sleeves. "Let's do this," he growls.

"DAD!" Dane shouts.

"SHUT YOUR MOUTH!" His eyes never leave mine.

"You wanna play tough, old man? Fine. Let's go." My hands shake. I don't notice until he points it out.

He lunges. Twists my wrist. Gun flies from my grip.

He grabs me. Gun to my temple.

"Hold it!" Frankie shouts.

"Dad, please!" Dane begs.

"Toss your gun!" Lewis orders.

"Don't do it, Frankie," I plead.

"I won't kill him if you drop it," Lewis lies.

Frankie tosses it into a nearby truck bed.

Lewis shoves me. Throws the other gun into darkness. I charge him. Try to tackle him by the waist. His knee crushes my chest.

Fist to my jaw.

I swing wildly. He dodges. Another kick. My ribs scream. White flashes in my vision.

I stagger. Punch. Miss. Swing. Miss. My arms slow. Another hit. Lights out.

A gunshot. Frankie fires into the ceiling.

The SUV's lights die. Black.

"Someone else here, boys?" Lewis asks as the room flashes red, then black. Red again, then black. The hazard lights all out of sync. He steps forward. "What is this?" Neither of us says a damn word. "Who else is here?" he yells. "Leave with your life, or stay and die!"

Dane pushes himself further into the corner, his wide eyes seeking mine.

The SUV wails and whistles as the alarm blares. The headlights flash on, illuminating the warehouse again. He pulls his gun on us as he looks over his shoulder toward the bright headlights, his free hand blocking the searing light from his eyes.

"Who's there?" he steps over a coil of wires and cords toward the warehouse's opening.

A small red light blinks near the corner of the exit—an electronic whir. A thick cord of woven wire cinches around his ankle, jerking his leg out from under him. His gun flies out the door as his body whips back. His head slams into the concrete as he flips upside down. He's hoisted upward, smashing against the metal rafters above, screaming the whole way. He reaches up to his ankle, tearing at the wires. There's a metal 'clink' from the shadows. The wires slacken, dropping him to his back. He groans, holding his head. Some mechanism releases, and the metal chains above fall free, sending the large engine block tumbling down.

It all happens simultaneously: the sound, crunching bone, and squishing meat. Chunks of his skull ricochet off the walls and rattle around the floor—the pungent smell, like swimming in a pool of pennies. The taste sticks in the back of my throat. Dark red spray coats the floor and splatters Dane. The headlights of the SUV drip with viscous streams.

"We gotta go now!" Frankie screams as he grabs me by the arm.

I grab Dane, who still stands in the corner. His eyes stuck to the mass of bloody flesh. I pull him outside, stumbling in the dirt. He opens the back of the SUV and pulls out a large gasoline container.

"We need to get out of here," I say.

"Nobody can know about this! They can't know about my dad." His eyes are wide and glossy. He pours the gas throughout the warehouse. I call out to him. He stumbles back outside, an old rag clenched in his fist. He lights it up and tosses it near his father. The flames grow to a blaze with a wicked flutter of fire. He leaps into the SUV and Burns out, leaving us behind.

Frankie grabs me and we just start running, following the first semblance of a road. My trembling fingers attempt to operate my phone. Ten missed calls.

A new message.

I stop. Stare.

"What?" Frankie pants. "What is it?"

I open the link. The horrid image of the mayor lying lifeless, his head smashed under the engine block. The warehouse, fully engulfed in flames. Another message appears.

We work well together, wouldn't you say?

I KEEP my window rolled down, praying the cool night air will keep the vomit in my throat at bay. It mostly works. We crawl to a stop in front of Frankie's apartment, eyes scanning the bushes along the sidewalk for any sign of masked psychopaths. The silence stretches long, taut, until the latch clicks and he steps out.

He leans down to the window, elbows on the passenger

door. His teeth chew at his lip before he speaks. "Delson…" I won't look at him. His hands frame my face, his forehead rests against mine. "I—I'm sorry," he murmurs. "We're done —I'm done. Promise. No more of this shit."

"Don't do it for me, man."

His head nods gently against mine. "Alright." His hand wraps around mine. "You got it." He clutches his ribs, limping to the stoop. He looks back once, before disappearing inside.

"Del. What happened?" Cordy asks, pulling away from the curb.

"Drop it, please," I mutter, staring up at the star-punched sky.

"Where've you been? Edward's been trying to find you."

"So he got out?"

"My mom, being the badass lawyer she is, marched in and put the sheriff in his place."

"Good. That's good…"

She glances at me. "Delson, I just need to know that everything's okay."

"Nothing's changed. He's still out there, leading us around like blind puppies. We're not on his level." I glance back out the window. The houses pass by, quiet, dark, and filled with prying eyes. "He's got us right where he wants us. It's like he's writing a horror story, and we're just characters made for cannon fodder. He's ten steps ahead. Swear, the fucker knows where we are at all times. Hears our conversations…"

"How's that even possible?"

Then it hits me. I don't know why I didn't think of it

before. "Whoever this is, he must be pretty tech-savvy, right?"

She shakes her head. "I don't know. I mean, I guess."

"Think about it. The entire town received the pictures he sent. The videos he sent us, after one viewing, the link expires. The police can't trace it for shit. Otherwise, they would have caught him, right?"

"Yeah, you'd think so."

"He's bugged our phones. Not just us, but maybe the whole town. He could be listening to this conversation right now."

"This guy work for the FBI now? Let's flip the reality switch back on."

"Interplanetary travel, artificial intelligence, the inability to distinguish what we see or hear online from fact or fiction. Hello? *Did the president really say that, or was it AI?* Nobody fuckin' knows. It's not science fiction; that's *our* reality. This isn't the 2000s; bugging phones is child's play."

"Point taken." She looks at her phone, suddenly uneasy.

"Turn it off, Cordy." I slide off my jacket, wrap my cheap phone in the sleeve, twist it hard until the thing cracks. I shake the pieces out the window. Glass and plastic hit the pavement.

"Now, Cordy."

She fumbles to shut her phone off.

"Can you take me back to Frankie's?"

"Sure—but why?"

"I have an idea." The tires squeal as she pulls a sharp U-turn.

I stumble out of the car, charging to the front door. "Frankie!" I pound my fists against it.

The door flies open. His eyes wide, a cloud of weed smoke trailing behind him. "What, man? Jesus!"

I shove past him. "Close the door."

He glances toward Cordy's car. "She coming in?"

"Close it."

His eyebrows jump, but he obeys. The apartment's small, not messy. Minimalist, but not by design. He's been saving for something—probably a house.

"Take a seat, will ya?" he drops into his recliner, grabbing the bong from the coffee table.

"You're getting high?" I snap. "Three people are dead, and you're getting stoned?"

"Yeah. And Courtney's still missing. Forgive me for needing to breathe."

"You killed two men tonight, Frankie."

"Pshh. Okay, Miss Marple," he scoffs. "It was them or us."

He's not wrong.

"Turn your phone off," I demand.

He exhales a thick cloud. "Paranoid much?"

I snatch the phone off the table, drop it to the floor, and stomp down until it's shattered into fragments.

His jaw hangs. He stares. "Five seconds. Better be good, or I'm kicking your ass."

"You have any burners?"

He clicks his tongue, pulls a Ziploc of joints from the cushions. "I mean—"

"Burner phones, Frankie."

He throws his arms up. "Yeah, a few! What the shit is going on?"

"Where are the phones?"

"Dresser in my room." He nods his head toward his bedroom door.

I barge through the door and scramble over his bed. I pull the first drawer out. It falls to the ground, just socks. The next drawer hits the floor. Condoms and fancy watches spill out. I open the next drawer.

"Hey, don't break my shit!" he yells as he stumbles through the doorway.

My heart stops. Tucked next to a neat stack of shirts, the smooth handle of a knife juts out from a large leather sheath. I unbuckle the leather strap and draw the knife. I feel Frankie's eyes on me from the doorway.

"Bottom drawer, asshole," he says.

I turn, taking a noticeable step back, knife clutched awkwardly and unsure.

His hands raise. "Woah, chill out."

"Why do you have this?" I press my back to the dresser.

His brows pull together. "I need to explain why I own a knife?"

"It's a *big* fucking knife," I say.

"It was just a gift!" he blurts. "From my dad, before he bailed. It belonged to *his* dad. It's old. Dull as hell."

It is.

He walks past me, opens the bottom drawer. A dozen burner phones stare back.

"Take your pick."

I slide the knife back into its sheath, place it back with the shirts. "I'll take them all."

"For what?"

"Don't worry about it."

"Well, I'm keeping one. Seeing as you went full American History X on mine." He sighs. "Just bought that thing."

16

DELSON

A LITTLE DEATH

A CHILL ZIPS from my scalp to my fingertips as I press my forehead to the glass. My skin—still damp from a blistering shower—squeaks out a hollow sound against the window. Cigarette smoke drifts upward, curling through the cracked pane above the sill, swallowed by the night. Aloneness. There are few things I fear more.

A soft tick. A tiny pebble taps the window from below. A figure stands beneath the skeletal tree in the front yard. She waves. I shove the window open and—like a memory ripped from some sweeter time—there's Alissa, staring up at me.

"Can I come up?" she whispers from the shadow of the tree.

A familiar scene from childhood—another life altogether, really. Like a long-forgotten song, all it takes is that opening chord, and the whole chorus comes spilling out of you.

"I-I'll be right down."

Each step down the stairs feels like a step in the wrong

direction, but also a step toward the inevitable. The deadbolt clunks as I twist it. The door—too large for the frame— barks open.

"Hi," she whispers.

I place a finger to my lips and lead her upstairs. The bathroom door squeaks open. She scurries toward my bedroom, freezing in place as Rick pokes his head out of the bathroom.

"Can I help you?" I ask.

His eyes bounce between Alissa and me. "Nope." He zips his lips, locks them with an invisible key, and tosses it over his shoulder like a drunken mime.

I shut my bedroom door and lock it, double-checking the knob just to be sure. Alissa leans against the open window, silhouetted in moonlight. The whole room glows faintly blue, like we're floating in some limbo between dreams and memory.

She smiles. "Should I leave?"

"Only if you want to," I say.

"Nah." She chuckles, slipping off her coat. The moon- light brushes her bare arms. She glances out the window. "I tried calling. You and Cordy. Her phone was off." She shifts, nervous. "I didn't wanna be alone tonight."

"What about your parents?"

"Dad's still out patrolling. He's been obsessed." She shrugs. "Mom's two bottles deep in a cheap merlot."

She leans against the windowsill, fingers tapping the wall near her hips.

We sit in silence, not feeling pressured to talk. Like slip- ping back in time, I can almost hear and smell that other life, hazy, dreamlike images and sounds—a smell I can nearly pinpoint but can't quite place. A feeling I forgot and now only catch in echoes, each one teasing somewhere in my temporal lobe.

"Déjà vu, huh?" she says.

"Yeah, a bit."

Her tongue clicks in her mouth. "Remember when we were kids, my dad would drink, and I'd sneak over and climb up the tree—" she giggles. "To crawl through your bedroom window?" I laugh, and she continues. "You'd make a little nest on the floor and insist I take the bed." She pauses. "Always a perfect gentleman."

Laughing unties the knots in my stomach. Dislodges the lump in my throat. My cheeks ache from smiling rather than fighting or crying.

"You always took care of me," she says.

"We took care of each other," I correct.

The moon flickers through her red hair like fire behind stained glass. I look down at the floorboards, heart spinning, as she lowers herself onto the mattress beside me. Her shoulder brushes mine.

"Kinda funny," she says. "I swear, there was one summer I slept in this bed more than my own." She grins, eyes on the window. "Remember those raccoons that used to raid your trash cans like tiny masked bandits?"

I laugh. "Remember when we planned to run away and get jobs?"

"Yup. Got as far as the bus stop before someone got *hungwy*," she teases with a pout.

"You're the one who bailed," I say.

"And just like that, our plan to open a bookstore was ruined."

"Technically, my plan," I smirk.

"Fine. I was just along for the drama."

"I haven't thought about that in years," I say.

She sighs. "I miss this. I miss *us*... what happened?"

"We got older and made other friends. You found Edward, and I found Rose." Saying their names flattens the flutter in my stomach, like tying marbles to butterflies.

Silence. A light breeze drifts in, cooling my neck.

"Do you ever wonder what it would've been like if things panned out differently?" her eyes watch the floor at our feet.

A jolt wrestles its way up my spine. My throat tightens. "In what way?"

"With us."

My stomach flutters again. I could stop this right now, put up another wall. But I'm sick of walls.

"I guess I'd be lying if I said it never crossed my mind," I say.

Her hand drifts over mine, and our fingers lace. Static jolts up my arm. I stand upright, releasing her fingers from mine.

"I'll take the floor, for old times' sake."

Rose, I can feel her pale arms pulling me down. I miss her warmth, the way her eyes would light when she smiled, squint when she laughed. I wrestle back the nausea when I remember she can't smile anymore. She can't laugh. She lies in a dark box under six feet of earth. Everything she was and ever could be, reduced to memories and whatever sphacelates in that box.

Alissa grabs my hand. My body betrays my heart. "Delson, it's okay," her voice is light. "I think we can share the bed."

"I don't—"

She interjects. "I just want somebody next to me."

Chewing on my cheek, I walk to the dresser and open the drawer. I grab a pair of sweats.

"Think these will fit?" I ask.

She nods as she grabs them and tosses them on the bed. Her hands fidget with her belt. I turn my back to her, cheeks burning—the buckle clanks on the floor as her pants drop.

"You can turn around," she murmurs.

I turn as she crawls under the blanket. I lie next to her—careful not to touch. She pulls the covers to our necks.

We talk for a while. Childhood memories. How we've changed. What stayed the same. I let her speak. I let her grieve. I don't have the strength to share my own.

If I hadn't gone out for Frankie that night—

"Maybe we'll wake up and realize this was all a dream," she whispers.

"What if you have to die to wake up?" I say before I can stop myself.

"Maybe we won't wake up at all." She shifts. "Delson, look at me."

I turn. Her breath warms my neck.

"Hi," I murmur.

"Hey." Her eyes glint in the dark. She moves closer. "I just want to try something."

Her eyes disappear behind lashes as her lips press against mine.

It's soft. Gentle. But inside, I burn. Less like butterflies, more like lightning crashing into a redwood—setting the trunk ablaze—sending scorched bark in every direction. Her lips part slightly against mine, and her hand grazes my cheek, then slides into my hair.

I pull away. Dizzy. My breath lost to her kiss.

"I—I'm sorry," I stammer, tasting her on my lips. "This isn't right."

Edward. What the hell am I doing?

Tears sting. Shame wrestles with need. One part of me demands loyalty. The other screams for something—someone—to make me feel alive again. Two primal forces wage war in my chest, determined to leave me a barren battleground.

Alissa stands. "Delson, we don't belong to anybody," she says. "We could both die tomorrow. And for what? Let's live first. Just this once... let's live."

I can't respond. My body betrays my heart.

She lifts her shirt over her head, lets it drop. Her lips graze my neck, a gentle touch at the base of my throat. My breath catches, dismissing all worries, abolishing all anxieties of loyalty and betrayal. All that's left is heat, skin, breath—now.

Only now.

Warmth pools in my stomach as her breasts press against me. She pulls me in tight as her kiss dances up my neck. Hot static zaps up my spine. Before I have time for another breath, her lips crash against mine. I grip the small of her back, the other hand tracing the curves going down. I pull her even closer. She tugs me tighter around her slender frame. My heart aches and yearns as her kiss deepens. I give myself over to it. Our clothes scatter the floor as the fire inside dictates my every move and I don't let go. I can't. So when I lay her on the bed, our eyes meet, and for just this once, we live.

———

Her love was like a funeral.

I linger in the memory of her touch—gone too soon. I was broken—split open and exposed—waiting for the crows to pick clean the cavity of my chest. And yet, somehow, I'm left mended. Her breath still dances steady and soft against my skin; a light moan purrs from her unconscious lips. Lips like knives. One to slice away tumors of guilt and grief, the other to stick in my best friend's back. But whatever happens to us, her body will haunt mine: a little love and a little death.

She curls up; the comforter bunched against her. The flesh of her hips, ribs, and back glow in the early morning sun. I brush her wild red mane from her porcelain cheek. Her tiny powdered freckles spot the bridge of her nose and drift under her eyes in equivocal patterns. Plump lips part, pale-pink and supple. I run my fingers down the length of her body—curvaceous and tight—slowing at her hip to circle her thigh and sail up again. Dark lashes shudder as she slumbers, threatening to end this almost perfect moment.

I'm so lost in her that I barely notice the knock at the front door. The voices from downstairs are of no concern. Real life and all of its burdens take a firm backseat. The staircase flexes and groans beneath encroaching footsteps. They advance up the hallway toward my bedroom.

A quick knock. "Del," he's muffled through the door.

The knob turns. I didn't lock it after going to the bathroom.

I freeze. The door swings open.

"Del, wake up—"

I jolt upright. "Eddie!"

Alissa scrambles, dragging the blanket to cover herself, pressing her back to the wall. Her hair a wild, fiery halo. My chest knots.

Eddie's mouth opens. His jaw locks, his nose crinkles. His eyes flick between Alissa and me, disbelieving, burning.

"Eddie, I—"

"Fuck this," it tears from him. He throws something across the room. The door slams, rattling the walls.

"Eddie!" I yell, leaping from bed, hopping into my sweats.

Alissa covers her face as I stumble into the hall. I nearly lose my footing on the stairs. Rachel shouts a question, but I blow past her and out the front door, barefoot and shirtless.

The cold air hits me. Eddie stomps across the lawn to his truck, fists clenched. I nearly slip in the damp grass sprinting after him.

"Eddie, stop!" I grab his shoulder.

He whirls. His hand snatches my arm, and he spins me, pinning me to the truck.

"WHY?" he roars. "Why HER?" His voice breaks. "How could you do this to me, Delson?"

"I'm sorry. It just happened—I didn't mean—"

"That doesn't *just* happen!"

"You're right. I screwed up... I *am* screwed up."

He scoffs, choking on the lump in his throat. "You're not the only one who's broken, you know. How long are you gonna play the victim?" He jabs a finger at my chest. "Just because you're hurting doesn't give you the right to do whatever the hell you want." He leans in, close. His eyes black with betrayal. "What would *Rose* think?"

She flashes behind my eyes—pale hair, sky-blue eyes, that wrecking-ball smile.

But now she's sunken. Hollow. Cold in the earth. I force the vision away.

"Shut up." I shake my head.

"No, really. What would she say? If she could see you now?" he hisses. "How would she look at you?"

I grit my teeth. My breath thickens.

"Drug dealing. Two-faced. Backstabbing bitch."

"Quit while you're ahead, Eddie," I warn.

His laugh is forced. Pained. "You gettin' mad? Do something, then!"

Rachel yells for Rick from the porch. Eddie's eyes don't budge from mine. I stare back, reining in each breath. Unsteady, shaken.

"C'mon. Hit me." He shoves me back to the cold metal. I shake my head. "Take your best shot, bro." He shoves me again.

"Start swinging if you have to, but I won't fight you," I say.

He grits his teeth. "Oh, but you'll screw my GIRLFRIEND!"

"I think that relationship ended when you fucked *Bridget*." My head spins from the blow to my jaw. I'm surprised the window doesn't break against my skull.

"WHOA, WHOA!" Rick shoves himself between us. "That's ENOUGH."

Eddie's fists tremble. He backs off, hands up, veins taut. His eyes never leave mine.

"Ya done?" Rick growls.

I hold Eddie's glare, rubbing my jaw.

"Yeah," Eddie says.

"Good. Cause I'll kick both yur asses." Rick sighs. "Now, figure this shit out the *right* way." He loosens his grip on us.

"I'm outta here." Eddie rips open his truck door, shoving me aside as he lifts himself in. Loose rocks kick up from under spinning tires, and he disappears.

I run back upstairs. Alissa stands by the window, hair wild. She chews on her thumbnail. Eyes wide. I bend down to grab the flash drive Eddie must've thrown.

"I hope you don't regret what happened last night," she says, stepping toward me. "Because I don't." Her voice is soft but steady. Her eyes search mine.

"I'm tired of living with bitterness, Alissa. I'm sick of feeling empty. Feeling dead even though I'm breathing. So, I can't bring myself to regret what we did."

The contents of the flash drive leave us quiet. Alissa stops the video. The image of her father, just a kid, committing murder. One of the murders for which my dad took the fall. But why?

"I understand if you want nothing to do with this, but—"

"What do you need me to do?" she asks.

"I need a ride to Moonstone Prison."

17

DELSON
MOONSTONE PRISON

THE HIGHWAY IS LONG, winding, and empty. Trees and mountains consume the right side of the road; to the left, the ocean thrashes against jagged cliffs and stone outcroppings rising from black water. Cold, salty wind blasts through my open window.

From the outside, Moonstone Penitentiary resembles an old castle more than a prison. Stone towers with arching doors overlook the ocean from atop a cliff. Barred windows stretch up the length of the walls. Gulls screech from the rooftops, watching over the prison and waves and warning all who draw near.

Once signed in, they pull me aside and pat me down. I only have my phone. A missed call from Rick flashes on the screen. They lead me into a vast, echoing room. Stone beams rise from floor to ceiling. Inmates sit across from loved ones at metal tables. They seat me alone at a secluded corner table. Two guards flank the entrance, their hands resting on holstered weapons. My cheeks tingle with heat as my throat tightens. I want to leave—want to change my mind. But I can't. The sweat from my brow goes cold against the back of my hand as I pull it away, and the door opens. The guards escort him to the table, one of them patting his shoulder as he sits. They join the other officers at the door.

He rolls up the sleeves of his slate-gray coveralls—the same color as the churning water below—and lays his hands flat on the table. A black crescent moon is tattooed below the first knuckle of his thumb, its tips just touching to form a full circle. The veins in his arms swell as he laces his fingers. His eyes—blue like mine, but deeper, darker—study me with a wide, soft gaze. His hair is just like mine in the old photo: dark, tousled waves pushed back behind his ears. A clean layer of scruff shadows his jaw.

"I always pictured plexiglass and corded phones," I say.

"Would that make you more comfortable?" he asks, his cadence slow and deliberate.

I shake my head. "We have to talk."

He leans in, crow's feet tightening as he fights the tears. I flinch.

"No physical contact, Heller," one of the guards calls.

"He's my son," my father says. "I didn't get to hold him as a baby. I've never seen him as a man. Let me hug my son."

"You know the rules," the guard says without emotion.

The veins shuffle in his arms. "Yes, sir." His gaze returns to mine. "Delson, I missed everything. I don't even know where to start."

"I know you didn't kill those people," I whisper.

His expression hardens. His eyes narrow.

"I saw the video," I say. "I know Mayor Lewis framed you. I need to know why." I hesitate. "People's lives depend on it

—not just yours. That man in the video... that was Beckett Reid, right? He killed Angela Webber. And all those other kids, too. Didn't he?"

"You listen to me, son. Don't go digging. Stay out of the dirt."

"It's too late for that."

"If Will figures out what you're doing—"

"He's dead," I interrupt. "Someone's following in Beckett's footsteps. They're tying up loose ends."

"Mind your own, and everything will be fine. It's none of your concern."

"You don't get it. The people in that video? Their kids are the ones being hunted now." I pause. "I already lost someone. So don't tell me this isn't my concern."

"Your mother, is she...?"

"No. She's just fine, killing herself slowly." Another pause. "Rose Bailey. A girl from my school. She was murdered—exactly one year after they killed another kid I knew, Ian Bloom..." I lean in. "I need you to tell me everything."

He sighs, eyes drifting to the stone ceiling. "It was our senior year of high school. Your mom and all our friends were there when we met Beckett. He was a few years older. Charismatic. Could charm the pants off a rattlesnake. We partied at his place up on the mountain every chance we got. Called ourselves The Moonlight Club." He rubs his chin. "Things got weird fast. We thought he was just eccentric. We wore robes, masks. Tripped on Skullflower. That house... it wasn't just a house. It felt like a temple. But the catacombs... those were something else."

"Catacombs?"

"You haven't heard that rumor?" he asks. "There's a tunnel system under Blackroot. The Society used them. Town blocked off the entrances after the first Founder's Fire."

"Sounds like bad fiction," I say.

"Believe it or not. Reid was obsessed. Said the tunnels held relics with mystical properties, blessed by Ingomar himself. This stuff was sacred to the guy. Whack-job. We didn't know he was trying to restart the Blackroot Society..." he sighs. "He murdered that girl in front of us all. He could control us while on the Skullflower. His word was like law. He stabbed her first." His eyes shake, lashes encumbered. "I can still hear her scream... the flower, somehow he altered it, turned us into zombies." He wipes his eyes. "Once we sobered up, and all agreed what had happened was real, I devised a plan to stop him. And we did." He pauses. "It took years for the guilt to eat me alive. I was going to be a father. I couldn't even look in the mirror. Will wanted it buried. Said we'd all go down. He made sure I went down alone. Bastard. Can't say I'm mourning him."

"Was anyone against killing Reid? Someone who'd want revenge?"

"No. We all wanted him dead."

"Think. Someone had to have known what happened. Did he have family? Siblings?"

His eye twitches. "A brother. But he wasn't there. He was younger. We never told him."

"Could he have seen something? Overheard something?"

He shakes his head. "I don't know. Last I heard, he dropped out. Left town. They were on their own."

"What's his name?" I press.

"Stop sniffin' around, son."

I press my fingers to my temple. "Fine. I'll figure it out myself." I push back from the table.

Two guards step in and lift him to his feet. My throat tightens—how do you say goodbye to a ghost?

"Delson," he says.

The guards ease up. He throws his arms around me, pulling me into his chest. His scruff scratches my cheek. He doesn't say anything. Just holds me. The officers grunt and tug, trying to pry us apart.

"In the attic," he whispers. "Far left corner. It's there. It'll protect you."

They rip us apart.

"What is?" I shout. "What's in the attic? Give me the name!"

His eyes lock on mine. His lips flatten.

"Rick Reid."

The name hits like a punch to my sternum. "Rick—wha... no." I stammer. "Are you sure?"

He nods.

***

ALISSA CLUTCHES her chest as I throw open the car door and slide in.

"Drive," I say.

"Delson!" she gasps as we hit the highway, begging for answers.

I call my mom. No answer. Again. Again. Still nothing. Alissa glances between me and the road. My voicemail icon flashes. Him. I don't listen. I call.

"Hey, Delson. I didn't want to worry you, but we're at the hospital again," Rick says, calm.

"What happened?" I bark.

"Pretty sure it's just anxiety. She thought it was a heart attack—"

"Meet me at the house," I cut in.

"Won't be much longer—"

"No. Just you. I need to talk."

"Listen—"

"You listen," I say. "I know who you are. I know who your brother was and what he did."

There is a long pause. He finally sighs. "You sure you wanna do this?" His tone is admonishing.

"See you there." I hang up.

Alissa's lips are a flat line. "Delson, please..."

I explain everything.

"Being Beckett's brother doesn't make Rick a murderer," she says.

But I only see red. It's the closest I've come to an answer. And I'm not letting go.

"Our parents killed his brother," I shout. "Buried him in the woods like garbage. Left him to rot. He had no one. No family. Alone. You think he didn't spend years plotting his revenge?"

She says nothing.

The windshield wipers whip at full speed, but they can't keep up. My fists tremble, pressed to my forehead. I rock in place. I'm slipping.

"Can't this thing go any faster?" I snap.

Alissa's knuckles go white. Trees blur green. The ocean

to our right thrashes in black and white beneath a stormy sky. Flashing lights in the rearview. Red and blue.

"I have to stop, Delson!"

I know. But I scream anyway. She flinches.

"Pull over," I growl.

My knee bounces. I chew my thumbnail to the skin.

The cop throws on a black hooded rain poncho and strolls up. Rain pours in as Alissa rolls her window down.

"I know I was speeding, officer, but—"

"License and registration."

"Asshole," I mutter.

"Got a problem, son?" he asks.

I stay silent.

"Step out of the vehicle."

"Fuck off. This is a traffic stop. Write the ticket and let us go."

Alissa shoots me a panicked glance.

"Remove yourself or I will be forced to remove you."

I climb out, soaked, and hand him my ID.

He studies it, then slaps it back in my hand. "Heller, huh? Any relation to Jason Heller?"

Of course. Always the same question. The same judgment.

"My father," I say through gritted teeth.

He chuckles. "Should I just book you now, or does blood-lust skip a generation?"

"You should hope so."

"Not smart to threaten an officer." He grabs me and shoves me against the trunk.

Alissa jumps out. Rain flattens her red hair to her skin. She yells for him to stop. He pins me to the car.

"You were provoking him!" she shouts.

"We take threats seriously," the officer says, smug.

"My father is Sheriff Lancaster. I'm sure he'd LOVE to hear about this, Officer..." She checks his badge. "Reynolds."

His grip loosens instantly. "License," he mutters.

She shoves it in his face.

Where's that smile now?

He releases me.

"Can we go?" she asks, soaked to the bone.

He huffs and trudges back to his cruiser. "Watch your speed," he mumbles.

We have forty-five minutes of driving ahead.

"Call your dad. Let me talk to him."

She dials and hands me the phone.

"Hey, baby girl," he answers warmly.

"Sheriff, its Delson Heller—"

"Where's my daughter, boy?"

"She's right here. She's fine, but the killer is Rick Reid," I say. "He should be at my house waiting for me. Now's your chance to catch this fucker." I hang up.

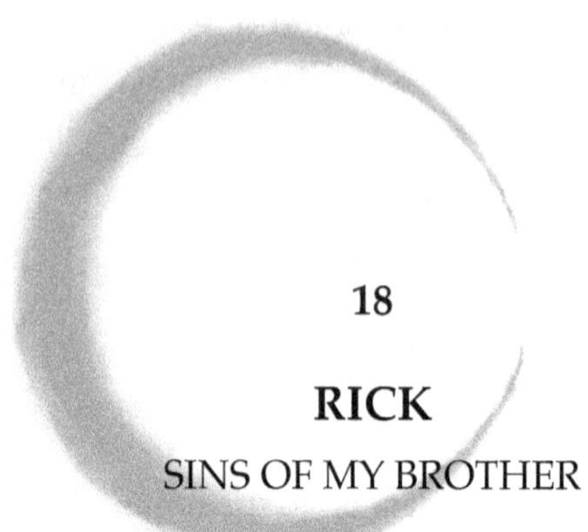

18

RICK
SINS OF MY BROTHER

FOAM HISSES as the can cracks open. A little buzz might calm the nerves. The house is too damn quiet. How'd he find this out? Who's Delson been talking to? How the hell am I supposed to explain this mess?

I didn't know who Rachel was when I first came back to town. Didn't recognize her at first. But it all came rushing back when I met the boy.

Damn kid. He's out for blood. Got his mother's mouth and his father's rage. I'd be lying if I said I hadn't wanted to smack him a few times. But that's not my place. He hasn't had it easy—not even close. I've seen his life before. I lived it. I know how it feels. That's why he's gotta get out of here. He could be something. Not like me. Not like the rest of us.

I've spent years trying to forget who Beckett really was. What he did. But these killings? These missing kids? They reek of him. His sickness. He set this in motion. He knew it wouldn't end with him.

I remember the night they found out what kind of

monster he was. I remember their faces through the crack in the cellar door. That girl—slaughtered like an animal. They all ignored me at school after that. Pretended I was a stranger. Pretended they didn't know Beckett was born evil. But I always knew. Same as our father.

I take a long swig. The cold beer bubbles down my throat, interrupted by the buzz of my phone.

"Delson, hey, I'm waitin'—"

"We've been waiting, too," the voices say.

The can slips from my hand and hits the floor.

"Who is this?"

"Beckett would be proud—knowing we are together. Knowing we'll be the ones to send you to him."

The voices meld. Distort. Blend.

"Don't act like you know me," I growl. "Or know who my brother was." I wipe the foam from my mustache. "Who are you? I'll kill you myself!"

"You're searching for answers you already have. That's why you came back, right? No distance could cure your affliction. Wherever you go, we follow. We've never left. We're all around you... even now."

"Where are you?" I scream into the phone.

The line goes dead.

"Where are you!"

I fall to my knees and hurl the phone against the wall.

"Right behind you," Beckett whispers.

The chillingly familliar voice skitters up my spine with too many legs, tightening the muscles in my back. Goose-flesh raises on my arms. Couldn't be.

The sound of metal sliding from a leather sheath rings.

I throw myself sideways, slamming into the busted-ass coffee table. He's standing above me.

Flowing black vinyl swims toward me. Hood pulled tight. That same pale, yellowed leather mask—stitched and warped. A long steel blade glints in the light.

He lunges.

I grab his wrist just as the knife plunges downward, the tip aimed at my eye. He presses down with everything he's got. I kick up with both knees, hurling him over me, crashing him into the broken table. Wood splinters scatter across the floor.

I scramble for the kitchen.

The blade slashes across my ribs. Cold steel burns as I drop to my knees. I twist, trying to block the next strike. The point stops inches from my face—held back by the surrounding flesh of my palm. The blade slips, gliding upward with terrifying ease, slicing my hand in half.

Black-red blood gushes from the split. I slip in it trying to stand.

The knife swings again. I dodge. Barely.

I grab his shoulders, reaching for his neck.

Slam! I drive him into the cupboards. Plates shatter. The knife buries deep into my back.

I howl.

Wet heat runs down the back of my shirt, turns to paste.

I smash his head into the counter.

His hands are empty.

I let go. The knife's still lodged in me, scraping bone with every breath.

The room tilts. My limbs buzz like a live wire. Then—white.

The cast-iron skillet collides with my skull.

I hit the ground. My body slick with blood. My hand crawls to the knife in my back. Teeth grind so hard they crack. Bits of enamel crunch between my molars. Like sand on my tongue.

"Your death was never predetermined," he says, crouching over me. **"It's just penance. The consequence of your own doing."** He yanks the blade free. **"Tell us... if you could go back, would you make the same decisions?"**

I swallow thickly.

"Every time," I rasp. Because I know this is it. This is how I die. And I'm not going out a liar.

He grabs a plastic grocery bag off the counter. I don't try to stop him. Couldn't if I wanted.

"And so, this day," he murmurs, **"you have spilled your own blood. Drown in it."**

The blade plunges into my neck. In. Out.

Then the bag comes down over my face.

Tightens.

I can't breathe. Can't swallow. I fall into him as the blood surges. Hot. Thick. It climbs into my ears. My mouth.

It's like choking on boiling pennies.

And the darkness?

The darkness ain't any better.

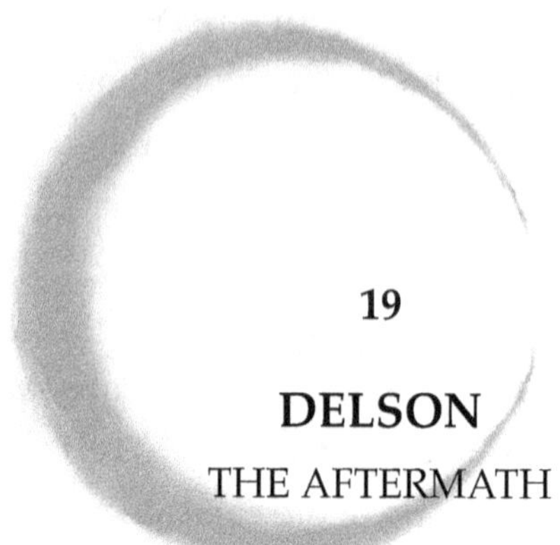

19

DELSON

THE AFTERMATH

WE CRAWL DOWN THE ROAD, my heart moshing in my chest. The brakes squeal as Alissa eases onto the pedal. The wet pavement glistens, painted red and blue by the rotating lights atop cop cars lining the street. Paramedics and EMTs litter the front yard like the meth heads that haunt downtown alleys—pale faces, shifty eyes, and nausea everywhere. A City Coroner van squats in the driveway. Invisible fingers tighten around my heart.

My foot scrapes the pavement before Alissa can stop the car. She calls out as I race toward the house, engulfed in panic, sweat, and fear. She runs after me, leaving her car in the middle of the road. I think she screams for me to stop, but I can't be sure. Officers try to block my path as I shove past them, squirming between their arms and ducking beneath caution tape.

Rachel sobs in the yard, closed fists held tight to her chest. Eyes stuck on some meaningless spot in the grass, hands and knees soaked in blood. Sheriff Lancaster stands before her, the butt of his pen twitching as he scribbles in his notepad. Other leering figures stand beside him in black coats. Detectives, FBI agents? Hard to tell.

"Mom?" I call out.

She busts into tears, the only thing she can manage is his name. Rick.

"Delson, you can't go in there!" the sheriff yells.

The living room is a war zone—broken glass, splintered wood. The walls and ceiling bloom with blood in constellations. Crime scene investigators buzz through the house like flies. Another figure in black stands in the kitchen, camera flashing with each step. I don't feel my feet move. The kitchen just gets closer.

FLASH. I shove through the blur of faceless people. Bile churns in my gut and claws at my throat.

FLASH. A plastic bag, split and oozing dark fluid, reveals his face. Painted in blood.

FLASH. His eyes—bloated and empty—stare at the ceiling. His jaw gapes open. Tongue curled back and drowning in a deep maroon pool. That metallic stench—I know it too well now.

Hands grab me. A creature, real or imagined, drags me deeper into the grave opening beneath my feet. The sheriff yanks me upright and hauls me outside. His mouth moves, but I can't hear anything over the buzzing in my ears. My head is hot. My breath comes in gasps, each one emptier than the last. Alissa appears. Her hands cup my face. I shut my eyes. Tune it all out. Tune everything out.

Then she's gone—pulled back by the sheriff.

Sobbing... Rachel. Mom. My name. People yelling my name.

The neighbors gather like a pack of vultures. Eyes sharp, glowing red and blue in the cop light strobe. They point at me. Upper-middle-class pill-poppers and wine-drunk bigots. They sneer, herd their kids behind them like I'm contagious.

Mr. Bruckner shuffles to the caution tape. Shirt two sizes too small, gut hanging out. His bare feet slap across pavement. His forehead glistens with sweat, even in the cold.

"Get out of town!" he barks. "Take your junkie mother and go. We don't want you here!" The mob behind him howls with him.

Trash. Toxic. Not welcome. Leave.

A smug grin breaks across his greasy face. "Lock him up with his father!"

Words. Just words. I could probably listen to myself on any other day, but I savor the moment my fist connects. The crack of bone. The split of flesh. I kneel over him, blood on my knuckles and none of it mine. It's a sick, burning satisfaction. But satisfaction nonetheless.

Sheriff rips me off him, holding my arms back as my body surges forward.

The sloppy bastard struggles to his feet, dropping to his knee more than once. His hand cups his mouth. "Sheriff, I want to press charges!" Blood drips through his fingers. "He hit me!"

"Well, what d'ya think was gonna happen?" he growls, his grip firm on my arms. He yells at the onlookers to get back inside. "That means you." He glares at Mr. Bruckner.

Jenna Darkly's sharp eyes catch mine. She stands across the street, her arms crossed.

I pull my sobbing mother from the gurney as they wheel out Rick's body, giving the city coroner enough space to load him in the van. She cries into my chest. Alissa's eyes imprison mine.

"Baby girl, you get home now," the sheriff says.

"No, Dad. I'm staying."

"Not askin', Sweetie. Now get in your car and get the hell outta here." He huffs.

"I'm eighteen. I'll leave when I'm ready."

His face turns a deeper shade of red. "As long as you're under my roof—"

"Then maybe don't make me want to leave your roof," she fires back.

His jaw locks, but the fight's already lost.

This house has never been safe. My mom's not safe here. Hell, she's a danger to herself. That's it... I make the call.

It takes hours for the responders to leave. The sun falls. The sky folds into darkness. My mom smokes on the porch, cigarette shaking between her fingers. I tell her what's going to happen. I don't ask. I report her myself—threats of self-harm, detoxing, her boyfriend murdered in the home. The officers arrive fast. They ask their questions. Then they tell me she'll be placed under a 48-hour hold in a mental health facility.

I feel like a traitor. But I can't protect her. Not anymore. At least in there, she'll be safe.

***

SMOKE CURLS up from my cigarette as Alissa rests her head on my shoulder.

"She'll understand," she whispers. "You okay?"

"Sure. It's fine," I mutter.

"No. Don't do that." Her voice sharpens. "You always—"

"What, Alissa?" I snap. "What am I doing wrong?"

She pulls her head away, eyes penetrating mine. "This." She shakes her head. "You've done this since we were little. You refuse to let anybody in. This negative self-image and outlook you project only harms you."

I flinch at her sudden analysis of me, speaking as if she'd prepared for this moment.

"You wallow in a perpetual state of self-deprecation. You work against yourself constantly. You push people away. But you can't push me away. So stop trying."

I wonder if that's true. I nod, putting out my cigarette. She follows me inside.

The gore in the kitchen has congealed, thick and sticky like syrup. I fill a bucket with scalding water and soap. The yellow sponge doesn't clean—it smears. Brown-orange streaks spread across the linoleum. On my knees, my reflection stares up from the slick pool like a ghost trapped beneath the floor.

"It's my fault he's dead." I drop the sponge. "I told him to meet me here alone. I—"

"Delson." She kneels beside me. "It's not your fault. None of this is." She kisses my forehead.

Two hours. Sixteen buckets of bloodwater. The kitchen still smells like death, but it looks passable. We stack the trash bags outside—sopping sponges, busted wood, shattered table legs.

Alissa walks me to the porch. Her hug is long and quiet. The kind that softens your lungs and slows your heartbeat.

I wait for her taillights to disappear before I go back in. Lock the knob. Throw the deadbolt. Slide the chain. I double-check every window—downstairs and up.

Then I pull the cord.

The attic hatch groans open. The ladder creaks like it hates me. The shadows press in as I climb. The air is musty, dead. I lift my phone and use the flashlight. Cobwebs cling to my skin. Something rotting lingers faintly in the air.

I go to the far back corner. Narrow. Tight. I'm practically crawling now.

Creeeeeak.

The floorboards flex under my weight. One plank moans louder than the rest. I rip it free—dust explodes into my beam of light. I toss it aside.

A gruesome face stares up at me.

I jerk back, cracking my head on a beam. I curse, rub the sting, and pry up the second board.

It's a mask.

Crafted from thick, hardened leather. Stitched crudely beneath sharp cheekbones. The empty eyes—jet black and almost human in shape—stare through me. The sockets are deep and skeletal. The bridge of the nose, long and sharp. Its lips are thin. Its cheeks are sunken, mummified. The jaw juts like an L. Two stubby horns sprout from the forehead.

I lift the thing from its dusty cradle. Leather straps hang limp. I raise it. Metal buckles clank.

And I look through it's eyes.

20

DELSON
HOMECOMING HORROR

It's been weeks since Rose and Sam's murders, the disappearance of Courtney Pierce. Nearly a month under curfew, and the town's getting restless. With a killer on the loose and the mayor still missing, it's strange that what troubles the residents most is how curfew affects local business and football—not the growing body count, not the missing. Night terrors and stress-induced nightmares plague Blackroot like it's trapped in an '80s slasher flick. And I can't shake the feeling that more and more eyes are on me.

I've never belonged here. Blackroot—Heller County— crawling with miscreants, lowlifes, and villains. They swarm down in the filth and squalor. Morally ambiguous ghouls hidden behind human masks preaching their sanctimonious platitudes. But this place was born of violence. We all bear the scarlet sobriquet as a birthright. An unwanted inheritance from an ugly heritage best left forgotten. The soil beneath our homes, our schools, and feet is spoiled. Sour. It's gone bad from all the blood. But they pretend. They smile.

Put on a grand show atop a crimson stage. Tonight, we dance on a mass grave.

———

CORDY BOOKS A LIMO TO drop us at the boardwalk. A boat waits to ferry us and the rest of our classmates across the marina to Bellflower Island. Fog coils low over the black water like breath on glass. The moon peeks between strangling clouds—casting silver glints across the rippling bay. I can taste salt. The scent of rot, seaweed, and damp mud clings to every inhale. A phantom buoy dings somewhere out in the dark, and I look back at the archaic silhouette of downtown fading behind us.

Alissa's dress is midnight black, hem above the knee, thin straps hugging her shoulders. Her mask—lace, mascara-smudged, horned—makes her eyes smolder under smoky red, glittering shadow. Her wild red hair engulfs her.

Cordy, in contrast to Alissa, dresses as a nun. Luca painted his face like a sugar skull, he wears a black tuxedo with skeleton gloves. Edward, who keeps his distance from me and Alissa, dons his usual go-to, a zombie quarterback. Dane sports a hockey mask and a blazer combo while Nathan dons a sleek-black boxer getup, complete with silken robe and pink boxing gloves that hang over his shoulders. Beside him stands Rowan, in all pink workout attire. A fluffy white puffball tail fastened to her butt-lifting leggings, and a pair of fuzzy rabbit's ears stand up from her swirling brunette locks, completing her 'gym bunny' getup. I wear the mask from my attic atop my head like a ball cap, hoodie up.

Luca flashes a silver flask. "Pre-game, anyone?"

"Obviously," Rowan chirps, swiping it with a grin. She glances at her livestream. "Ew, stop sending the cowboy hat. I do not look good in a stache." Then: "Ooh, let's play a game. Here, I'll start. Last year, I—"

"Allegedly," Nathan says, deadpan.

She smirks. "Allegedly replaced someone's special shampoo with Nair." She sips. The group chokes back their laughter, realizing she's serious—except Cordy, who just raises a brow.

Nathan grabs the flask. "You know she changed schools because of that, right?"

Luca takes it next. "I'm the one who egged Meyer's car last year."

"Maybe end the live," Cordy says. Rowan complies.

"Mid," Dane mutters. "Give us a real one. Something that keeps you up."

Luca stares at the ground. "Alright. Fine." His grin falters. "Couple years back, I went hiking solo past Ingomar Hills—Redwood Canyon. Found an old tunnel entrance... I heard someone calling for help. I bailed."

"We want confessions, not creepypasta," Rowan says.

"I swear." He shrugs. "Whatever." He offers the flask to me.

"You don't have to," Alissa says softly.

"Nuh-uh. Fuck that," Dane says. "Let's go."

I take it. The oaky burn hits my nostrils. "I, uh—I was supposed to stay with Rose. Her mom was out of town." I glance at Eddie. "But I flaked. Went to a college party in Ingomar Hills instead. That was the night Rose died." A pause. "I could've been there. I could've protected her. But I went to make a quick buck. She paid the price."

No one says a word. I drink. Fire pools in my gut. Eddie lowers his head. Alissa touches my shoulder.

WE POUR off the boat like prisoners to the gallows. Bellflower Manor—gothic, towering—looms over the island. Staff and parent chaperones lead us through tacky webs and dollar-store pumpkins into the ballroom. A beat pounds through the walls.

Principal Myers lurks in a corner. Inside, the decor is laughable: plastic skeletons, large rubber spiders hanging from the ceiling, and 'spooky' scarecrows towering from atop bales of yellow hay. The moody lights fade from red to purple, orange, green, and back.

"We shouldn't even be here," Dane grumbles.

"Like it or not, we're safer together," Edward says.

He's right.

Luca scoots toward us. He opens his jacket, revealing another hefty silver flask. "Let's make this more interesting," he says with a wink behind his sugar skull face paint. "Dane, cover me." They slink to the sprawling table of refreshments and food.

Rowan grins. "Punch?" she spins around and strides toward them with Nathan quick on her heels.

Edward joins them, as well as Cordy.

Alissa grabs my hand. "Come on. Let's try to have some fun." Her eyes peer at me from behind the lacy black mask.

Luca shoves the flask back into his jacket as he stirs the punch. He passes a cup to each of us, filling them to the brim. I try to pass it back to him.

"No, no." He grunts. I shake my head. "Delson, it's like over three parts punch, less than one part booze. Chill."

"You don't have to." Alissa nudges me. "You already had some..."

Edward's eyes flick to our clasped hands, then dart away as he gulps the fruity red liquid. I pull my hand free from hers.

"I guess it won't hurt." Luca was right. I can't even taste the liquor.

The dance floor shakes with pummeling base and dancing feet. All drenched in the shifting colored lights, we join the dance floor. It's hard not to watch Edward down cup after cup of the spiked punch. But he loosens up as he dances with Cordy. Dane hangs back near the punch bowl, his eyes scanning the crowd. Rowan lets loose more than anyone, dancing around the crowd, accumulating a sizable collection of jealous, judging stares as thirsty eyes gawk at her from the arms of other girls. Nathan trails behind her, as usual. Alissa pulls my wandering gaze back to her with a nudge to my jaw.

"I'm not much of a dancer," I say.

"Nobody's watching." She grabs my arms and begins moving them with her, jerking me around as she shows a side of herself rarely seen.

My guard drops as my skin buzzes and warmth radiates from my gut. She pulls my mask down over my face and I stare at her through new eyes. I follow her lead.

The following several songs pass in a blur of sweat and aching smiles. I feel my body, smooth and bubbly, loose. I go in any direction she takes me, my ambition lowered. *Focus.*

The room sways. The lights shift. Red. *Focus.* Hard to breathe? Noise roars in my ears.

"Delson?" Alissa says.

I exhale a sharp breath. "Something isn't right." I attempt to shake off the foreign sensation with a quick rattling of my head back and forth. I lift my mask back up to look through my own eyes.

Her voice becomes a sloshing sound mixed in with the booming bass and beat. I scan the dancing crowd. A pair of eyes lock onto mine. Principal Myers stands, his back to a door leading out of the ballroom, his arms crossed. His face, emotionless. I try to pull in a breath but my lungs seem to fight, pushing it back out before satisfaction. A chill shudders down my spine and panic cramps in my chest.

Myers lifts a finger to his lips, eyes peering over the pit of sweaty dancers jostling about, unbothered. Rowan circles by us again, her arms waving in the air. She slows. Everyone does. Her arms leave tracers behind as she sways. No longer is it the base shaking the hollow-feeling floor beneath my feet, but my very own heartbeat. It's all I can hear.

Thud-thud. Motion speeds back, then slows again. *Focus.* With each labored breath, colors bleed and shapes elongate, melting into the light.

Thud-thud. Purple. No. Orange. Principal Myers. *Focus.*

He's gone.

Thud-thud. The door where he stood closes.

"Delson!" Alissa shouts, several feet behind me.

When did I move?

I'm next to Dane. No idea how. I grab his cup. Smell.

Sulfur.

Skullflower.

"We've been drugged," I pant. "All of us."

Luca's beside me. "Just booze!" he says. "But I'm... I'm feelin' somethin'..."

"Somebody spiked the punch before we got here."

Shapes bend. Colors slide. I touch my mask. My face. Mask again. I'm being pulled. No—Alissa grabbed me.

"Delson, I need to get out of here!" she yells. "Something is wrong..."

I tell her to stay put. The crowd of sweating creatures, all dressed up like Halloween, stare at their hands. Bodies still moving to the music. I try to avoid contact, but a new ghoulish figure illuminated by the ever-changing lights meets each step I take. My feet sink into the floor, which changed from wood to bay mud. But I trudge forward through the swampy ballroom floor until I meet him. He stands still amongst the blurring, shifty dancers. All black. Hood pulled up. That monstrous face, fleshy leather. Those hollow black eyes, misshapen, pained. Held together with thick, tight stitches.

"Who are you!" I scream.

He lifts a finger to his black lips. Blurred, gyrating figures obstruct my view, and he vanishes.

I rush toward the closing door as a black shape slips through. The hallway elongates with every uneasy step. I hold on to the walls to keep myself from sinking, suck in as much air as possible, fight back the suffocating anxiety. Pale arms reach down from the blackened ceiling, and from the walls, fingers outstretched. Framed portraits watch me, their eyes following my every move. The walls breathe. Close in. I glance up the dark staircase. Principal Myers stares back at me over his shoulder. I scream for him to stop. He doesn't.

Hand's grip on my arms from behind and spin me around. I raise my fist. Jenna Darkly.

"Delson! Stop!" She shakes me. "What's going on in there?"

I try to swallow. I can't. "We were drugged." I blurt. "Principal Myers! Get him!" I point up the stairs.

She draws her gun and slinks to the bottom step.

The hooded figure ruptures from the darkness of an adjacent hallway, tackling Jenna. They smash into the steps. Her gun falls to the floor. Dim light glints off the long, thick blade. The knife slashes down. Jenna's arms cross before her, blocking the savage weapon. The skin splits like wet tissue paper. Her boot bashes into his chest, knocking him back. She snatches the gun from the floor and points it as she scrambles to her feet. But it's too late. Gloved fingers grip my hair, pulling my head back. The blade set firmly to my throat.

"Drop the weapon!" she orders down the barrel of her gun.

He pulls me back slowly down the hallway. "**Take another step, and I saw until I hit the spinal cord.**" The voices coil out past my ear. The hard leather chin rests against my cheek. "**We prepared them for you, Delson,**" he whispers in my ear. "*It's easier than you think.* Kill for me, *and I can come back.* Make my sacrifice *mean something!*" Rose screeches.

"You don't want to do this." Jenna edges forward.

The knife presses deeper into my throat. She holds up her hands. The masked man pulls me down the hall. Rose stands between me and Jenna, screaming in silence. Cold steel presses to my fragile flesh. Like a blast of the frigid vacuum of space, the icy air barrels in from the open door behind me.

"Move the knife from the kid's throat, now!" Jenna screams. Her gun pointed back down the hall.

"As you wish."

An icy whisper of steel rings across my throat, and warmth spills into the air. He shoves me down, fleeing into the darkness.

Jenna hovers over me. Panic. Her hands press to my throat. She screams for me to stay awake. Stay with her. Her image shrouded in shadows. Her blood-soaked hand holds a phone to her ear.

"I need an ambulance and police on Bellflower Island, now!"

Darkness.

21

JASON

THE TRANSFER

"RUMORS TRUE, then? You're outta here?" he asks from the bottom bunk.

"Just trading one set of bars for another," I say.

"Still, change of scenery'll be alright."

I nod, sullen.

My cellmate for the past four years holds out his hand. I shake it.

The guard clamps the restraints on my wrists, then crouches to shackle my legs. The cuffs snap around my ankles. His fingers fidget with my sock. I feel the cold little piece of metal as he slides it in the elastic, replacing the wad of cash.

He escorts me to the line of inmates following Raker. The cell blocks loom overhead like stone sentinels, their walls scarred with the memories of the men who've rotted here.

I shuffle through the cold corridors. Each block has its own identity—but they all suffer the same. Some whisper with despair, others echo with the bravado of hardened souls, all of them sharpened by loss, regret, and pain.

We emerge into the yard. The air hums with tension. For the first time, I feel truly vulnerable. My hands are cuffed and chained to my waist, ankles shackled with only a foot of slack. Inmates line the yard, watching our small group led by Raker—his hand on his revolver—as we march not toward freedom, but something new.

When you've stared at the same stone walls and iron bars for years, sometimes *anything* new feels like freedom. And sometimes, that very idea is the most terrifying thing in the world.

Eyes flicker with hope. Resignation. Resentment. The sun struggles to pierce the walls, casting long shadows that grip the yard.

An alarm shrieks once. The tall chain-link gate groans open.

A young officer, shotgun in hand, waits beside a gray half-bus. Its windows are reinforced with steel mesh. Balding tires wrap around rusted hubcaps. The door hisses open.

"Afternoon, boys," says the old man in the driver's seat. "Lenny," Raker nods. "I'll be joining you on the transfer."

"Barry ain't comin' then?"

"No, Barry's still goin'."

The younger officer's shoulders slump a little.

"Given the circumstances," Raker says, glancing at me, "I'd like to make sure everything goes smooth."

"Always does," Lenny mutters.

They load us in one by one, chaining us from the metal

posts beneath the seats to the cuffs around our wrists. Raker seats me in the back, away from the others.

The bus rumbles as we pull away. Metal groans. Seats tremble. The soles of my shoes buzz against the floor. Sunlight glares off the window's metal trim, forcing my eyes shut.

All things I didn't know I missed—until now.

As the prison fades behind us, Raker strolls down the aisle and takes the seat beside me.

"Gotta admit, Heller. It's goddamn convenient. Murders start, your boy visits, and now you're gettin' transferred?" He doesn't wait for an answer. "You schemin'? Or runnin'?"

"We're all running from something," I say.

His hand rests on his weapon.

"Just remember, I got six itty-bitty little friends, and they all run a helluva lot faster than you."

Raker's a prick. A nosy, dick-swinging prick who's convinced I murdered his little brother all those years back. And honestly, I don't blame him. Were I in his shoes, I'd be worse.

THE STEADY RUMBLE of the bus lulls me damn near to sleep. Feels like long car rides with my folks when I was a kid. Nothing soothes like the hum of an engine and the rhythm of the road.

Redwood giants line Bigfork Avenue, stretching into the charcoal sky. Swollen purple clouds choke out the stars. Rain starts slow and light.

Fifteen minutes later, it's dumping. Windshield wipers

squelch back and forth in a hopeless but determined rhythm.

Raker, bitching from the front, tells Lenny to switch on the defroster.

"Been actin' up," Lenny says. The bus makes an ugly sound as he tries. He shuts it off.

"Alright, let's get these windows open," Raker says.

He and Barry inch down the aisle, sliding open every other window. Rain jets inside, breathing out our stale, humid breath into the night. I shield my face from the icy spray.

"That oughta do it!" Raker says, heading back up.

But he doesn't sit down. Instead, he crouches behind Lenny.

"WATCH OUT LENNY GODDAAA—"

I brace myself against the seat ahead of me as the bus swerves, its steel frame groans as we slide, tires skidding on the slick dark pavement. The bus lurches forward and whips back the other way as the driver overcorrects his initial swerve. My body floats from the seat and I realize we are tilting, *rolling*. I'm weightless as the world spins in dizzying cartwheels of screeching metal, levitating men, and a shower of glass and rain. Sheets of white flash into vision as my body slams into metal, glass, and more metal.

Amidst the cacophony of men screaming and crying in our steel-rolling death box, the primal instinct to survive kicks in. The adrenaline surges through my veins like hot rage.

Then, as suddenly as it began, it ends. Only the eerie silence of afterthought remains. The chaotic drumming of the rain hammers against the metal of the bus's undercarriage. I let gravity open my eyes. The bus is upside down.

A figure stands against the sky. No, the road. A woman—naked, bloody, hands bound. A sack over her head. She stumbles into the trees.

I look around. Bodies hang from their chains. Some moan. Others don't move.

Barry lies in a broken pile—limbs twisted, flesh torn open. Lenny's draped over bent metal, skull caved in, back twisted in a way that doesn't make sense.

Raker's facedown, leg bent at a brutal angle.

Blood rushes to my head. Veins pulse. I groan and reach for my feet—still shackled. The chain holds me fast to the ceiling.

I snap the elastic on my sock. Metal clicks.

"Fuck!" I choke out.

I reach.

"Come on, Heller! Get us the fuck outta here!" someone yells.

"I can't reach!" I say.

"Yeah, you can—fuck yeah, dude, get that shit!"

I stretch. The cuffs slice into my wrists. Fingers tingle. Numb. Blood drips in tiny black-red beads.

One drop lands on the key.

I smear it with a fingertip. My breath catches. I didn't know I was holding it.

Stretch. Nudge. Nudge.

The key snags the light fixture. I guide it onto the metal lip—

Got it.

I free my hands first, then my feet. I drop to the floor—

The ceiling, I guess.

Inmates cry out. Plead. Cheer.

I find Barry's shotgun by the shattered windshield and step over Raker.

"Come on, Heller! Please!"

"Let us out, man!"

I ignore them. Crawl from the windshield into the pounding rain.

"Stop right there!" Raker yells.

I turn.

He's dragging himself out, revolver in hand. Leg useless. Blood soaking his pant leg. He braces himself on the bus.

Eyes locked on mine. He means to see me dead before he lets me go.

I'm already aiming.

"Drop the weapon! Get on the ground!"

He says it again. And again.

Then—

BANG.

The shot rings out through the rain. I stagger, rage and fear blurring my vision.

I fire.

The blast roars through the woods. Raker crumples into a lifeless, broken pile.

The storm rages on.

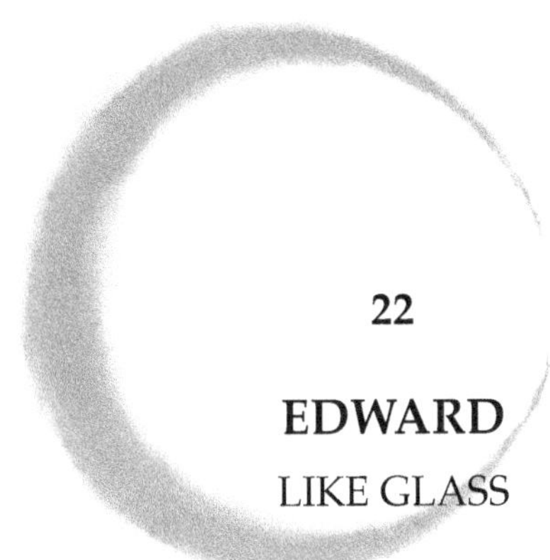

22

EDWARD

LIKE GLASS

IT'S ALREADY past curfew when Alissa calls.

"Delson's missing," she says, breathless. "He's not in his hospital room."

My gut sinks. "What do you mean, missing? He just walked out?"

"I don't know. No one saw him leave. I'm heading to his place—just in case."

"Fine. Me and Dane'll start driving around. We'll find him." I hang up.

The streets are dead quiet, shadows pooling under every streetlight. Then, less than an hour later, we spot him—Fourteenth Street. Hood pulled up, hands jammed in his pockets, like he's trying to disappear into himself. He walks slowly, like the world doesn't care that he's breaking.

Dane honks as we pull over. "Hey, dumbass, hop in. I'll give you a ride back to the hospital."

"Not going back to the hospital," Delson says, not slowing.

"Wherever you need to go, then," I tell him.

He stops, eyes still fixed ahead. Rain dribbles off his nose and chin. He gets in.

Alissa's car is already in the driveway. Curtains shift as we pull up. I shuffle Delson's unconscious body from the back seat, his eyes fluttering as he grips my shoulder. The front door bursts open, and Alissa rushes out into the rain.

"Oh my god! Is he okay?" she cries.

"He's fine." I hold him steady, his arm slung over my shoulder.

Her eyes widen with worry. Her need to protect him is more real than anything. It messes with my head—knowing she'll never feel that way about me again. It's just... strange. Stranger to think all that love, all that feeling, is his now. Maybe it always was. Maybe they were meant to be, and what happened between us had to happen to lead them to each other—like fate or some shit.

Or maybe I just want to believe that so it doesn't hurt so bad.

Fuck fate.

Delson coughs into my chest.

"Dane, help me get him inside."

He grunts and lifts Delson's other arm. Together, we carry him upstairs and lay him in bed. Alissa stands over him, fingers brushing through his hair.

"Have Del call me tomorrow..." I mutter as I follow Dane back downstairs.

Alissa stops me at the door. Dane rolls his eyes and trudges to his car.

"What is it?" I snap.

"W-what is it?" she echoes. Her hands push soaked red

hair from her face. "Don't you think we should talk about this? What are we doing? What's next? I feel like we—"

"Just go take care of Delson." I don't like the way his name sounds in my mouth. Neither does she.

"This isn't about your feelings, Edward. It's not about us." Her chin dimples as she fights tears—a tell I know too well now.

I roll my head, bite my tongue. "Never was. Was it?" My lips tighten. My chest pounds. "How long have you been in love with him?"

Her eyes dart away.

"No, really. I wanna know."

"Stop it—"

"Was it when you found out I cheated? Earlier, maybe? When we got together? When he was with Rose?" I press. "Is that why you two stopped hanging out so much?" I scoff. "Once she died, you just had to take the opportunity, didn't you?"

"Shut up." A tear slips down her cheek.

"I don't know how to! Don't you get it?" The words rip out of me like splinters. A dam breaks. "You think I *like* feeling this way? That I get off on this pain? I can't fucking stand it. But I can't stop it."

Then I hear what I've said.

I *know* what I've said.

This anger—it's not some outside thing that's been controlling me. It's me. It's always been me. All the worst parts.

My fault.

Only I can fix it.

Arms wrap around me, and I fall into her shoulder. I cry

into her like I never left. It feels both familiar and foreign. I don't pull away. I let her hand stroke the back of my head. My heartbeat calms.

"There are bigger things than this," she whispers near my ear. "None of us knows what to do. We don't have a plan. We don't know what's next. But drinking, screaming... wallowing in grief and hate won't help."

Her voice steadies me.

"However this ends, just know I care about you. And I wish things could've been different. I don't want to die knowing you hate me, Edward."

I sniff. "I don't hate you... I never could." Pull my head away. The image of her holding Delson, when I close my eyes, leaves an empty-feeling ache in my chest, but also some strange sort of comfort. Comfort for him and for her. "He needs you more than I do. Deserves you more." I wipe the snot from my upper lip. "When all this is over, I'll still be here." My head drops. The voice in my head tells me not to say another word, but I do. "And... maybe I can become somebody deserving of you again."

"Maybe..." she whispers.

Dane's horn sputters a few beeps against the pouring rain.

I glance back with a nod and head through the door.

"Where are you guys going?" she asks.

"Back to Dane's, I guess." Rain still reaches me under the overhang.

"Take Craven Creek Road. There was a huge wreck on Bigfork."

CRAVEN CREEK ROAD is one long, curvy stretch of shadows, the entire way absent of streetlights. Open pastures frame both sides of the road, dark and wet. Empty. Faded yellow lines streak by on the black pavement, pocked with potholes. The applause of the rain comes back, reminding me of easier times. The stands at Blackroot Stadium filled, locals cheering for the team, for Ian. Delson taking photos for the school paper, Alissa holding me in her gaze no matter where I was on the field. When I took a hard hit, I'd swear her heart stopped. She *really* cared. So, yeah—I played it up some-times. Felt good knowing she watched out for me.

Now it feels like we're in some alternate reality. Like the dickheads at CERN tore something in the timeline. Some Mandela Effect glitch. But this isn't about cereal mascots or misquoted movies.

This is worse.

A figure catches my eye.

"Wait!" I blurt. "You see that?"

"Some chick. So?" Dane shrugs.

"Go back."

"Hell no."

"Dude. Go *back*," I repeat.

The car screeches to a stop. "I'm not picking up some tweaky lady."

I unbuckle and step into the rain, ignoring Dane's complaints. I run back toward the woman. The red glow of taillights shines on the slick road as Dane reverses, still cussing.

"Hello?" I shout into the blackness.

"Help me!" she screams.

Her voice isn't far. I sprint. The red taillights follow still.

Her pale skin glows red in the light. A filthy, injured figure stumbles. Her bra and underwear are barely clinging on. Covered in cuts and bruises. A sack over her head. Hands tied.

I race to her side, yelling for Dane. He stumbles from the car, staying a few feet back.

"Oh man, she's *really* hurt," I stutter.

"Bro, we gotta get her to the hospital or something."

I glance back at the drenched figure. Rain bringing some gooey life back to the blood crusted to her skin. She hasn't been in the rain for very long, but there aren't any houses nearby.

"Miss, I'm gonna remove the bag from over your head, okay?" I try not to trip over my own words.

"O-okay..." Her voice is warbling and weak. And *familiar*.

I reach for the dark sack. Dane hits the ground before I have a chance. The black shape rolls on top of him. A single blow knocks his head into the concrete, and his eyes roll back.

I lunge at the figure. The broken girl wails at the commotion. My arms are restricted. Grabbed and held behind me by an unseen enemy. I squirm to break free. A needle plunges into Dane's neck.

The figure rises. Cloaked in darkness. The mask is hideous—its shape barely visible in the red glow.

He turns to me. Brings the needle.

I lift off the ground—arms still pinned by the man behind me—and slam both boots into the other's stomach. He stumbles back.

I lose my balance. My face hits the concrete.

Cold water floods my nose and throat. I gasp, choking. It tastes like metal, dirt, and something chemical.

Then—

The pinch of the needle.

Fire in my veins.

And everything fades.

23

DANE
I FALL ALONE

THE SUN'S white-hot light reflects off sleek, shallow puddles on the roof. The glare stings my eyes and—oh god, I wish I could close them—I'd give my left nut—fuck, honestly, a bullet to the head is better than this. For the first time, I understand the expression "screaming on the inside." I'd rather be dead than live another second without control of my own body. It's simple, right? You just think it and it happens—like, think about making a fist, or clapping, or wiggling your big toe. Shit, you almost don't even have to think. But it's not working. I can't move a fucking muscle.

Town Square looks like an ant farm from up here, so busy you'd think it was already Halloween. My eyes still burn. That doesn't stop. I try to scream. I think it. I scream on the inside, but that doesn't help. That doesn't get somebody up here to hold me down, to stop me.

I'm reminded I can't swallow either. The saliva just keeps filling my mouth, slowly dripping down my throat. At first, the spit was leaking into my lungs, causing my body to cough, but now it's going all the way to my stomach. I hate this feeling the most.

The alarm goes off. Where is it? What alarm? Oh, the one he set on my phone. One foot moves forward after the other, slow and steady.

No! The alarm! That's right! Please let this be a nightmare. Let me wake up! I don't want to hear the last alarm, no, please please please.

The stone steps, sidewalk, and busy street wait below. There's gotta be a way out of this. I won't go out like this. Hell no! I can't die like this!

Fuck, my eyes burn.

I picture Sam, the dumbass. Why couldn't you just leave Rose alone? You died for nothing, Sam. For. Fucking. Nothing. But I don't want to die. I really don't want to die. But I also want to blink and swallow, and if I can't even accomplish that much, then I'm probably as good as dead. God, Sam, what the hell is Mom gonna do without us?

I wanna rub the sore spot on my neck where the needle stuck me—big damn needle. My memories are a bit fuzzy. Ever since then, I've been forgetting. What's happening? Why do I do everything he... they? Tell me? Forget what they want me to forget? Remember what they tell me to? Where is Edward? He was right next to me.

I can't control my limbs, but they move. No matter how hard I try to command my body, it follows their orders instead of mine. I'll wait here on the edge. I don't jump. Not yet.

24

DELSON
THE MOONLIGHT CLUB

THE GRAY LIGHT streaming through my bedroom window pulls me from the blood of a violent nightmare, and I wonder—am I now accustomed to loss? Desensitized to suffering? Is this what I've become? A victim? A victim by choice, or by fate? But I don't believe in fate. It's bullshit. And I didn't choose to be a victim. I didn't choose a fucking thing. But then, that's not true, is it? Haven't I chosen this? The warmth of another body. Her body. No... not her. It could never be her. The White Rose of Blackroot doesn't exist. Maybe she never did. Who's to say? All that's left of her now are hollow things—pictures, memories. I wake beside comfort. My escape from the cruelty of reality. From wickedness. I seek asylum in her embrace. In her kiss, her hips, her thighs...

She stands by the window, slipping into her clothes before sitting—legs crossed—on the foot of the bed. She opens her laptop, still somehow buried in book reports and essays. Of course, she'll probably get into any university she wants. I'll end up at some junior college. End up stuck at some entry level job in my 30s. Alissa will be a professor. Or a fashion designer. Or anything she sets her mind to.

"Why do you always look at me like that?" she asks.

I shake my head. "Like what?"

"Like you're somewhere else." She slides her laptop aside and crawls over to me. Her fingers thread through my hair. "Where do you go?"

I notice the bruise under her left eye. The puffy cheek beneath her fading makeup. "What happened?" I sit up, brushing her hair from her face.

She flinches, hiding the bruise again. "It's literally not a big deal." Her face turns away.

"You can tell me what happened," I say, more forcefully than I mean to.

Her eyes fix on the corner of the room, high and away from mine. Glossy. Lashes trembling. "He said he didn't mean to." Her voice is a pathetic squeak.

My neck and face flush with hot blood. The stitches in the tender, itchy flesh of my throat tug, threatening to open.

"Tell me everything." I let go of her arm only when I realize I've grabbed her.

She snivels. "My dad just drank a little too much. I shouldn't have—"

"He HIT you?" I tilt her face for a better look.

"I just k-kept picking at him. I was screaming in his face. He wouldn't listen. I smacked the drink out of his hands, and he... h-he—"

"Okay," I say, numb.

"It was just a slap. It's not like he slugged me. He's just got so much on his plate right now with everything, and—"

"He's gonna be at the Town Hall meeting today, isn't he?" I yank my clothes from the floor and leave her behind with her hesitant reply.

She comes after me, yelling for me to stop. The neighbors peek through their blinds as we storm off from the yard and down the sidewalk. Windows crack open halfway so they can catch the drama. Shaded faces peer out like sickly ghouls, or maybe like some demented motel owner who's got a real dangerous voyeur kink, transfixed by our bodies, our lives, feasting on us against our will.

"Nothing good on Netflix?" I shout at the onlookers. Mr. Bruckner, the sonofabitch on his porch, arms crossed, ugly smirk on his greasy face. "You have a good-fucking-day, sir," I say, flipping him off as I pass. He steps back into his house.

"Delson!" Alissa screams. "Get in my goddamn car. Right. Now." She points the key fob. The car beeps.

She rattles off every detail about her and the sheriff—how it's not so bad, how she provoked him. She defends him. Actually *defends* him. Her eyes barely stay on the road. She tries to calm me down, tries to convince me not to make a scene. Truth is, I don't even know what I'm going to do. I could confront him. Call him out in front of his colleagues, his bosses.

Cars clog downtown. I take my chance at the next stop sign, ditching Alissa and her car.

I push toward Town Hall, weaving through the slowed traffic as I pass the clock tower. My sternum jolts with each step up the stone stairs. I don't stop to brace myself. Not to catch my breath or to give a thought of what I might do. No plan. No sense. Just rage.

The large wooden doors stand propped open. I slow my pace at the sight of the crowd. Hot breath, strong cologne, and ubiquitous chatter. Pressed shoulder to shoulder, the people line across the meeting room in benches like church pews. Row after row of paranoid faces look to the front of the room, desperate for resolution. Fear controls them, like everybody.

A sandy voice rattles through the PA system. "Please, can we bring down the volume?" the blond woman in an ugly pant-suit rasps out into the little microphone on the podium before her.

They gawk in anticipation up at the city officials sitting in their spots, all lined up like some bullshit counsel—small microphones crack and feedback. A large mounted flat screen hangs on the wall behind them. Sheriff Lancaster sits beside the blond woman. He holds his hand over his microphone as he whispers in her ear.

My teeth creak as my jaw tightens. I'm pulled from the fury. My name being whispered. Frankie gestures for me to sit beside him. Only then do I realize I'm being watched. Multiple sets of eyes hang on me. Some even sneer—judgmental pricks. I squeeze in beside Frankie, throwing eye contact to as many nosy faces as possible.

"What the hell are you doing here?" I ask.

Dark rings hang beneath his eyes. "Cheaper than the movies." He smirks. "Like the county fair in this sumbitch." He pulls his hood over his mouth to stifle a cackle.

Sheriff Lancaster starts. "Alright. Think we'll begin with

the temporary shutdown of our schools. I know you've got a lot of questions, and—"

"Here's a question for you," a wiry man stands. "Why are *you* the one talking to us? Where's Mayor Lewis?"

"Are the rumors true?" a journalist chimes in, recording with her phone. "Is the mayor missing?"

"Now, hold on—"

Before he can finish, the woman keeps going. "If so, why has it been kept from the public? The people of Blackroot have a right to know. Why all the secrecy?"

"There is *no* secrecy," Lancaster snaps. "Information is processed and released in stages." He sighs. "Yes. It's true. Mayor Lewis' whereabouts are currently unknown. We have people on it."

"Any reason to believe his disappearance is connected to the murders? Or last year's case?"

"No. We don't believe so." He grunts. "There's not enough evidence to suggest—"

"With the disappearances, murders, and all the drugs on the street, it seems like you're in over your head." She clears her throat. "Will you be calling for outside help?"

He rolls his eyes. "We can handle it." His professionalism starts to slip. "Hell, you remember last time outsiders came in? Whole damn town flipped. Trust-fund babies playing crime-fighter. They don't care about towns like ours. People like us. This ain't anything we can't handle with good old-fashioned police work."

A white couple stands. The husband squeezes his wife's hand.

"How do you expect us to trust you when our daughter is

still missing?" His eyes are red. Her cheeks streaked with tears.

They just want answers. But we all know Courtney Pierce is dead. Even they do. The sheriff says nothing.

"Doesn't look like your old-fashioned police work is cutting it, Sheriff." The Journalist scoffs.

Before anybody has another chance to slam Lancaster, the large, mounted flat screen behind the city officials turns on.

Muffled, shallow breaths. Panic. Fear. As we all focus on the large screen, the cavernous room falls silent. Breathing. Struggling for breath. A light groan. A thousand different jingles ring out from the pockets of everyone in Town Hall. I don't grab my phone. I already know what it is. The panicked breathing engulfs us in surround sound as it struggles through every speaker on every phone. Strange that nobody screams. They all wait like I wait, like Frankie waits beside me. Eyes fixed on phones or the seventy-inch screen mounted above.

An image finally appears. The white light of the bone-colored sky pierces through the screen. The white slowly fades as a sidewalk appears and then the road. Cars parked all along the street. Hands pull up into the image—black zip ties cut into the wrists. The pale flesh is grimy, crusted, and stained with coagulated blood. Town Hall comes into view. It's then that everyone gasps, just before all the air in the room vanishes. It's then that we realize what is about to happen. We all slowly turn around in our seats, away from the screen.

A gangly figure. Narrow. Sharp. Ribs traceable through skin. Her flesh coated in filth and blood. Little cuts run all along her petite frame—random placement, some larger than others. Most bled, but not all will scar. Her bra and panties barely hang on to her with how much weight she has lost. A small camera hangs from a strap on her neck. Capturing the live footage of our reactions to the grisly return of Courtney Pierce.

Frankie grabs my arm. "She—she's alive." His voice cracks.

She stumbles inside, eyes darting, confused. Her greasy hair clings to blood-caked skin. Her knees give. Her scream shatters against the high ceiling and crashes back down like thunder from a vengeful goddess.

Her parents launch from the crowd, clawing past bodies to get to her. Lancaster vaults the desk and rushes over, shouting for people to move.

Radios chirp. Officers call for backup and EMTs. Others storm out, weapons drawn.

Courtney curls into herself—knees tucked, cheek against the floor. Her hair falls forward, revealing Polaroids stapled to her back.

I have to see them.

I leap the bench, push through shoulders to get closer. Sheriff Lancaster gawks at the photos.

Rose's photo sticks out like a sore thumb, last year's photo for the Year Book. Sam Lewis, his picture beside hers. Mayor Lewis. Bridget Bailey. Ian Bloom. Below that is another set of four photos. I recognize them. They were victims of Beckett Reed. My body trembles at the thought. What is about to be revealed? Finally. Now, the public will see that these murders are connected. Now Lancaster and the rest of them will know. You can't outrun your sins.

There is something beneath the photos etched into Courtney's back. She cries and grumbles as Lancaster lifts the Polaroids.

"I'm sorry, darlin'." He grimaces as he pulls the staples, tugging on the flimsy pictures.

The flesh of her back is carved up, the skin pulling away from itself like a hotdog split open in the microwave.

MOONLIGHT MATTERS

The freshest wound on her mangled body. Her parents cry over her, covering her exposed flesh.

The surround sound of Courtney's cries stops. The large screen turns black, and the voices speak.

"**Are we… interrupting?**"

Everyone's eyes jump to the black screen.

"**Well, now that we have your full attention…**"

A pause.

"**Mourn not the blood spilled, for we will use it to mix the mortar.**"

Another pause.

"**As a show of good faith, the girl has been returned. I want the Moonlight Club.**"

"Beckett Reed is dead!" Lancaster growls. "This whole thing died with him! There is no Moonlight Club! You think you got us? HA!" He stands. "When we find you—and we *will*—there won't be a cell waiting."

A scream outside.

A body crashes onto the stone steps.

An alarm chimes beneath it.

"**We do not give second chances.**"

The feed cuts out.

25

DELSON
THE HACKER

Sirens fade as the ambulance carrying Courtney races to the hospital. They load Dane's body into the back of the coroner's van, and I don't look away until the doors shut—not because I want to see it, but because I need to. Alissa pushes through the crowd toward me and Frankie, and I feel like I can finally breathe once she gets me to the car. I send a group message and try to collect myself during the drive back to my house. Never thought I'd see Frankie speechless, but he sits in the back seat without a single word.

Once we get home, I light a cigarette. Smoke drifts into the living room, where Cordy and Luca sit on the couch with their heads down.

I focus on the soft taps of Alissa's keyboard as she types out the final edits of some essay or report. The typing slows, then pauses. One last click. Then silence.

I glance back. Her brows furrow over her eyes. Then her gaze snaps to mine. She sets the laptop down on the couch and rises slowly. Her steps are careful.

"We're being watched." Her lips touch my ear with a whisper.

There's a cold thud in my chest as the hairs on my arms stand up. She nods back to the couch.

"The red light on my laptop is on…" She nudges me outside. "He's watching me through my webcam."

"Oh shit. Wait, that could make things easier for us," I say as I text Nathan, filling him in. I tell her to go back to her work, act normal. She does.

Rowan's sleek car pulls into the driveway. She steps out, her large oval sunglasses taking up a quarter of her face. She scoffs as she walks, head down, through the doorway past a faint coil of cigarette smoke.

"How's Court?" Alissa asks. "Is she awake?"

"They can't get her to stop screaming. The cops are up there trying to get whatever they can out of her. They wouldn't even let us in to see her."

Nathan emerges from the passenger side, a backpack and laptop bag slung over his shoulders.

"You ready?" I ask.

He nods slightly, adjusting the heavy bag.

I nod back, flicking my cigarette into the gravel.

"Edward texted me. Said he'll be here soon. We'll start without him." I head back inside.

Nathan sets up on the nightstand, connecting to the Wi-Fi.

Frankie huffs to announce himself, then meanders over from the recliner in the corner.

"No Ed-boy?" he mutters. "Is that not—I don't know—*stupidly* sketchy?" We all shoot him sharp looks. "I'm just sayin', like, did he even say what's up?" His hands rise in defense.

"No," I say flatly.

"Bro, I get it. You're hooking up with his girl or whatever and it's awkward as shit, but—"

"Excuse me?" Rowan lowers her sunglasses, eyes bouncing between us.

Luca shudders theatrically. "You guys bangin' is absolutely diabolical."

Alissa claps once. "OKAY. Can we *not*?" Her hand flicks between us. "What Delson and I are doing—that's our business."

Frankie's eyes bulge as he slinks back to the recliner.

I turn to Nathan. "How long to trace the IP?"

"Not sure, but since we know he hacked Alissa's laptop, there's a good chance we'll get more than just the address."

We gather close as the muddy orange sun slouches behind thick clouds. The soft glow of Nathan's monitor paints our faces—anxious, angry, focused, afraid.

"Okay, everyone chill. Let the master work," Nathan says, setting Alissa's laptop beside his own.

Luca taps his fingers on the nightstand. Frankie paces. Nathan exhales quietly.

"I'll start by analyzing the breach. Look for system anomalies." His fingers fly across the keyboard. Lines of code race down the screen. "Think I found the entry point. Got it. Now let's see if I can trace the IP…"

A distant siren wails, reminding me that Dane is gone. *Really* gone.

Nathan opens his network tracing tool, typing in the IP.

"The hacker used a string of proxies to mask the location," he explains. "Obviously."

Luca snickers. "*The Hacker.* That's it, that's his name. Because he hacks... people. With a knife." He pauses. "Also, comput—"

"Can you break through?" Rowan interrupts, ignoring him.

"Yeah, should be able to," Nathan mutters, his fingers a blur. "Using a combo of backdoor protocol and some trusty decryption—hold up..."

He clicks his tongue. A grin breaks. "Got it. Found a loophole. I'm in."

All of us go quiet. Even Frankie joins us at the monitor. Seconds stretch. Then stretch again.

Nathan exhales. "Wait... there's something else—a live feed." A couple of clacks on his keyboard, and the feed pops up.

Cordy gasps. "Is that Edward?" Her hand covers her mouth.

I lean in. It is. He's tied to a chair in a dark room. Hard to see much beyond him, but he looks rough, beaten up and bloody. Might even have stab wounds. Can't be sure.

"Shit!" I shout. "Where is he? Find out where he is!" I demand while drowning in a sudden wave of guilt.

"Okay, I'm-I'm trying!" Nathan says, but before he can touch another key, the screen turns blue.

"What's happening?" I ask.

Nathan starts clacking on the keys. "No no no." His head drops. "Probably no better than a freaking paperweight now."

"What? He just *crashed* your computer? Just like that?" My fingers clasp behind my head, reality weighing down.

Nathan stands. "We might not know where Eddie is, but the IP address was tracked to the high school. So, unless someone has a better idea..." He winces. Glances around. "No? Okay, then I guess we start there."

***

THE FINAL SMUDGE of orange in the sky suffocates beneath the encroaching Tartarean darkness. Night has come, and with it, uncertainty and fear.

Frankie heads to the hospital to see Courtney while the rest of us pile into Rowan's car. Nathan drives—and to Rowan's dismay, I sit shotgun. The streets are dead. Sidewalks empty. Children's bikes lie abandoned in front yards littered with orange and brown leaves, the same leaves scattered across the road. Blackroot is a ghost town with curfew looming. I squeeze the crowbar until the skin on my fingers burns.

Not a single car in the school parking lot. No skater kids doing flip tricks off the front steps of the Lecture Hall. No janitor van. Not even security. The place feels dreamlike, unreal, disconnected—like some half-rendered memory pulled into reality.

Wind bellows as I step from the car into the swaying drizzle, orange streetlights flaring off the rain. The air is warm, like breath from some unseen beast—a storm waiting to break.

Alissa and Cordy step out behind me, huddling close in their sweatshirts. Luca follows.

"We're not waiting in the car," Alissa says.

"I'm perfectly happy waiting in the car," Rowan calls from the backseat.

"Samesies," Nathan agrees, hands still gripping the steering wheel.

"Nathan, I need you. Assuming I can find the receiver, I wouldn't know what to do when I got there," I say.

He huffs as he gets out of the car. Mumbling to himself. "If I die in this school, I'm haunting your ass. On god."

"Hey!" Cordy grumbles. "None of us are dying. We stick together."

"Bet," Rowan says as she scoots out of the car. "I'm not going to wait here alone just to be skinned and turned into a coat or a lampshade or whatever."

Hoods up, we jog through the courtyard. Don't think anyone saw us. My steps quicken as a small precursory dose of adrenaline hits, snaking its way through my veins. We move as a group down the exterior corridor to the double doors on the school's side entrance. A separate walkway to our left leads past the office windows and out to the street. We duck behind the parapet as headlights flash overhead.

Alissa squeezes my hand. "What if an alarm goes off?"

"It's a risk," I say.

"That's not exactly comforting—"

Luca cuts her off. "It probably doesn't work. They haven't updated this place since, like, 2015. Besides, first offense, right?"

"Right..." she mutters.

I scan the dark for shapes. Hoods. Movement. Shadows. I can't tell if I'm paranoid or if someone's actually watching. But I feel it—that prickling alertness in the back of my brain.

Like something primitive. Evolutionary. The old survival sense. The kind that told cavemen when a predator was near. I don't know if it's real, but I believe in it.

I glance through the wire-mesh square window in the metal door. Alissa's hand rests on my arm.

"Watch out," I say, raising the crowbar and slamming it into the glass. It takes a few hits before the pane and mesh start to give. I reach through the jagged hole, stretching my fingers toward the push bar inside. I grunt. Can't reach.

I pull out, jam the crowbar through instead. Use it to press. Still not enough leverage. I push up onto my toes, wedge my shoulder into the opening. Headlights bounce off the street. The others duck. My arm stays stuck, muscles screaming. Something pinches deep in my shoulder.

The crowbar slips—then I catch it by the curve. Gasping, I steady it against the bar. My fingers push again. No good. I rotate the crowbar, grip the straight end, and press the curved teeth into the push bar. I strain with everything I've got.

The lock unlatches. The door swings open.

I exhale, lungs on fire. The crowbar clatters to the tile floor. I yank my arm free, shoulder throbbing. Step inside.

"No alarm," Alissa sighs.

I grab the crowbar and lead them in.

"This way," Nathan says.

We follow as he stares at his phone. The red lockers look black in the dark. I stay close to him as we make our way toward the offices. Then I hear it—the screeching alarm floods the corridor, slicing the stillness apart.

"We gotta go!" Nathan yells, stumbling back.

The others cluster together, retreating on instinct.

"No! We're too close. We can't stop now! Which office is it?"

He holds up his phone, shaking. His flashlight bounces. His hands tremble.

"Which is it!" I shout.

"Main office!" he says, pointing.

I lunge forward and wedge the crowbar between the door and frame. Pull hard—nothing. I slam my shoulder into it. It slips out. I jam it in again, grip tight, press with everything I have.

Luca jumps in beside me, gripping the bar with both hands as he shoves forward until his muscles shake. He wriggles the bar back and forth with me until it slides further between the seam, cracking the wooden frame more. We wrench our bodies to the side.

THUNK! Loud and metallic, the lock breaks.

"Hell yeah, that's how it's done, boys!" Luca laughs victoriously.

The heavy door swings open. We rush in.

"There!" Nathan points to another door.

The alarm continues to blare and I know the police are coming. Could be here already. I jam the crowbar between the door and the frame. Goes in easier this time. I clench my fingers around the curve of the bar for cushioning as I slam my chest and ribs into my fingers. The bar cracks further. I pull to the side. Frame splits, door cracks, and we're in. Only then do I realize where I'm standing. Principal Myers' office.

Nathan opens the laptop on Myers' desk. His fingers stumble and shake over the keys.

A sense of familiarity... déjà vu... a memory. Principal Myers at the Homecoming dance. He watched me on Bellflower Island. He *saw* what was happening to everyone, and he just *left*. I followed him... Jenna Darkly was there.

My fingers drift up to the tender wound on my neck. The bandage, soggy, stains of red and orange. The alarm reminds me again of the urgency.

"It's Myers..." I realize aloud.

Nathan looks up. "The live stream's feeding straight to his computer." He wipes sweat from his brow. "He's our guy."

"Let's go!" I shout, herding everyone out.

We tear through the halls. Lockers blur. The alarm drowns everything out. Only the glowing EXIT signs guide us. I slam into the same side door we entered through, glass crunching underfoot. Rain and hail hammer the metal awning overhead like machine-gun fire.

We bolt through the lot. Alissa grips my hand. Cordy holds hers. Rowan gets dragged by Nathan up front. Luca slips, knees skidding.

"Save yourself, dipshit!" Rowan yells back.

"I'mma remember that, girl!" he groans, popping to his feet. He nods for us to keep going. He's behind us again by the time we hit the car.

Nathan fires up the engine before the others finish piling in. I slam the passenger door shut just as the first cop car screeches into the lot. I reach across and kill the headlights. The SUV idles, spotlight scanning the building. Two more cruisers pull in. Officers climb out.

A beam blasts through the windshield, locking onto us.

"Drive!" I bark.

Nathan slams the gas. Tires scream. We rocket out, sirens igniting behind us. Red and blue lights gleam on slick rooftops and windows in the distance. We park in an alley for a quick minute before the sirens grow louder again. In a flash of black, white, red and blue, the cars bolt past the alley's mouth. The sirens sink to a whisper. We waste no time before fleeing our hiding spot.

I've never been so happy to pull into my driveway.

"Nathan, your mom owns Barclay Electronics downtown, right?" I ask.

He nods as his eyes narrow.

"Can you get us in there? We need some stuff." I say.

"Yeah, no." He scoffs.

"You work there on weekends, don't you? You have a key."

"I mean-yeah, but-no." He shakes his head, shifts his feet. "We're not robbing the store, so..."

"We'll return everything we take. C'mon, it'll be like nothing ever happened, okay?" I press.

He sighs, the space between his brows wrinkles.

"Nathan, trust me. If anything goes wrong, I'll take the blame."

He agrees after a long moment.

"This is a long shot, but do any of you have an empty space for tonight? I mean empty house, family cabin or something?" They glance at one another. "Any parents out of town?" I probe.

Rowan raises her hand. "Actually, my parents have a place in town. It's our Airbnb." She pauses. "Why?"

"How do you feel about being bait?"

"I'll do it," Cordy says.

26

DELSON
UNMASKED

"Just drive slowly, and take back roads," I tell Nathan.

The car hums to life, and the little green gel air freshener blasts out pine scent as the fan kicks on.

"This is stressful. You're a stressful person. You know that, right?" his eyes widen.

"The worst," I nod. "Drive, please."

His tongue clicks against his teeth as he mutters something under his breath.

"We're an hour past curfew. When we get in, we have to move fast," I say, glancing out the window. Houses blur by. Jack-o'-lanterns, fake spiderwebs stretched from porches and trees. A few foam headstones, zombified limbs reaching from faux dirt. A wooden black cat behind a tree. An inflatable hearse. Even a real black cat perched in the twisted branches, eyes glowing.

Nathan glances back at me, squinting. "This is exactly why you don't have a lot of friends, Delson."

I chuckle. "My circle's small because authenticity's rare."

"And you're the realest? Mr. Authenticity?" he teases.

"Didn't say that…"

Clouds churn overhead—inky, bloated, dragging across the sky. The wind wails like something wounded. Leaves barrel down the road, glistening in the orange glow of streetlights. Nathan pulls over a block from the store. We grab our bags and flashlights. He pulls his hood up as we move quickly down the sidewalk. Leaves crunch beneath our feet, dissolving into sludge in black puddles.

He ducks behind a trash can, wide-eyed, then shuffles behind a bush.

"Will you come on!" I hiss.

He fumbles with the keys at the back door, hands shaking. The lock clicks. He yanks the door open and pulls me in by the arm. The keypad beeps as he punches in the code, disarming the alarm.

"Okay, let's move." I hand him the list of what he needs to grab. "Where are the mini DV cameras?"

He points me in the right direction. The beam from my flashlight is a harsh white. I try to keep it from shining through the store windows as I creep down the aisles. It takes longer than I thought it would, but I find what I'm looking for. I fill my backpack with the equipment.

Before I can zip up my bag, the glossy shelves and reflective equipment shimmer from encroaching headlights. I freeze.

"Cops!" Nathan slams into me. We fall to our stomachs on the floor. We fumble our flashlights as we scramble to shut them off.

A cop parks outside the store window. His burning spotlight searches from the other side of the glass like some sentient lighthouse, or maybe a cyclops with some sort of heat vision. Red and blue flash silently from atop his cruiser. The beam sweeps across the store a few more times before the red and blue flashes stop and the car creeps away.

Nathan hyperventilates against the linoleum tile. "It's been like a day and I already need a vacation from being your friend."

"Friend?" I question.

"I'm the most authentic person in this town, okay?" he gets to his feet. "Come on." He reaches out a hand to help me up.

We meet with the others at the Airbnb to set up all the cameras. It's a five-bedroom house, two stories, with a backyard. Plenty of bushes and trees for Luca and Nathan to stay concealed.

Cordy paces in the living room, biting at her nails.

"You sure you can do this?" Alissa asks.

Cordy's eyes go wide. "I-I don't know. I'm freaking out. I mean—"

"Luca and Nathan are right outside," Alissa says gently.

"And we'll be watching on the cameras. If anything looks wrong, we'll get you out immediately. We'll call the cops. He's not leaving that house," I say.

"Right. Fine. Just go before I change my mind." She huffs. "Wait, no—I can't be in here alone."

"I'll stay with her," Rowan offers. "I doubt the two of us are much of a deterrent, but with a few girls' night selfies, maybe we'll actually draw him in."

Alissa and I set up a couple blocks away in her car. I dim the laptop screen. All the cameras are working—one in each bedroom, one in the upstairs hall, and two downstairs.

Cordy and Rowan confirm their phones are turned on.

"This doesn't seem very safe," Alissa mutters.

"It's not," I say.

No movement. All rooms quiet. The girls lounge on the couch. Cordy still bites at her nails. Rowan plays with her hair, checking herself in the front-facing camera.

I check in with Luca and Nathan after a few hours. Still nothing. I keep Cordy and Rowan updated through their burners.

"Is everything okay?" Alissa asks, eyes fixed on the monitor.

"As okay as it can be."

"I mean with you and Edward."

"He knows I'd never hurt him on purpose."

I feel her eyes.

"What about us?" she asks quietly.

"We'll have to survive to find out."

"He knows you'll come for him. Any of us would."

"I hope so." The pressure. What if he really knows and is counting on me to find him? To save him. If I fail... no. I'm gonna save you, Eddie.

The girls sit and talk for another hour or so. Then Rowan flags me down in one of the camera feeds. She points to her phone. I open the screen share window. He made contact.

> You are trusting your life in the hands of a
> child. Delson can't save you. He can't save
> any of you. All he can do is watch as you
> die and beg for mercy. It's his... destiny.

I ready my response, fingers on the keys. A message appears. Rowan responded on her own.

We know what you've done. We know who you are. And we're going to make sure you go down!

The cops are already on their way. They'll probably be knocking down your door any minute. We aren't running or hiding anymore!

He doesn't respond. "Come on…" I grit my teeth.

Rowan's phone rings. She glances at the camera—at us—then answers.

The voices buzz through the speakers on our end.

"Not too wise, taunting with a knife to your throat." Static, sizzling. **"Rumor is you're a bright girl—or at least you *think* so. I see now though… you really are dumb."**

"You want to know what I see?" Rowan growls shakily. "I see a prison cell. Just for you. With a very large cellmate who *loves* to cuddle. But I don't see a knife."

"I want to speak with Delson." The last words come in Rose's voice.

Rowan doesn't catch it. "I-I'll pass it along."

"Poor little girl. You're already dead. You may perceive life's moments linearly, but you've already felt our blade cut into your throat. Saw through your spine. Your head's already rolling!" A sharp laugh. **"Tell him this is his fault. Only he can stop it! You tell him I'll carve up every single one of his friends until he comes face to face with me."**

A pause. **"Did you get that?"**

Silence.

"Guess I'll start with you…" Laughter.

The line goes dead.

"Wait, did you see that?" Alissa points at one of the camera feeds. "I thought something moved."

The feed goes black. My jaw tightens until my teeth creak.

"He couldn't have access to the feed, could he?" she asks.

"No. Nathan said it's a closed network." I click on the black square. Nothing.

Another feed crackles before going dark.

I scramble with my phone.

"Go for Luca," he answers.

"Have you guys seen anything? Something is going on with the cameras."

There is a long pause. "What are you talking about? You said to drive by Principal Myers' house to scope it out."

"No, Luca!" I drop the phone. "Shit!"

"What's happening?" Alissa yells, shoving the laptop up onto the dash.

All the cameras go dark.

"Call the cops!" I shout, stumbling from the car.

I race down the sidewalk. Wind slaps against me, slowing my steps. Rain comes in sheets, sideways, cutting down from the sky. I skid across the front yard and nearly fall. I catch myself and pound on the red door.

"Rowan! Cordy! Open up!"

The door flies open. I shove through, slamming it behind me. Rowan and Cordy stand frozen, shaking.

"What's happening?" Rowan demands.

I scan the room, lungs burning, soaked clothes sticking to my skin.

"Delson!" Cordy screams.

I grab them both. "Come on," I say, pulling them back.

I open the door. The figure in black—a twisted, stitched face with hollow eyes—stares back at us. He lunges forward, knife raised. Rowan screams as I slam the door, but his arm blocks it. I throw my full weight against the door, wishing I had the sheer mass to lob his arm off.

"Run!" I shout.

They vanish. Their pounding footsteps fade out behind my heavy breath as I heave against the door. The door crashes open, slamming into my head, knocking me off balance. I stumble over the bunched-up area rug, losing my breath as I hit the floor. The drywall caves in around the doorknob. He stands over me, long black poncho—like the ones provided at school—dripping wet. The warped, yellowing leather face glares down. A single gloved finger lifts to the dark, frozen lips in silence.

I scramble away as he steps forward. Get to my feet, but he's already on me. I jump back, clearing the first slash. He springs forward, blade cleaving down. I twist to the side, lifting a painting by the wooden frame from its hooks as the knife disappears into the wall. Glass shatters and wood splinters as I smash the frame over the back of his head. I leap over the coffee table and race upstairs toward Rowan and Cordy. I run down the hall, calling for them. I rip open a door. Bathroom. Empty. Check another room. Empty. Cold. Notice the open window. I run to the window. A wide section of roof sits just below. I call their names, unsure I can even be heard over the wind and rain. No answer. I race back to the hall.

A door swings open!

"Delson!" Cordy cries as she and Rowan huddle next to me.

"You guys open that window? It wasn't open before."

They shake their heads.

Another door bursts open. Light glints as the blade slashes my arm. I shove Rowan and Cordy into the nearest room and slam the door behind us. I hurry them to the window. They climb out just as the bedroom door swings wide.

I slam the window shut and follow them.

"Go!" I shout as I step onto the slick roof tiles.

Rain whips across the sky. Wind howls, threatening to shove us right off. We edge along the roofline. I check each window we pass—locked. When we reach the front of the house, the yard waits far below.

"We'll have to jump," I say.

"No fucking way," Rowan snaps, stepping back.

"Just scoot down and hang off the edge."

Rowan glares at me, but Cordy grabs her hand. "Come on," she urges, pulling her to the edge.

I crouch above them. "Okay. Let go."

They drop.

I roll to the side, nearly slipping off as heavy footsteps close in. I catch my footing just as the blade flashes for my gut. I twist. My head cracks against the ledge above the windowsill. The knife slams into the wood, inches from my face. I drive an elbow into the leather mask. He staggers.

I yank the blade free from the siding and swing. He jerks back, the knife missing by inches.

I lunge. The blade cuts through rain. He ducks, slamming into my chest. My back hits the roof hard. The knife plunges into his shoulder like it's butter. His own weight drives it deeper. He groans, lifting himself off the blade. The vinyl poncho crinkles.

I surge forward, gripping the handle. I drive my chest into the hilt, pinning him to the shingles. A ragged gasp warbles from behind the mask.

With a sharp roll, he tosses me off. I go flying. My lungs collapse on impact, air sucked from my chest like a space shuttle door ripped open.

I tumble through the drenched yard. Cordy kneels beside me. Alissa runs to us from the street. I lose sight of him. Sirens whistle and bleep as the cops converge on the house.

"The killer's in the house!" Alissa screams at the officers.

Guns draw as they approach the front steps. "Stay put!" they order with a sharp glance back at us. One of them mutters something into his radio on his shoulder.

"Police! Come out with your hands up!" the dark-haired lady cop shouts. "This is the pol—" She's interrupted as the door opens. "Hands up! Now!" Both officers' guns point at the dark figures in the doorway. More police arrive. Lights cascade through the wet street, the house shifting from red to blue.

"Both of you drop your weapons!" the police officer orders.

The two black-hooded figures step out onto the porch. Metal blades clink at their feet. Their hands raise. They pull on their hoods.

"Don't move!" the older, heavy-set cop warns. "I said— don't move!"

They don't listen.

The masks fall into the wet grass.

It takes too long to register what I'm seeing. I expect Myers. But not the other one.

Not Adele.

Suddenly, my skin is too tight. My chest cramps and my knees feel weak.

They stand in matching black, eyes hollow—just as vacant as the sockets of their discarded masks. Officers wrench their arms behind their backs, locking the cuffs tight.

No resistance. No emotion.

Yet tears still stream from their dead eyes.

27

JENNA
THE SWORD

Rain beats against the windowpane—a somber percussion mirroring the chaos in my head. The red light from the vacancy sign outside hums on and off, reaching through the gaudy motel curtains. Like nimble, spine-like fingers, the red glow crawls across the ceiling.

Hmmz... On and off.

My eyes ache from hours spent staring at my monitor, combing through evidence—or the lack of it—scrolling articles, retracing routes on Google Maps. The little desk in this one-person motel room is a mess of photographs, news clippings, and maps I bought from the local inquiry office. A visual web of desperation under the weak orange glow of a dying table lamp.

"One step away from a corkboard and yarn, Jenna," I mutter to myself, like I'm standing just over my own shoulder.

A photograph of Edward Bloom stares up at me from

beneath my fingers. I tap the desk, mimicking the rhythm of the rain. His youthful innocence—if you can call it that—feels grotesquely mismatched against the darkness that's swallowed him and all of Blackroot.

The anguish in the Blooms' faces haunts me. It drives me to find the truth, to peel back whatever's festering underneath this town. I've spent weeks chasing a demented trail, one I thought belonged to a serial killer. But now... it feels like something worse is in the wind.

The Blackroot Butcher. That's what the papers are calling him. No tact. No shame.

"The Butcher, huh?" I say aloud.

That's really what they're going with? I couldn't believe it when I heard. The sheriff's office arrested two suspects—Clark Myers and Adele Madot. The high school principal and the lady with the creepy little coffee shop. They've got those kids held for questioning too: Alissa Lancaster, Cordelia Krueger, Luca Reyes, Rowan Riley, Nathan Barclay, and Delson Heller.

Sheriff wouldn't give me anything else. Wouldn't even let me speak to the kids.

I nibble at the peeling skin on my bottom lip and take another sip of lukewarm coffee. They searched for the Pierce girl for a month and covered a lot of ground. I joined in on a handful of searches, gathering as much information from the locals as I could. I'm sure that Edward's been taken to the same location she was kept. Now, if I could only figure out where that is.

Staring at the map until my eyes burn, afraid this is a blink-and-you'll-miss-it kind of situation, I consider the routes taken by the search parties. The dim table lamp casts its orange hue over the oddly average depiction of Heller County.

"Damnit," I say to myself, pulling the map from the desk and placing it against the wall. I smooth out the large sheet, sticking pins in the corners. I race to the hobby shop down the block before it closes for curfew. It doesn't take ten minutes till colored pins scatter the map, each representing a search party's starting point. White threads connect them, tracing their routes through dense forest, alongside rivers, across meadows, mountains and trails.

I stand back, arms crossed, staring down the pattern. Edward's last known location is marked with a black X—his home. But Alissa Lancaster says Edward left with Dane Lewis. The deceased. His car was found abandoned a few miles out on Craven Creek Road. No signs of struggle. Just left there. Same stretch of road where Courtney Pierce's car was found the night she vanished.

"Every search party started from somewhere logical. They covered everything they could," I mutter, dragging my finger along the threads. "So why no trace of him?"

My finger stops. Hovers. A thin patch of map—almost nothing. Maybe trails. Maybe a road? A few miles from Craven Creek.

Hmmz... The red light still pulses through the curtain.

I've seen this area before, but something looks different here. I check Google Maps. It's a shaded region. Denser than the rest. Almost impassable—thick brush, tangled undergrowth. But farther up the mountain, a small road cuts into it. Hidden beneath old-growth canopies. Barely noticeable.

There must be something there. A structure. A clearing. It's small. Easy to miss. Especially if people assumed it was too dense to bother with.

I stab a red pin into that spot. "It's a long shot," I murmur. "But every mystery gets solved by looking where no one else has."

The buzzing of my phone jolts me. My eyes never leave the map.

"Darkly," I answer.

"Jenna, hey." Static cracks. "This is Del—"

"I got it," I cut in. "Sheriff done questioning you? Where are you?"

"I'm heading home now. Wanna meet me there?"

"On foot? He didn't give you a ride?" I ask.

"What a dick, right?"

I glance at the clock. Curfew's been active for over an hour. Why would Lancaster release a minor to walk across town alone, curfew or not? Even with the suspects in custody, that doesn't track.

I stare at the motel's corded phone, sitting on the desk's edge. "Hold on. I'll come get you. Stay at the station."

Keeping Delson's voice on my cell, I lift the motel phone and dial the sheriff's office.

Nothing. Line's dead. It worked earlier when I called the front desk to request a new room because of the couple next door—loud, drunk, probably passed out now.

"I'll just meet y—..." Delson's voice breaks into static. Then silence.

"No wait, I—" The call ends. "What the—" My phone shuts off in my hand. "I just charged you." I murmur to the phone, trying to turn it back on.

THUD! Thud!

Two heavy knocks at the door send my shoulders up and the hairs on my neck standing.

Who the hell? I grab my pistol from the desk.

"Who is it?" I keep an authoritative air.

The nasally voice muffles through the door. "It's, uh, front desk."

"And?"

"Oh, you, yeah. Sorry, yeah, uh, you have a call... waiting for you." He pauses. "It's D-something. D-uh, Delbert?"

"Delson?"

"That's it, yeah. Your uh, room's phone, yeah it doesn't seem to be working, so..."

I crack the door, leaving my left hand on the knob, and my Beretta in the right, trigger finger resting lightly along the length of the barrel. Patrick—his name tag pinned on crooked—stares back at me from behind his greasy dark hair, bad mustache and thick glasses.

"Great, thanks. I'll be right over there." I shut the door on him. I feel my eyes tighten with confusion. Delson?

I check the desk, the nightstand—then find the room key in my jacket pocket. I grab the car keys too, just in case. I holster the gun, shut the laptop, and take down the map from the wall. The pins and threads go in the trash. The map, folded.

I wait a few seconds longer, hoping Patrick's shuffled back to the lobby.

But no. He waited. Apparently wants to escort me the whole thirty-eight feet.

His steps are slow, gravel grinding under each lazy shuffle.

He's halfway there by the time I pick up the lobby phone.

"Delson, how'd you get this number? I never told you where I was staying."

The yellow ceiling light sways above me with the spinning fan. A single red thread hangs from the chain. A jingle bell dangles at the end—moving gently, but silent.

Silence.

"Hello? Delson?"

Just a dial tone.

I set the phone back in its cradle.

BRRING! BRRING!

I snatch it back up. "Yes."

"Jenna, please help me…" Delson whispers. "They got me. They fucking got me." His voice trembles, ragged and breathless.

"What do you mean? Where are you?" I grip the edge of the counter.

Silence.

"Delson, what do you see? Buildings—cars—roads—trees? Anything?"

Sniff. "The fucker really sliced me up," he mutters. "Shit—it's a lot of blood, Jenna."

"I need you to focus. Tell me what you see."

"…It's dark. I see a thread. A crimson thread…"

The word crackles with static.

"I see Edward too."

"Okay—okay, good. But how do I find you? What else?"

"I see a sword." Static again. "Above his head."

"A sword? Over whose head? Edward's?"

"It's over yours too, Jenna..."

His voice warps into a tangle of whispers.

Shunk!

The power dies. No dial tone.

Hmmz...

The red vacancy light outside pulses on and off, casting its sickly glow across the lobby like pooling blood.

This isn't an outage.

Someone flipped the breaker.

Cut the phone line.

I place the phone down, eyes adjusting to the dark. My ears tune in for the scrape of Patrick's steps. For the jingle of the front door chime.

Nothing.

I draw my weapon, stepping slow, measured.

Back against the wall.

I scan the windows—the parking lot.

Only red light. No sign of Patrick.

Shadows stretch, vague and unmoving.

Cling.

The bell on the red thread jingles.

"A single thread, fragile, thin," Patrick mutters from the dark shapes, "held the sword, that weight of sin. Symbol of fate... of power's cost. A truth that all would not be lost."

"Hold it," I bark.

"A single thread. A single thread. A single thread."

The chimes above the lobby door rattle.

Debby—the blond from the room next to mine—walks in.

"'Scuse me, but the power's out—"

"Ma'am, do not move!" I snap, adjusting my aim.

"Wha...?"

A single thread.

I turn the barrel back toward Patrick—

—but something tightens around my throat.

I claw at it with my left hand.

The phone cord.

It digs into my neck as someone yanks from behind the counter.

The gun slips free with the first hard pull.

I'm dragged up and over, flipping across the counter.

Debby's husband. Fuck. They're in on it. I hear her now, cackling in the lobby.

He straddles me, my back flat on the floor. His arms pulling further and further to either side as he leans over, grunting. Blood vessels burst. The cord digging in deeper and deeper until my eyes feel like they could rupture. A fleck of red light glints off the silvery butt of the knife strapped to his hip. I reach for it, my vision tunneling like falling down a black well. The metal button snaps as I rip the knife from its sheath. No time to think. The well's opening is shrinking and drifting farther away. I sink the long blade right between his ribs. Angle it from the back.

He shrieks, releasing his grip on my life. He stumbles back, gasping. Short, rapid heaves for air. Collapsed lung. He reaches for the knife, but his meaty arms are too big to grab it himself. I stagger to my feet, climbing out of the well. In one spiteful motion, I tear the knife from his back.

"Where's Edward Bloom?" I demand.

I clock Patrick rushing the counter. Goddamnit. I palm

the counter, swing my legs over. Gotta get the gun! Patrick leans down to snatch it before I can. I sink a boot into his face, knocking him back. Before he knows what hit him, I fire a round in his kneecap. Watch him crumble to the floor. I glance back, big guy passed out.

"Where's the kid!" I shout, ready to fire another round. Debby still stands near the front door, cackling.

"In shadowed halls where secrets dwell, in shadowed halls where secrets dwell." Patrick repeats. "A single thread…" He swings wildly at me with a small knife as he pounces forward.

I fire two more rounds, center mass. He drops as quickly as he stood. Debby still cackles like a witch in some nightmarish fairy tale. I holster my weapon, grab the corded phone from the counter, receiver and all. The long spiral cord trails behind me as I move toward her, stepping over Patrick. Laughing and laughing, all the way up until I smash the antique upside her head. She drops like a bag of rocks. Who's laughing now?

Hmmz…

Red light floods the room again.

I leap back over the counter.

There's a door behind it. A break room.

Probably where the big guy was hiding.

I spot the breaker panel. Flip the power back on. The ceiling fan stirs the air again. Yellow light swings lazily across the room.

I scour behind the counter.

Looking for anything.

Any sign of who gave these people orders.

This isn't just a killer. Not even two.

This is a cult.

Of course it is.

Tradition.

A crumpled yellow paper catches my eye, pinned beneath my boot.

I unfold it. Read the ballpoint scratch:

A single thread, fragile, thin, Held the sword, that weight of sin. A symbol of fate, of power's cost, A truth that all would not be lost. For kings and rulers, heed this lore, The sword that drops forevermore. In darkness, it swings, a dire decree, that power comes with uncertainty.

"What are we?"

The voice buzzes from the speakers above the front desk —where smooth jazz used to drone.

"Fate," I answer aloud. "Guess I've got a thing for moral parables."

I shut the break room door behind me.

Back against it.

"The sword of Damocles?" I ask, taunting.

Zzcht. Static hisses through the speakers.

"You think you're clever, don't you?"

It takes me a moment to register—

It's Edward Bloom's voice.

"But you couldn't save me," Edward says.

A girl's voice now—young. Familiar.

"I was helpless, screaming and crying while they tore me open. You couldn't save me."

Rose Bailey.

"But how could you? You couldn't save your father... or your brother. Not even yourself."

My voice screeches back at me.

Delson: "So what makes you think you can save me?" A pause. "Death would be a favor to you." He mimics me again.

"After all, how can you live with yourself?"

"I'll go to therapy."

I pull my firearm before stepping out of the lobby.

The chimes cling as the door swings shut behind me.

The sound fades into the stillness of the lot.

Hmmz... Dark and empty aside from the recurring red glow of the vacancy sign and my car parked at the other end right in front of my room. There are twelve rooms at this roadside motel and the door to every one is now left hanging open. Black, uniform cavities in the red light. My finger rests on the trigger as the red glow subsides. Slow steps, passing the first doorway.

Hmmz...

Unmistakable in the hellish light. Slumped shoulders, narrow and statue-like. Invisible eyes watch me from the silhouette on the other side of the door, deep in the room. Or — was that a mannequin?

As the red light fades again and darkness swells, I'm left floating in the middle of a vast ocean. Cold black open water in all directions with nothing but my own thoughts and *whatever* may lurk beneath my feet. My feet, that dangle over something so profoundly deep, my body could never make the journey to the bottom before collapsing violently inward on itself, due to the sheer immensity of the pressure. Even still, it's the *unknown* in that deep darkness beneath that fires an icy chill down my spine. Makes the tiny hairs on the back of my neck stand at attention and tells me to pull my knees to my chest and disappear.

Hmmz...

Another shadow person watches me from room 2. Tall, slender, and feminine in the bloody light. Her head cocks like some monstrous, predatory bird. Or lizard? She moves like slowed stop-motion. Stepping toward me robotically, as if her joints moved thanks to a series of gears and cogs and springs.

A few quick and quiet steps back deeper into the parking lot—near the sign—puts me at a safer distance. I keep the figure in my sights and my finger on the trigger. When it comes down to it, it's me or them and it sure-as-shit ain't gonna be me.

The ruby glow chokes out and I take a cautionary huff in the darkness, holding my breath.

Stomp stomp stomp stomp!

A broad shape rushes me from the black maw of Room 3. The figure—target—doesn't slow, charging full speed.

POP-POP-POP!

I squeeze off three rounds just as the red light flares again. The target collapses mid-run, nearly flipping ass over end in the gravel. I don't give a damn about the crap in my room anymore—I just want my car. I want this fucking place in the rearview.

I keep the gun trained on the motel, sweeping in a controlled arc as I side-step toward my car. More figures watch me from the glowing red and deep black of the twelve rooms—except Room 3. The red light pulls back, receding like blood into water, and the blackness becomes bottomless. Cold and alive. It stretches forever.

Crunch-crunch-crunch-CRUNCH!

Boots in gravel—too close.

POP-POP-POP-POP!

Four more rounds, center mass. The shadowy man folds, crashing at my feet. I stomp his head. Gravel digs into his eyes, pours into his mouth, cracks his front teeth, top and bottom. I shot Patrick three times. Same with the one from Room 3. I'm willing to bet they know as well as I do, with a restricted clip capacity of ten rounds, that I'm empty.

Ten rounds—

Hmmz...

The red vacancy light buzzes back to life, casting its glow over my shoulders and across the gravel. Cherry-red gleams off my bumper—almost there. Almost free.

But *he* watches me now. From outside my room's open door.

The crimson light deepens the black in his eyes—voids, wormholes, portals to some dimension Lovecraft never lived long enough to name. The expression on the counterfeit face is so ghoulish and off-putting—I've seen it before in pictures, but in this light it lurks somewhere between the uncanny valley and hell. It makes me *believe* in monsters. Monsters in masks and black hoods. His boots scrunch into the gravel, long legs ready to bolt. His black rain poncho drapes past his knees and he steps forward like some lurching creature covered in scales, slime, and seaweed. Some swampy manifestation of Death. The long ruthless blade he holds in his left hand shimmers in the gory light as he propels himself and his reaper's scythe forward, closing the distance between us. I grip my Beretta M9 semi-automatic pistol.

—**Eleven** with one in the chamber.

POP!

I tag him, bury it right in his chest. Upper-left, blows his shoulder back. Sends the knife flying from his fingers. He still crashes into me, a shambling, off-kilter lunatic. Darkness again. We roll in a mad scramble in the gravel lot, but he overpowers me, my shoulder blades smashing into the small jagged rocks while he gains side control, pinning me down. I try to sweep to escape my inferior position, but he drives two fast elbows across my forehead. A hot rush of panic knots in my throat as I slam my free fist into his body. The icy realization pours over me, up past my chin, drowning me. I can't overpower him, not physically. Not on the ground.

He places his right knee down on my chest, digging hard into my sternum, squeezing and pinching my breasts under my leather jacket. His left leg extends out to the side to hold his balance. His right hand pins my left arm to my stomach, just below his knee. His left hand finds its way to my throat. My legs kick with desperation as I struggle, trying to buck him off me. I can't, he keeps full control in the dominant position. His hand squeezes around my throat, thumb and fingers pinching my windpipe. A wheezing gargle huffs from my mouth as I slam my free hand into his stiff arm. Nothing. I see now, with him on top of me, that he's wearing a kevlar vest. Where are the others? The lesser sharks, swimming below, waiting to pick from the scraps left behind?

Hmmz...

Seeing red again. I'm NOT someone who needs saving. I'm NOT some helpless damsel in distress. And I DON'T go down like this. I let go of his arm. Find my keys in my jacket pocket.

The engine roars to life at the push of a button. Headlights flare, bathing the lot in sharp white light. The Butcher

—straddling me like some sleep-paralysis demon—recoils, loosening his grip.

He turns, panicked, toward the phantom driver.

It's enough.

I drive my keys—spread like claws between my fingers—straight into his face. I hope they pierce through the mask. Hit an eye.

I roll left. He loses balance and tumbles onto the gravel.

I pop the trunk and sprint for the car. Figures emerge from the rooms—only four. Maybe the others were mannequins after all. I grab my aluminum bat. A tube sock stretches down from the barrel. Dad's old trick. I turn.

The masked maniac rises, slouched and seething. His blade gleams in the headlights.

I step forward, both arms raised, bat lifted high. I scream as I bring it down.

Thunk!

He catches it. Tries to rip it from my hands.

But all he grabs is the sock.

DINK!

The bat rings off his skull.

DINK!

Again. He drops to one knee.

The other four now shuffle into the headlights. Their eyes are blank. Distant.

I scoop up my gun and bolt for the car. I dive inside, slam the door, and lock it. Throw it in reverse. Gravel spits in every direction as I whip the car into a skid.

I throw it into drive. The engine growls. I aim at him.

He stands, arms loose, challenging me.

Tires scream. Gravel flies. The car surges forward.

I scream with it.

He flies over the hood, off the windshield.

I don't stop.

They watch me as I watch them.

And then they vanish in the rearview, along with the motel.

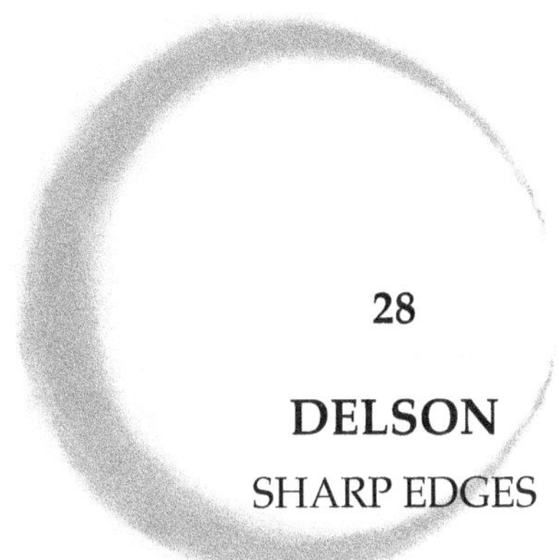

28

DELSON

SHARP EDGES

THE CIGARETTE SHOULD BE SATISFYING. Should melt away the ice on my shoulder, but Alissa can't pull me away from The Serpent. The gray, swollen sky weeps for me. I couldn't save them. Rick. Dane. Rose. The psychopaths responsible for this may be behind bars, yet doubt still burrows deep. I couldn't save them. What if I can't save Eddie?

I disregard Alissa's soft plea as her hand tugs at my arm. The CLOSED sign hangs on the inside of the windowed door. Chairs sit neatly stacked atop the wooden tables while voodoo masks fixed to the walls peer out from the shadows of the empty shop. Phantom scents of fresh coffee and pastries lap at my subconscious. I can almost feel the warmth, taste the bitter brew.

"You're torturing yourself." Alissa sighs, weakness on her tongue. "We survived. Smile... please?" Her cheek rests on my chest as her arms tie around my waist.

"I'll smile when we find Eddie."

Her head lifts. Chin set to my sternum. "The Police are

out there with search parties all over the county. They WILL find him."

"Yeah, like they found Courtney?" I pull her arms from my waist.

"But he's safe in the meantime. The killers are behind bars." Her head shakes. "It's only a matter of time before they get some kind of offer in return for his location, right?"

I start for the car. "Did you see the look in their eyes when the masks dropped?" I ask. "Those two are insane. No deal in the world would make them spill. Eddie could be anywhere."

The car starts and we sit. Rain sputters in slow plops against the windshield. Eyes dry as the air blasting from the dash warms.

Small veins puff under the delicate skin of Alissa's hands as she grips the steering wheel. "Too bad the founders burned down the Society's temple. That's the first place I'd look."

"What'd you say?"

"They brought their victims to their temple in town, right?" she recalls of Blackroot's muddy history.

It strikes me. "You remember the house where it all happened? Where our parents killed Beckett?" I clarify. She nods. "That was his house. When I spoke to my father about that night, he even referred to the house as a temple."

Her eyes stagger to the side in hopeful thought. "I'd say it's worth a try."

"You're damn right it is."

Rowan's car sits alone in the gym parking lot. Raindrops bead on the sleek blue paint, bulging over and spilling down in rivulets. The gym, as empty as the second week after New Year's, aside from the sound of muffled fists hitting pads. Rowan and Nathan square off in the ring. She strikes the hit pads on Nathan's hands, ducking as he tosses an arm around to her head. She straightens back up, delivering a short combo of blows. She pounds a final hook into the hit pad before her reluctant eyes set on us.

"I just need to see the recording of Edward one more time," I say as Nathan dips down from the ring, sliding between the ropes.

He sighs, wiping sweat from his brow as he reaches for his bag on the bench behind us. Rowan leans over, glancing down at us. Salty skin shimmering beneath the fluorescent lighting.

Nathan complains as he retrieves his laptop. "Man, we watched this thing at least a hundred times."

"Then a hundred and one won't hurt," Alissa says.

Edward sits bound and gagged in the old, rotting chair. Eyes half shut. Chest rises and sinks at a slow, steady pace. His head drops. Sways back and forth. Sluggish. Exhausted. He'd already given up three days ago. I cringe at the image of what may wait in that chair now. Alone, filthy, and forgotten. What if I'm too late? What if he died thinking I failed him? Or that I didn't care?

"This place, it must be Beckett Reid's house," I insist. "Digging up the address can't be difficult."

Nathan shakes his head. "That thought crossed my mind already. I looked into it. It's like all those records were scrubbed from the internet. Like some real coverup-type-shit."

Rowan finishes a swig from her water bottle. "You've tried tracking his phone?"

Nathan nods. "It's at his house. Didn't have it on him."

Rowan scrunches her face. "Who just doesn't keep their phone on them?"

It's so obvious. "Because he was using a burner phone!" I shout.

"Can you track that?" Alissa asks.

"No." Nathan sighs. "Kinda defeats the purpose of the burner."

"What about his Apple ID or something?" I ask. "All the burners are capable of downloading apps, if he signed in to one..." I open up the Find My app on my burner. Have Alissa type in his email address. After the third or fourth try, she gets his password correct. I count the blue dots on the map. One dot sits a few miles out of city limits just off Craven Creek Road, just a cow pasture. Likely where he was abducted. I feel so stupid, such a simple solution. Of course, it wouldn't be that easy.

Nathan sighs. "I'm sorry, Delson."

"I'm going to find him," I say.

So focused on saving Edward, I blow past the woman outside the gym's doors.

"Hold it!" she shouts. Her grip, already on Alissa's arm. "We've got a real problem."

"We don't have time for this. Don't you have a job to do?" I ask Jenna.

"Not officially, not anymore." She lets go of Alissa. "The Blooms fired me." She looks like she's recovering from a bar fight. Or worse… I take note of the bruising around her neck. "But as a decent-goddamn-human being, I have a duty. Moral obligation and all that." She wipes at her chin with the top of her wrist.

"So, then what?" I grab Alissa's hand. Pull her toward me.

Jenna steps forward. "The killers just gave themselves up? No struggle, nothing?" she sneers. "They're both reciting the same inane story. Saying they have no recollection of the attack. Claiming they've got gaps in their memory. Both of them even say the blackouts started happening around the same time, about three weeks after Rose Bailey's murder." Her jaw tightens. "Now they could be full of shit or not. Probably they're full of it. I can't say one way or the other for certain." She takes another step, emptying a shallow puddle with her boot. "But what I can say is that they weren't working alone. There's more of them."

"Bullshit," I say.

Alissa squeezes my hand. "No. That's just not possible."

"Someone attacked me last night at my motel." Her hands find her hips. "I got out by the skin of my fucking teeth. They burned the place down, too, according to Blackroot News Daily."

Passing cars splash the water buildup in the street gutters onto the sidewalks as they speed by. I can't help but picture that murky water as blood.

"And don't trust anybody over the phone. They're using some kind of AI software to mimic people's voices. They called me as you, Delson…"

"…We need to go to the police," I say.

Her eyes narrow. "Get in. I'll drive."

Sheriff Lancaster blocks us as we head inside the station.

"What the hell you kids doin' here now?" he grumbles. Lucky I don't knock him out. His eyes land on Jenna. "What the hell are you doing, Darkly?"

"Last night I was attacked by the killer and he wasn't alone."

"No no no. We got 'em." He holds out his hands, furious but pleading.

"Sorry, Sheriff, but you've got a cult on your hands." Jenna's nostrils flare.

"You've been nothin' but trouble! Ever since you showed up, shit's been bad." Spit flies.

I butt in. "If you won't take us serious, at least tell me where Beckett Reid's house is."

He groans, shoving me out the door. "Don't know what you're talkin' about, boy."

"Stop lying, Dad," Alissa snaps.

"You knock this shit off, Alissa, you hear me?"

"Edward has to be there," I say. "Please tell me where it is."

"I'm sure that old place has long since been torn down. Damnit, you aren't the police, let us do our job. I'll send somebody out that way."

"No way, I don't trust that. I need to do it myself," I say.

"Not gonna happen." He almost laughs at me.

I feel the heat in my neck climb to my head. "We know, Sheriff. We know everything. The kids who were murdered all those years ago. The Moonlight Club... you still have the tattoo, or did you get it removed?" I lean in, glimpse the small dark tattoo hiding under the band of his watch. I quiet my voice. "We know who killed Beckett Reid, and I have undeniable video evidence."

The skin around his eyes wrinkles as they narrow.

"Be a shame if that video got leaked to the press." I smirk. "I can see it now. Sheriff Emmet Lancaster of the Blackroot Sheriff's Department—"

He cuts me off. Shoves me outside. Alissa and Jenna follow. "Shut your damn mouth, boy. That video proves one thing and one thing only; I killed a madman hellbent on fillin' these streets with blood in pursuit of some psychotic prophecy. He was dangerous and deranged. You got nothin'."

"What about the man who took the fall? Who you helped send to prison? Labeled as a monster. Ruined his life, my mom's life. Mine... ruined yours too, didn't it?" I look into his weary eyes. "Do you sleep well?" I ask.

"Get out of here before I arrest you." His words are slow. Tone, mild. Eyes down.

"I'll go," I say, backing down, not wanting to spend another thirty-six hours here. "Someone's got to save Eddie."

He tries to stop Alissa from following me and Jenna.

"Don't!" she shouts, ripping her arm from his grasp. "Leave me alone." Her voice cracks as she leaves him standing on the sidewalk.

He mutters into the radio on his shoulder as we pile into Jenna's car.

"I KNOW where the house is. I figured it out last night, just before I was attacked." Jenna white-knuckles the steering wheel. "I don't think they know I know either..."

"We need to get there now, Jenna. Please, we gotta save him," I plead. Alissa clutches my hand.

Jenna whips her car around every corner, my heart pounding like it's trying to crack through my ribs as we hydroplane. She keeps her wits as we tear through the perpetually soaked streets, blowing through intersections like the lights don't apply to us. She ignores every stop sign. Misses other cars and pedestrians with the precision of a stunt driver. Sirens blare and lights flash from two police cruisers chasing us once we hit Craven Creek Road.

"We stopping for the boys in blue?" she asks.

"They'll only slow us down. We have to get to Edward! It won't matter once we find him."

Her eyes never move. But her foot sinks deeper into the gas. She shifts up. The car screams louder. Alissa shrinks into the back seat, her grip on the handle above the door a vise.

Four cops total by the time we pass the old gas station.

Jenna checks the mirror. "I'm definitely going to jail today."

"If Edward makes it out of this alive, I'm sure the Blooms will pay your bail," I say.

Jenna yanks the wheel. The back wheels skid on the slick gravel, then catch as we rocket down the old mountain road. Cement gives way to gravel, gravel to mud. The cruisers stay close, tires chewing through the slope. More lights. More sirens. The road narrows as it winds around the redwoods. The car jolts and shakes as we bounce over roots rising through the mud.

"Not too far now. The search parties didn't get much past this point up ahead." The road narrows again, then spreads wider as we climb. Jenna points to the right. "If I'm right, the house should be up through those trees!"

"Stop the car!" I shout.

"What?" Jenna eyes me.

I throw open the passenger door. The brakes slam and we lurch forward. The car slides sideways through the mud. I rip my seat belt off and leap out before we stop. I hit the ground hard. Mud soaks through my jeans, squishes between my fingers. I push up as the cruisers fishtail into each other, smashing and grinding to a halt.

"Let's lose 'em on foot through the trees!" I yell.

"Okay, that way!" she shouts, pointing to the wall of brush, ferns, and trunks.

The closeness of the trees recharges me as I run uphill through moss and mud.

Cops burst from the road behind us. Three charge toward the car. Jenna throws open the door and grabs Alissa's arm as she bolts after me.

"Run, Delson!" Alissa cries. Her voice breaks. So does something inside me. I push harder.

I clench my fists until my fingers hurt. What if I'm too late? "No." I say. "The house is here. It has to be!"

I keep running. Shoving through thickets of brush, rotted logs, and felled branches. Jenna and Alissa on my heels. The cops shout as they run us down. Feels almost like not moving at all. Every tree that we pass is just as red, towering, and ancient as the last.

The distinct sound of flat dirt beneath our feet. No more moss. No twigs. No foliage of any kind. This was a small road at one point. Seems like it's been used more recently, too. With a desperate gulp for more oxygen, I push forward following the small road. Alissa staggers behind, slamming into the dirt road as a cop wraps his arms around her. I keep pushing. Have to. Jenna stays with me. Her breath is steady. Focused.

I can't believe my eyes when I see it. Atop the fern-covered slope, encompassed by the redwoods, sits the old dilapidated house. The paints all but peeled off. The back porch has caved in. A nest for the forest's critters. I run up the hill. The foundation is rotting, leaving the house sitting at a slant.

"Eddie!" I scream out. I call him again. Ignore the scattered voices of the police moving in on us.

I hear a muffled cry. The kind of scream that leaves your throat bloody and raw. I drop to my stomach in the damp moss and ferns. A small rectangular window, partially sunken in the dirt. I scrape off the mushrooms and moss that have grown against the old glass. The gray light shines in to the cellar below, a faint neutral beam. Eddie's eyes catch the light. A black scarf cinched from his mouth to the back of his head. The cloth has pulled back into his mouth. His lips are crusted and bloody. His eyes finally drift to mine. A small moan.

"Everything will be okay!" I shout down at him through the thin dirty window. "I'm here. I'm here. Everything's okay!" I repeat.

"Go around to the front door!" Jenna orders. "I'll deal with the cops."

I don't think about it. We've won. That's all I know. All that matters. Lungs burn, muscles scream, but I sprint full tilt to the front porch. The old soft wood gives beneath my feet. Elbows slam to the floor. I claw my way upright, still pushing forward. I search the bottom floor. The empty living area is a cathedral of mold and rot.

I find a door leading to the cellar. Each soggy step threatens to give under my weight as I trample down. Another door waits at the bottom step. I twist the knob. It's not locked!

"Eddie!" I push the door open.

He already knew.

Knew from the moment they tied him up and left him to rot.

Knew it when I called his name.

When I ran to the door.

He knew I'd be the one to kill him.

His eyes widen—scream louder than his mouth ever could.

A yelp.

Then—

An arrow slams through his throat.

It goes straight through. Embeds into the wall behind him.

His eyes don't leave mine as black-red blood spurts from both sides.

I scream.

Fall to my knees.

Clasp my muddy hands over the holes, trying to stop it. Useless.

"EDDIE! No, Eddie, no. I'm sorry! I'm sorry, fuck! I didn't mean to hurt you! I didn't mean it!" Tears burn down my face, hot and stinging. His eyes start to roll back.

His cheeks are sunken. His body smells like death. Like shit and sweat and rot.

"Eddie, please don't go! Please, fuck, please. I didn't mean

it! You're my friend. You're my fucking friend! Please don't—
NO! No no no! God damnit!"

His head drops.

I pull my fingers from the holes in his neck, rub my eyes
to try to vanquish this version of reality.

"You're not dead! You're not fucking dead!"

Boots thunder down the stairwell.

Something slams into me. My teeth grind into dirt.

Blood on my hands. The weight of failure—on my chest.

29

DELSON

THE LAST SONG YOU'LL EVER HEAR

I KNOW what it's like to really, truly wish to trade your life for someone else's. I know what it's like to be haunted. Haunted by phantoms... ghosts that don't go away, even when you beg them to. To be trapped inside a scary story. Reading alone in the dark. Life like a horror novel. I know what it's like to try rewriting the pages, starting a new chapter—wanting nothing more than to slam the book shut and turn on the lights. I know what it's like to be stuck.

An hour passes, and I haven't said a word. I don't know what to say—got nothing to say. Crime scene investigators funnel in and out of the house, bathed in flashing red and blue lights. Alissa sits in the back of a police cruiser while Jenna argues with officers further down the road. I zone out, staring at a cluster of ferns at the base of the slope, my back resting against the trunk of the sheriff's cruiser. He says my name again. He's been trying to get me to talk for over forty minutes.

Finally, I speak. "I don't understand what happened down there."

"They strung up a seventy-five-pound compound bow with a trigger release. Attached it to the door with twine..." His hands drag down his face. "It's not your fault, boy." He sighs.

Another moment that lasts a century. Eyes on the mud and moss. "I need to talk to Myers and Adele. Take me to the station."

"They ain't there, Delson." His answer is flat. "Been released."

"What do you mean RELEASED?" spit flies from my teeth.

"Their story, the blackouts, the memory loss... we've had other reports like that. For weeks now." He sighs again. "Toxicology came back. They had Skullflower in their systems. Same as Dane Lewis and the Pierce girl."

"What are you talking about?" I ask, shaking, furious, confused. Tears threaten. My heart slams against my ribs like a lunatic in a padded room.

"When Skullflower's synthesized a certain way, the effects... change. It's goddamn mind control, boy. We got nothin' on 'em." He presses his lips together, then exhales hard through his nose. "Fact is... we got a maniac on the loose. Maybe more than one. Bastards are resourceful. A booby trap for the police?" He spits. "That's one for the books."

"Wasn't for you, Sheriff."

He hacks something awful out of his throat and hurls it into the ferns. "Who then, you?" A short, dry chuckle. I nod. "How you figure?"

"Because they know me. They know all of us."

"All of who?"

"The children of the Moonlight Club." I list all our names, ending with his daughter's. "We're the ones paying the price. For some loose end left behind by you and your damn club."

"Ancient history." His voice is low and bitter.

"Open your eyes, Sheriff. No matter how hard you try, you can't kill the past."

He doesn't move. Not an inch. Chin flexed forward, jaw tight. "Jason was always Beckett's favorite. For your sake, I hope you're wrong."

"What do you mean?"

"Should be your dad tellin' you this, but... he's vanished. Gone from Moonstone. Warden asked me to keep it quiet. But this whole damn county's comin' apart." He pauses. "Reason Beckett took such an interest in your father was some old blood contract—nearly two hundred years ago. Two men, heads of the founding families, started the Blackroot Society. Victor Ingomar and Thomas Heller. According to Reid, the Society couldn't return unless both bloodlines were represented."

"But Victor Ingomar burned to death in the temple fire. He had no children. The Society would've died with him." I insist.

"Victor Ingomar had a sister." He scratches at the grizzled hair on his jaw. "Reid traced the ancestry. All the way back. She's his line."

"So what? I'm part of some creepy prophecy?"

He leans in. "I'm not sayin' anything. But if *they're* really out there doin' this—and I mean doin' this right—they won't stop until they get what they came for." He jabs a finger at my chest. "I'm only gonna say this once. Stay away from my daughter. If this is real, they'll cut down everyone you care about. Just to get to you. To break you. I won't let my girl be one of 'em."

"Would this even be happening if it weren't for me?"

His eyes lower. "If you didn't exist, I guarantee the people of Heller County would be gettin' better sleep. This whole thing—ain't exactly the town's best-kept secret. Catch my drift?" He nudges me. "You know how people get with mass hysteria. Especially the dumb ones. I'd lie low if I were you."

"Delson, you need a ride?" Jenna asks, keeping her distance from Sheriff Lancaster. I nod.

"Miss Darkly, your job's done here. After you drop off the kid, do us all a favor and get the hell outta Heller County."

"Think I'll stay a while longer, Sheriff."

<hr>

I DON'T INVITE Jenna in. Don't say a word. It takes her too long to drive away after I close the door behind me. I'm left with the taste of dirt still on my tongue. I can't stop the images. I can't stop the voices. My mind—like a shuddering film projector—casts visions. Snapshots of Edward. Of Rose. Even Dane. Rick. Closing my eyes only makes it worse. It darkens the room. Sharpens the picture.

If I didn't exist...

It's hard to look myself in the eyes. Reflections gone bad. I am my own worst enemy. My fingers trace the scarring on my throat. They couldn't finish me off. They need me. The white cap pops from the orange bottle. It clatters in the sink, rolling on its edge before lying flat over the drain. All it takes is a handful... a glass of water. A bed. Maybe music.

If you could choose, what would be the song to play during your death? Would it fade out, gentle as a dream? Or end suddenly? Would you carry some echo of the melody with you? Maybe there's no song at all. Maybe silence is the point. Maybe you just... shut it all off. Or maybe I'll see them again... couldn't that be possible? Why not?

What about Kenzie? Could I really leave her behind?

She'd probably be better off without me...

I clutch the bottle to my chest. Curl up on the tile floor. My throat still burns from screaming. The cool ceramic kisses my skin.

Just sleep.

30

JASON
MOONLIGHT MATTERS

THE SKIN on my ribs stretches outward—tender, aching putty—as Manuel pulls away the old bandage. Crusty, blood-soaked gauze and tape flop to the cold pavement floor. The garage is dingy, lit only by a dim lamp near the workbench in the corner. I consider it tidy in here, but there's still a trace of mildew in the air, reminding me of my cell at Moonstone.

"You know, you're lucky this thing went all the way through, man. Even luckier it didn't hit your lung." Manuel's eyes flick up from the wound. "Stupid fucker."

"Yeah, thanks for saving my ass." I choke on the cough sitting in my throat to avoid the pain. Probably makes it worse. "Hey, and Manny, thanks for letting me crash in here—"

He cuts me off. "I took an oath." The icy liquid he sprays on my ribs burns the edges of my very soul.

"Right, right, *Doctor* Reyes." My grin probably looks painful, but I can't tell for sure.

His face scrunches. "Not what I mean, fuckhead." He dries the wound and presses on a fresh foam dressing. Smooths it down with both hands, making sure the adhesive sticks, like he did with the exit wound.

"Not following," I say, pulling on one of the clean shirts he lent me.

"When we were kids, fool. We took an oath. You know, The Moonlight Club. We always said we'd have each other's backs. I still believe that. All that shit with Beckett aside, man. I still believe that." He holds out his hand, palm up, revealing the small black crescent moon inked on his wrist.

"Never got it removed." I state it more than I ask.

"And neither did you, Jay." He grabs my hand, turns it until he sees the black moon above my thumb. "We can try to hide from the things we've done, man. Try to cover it up. But just because you can't see it anymore doesn't mean it's not there."

"Maybe you're right."

"I am. But us—the Moonlight Club. Man, all of us. That was us before Beckett, and it still is now. I believe that."

It's painful to look back on the old days, when we were young. Not just the mess with Beckett. No, even before that —even the good times. It aches because those people are dead. We walk around using their names, sharing their memories and hurt, but we aren't them. Not anymore. The toughest pill you'll swallow in life is realizing your childhood is gone. That so much was taken from you. That the kid you were is dead now.

The flames lapped up from the pit, casting tendrils of throbbing orange light against the redwood canopies above.

Jaw flexes. Teeth clench. I try not to go back there when I can help it, but hearing Manny talk like this... damn it. I sigh.

———

ALL OUR EYES met over the fire as Beckett lay dead and bloody in the dirt. I remember the groaning redwood trunks surrounding us, creaking under the weight of the wind.

The drugs had worn off. We felt different. Changed—but with no memory of how or why. We had gone along with Beckett, played our roles, but never swallowed another capsule. Never took another drink. He hadn't suspected a thing. We'd come to our senses and built a plan—then followed through. We murdered our leader and friend.

I remember Rachel's grip on my arm. Her fingers laced with mine, though she might as well have been grasping my heart. She had more hold over me than Beckett did... or so I'd believed for a time.

Bridget threw her arms around Will, sobbing into his chest. "I can't believe it's over. It's finally fucking over."

Emmet pulled his dark cloak from his shoulders and threw it in the bonfire. I thought the heavy cape might smother the flames, but it proved no match for the inferno. The cloak charred and turned to flying orange flakes propelled far into the misty forest.

Emmet spat in the fire, on what remained of the fabric. "C'mon everybody, get movin'. Burn those damn things so me and the boys can figure out what to do with the body."

Nancy shook her head. "We NEED to call the cops." Her wild, dark curls bounced in the wind. She pulled her phone from the front pocket of her jeans. It made a slight click sound as she flipped it open with her thumb. "Have you lost your mind?"

Emmet stepped toward her. The fire danced in his eyes as he loomed. "I could ask you the same thing." He scanned the group, then locked back onto her. "What the hell do you think's gonna happen to us, huh? We KILLED people. WE did. Understand? Beckett didn't do this by himself."

I squeezed Rachel's hand a little tighter. Prepared for the violent refutation. But there was only the wind and crackling fire.

Finally, Will said. "I didn't do shit. I'm not going down for this. I didn't kill anybody!"

Bridget pulled herself from Will's embrace. "Neither did I. It had to be Beckett." Her white-blond hair lashed in the roaring winds that whistled between the giant tree trunks.

Then Manny spoke. "Hey man, I didn't kill nobody."

Everyone agreed—except me.

Emmet pulled his cap from his back pocket and wiped his forehead before putting it on. Always the same routine: he'd pull the bill down near over his brows, pinching the tip of the bill with his finger and thumb, then his free hand would slide behind his head to nudge the back of the cap down some. I assumed to fix the hair that stuck out the back.

His eyes peered out from under the narrow bill. "Ya'll gonna fucking stand there and lie to me? To each other?" he spat into the wind. "Tell me—look me in the goddamn eyes and tell me you ain't havin' those fuckin' nightmares?" he pointed the gun to his own head. I hadn't even realized he had the gun. "Tell me right now. I swear to GOD. Tell me I'm the only one and I'll blow my goddamn brains out right here!"

Nightmares. Shit—yeah. I'd been having nightmares. Every. Damn. Night. And they were always the same. Some poor girl, running for her life. Shambling. Her legs weak, muscles atrophied from weeks bound in one position. She stumbles over a thick root, rolls down a fern-covered ravine, and crashes into the scorched stump of an old redwood. The tree had been hollowed out by fire after a lightning strike.

Her face red, her neck taut with strain. Veins bulged at her throat and temples. But her scream was pathetic—barely more than a rasp. Too raw from the screaming she'd already done. I came down after her, numb, but aware. Knife heavy in my hand. Jug heavier still. I knew what the right thing to do was, but I wasn't sure I had the strength to do it. Her blubbering wet eyes pleaded as I strode down the side of the gulch, grasping the ferns to slow my descent.

I could feel his eyes on me, like he was over my shoulder. I still feel them. His voice echoed against the walls of my subconscious, telling me what to do and how to do it. And what GOOD would come from her small sacrifice.

And what a momentous immolation it would be! Consequential! Key, really. Beckett's voice would rattle around in my skull.

The first stab was so she knew she was fated to die. The second was for Beckett. And the third was for me as much as it was for her. Gasoline was for the fire and fire was for the cleansing. A part of me died with her that night, and every night thereafter, she reminded me.

And then in the silence, with only flames and wind came the sobs. The retching. We all looked at each other, sick and ashamed. I held Rachel close while she cried over the boy she killed in her dreams. A boy we all knew. His face had been on every flier in the county. His body had been stuffed into a shallow hole, lit on fire, buried and forgotten. His final words—just a plea for help, somewhere in a dream.

Manny's phone rings on the milk crate beside him. He glances at the caller ID. I see it too.

DAVEY BLOOM.

<hr>

MOONLIGHT MATTERS, David had said. That's all he said before hanging up. Just like when we were kids. Back then, it could've meant something good or something bad—probably the latter this time—but one rule was sacred: you show up.

Manuel's car is one of those weirdly silent electric cars. Not even a hum as we idle in front of David's house. The wipers swish slow, clearing bulbous drops, only for them to return. The sky is locked in a paradox—feels like both twilight and dawn. Like time itself can't exist in something so gray, so vast in its nothingness. The only thing breaking the emptiness is a cop car in the driveway.

With a button, the noiseless vehicle shuts off. Manny sighs. "Wanna bet that's Emmet's cruiser?"

"Of course it is. Moonlight matters." Just saying the words transports me back to our high school days; finding a note in your locker with the phrase sketched across it in bold black sharpie, passing the message on to the next once you bump them in the hall.

David's front door opens just as Manny and I step foot on the porch. It's Emmet, his dark gray-specked hair pushed back with sweat or rain. Grief hangs from his hard eyes. Eyes that damn-near jump from their sockets when he sees me.

"Jay?" seems like he doesn't know whether to shoot me or hug me. "What the hell you doin' here?" he asks.

"Same thing you are, I suppose," I say.

"Jason, you just expect me to look the other way?" He squints. "You're a wanted fugitive."

"Moonlight Matters," I say.

"Please come in," a drained voice says from behind him. David stands in the hallway. "We should talk."

For a second, I think Emmet might cuff me. But instead, he gives me a quick hug and steps aside.

We gather in the back room. A fire burns low in the cobblestone fireplace. The wide plate windows look out over the ravine. Redwoods stretch up into the gray, wet sky. Rain taps the glass like slow applause for our shared silence.

I speak first. "David, who else did you call?"

"Everyone," he answers. He winces as ice clinks in a glass behind him.

His wife pours liquor over a perfect sphere of clear ice. She looks like she wants to speak but doesn't—maybe the mountain of grief is just too steep to climb right now.

Emmet finishes texting. "Regular goddamn high school reunion."

Manny chimes in. "Shit, not counting Jerome, Jenny, Will, or Bridget..." He hangs on that last name.

Emmet grunts. "Yeah, well, consider Jerome and Jenny lucky they never had to see this shit come to pass. Rest in peace, of course... Can't say Mayor Lewis'll be missed much, though. 'Least I won't be missin' the sonofabitch."

David sighs. It's hard to look at him, a man who lost his

children. His youngest—my son's age—dead now. His body under a sheet in some small cold room waiting to be cut open and sewn back up so it can be pumped full of chemicals.

At least David got some time with his boys. Got to see them grow and learn and play and thrive. Probably saw them fall in love once, maybe twice. Witnessed their hearts break. Even taught them to drive, I bet. More than I got with my boy. But Delson... such trivial things shouldn't be considered crucial to his upbringing. He's meant for more.

Knock knock knock.

I brace myself for what waits on the other side of that door at the end of the hall. I can only assume it's Nancy Krueger, but the gnawing possibility of Rachel standing outside the door leaves me rooted to my chair. Breaths shallow and rapid. A bulky dry knot twists behind my sternum. Hesitation hangs in the air. I keep my eyes on the floor, transfixed in a made-up scenario where seeing Rachel again wouldn't tear me in half.

Emmet says, "Don't everybody get up at once." He sighs as he stands and starts for the hall.

Feels like my body moves before I do and by the time I'm cognizant of my surroundings, I'm already pouring some Jack over one of those fancy ice balls. I avoid a direct glance at the pretty blond woman who mourns her dead sons, face-down in a glass of whiskey. I grip my own glass. The ice chatters as I raise a shaky hand to my lips. The consolatory liquid singes my tongue. Cold and hot in chorus, it goes down like something on fire. Like when something is so exponentially hot it feels cold... or is that the other way around?

I refill the glass two times before Emmet wanders back into

the dim light exhaled from the cobblestone fireplace. The rain still smacks the large plate windows, now a drumroll battering my heart as I finish a third drink. Nancy strides behind Emmet, claiming a spot on the green sofa near the windows. The orange glow of the fire turns gold against her creamy-dark complexion.

David nods. "Nance..." A solemn greeting.

"I'm so sorry, David."

"Please." He shakes his head. "We have other matters to discuss now."

She offers a look of understanding. "Are we expecting anyone else?" Her eyes scan the room, landing on me. "You're supposed to be in prison."

I pour another measure of amber over ice. Fourth time. "Good to see you too, Nance." I lift my glass with a half-smile.

She bounces up. "It is." Long legs carry her across the room fast. "Good to see you, I mean." She gives me a short hug.

Knock. . . knock knock.

I sigh at the particularly unmotivated knock on the door. Take another drink, trying to combat the growing tension slinking into the room like low fog settling below our knees.

"I'll get it." I slam the glass down on the bar harder than I mean to.

Rachel flinches when the door opens, then freezes solid when her eyes—hidden behind oversized sunglasses—lock on mine. She stares, jaw jutting forward the way she always did when she was pissed. Her lips part, say nothing, then press flat again, nearly pulled inward. Her nose scrunches behind the bridge of her glasses, and though she's doing everything she can to hide it, a single rivulet spills down her cheek.

"I can explain," I say, closing the door behind me and pushing myself onto the front porch with her.

"What the fuck…"

"I—I can explain—"

"What the fuck?" She gasps sharply. "Jason—what the fu —what are you doing here?" Her voice cracks, and suddenly she sounds like the sixteen-year-old girl I once fell in love with. "What the fuck, Jason!" Her sobs crumble against my shoulder the second I pull her in.

I hold her tight like I used to. I shush her, feeling as though I might appear condescending rather than caring. How could she see me as someone who cares about her now?

"Why'd you never l-let me see you? I tried to visit you I-I tried to bring Delson to see his daddy! I tried for years!" Her voice breaks more and her sunglasses fly off as she twists her head away from me. The black leather strap of her little black purse slips from her shoulder, catching on her forearm.

Her eyes are still those boundless blue wells of life I remember from our youth. A dozen flash memories flicker through me. Images mostly. Some sound. Her smile, always infectious. Her laugh—raspy and squeaky at once. Long drives. Beach bonfires. The quiet symphony of our bodies tangled beneath her sheets or in the bed of my old man's Tacoma.

"I could give you a thousand reasons, tell you everything, but I can't take any of it back."

"No, you can't." She wipes her cheeks with the loose sleeve of her sweatshirt.

"I'd understand if you left. I wouldn't wanna be here either if I were you. I think they'd understand too." I say it, but I don't know if it's meant to help her or relieve my guilt.

She picks up her sunglasses, wipes them off with her sleeve. Shakes her head and looks to the purgatory-gray sky. "It's not about wants, Jason." She slides the glasses back on. Sniffs. "Moonlight Matters."

"IT OKAY to smoke in here, or what?" Rachel asks, pulling a crumpled pack from her purse. David nods. "Great. Anybody else fiending? Because in the next ten to fifteen, I'll be lighting my lucky."

Lucky. "I haven't thought of that in years," I say aloud, studying her face in the pulse of the firelight.

"Yeah, well." She drops her head and slips off her sunglasses, placing them in her purse. "Make your own luck." She pulls out a small white Bic lighter.

Then, an unexpected voice murmurs, "I'll have one." David's wife lifts her head, vacant eyes pull away from the empty glass in front of her.

"Sure thing." Rachel says as she lights the one in her mouth. She walks to the bar and hands the lit cigarette to the grieving mother. She snatches another from the pack using her lips, then clamps it softly in her teeth before lighting it. Her blue eyes catch the flame of the lighter. She looks so much the same as she used to. Somehow, the abuse she has taken both mentally and physically over these years hasn't carved its violent path through her flesh. Sure, she has lines in her face now that weren't there before, others deepened from years gone by. But her beauty shines through. She holds out the pack one last time. "Anybody, Nancy?"

Nancy shakes her head mildly. "No thanks, I quit years ago."

"Smart." Rachel returns the pack to her purse. "You look good, Nance."

"You too, Rach."

A small, caustic chuckle escapes Rachel's lips past the cigarette clamped between her teeth.

"What's a *lucky*?" Bloom's wife mutters. Her swollen eyes drift through the smoke, unfocused.

"...When we were kids," I answer, "every time one of us opened a new pack of smokes, we'd flip one upside down. That was the lucky cigarette—you save that one for last."

"Why, what makes it lucky?" Her eyes still drift, like she's trying to see her boys again—just one more time, even if only in smoke.

I give the same answer I gave back then. "I always heard it started with American soldiers in World War II. They said you were lucky if you lived long enough to smoke it."

A soft "Hmph" slips out through the blue-gray haze. "In that case, smoke 'em if you got 'em. You all need the luck."

Manny leans forward in his seat. "Actually Rachel, can I get a drag of that?"

Without pause, Rachel conjures up her mock bewilderment. "No, Doctor, you of all people should know better." She holds the cigarette out to him.

Manny steals a couple puffs. "Just don't tell my wife." He passes the cigarette back and takes his seat again near David.

"Here we are... Surreal, isn't it? After all these years—The Moonlight Club meets again." It's not excitement in his voice, but consternation.

Rachel blows a cloudy puff up toward the vaulted wood ceiling. "Considering the circumstances, I can't say I'm thrilled."

Nancy scoots forward in her spot on the couch. "And what are the circumstances, exactly?" her question is directed at Emmet. "Got any leads, Sheriff?"

He crosses his arms, his natural position. "Whoever's doin' this... whoever they are—and I assure you, there's more'n one of 'em—they ain't just picking up where we— where Beckett left off. They're takin' credit for the murders, all of 'em including the ones we—"

David interjects. "WE never killed anybody. It was all Beckett!"

For a long second, no one speaks.

Emmet sighs. "Guess that's a matter of opinion. Point is —they know things. Things only we should know."

I pour another splash of Jack over what's left of the ice ball. "Maybe that's it," I say. All eyes shift toward me in the flickering light, unsure, wary. I take a sip. Then, "Hasn't it crossed your minds that this person might already be in the room?"

Nancy leans back slowly. "It has now."

Manny shakes his head. "We've been through too much together to—"

Rachel scoffs. "*Together.*" Her eyes roll as she puts her cigarette out in the glass ashtray on the bar. "When did The Moonlight Club last mean something to any of you? Because I sure as hell don't remember the last time one of you reached out to me. Hmm? Sometime after Jason went to prison? Maybe?" She lights her lucky. "I haven't had a friend in a long time—and I look at all of you, and it just makes me sad... and pissed off. Pissed that I ever thought any of it mattered. So yeah, I see a room full of suspects." She takes a deep drag. "Christ's sake, it took almost twenty years and a string of murders just to get us all in the same room again." She laughs—jagged and bitter. "And wouldn't ya know? I only see six out of ten." Her smile cuts like a blade.

Emmet squares his shoulders. "That ain't fair. Jerome and Jenny died years ago. And Bridget—"

"And where the hell were we when she needed us?" Rachel fires back.

I don't dare take my eyes off her. I won't shuffle them around the room, uncomfortable and ashamed—settling on the floor—like everyone else.

"You're right," Nancy says. "We have let each other down again and again. We've let our kids down—all of us." She pauses. "This started with us—let's make it end with us."

Emmet shakes his head. "Easier said than done." His arms stay folded tight across his chest.

Manny stands. "Nance is right though. They both are." He walks to the big plate window, peering out at the clouds as they break—letting a slow orange haze spill down through the glittering canopy.

"Where's that leave us?" I ask.

Nancy answers, "Well, we're here, so we start with the odd ones out—Jerome, Jenny, and Will. We can all agree whoever's behind this knows about our past. Our secrets. Maybe they spilled to their partners. Maybe someone figured it out."

Emmet cuts in. "Will's missin'. Doubt his wife's gonna wanna talk to any of us about this shit."

Rachel adds, "Right. Those kids died—his older boy and Bridget's girl, Rose. And Bridge tried to warn us—at the vigil. She said it wasn't over. Said we'd have to answer for what happened. Then she winds up dead, and Will just disappears?" she takes a drag. "As for Jerome and Jenny's other halves, I don't know them. Which means I don't trust them."

"LISTEN TO YOURSELVES!" David explodes, launching to his feet. "For fuck's sake!" he storms to the fireplace and grabs a dark iron poker. The glow of the flames flickers against his face. "Sometimes the answer's simpler than you make it out to be." He jabs at the embers, tosses in a few logs.

Nancy folds her hands. "So what are you proposing?"

"The reason this person knows about our past—and is taking credit for everything Beckett did—is simple: because it *is* Beckett."

Emmet groans, rubbing his temples like he's trying to erase the thought. "Goddamnit, David, not this shit again. Beckett Reid is DEAD. D-E-A-D. What's it gonna take to make you believe that?"

"A body," he says coldly.

I set my glass down, unable to hide the smirk at his answer. "You were there that night. You know as well as any of us—hell, *you* helped me and Manny get rid of the body."

"You'll have to forgive me, but MY MEMORY OF THAT NIGHT IS A LITTLE FUZZY!" Spit sprays from his teeth.

His wife flinches at the outburst.

He presses on. "Where's the proof, huh? We didn't blow his fucking brains out, I know that much. What if it *is* him?

What if—after we left him to rot in that fucking hellhole—he got his happy-ass up and walked out? Hiding all these years. Waiting for the perfect moment to take his revenge?" His eyes land on me. "He always was a patient bastard, wasn't he, Jay? Had a flair for the dramatic too, right?"

Emmet growls. "Don't be a goddamn fool. He's dead."

I add, "It's impossible, David. If he got up and walked out of there, then whatever made it out wasn't human. No one could've survived that kind of damage."

He shrugs, unimpressed. "Call me superstitious then. When's the last time any of you were in the catacombs?"

I hesitate. "That night. I haven't been there since."

"I assume that's the same for Manny. And for me."

"So what's your point?"

"My point is that until we see a body, we can't rule him out as a suspect."

Emmet stands up. "Listen—"

"No, *you* listen!" David snarls. "Both my boys are dead. Gone forever, god damn it. I'll never see their faces again, and there's this pit in my stomach. This black ball of fucking pain and hate. And something else. I can *feel* him. I swear I can."

Everyone lowers their heads, too ashamed or too scared to meet the eyes of a man who's lost everything. Maybe they feel it too. I know I do.

"Alright, David. You win." I place a firm hand on his shoulder. "Us three—you, me, Manny—we'll go down to the old tunnels. Bury Beckett once and for all." I look around the room. "Rachel, Nance—why don't you go with Emmet to talk to Jerome and Jenny's families? Maybe they know something they aren't spilling about Will's disappearing act—"

Emmet cuts in. "Sorry, Coach. I'm bowing out."

"We need to stop this, Emmet," I press.

"I got my baby girl to worry about." His eyes flit between the grieving parents. "Now, Dave, I'm sorry for what you and your wife are going through. Truly. But my daughter's still breathing—and I intend to keep it that way."

"So you're just gonna leave?" I ask, deflated.

"I'm gonna get Alissa as far away from Heller County as I possibly can," he states.

Rachel's eyes land on me, an urgent halfway-hopeful look. "Maybe that's the smart thing to do. Just remove ourselves and our children from the equation completely." She looks back to Emmet. "Where will you go?"

He shakes his head once. "You know I can't say where I'm goin'. But by the time the first fire lights, me and my kid'll be long gone."

Rachel's eyes fall back to me. "Jason, let's get Delson out of here too. We can just drive. Just drive. Drive and not look back."

I let the thought steep for a moment, heavy and warm. Then I speak. "It won't change anything. This is our responsibility. Emmet can leave, take his daughter and run—I don't blame him. And I won't blame any of you if you do the same. But I'm staying. I'm going to end this. So whoever wants to see these motherfuckers—whoever they are—*die screaming*, stay. Help me finish this." My eyes flick to Emmet's. "Wanna outrun the Devil? Better hit the road."

31

DELSON

KINGSIDE

THERE'S a groggy sloshing in my skull—pulsing behind my eyes—as my head lifts, ears straining to isolate the sound of creaking floorboards. I can feel the vibrations in my chest, in my chin where it rests against the floor. The steps are slow. Cautious. The last streak of daylight stretches down the hallway from the window at the end. Grayish spots of mold pock the chipped white paint. Orange streaks bleed across the floorboards, leading toward the bathroom where I still lie—unsure of my next move, unsure if moving is even possible.

Listening to my intruder. Another slow step. Hushed moans from the floorboards. I scan the room. A bar of soap. A bottle of shampoo. Body wash. I could rip the towel rack from the wall. No, it's hollow. Wouldn't do enough damage. I push myself to my feet and the world tilts. I anchor to the sink. Scrape at the pills still embedded in the flesh of my forearm. Small dents in the skin. I could take the whole bottle now. I'm no good to them dead. No. Too risky. They could force me to vomit. Sedate me. Bend me to their will. I can invent a thousand excuses not to do it, but deep down I know the truth—I'm just too chickenshit.

Quick step from the bathroom doorway. I slip into my mom's cluttered room. Clothes piled on the floor. Boxes, knick-knacks, shoes everywhere. Try not to trip. Mom's a goddamn hoarder. Bound to be something—there. I grab the roque mallet. Solid wood. Like a croquet mallet but heavier. I grip it with both hands. My lungs beg for air. I hold it back. I'm afraid to breathe. I press my back to the door frame. Inch my head past it. The hallway's empty. My bedroom door's open. I *know* I closed it. They've come for me. One foot creeps past the other. I slink down the hall. Fingers sting. Knuckles pop from how tightly I'm squeezing the mallet. I hyperventilate in silence outside my door. Bed creaks. I can picture the grotesque leather mask—shrouded in black—drifting down over my pillow. Catching my scent. Some ancient supernatural law tethering the monster to its destiny. To mine.

No. That's stupid.

Just some sick fuck. Flesh and bone. Killable.

Already screaming, I burst into the doorway. Mallet pulled back over my shoulder, ready to cave in skulls.

Alissa screams as she falls from the edge of my bed. "Delson, it's *me!*" She scoots back until her shoulders flatten to the wall.

Her eyes bulge. Hands up to defend. Teeth bared as she sobs at what must be a frightening image. Me, veins throbbing at the surface of my neck, blood rushing to my face. Leaping through the door like some nearly naked maniac. I've lost it. I recognize that. Because I see it, I *should* be able to isolate it. Fix it. Change it. Grow. I want to, but I don't. The anger boils in my skull. Trembles in my fingers. It aches beneath my ribs. I want the anger to make sense. Want it to feel justified.

"Jesus Christ!" I shout. The mallet clunks against the boards at my feet. Bounces. Smacks a toe. Just pisses me off more.

"Sorry—"

"Can't I get *one* night?" My voice is a toxic sludge. "Just one night t—to, to—"

"I said I was sorry!" she yells through tears.

"You can't just—I mean..." I stumble. "You could've called."

Her eyes narrow as she climbs to her feet. "Check your phone. I *texted!* And when you didn't answer, I called. Twenty. Damn. Times."

I shake my head. "What are you even doing here, Alissa? The sheriff was *very* clear about me staying away from you."

"Don't take it like that—"

"Who said I did?" I scoff. "I agree with him. The fact that you're here—I mean, are you stu—What were you thinking?"

"You don't need to worry about me or *my* decisions. Stop treating me like I'm some antique porcelain-fucking-doll. I'm not gonna break. We're in this together. Right? Because *that's* what I thought."

My hands scrub my face. The motion makes me dizzy. I forget for a second where I am. "It's because I worry about you. Don't you get it?" I grab her shoulders. My vision blurs. Wet heat drips from my lashes. "I don't know what I'd do if anything happened to you. I *can't* let it. I *won't.* If I weren't alive, you'd all be safe. Edward would still be here. Rose wouldn't be dead!" I shake my head. "It's all because of me. Don't you see?"

"Delson, you're scaring me." Her hand finds my cheek.

"Good," I say coldly. "You *should* be scared. Now get the fuck out of my house."

Lines crease between her brows. Her eyes peer up at me, confused. "Del—"

"Please don't make me ask again."

Her head drops. She shuffles to the doorway. Hesitates there. "I came to tell you my dad's taking me out of town." She sighs. "We're leaving tonight. I begged him—and he said if you want, he'll take you somewhere safe too."

"With you?" I ask.

"No. But you wouldn't be here. Nobody would have to know."

"We both know running won't solve anything. Not for me."

"Maybe not. But my dad seems to think whatever's coming... it's happening *tomorrow*."

"Why tomorrow?" I ask.

"The Founder's Fire. Talk of the town is they're going ahead with the celebration, curfew or not." She turns to face me. "You being gone—it wouldn't change anything. This person, or these people—whoever they are—they do what they do because they *want* to. Or because they *think* they need to. It's them. It's always *been* them. It *will always* be them. There's no one else to blame." She shakes her head. "If it weren't you, it'd be somebody else." She hugs me. I didn't even see her move.

"I wish you would come with me. Or I wish I could stay."

"I wouldn't ask you to stay."

"Couldn't if I wanted to. Sheriff's downstairs waiting."

I hug her back, her face pressed against my chest. "I *will* see you again," I promise.

She lifts her face. Her eyes drift up to meet mine. "I'm counting on it." I try not to linger in her kiss. No time would be enough, so it's easier to pull away.

She meets my gaze from the passenger seat of her father's cruiser. I hold her eyes through the window from my bedroom. Saying a silent goodbye as the trees stretch across my view like arthritic fingers.

What if she's right? I want to believe that. I'm *done* thinking this is because of me. I didn't do this. *They* did. And even if I weren't here, they would've found a way. But what if she's wrong? How far does this psychotic rabbit hole go? What if my death *really would* end it?

No. That's not the question. I *can't* think that way.

The question is—if I'm here, if I'm alive—*can I stop this?* Put an end to it all?

Because if I don't... who will?

This whole time, I've been playing their game. They've led me like a dog on a leash. Every move—mine—has been theirs. They know how I think. What I'll do next. And they're right. They've had control this whole time. Every situation. Backup plans for backup plans. Mind control. Paranoia. I don't remember any blackouts—but then again, how could I?

I've been going at this all wrong.

What are they expecting me to do?

That's what I need to figure out. *Think like them.* Get in their heads. But I tried that. I tried to lure them out like I was setting bait out for some predatory mountain cat. It worked so well for them. Stupid. How could I be so foolish? I can't outsmart them. I can't lure them out. Can't track them. It's like chess; every move calculated. Gotta think ahead. They're sitting on checkmate, just waiting for my misstep. They will kill the ones I hold dearest just to get to me. Break me down. Make sure I've got nothing else to live for... so if that truly is the case, I know their next move.

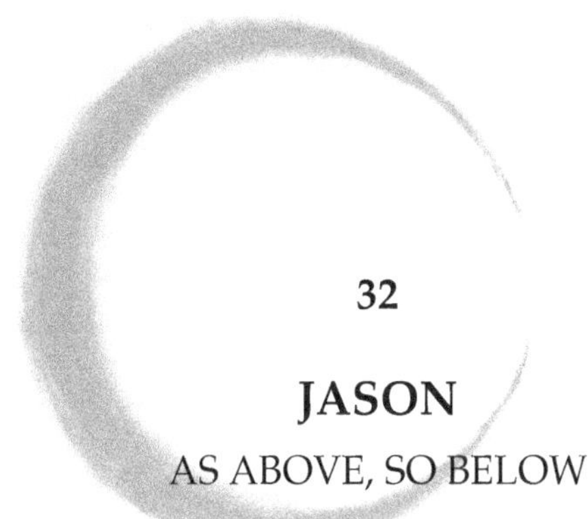

32

JASON

AS ABOVE, SO BELOW

"LET'S GET ONE THING STRAIGHT," Rachel says over her shoulder. "We aren't doing that Scooby-Doo shit." As she pulls open the glass door, it fogs, her shape blurring like a memory. She grabs a large can of Monster.

"How do you mean?" I ask, picking up a small bag of beef jerky from a corner rack and one of those—highly caffeinated—Starbucks canned coffees from behind the same door Rachel used for her fix.

"Splitting up. Nance and I talked about it. We ALL go, or nobody does. We're already down five." Her boots clunk across the scuffed tile floor as she makes her way to the counter. "And a pack of Marb 100s," she says to the clerk.

"Sure." He sighs, pulling a pack from the top rack behind him. He looks familiar. Graying, balding—probably around our age. An old, dusty face from high school.

"These too," I say, setting my items on the counter. "I got it." I mumble to Rachel, digging out a couple of crumpled twenties.

The clerk scans our items with his little barcode gun, then pauses, eyeing me as he takes the cash. "I know you, don't I?"

"Don't think so. From outta town. Just driving through," I say, almost convincing myself.

"No, no. I *know* you. I know both y'all. Y'all went to Blackroot High?" He opens the register and counts my change like it's a bribe he's not sure about.

I shake my head, eyes low. "Just got one of those faces. Everyone thinks they know me from somewhere." I glance at the money in his hand, hoping he takes the hint.

Then his face lights up. "Oh holy *sheeeit*. Jason? I'll be goddamned. Jason Heller?"

I shake my head, hanging onto the threadbare charade with shredded fingers.

His cheeks puff as he grins at Rachel. "Can't believe you're still slummin' it with this sorry S.O.B." He chuckles.

Rachel hums out a nervous pity-laugh.

"You got us," I say, putting on a half-smile, switching to another performance. "Good to see you, buddy. But we're actually in a hurry, so..."

"Oh, a'course. My bad, Jay, my bad." He hands me the change. "Need a bag?"

"No, thanks." Rachel's already heading for the door. I follow.

"Say, ain't you supposed to be locked up?"

"Good behavior," I mutter over my shoulder. The little bell jingles behind us as we step into the rain.

As the downpour picks back up, I throw my hood on. "Okay, no splitting up. Fine. You, me, David, Nance, and Manny—we head for the catacombs tonight." I crack open the coffee, take a sip of the sweet, jittery stuff. "But I'd really rather you and Nance stay in town. Maybe together. Get Delson with you. Keep him inside. Keep him safe."

She shakes her head. "This is how I help Delson. How I make it up to him. How I keep him safe." Her Monster drink hisses as she pops the tab.

"We," I say.

She nods. "We. We end this. Once and for-fucking all." She packs her smokes by slapping the entire pack against her palm, packing the tobacco in tighter. "He's a good boy, you know, regardless of—fuck, everything." She flips her lucky and pulls out her first cigarette. I block the rain and wind so she can light it. "He deserves better and he's been blessed with a plate full of shit."

The neon lights in the window of the gas station gleam off the black puddles near the gas pumps. Her face holds steady in the blue and pink glow, eyes sharp like she's trying to see through me. I put my arm around her, leading her back to David's house where the other's wait, aside from Emmet who left a couple hours earlier. He said quick good-byes before he left, and though I feel it wasn't a conscious decision, those goodbyes had a sort of finality to them. He didn't believe he'd be seeing us again.

"He's our son," I say. "We need to do right by him, and we will. I promise."

"I'm sorry. I can't go," Nancy mutters, slipping on her jacket. The fire's soft orange-gold still glows on her cheeks. "After thinking it through—and after Emmet left town—Cordelia was supposed to be staying with Alissa tonight, and I can't leave my daughter alone. Honestly, I need to go. It's already dark."

Rachel crosses her arms, still shivering from the cold walk back. "But, Nance, you said—"

"Beckett-fucking-Reid is dead. I'm not spelunking into some old-ass subterranean tunnels to prove that *very* simple fact to David." Her face contorts. "I'm sorry, really. I truly am sorry for your loss. I want to help. But I'm not going down there, David. Beckett is dead."

"Then leave," he says.

"I can't leave Cordelia alone at night—"

"I don't blame you, Nancy." David softens. "Just go."

She stammers out a few more apologies before slipping out the door.

"And then there were four," Rachel sighs, glancing around the room.

Manny smirks. "Shit, just like old times, huh?"

"What are the odds..." Rachel mutters, flatly. Like she knew it would come to this.

I almost can't believe it myself, but when I look around the room—David's wife not included—it's the same group from that night... the night we——

——*We gotta get rid of the body," David had said. "But according to Emmet, the ocean or bay's a no-go. We can't count on sharks to eat all of him. If the body's recovered and the bullets get traced back to his dad's gun—"*

Rachel groaned. "Yeah, we got it, Davey. We were there. Stop. We're thinking, alright?" She wasn't trying to be mean. She was panicking.

Manny—sitting shotgun in my dad's Tacoma (I was driving)

—slapped my arm. "I got it. We'll dump him in the Chamber of Secrets."

Rachel snapped, nitpicking instead of facing reality. "I told you, that's Harry Potter. It's the Chapel. Just the Chapel."

He shot her a quick glance. "Right. The Chapel. That's as good a place as any."

I checked the rearview, watched the wind catch Beckett's cloak —black fabric flying from the truck bed—as we sped down the road. Rachel and David caught my eye. They seemed to agree.

"Alright then—"

"Let's get it done," I said.

THE LONG AND winding road through Ingmar Hills is one that seems could go on and into the void forever. Unfortunately, it is—as memory serves—indeed finite. The road ends, and the forest begins. The five of us—including David's wife who refused to stay home, and who could blame her?

David's truck shuts off. We step out and———

———Stood around the bed of my Pop's Tacoma, watching Beckett as he lay cold and still. His sandy hair fluttered in the damp wind, bluish gold streaks in the moonlight. But his eyes— his eyes stared back—still, unmoving like you'd expect from a dead person. Yet, they seemed so focused. Determined, obsessed— even disappointed. But what scared me the most was the deadness in them. Even behind all the other stuff, those were dead eyes. Or maybe because of all that other stuff—still lingering behind those eyes—maybe that's what made the deadness that much more frightening.

"How about one for the road, Heller?" David suggested.

"Sure," I said, sliding the silver flask from my back pocket. I took a swig, passed it around—Rachel, then David, then Manny. I took another when it came back to me. I wouldn't call myself an alcoholic. My father was the boozehound. But a little whiskey here and there steadied my nerves. And that night, every nerve needed steadying. The——

——salty wind yowls, blowing a damp and sour chill past the old redwoods that taper up into the darkness above. The wind rips at the scale-like leaves and flat dark-green needles as they twist and dance by force to the glossy wet, uneven pavement at the road's end. We step into the forest———

———dragging Beckett's body, wrapped in one of the canvas drop cloths from my dad's toolbox. His head swayed between his shoulders, bouncing over moss, mud, and sharp roots. His eyes still stared. Down at Rachel and me. David and Manny were pulling. Rachel and I were just keeping him on the tarp. The tarp I'd have to leave behind—soaked in blood, printed with my dad's business logo on all four corners. And I was supposed to inherit that business. Soon, if Dad kept going the way he was. The beams——

——of our flashlights scatter across the forest, flickering on a path that's old, but familiar. The ground is soft, wet and mushy, stagnant with the stench of decomposing wood, rotted brush, and living earth. Diamonds blink through the canopies above, piercing down from the black sheet of the sky. The forest feels eternal, endless. A plane of shadows, whose toxic capillaries branch out beneath, stretching far and away from here, under the whole county. Pumping its infection. Gulls cry from beyond the canopies, screeching out for the dead sailors lost at sea. Feels like eyes are peering from the dark spots—behind the trees and between, from inside the hollowed log or any other empty place, that now doesn't seem so empty.

Manny's scream is about lost in the groans of the trees. He tumbles—foot catching a gnarled root rearing up from the crowded forest floor—he face plants. But his foot doesn't come loose. He twists his ankle pretty good. I help him up. It's not broken, or at least he doesn't think it is, but he can't put much weight on it.

"Fuck. I busted my ass already, man." He laughs at himself, but I can see the frustration behind his eyes.

"Can you make it?" I ask.

His eyes scan the ground, flashlight beam cutting across dewy ferns and gleaming insect eyes. He jerks his chin up. "That branch."

I follow the beam, spot the stick. It's more of a limb than a branch—but weirdly clean, like it's already been used as a walking stick. Doesn't seem to match any of the surrounding trees. "This'll work?" I check.

He tests it, leans into it, takes a few steps. "No sweat."

"Good. Let's keep going," David urges.

With another lurching gust of wind, the forest turns into a psychotic disco beneath the moon's silver torch. But like the road we left behind, the madness leads to a more staggering end. The black ocean roars beneath the cliff's edge, its fury so profound it feels like the forest floor shudders with every wave.

"It's still there!" Manny shouts over the crashing surf. He points his light over the cliff.

I inch to his side, aiming my beam down. "Won't lie, I'm

surprised," I mutter, looking at the flat stone ledge—a crooked oval five feet below. The entrance is still there. The large circular wooden slab we used to seal it, too. "I thought it might've slid into the sea by now—especially after that quake in, what, 2010? 2011?"

"You were hoping," David says with a sneer.

I nod. "Guess I was."

David——

——*dropped to the platform first, then Manny. Rachel shined her light down as I helped lower the body—bundled tight in the canvas cloth—over the side.*

"Got it! We got it!" David called from below.

"Come on down!" Manny huffed.

My chest scraped the cliff face as I descended to the platform. I reached up to guide Rachel's hips as she slid down after me, steadying her. Help——

——me move this," I say, and shove the wooden sheet. David and I roll it off the cliff side. It smashes into pieces on its way down, disappearing into the black hungry water, its white-capped waves like fangs chomping down on any object unlucky enough to fall in its mouth.

But it is our lights that are swallowed down the dark esophagus of the cliff side.

"Lianne, babe, I got you," David says as he helps his wife down onto the platform last. I can see the physical shudder roll through Lianne's spine as she stares down that long, dark arterial corridor.

Manny cups a hand around his mouth. "Hello! Is anybody down there?"

Rachel shuts him up with an elbow to the ribs. "Are you *kidding* me?" she hisses.

"Doesn't matter," I say. "Only thing we'll find down there is a pile of bones and a duffle of pipe bombs." I see recognition light up in each of their faces. "You remember that?"

Manny gasps. "Oh man, the bombs! I forgot about the bombs…"

Lianne's eyes flick across our faces, somehow even more horrified than before.

David shakes his head, like trying to rattle the memory loose. "I say we blow the catacombs. Collapse the whole fucking tunnel. Send the cliffs into the sea."

I take the first step inside. "Let's prove what we came here to prove. We can decide what to do after." I pull the flask from my pocket, hold it up. "One for the road?"

I take a quick swig and pass it to Rachel. She drinks. Then David, Manny, and finally Lianne, who nearly polishes it off.

"UGH…" Manny's face contorts. "What the *fuck* is that?"

"Guy I know makes it in his cell," I say.

He winces. "Like toilet wine?"

"Something like that." I leave it there and lead the way in.

Dirt. Rock. Salt. Rot. The stench of old earth thickens with every step. And they follow. They follow me toward the truth. Toward *him*.

I keep my eyes on the jagged floor. My legs move forward —guided not by will, but by memory. My breath hangs thick in the cold beams of our flashlights. Every fifteen feet or so, a rusted torch juts from the wall—long dead.

"What the fuck is this? This is real?" Lianne stumbles, clinging to Rachel's arm.

Rachel lights a stogie. "Every town has some bullshit story about underground tunnels. In our case, it's true."

As we make our way deeper into the tunnel, slowly but surely, the walls and ceiling drift further apart. What was once a narrow cylindrical passageway has now morphed into a tall and rectangular corridor.

The stone walls, now uniform in appearance and texture, the ground resembling something closer to a walkway, smooth and even. Our steps echo all around us, clattering in the long, deep darkness. Something flaps overhead, dashing past Lianne. A scream rips from her throat and bounces down into the shadows and back again. And again and again, like some mad banshee lost in the depths of these tunnels.

"It's just a bat, babe!" David shushes her. "It's okay."

"Fuck *you*, David! None of this is okay." Her hands are up, fingers spread, hair in scraggly tufts from digging around for scalp-eating bats.

After another five or so minutes, the tunnel splits into four passageways. I veer slightly right, taking the second-most-right path. The corridor narrows—cut more precisely. The walls close in. My shoulders nearly scrape the sides as we move single-file—David behind me, then Rachel, Lianne, and Manny at the rear. I have to twist my torso every few feet to avoid knocking loose the ancient torches, held in place by knotted rope loops.

Our collective footsteps sound like Grand Central Station in a parallel world where no one speaks. Just move-ment. Manny's dragging his foot now. His stick's not doing him much good in here. Maybe he's tired. Maybe the tunnel's too narrow.

Dragging——

——*Beckett's corpse down this suffocating stone throat. The walls closing in. His eyes still locked on me. We'd gone single-file then, too—me in front, pulling his feet by the tarp corners. David at the head. Rachel. Then Manny.*

"How far till we're there?" David asked, dropping his end of the tarp.

Beckett's boots clunked to the ground as I dropped my corners with a grunt. Rivulets of sweat ran down my forehead, dripped off the tip of my nose. My tongue was dry and sticking to the roof of my mouth, still, I gathered some sticky saliva to spit at the stone wall, hands on my hips as I caught some breath. A small passive glare shot at David, not meaning for him to catch, but he did.

"What?" he asked. "WHAT?" he asked again, this time a little pissed that I didn't answer.

"You'll know when we get there. Can we keep moving, or what?" I snapped.

"Oh, sorr-ry, Jay. So sorry we weren't all Beckett's favorite. Not all of us got invited to the 'Inner Sanctum.'" He air-quoted it, laughing bitterly.

"Chamber of Secrets—"

"Chapel!" Rachel corrected Manny again.

"You're not questioning my loyalty now, are you?" I turned to face him fully, my shoulders nearly scraping the tunnel walls. "Not after I've already led you this far."

The flashlight washed over his pale face. "Y-you..."

"Am impatient. And fucking with you." I knelt down to grab the corners of the drop cloth. "Lets do what we came here to do."

"I knew he was playin'," Manny assured Rachel and David.

The air in the tunnel grew heavier, thicker as we descended. Each step amplified the weight of our secrets, sins, our burden. Eerie shadow puppets danced along the walls as the flickering beams of our flashlights gave them life. After another several claustrophobic minutes we reached the gate—five dark iron rods that stretched from floor to ceiling, held together by two horizontal bars crudely soldered across—blocky hinges bolted in the rock. My fingers squeezed around the cool iron and I let out a slow breath as my forehead felt the bar's icy touch before I push——

——the old metal sticks. I put more force behind it. With a grinding shriek, the door gives, rattling and squealing into an upward whistle. The way is clear.

One by one, we step into the Chapel. Our footsteps echo in the cavernous dark. The ceiling stretches out of sight. Stalactites hang down, like tendrils reaching out of a darker world. *His* world. Long-dead torches line the walls, their wax crusted. There are other passageways, all sealed behind similar gates.

In the center of the chamber sat a dais, blackened altar carved from bone and hide. Jagged antlers frame its peak. An iron bowl rests in the middle. At the base—slumped—an old JanSport backpack. The floor is a cracked mosaic of moss-covered stone, etched by time and... other things.

"We tossed him down there, remember?" David says, heading past the dais to where the floor gives way. A dark pit. A sheer drop.

He points his light down. "My god..." voice hitching in his throat.

I stand beside him, looking down at the battered shape, sunken and lodged between the serrated stones. Still wrapped in the drop cloth, stamped with my father's business logo, that red **H**.

"He *is* dead," David whispers.

"So it would appear," I say.

He looks at me, eyes wet. "Damn it," he breathes. "I just

thought—" His pupils widen. Irises shrinking to rings. He's feeling it.

"Duh-does a-anybody hear thuh-that?" Lianne stammers, flashlight whipping around. "He's tuh-halking t-to mm-m-me." Her lips quiver. Sweat dripping from her face. "Oh! He's hungry!" she shrieks.

"...So... *so* hungry," Rachel agrees as she falls back onto the dais, her laughter bubbling. Her cheeks ball up as she smiles, examines her outstretched fingers, and the rings upon them. She closes her fists, then opens them again. Awed by the sheer brilliance.

Manny vomits, dropping to his hands and knees. His walking stick clatters to the floor as the room swells, expanding further into the darkness. The blackness above gets deeper as the stalactites get longer. Some even begin to twist and undulate, becoming more flesh than stone. And I *hear* him. Putting his parts back together. Rustling under the canvas tarp, his flesh stringing out, peeling into reality from his deadland. The scuttling of his guts—dry and porous—as they move to the correct spots. Then the squelching of his insides as the fluid and moisture revitalizes the tissue.

David rushes to his wife's side, staggering as he does it. He tries to calm her, struggling to keep his own composure. "Just breathe!" he shouts. "It's only going to get worse, hold on! It'll pass..." His eyes—now nearly black orbs—glare at me as he slips into *his world*. "What was in that flask?" he questions me, not with suspicion. No, that's out the window. He knows it was me.

"You can't see him without it," I say.

Rachel stares at me, breath ragged. Her voice cracks:

"Skullflower," she says to David.

33

RACHEL
GOOD GOODBYE

I SHOVE myself back on the rocky platform, boots scraping against moss and loose stones. The skin on my fingers and palms bursts with *sensation*—pain, pressure, panic—as I scoot across the cold stone. The room breathes—a massive stone lung. And color, even in the dark, swirls and pulses in impossible patterns with stunning clarity. Flashlights roll across the floor as they drop, their beams streaking over stone, casting long-limbed shadow people that dance across the walls... until they find the secret path off the wall—and stand here, with us.

You drugged us! I say—or think I say.

"You gave us Skullflower!" I definitely say that time.

"You—you—y—"

"*You cut open my throat,*" the tiny voice says. "*You cut me open and hid my body in a hole. You burned me up.*"

"Oh God!" I choke. My body forgets how to swallow, but it remembers the boy.

"*I miss my mommy and daddy,*" the voice says as he pulls

himself up from the fissure. The old bloody tarp comes to a tall uneven cluster of points—as if it's hanging from some haggard tree branch—the shoulders slump down, and the thing stands. He lumbers behind Jason, two feet taller at least, cloaked in that old blood-spotted tarp we dragged Beckett down with. The red H's mark every corner draped out around the figure.

Lianne's scream wraps around me, enveloping the entire space as she see's it. "Oh my FUCKING God!" she cries out, clinging onto David. "What is that? What is that? *What is it?*" she gasps in his arms. "No—no—it has Edward, Ian too!" she rips free from David's grip. "My baby boys!" she sobs, running toward Jason and... Beckett? Maybe it's not him. But it *feels* like him.

The chamber flashes white. Thunder detonates like a god's slap. Lianne tumbles forward, her shoulders rolling until she lands face-first with a sickening thud. Her bottom lip stretches back like strawberry taffy. Her eyes still leak tears as a dark red syrup streams from the crater in her forehead. Her golden hair stains red. The back of her skull—a broken pit of bone and brain. Bits of it speckle my sweatshirt.

Jason stands with the gun still smoking. "She's not part of this." One corner of his mouth lifts. "You really shouldn't have involved her, Davey-boy. How selfish. First your boys, now your lady." He makes a '*tsk* tsk' sound in his teeth.

The thing behind him—Beckett, maybe—shambles forward under its canvas cover, an eight foot tall bedsheet ghost covered in old blood and rot, sending the three of us scuttering back in terror. David now on his ass like me and Manny. The thing bounds forward, its long fingers—through the canvas tarp—grabbing hold of Lianne's hair. The fuckin' thing pulls her back, her shoulders lift from the floor as the *Beckett-thing* hoists her up. It breathes in deep, a clotted breath of dirt, moss and bark. You can hear her body lodge in-between the rocks after he drops her into that black serrated hole.

"Lianne!" David screams.

Jason stuffs the gun in a holster hidden under his coat. His other hand joins the party with a knife—a big hunk-of-metal-for-a-blade kinda knife. "She's being di-ges-ted. Can you feel it?" he grins.

I can. The satiation. But the hunger's still there too. Familiar. It's like before—before———

———*shit was so simple before," I'd said. My hands on either side of his jacket. Breathing him in. Even then I knew. I wouldn't have him for long. Even with him near, holding me, I already missed him. "Wasn't perfect, but it was easy," I said. "There's no way I do this without you, Jay."*

"I've got you," he whispered. It wasn't a promise—but he meant it. He believed it. And so I did too.

We'd driven back from the caves in silence. I trusted him. He was all I had. But I already lost him to Beckett. I just didn't know it yet. Before———

———we killed Beckett, I'd felt the same way during his rituals. High on the same goddamn drug. This is in my head. Like before.

None of this is real. None of this is *real.*

I'm real.

The voice—like gravel soaked in bile—whispers inside my mind. I open my eyes and the cloaked figure is inches from my face. Crouched like a beast beneath the tarp. I *feel* its eyes on me. Even through the canvas. The cloth pulses with its breath—reeking of wood rot and the sweetness of death. It straightens, then turns to David—who hasn't stopped screaming his wife's name between the sobs and gagging. The Beckett-thing steps back, leering from the shadows.

"You sonofabitch!" Spit flings from David's lips. "Why couldn't you leave it in the past? This whole thing *should've died* with Beckett!"

Jason runs the tip of his index finger up the length of his blade, stopping at the point. "Funny thing about the past, it isn't dead. It. Is. *Naaw-T.*" Jason takes a step toward David while Manny scoots my way. "And neither is Beckett." He finishes.

Time stops, or slows in this instant. Even the pulsing chamber seems to hold its breath before Jason rams that heavy-bladed thing into David's chest. His sternum crunching as Jason heaves his weight down, again and again, until David's chest caves inward around the blade. His screams stop fast. Blood gushes down his torso in thick ribbons, soaking his jeans, filling his shoes. The puddle around him grows fast.

Kerplunk.

That sound when Jason pulls the knife free. Something slides off the blade—wet—splats to the ground.

Jason lets go of David's collar. His body crumples. Joints gone soft. He was dead long before he hit the ground.

"When I say go—" Manny whispers beside me. His eyes fixed on Jason, then on the Beckett-thing lurking in the dark. A puff of breath, faint and visible, steams out from behind the canvas. "When I say go—"

"WOO!" Jason yelps, spinning.

Manny tilts his chin—a nod toward the altar. "Grab the backpack. Don't wait. Just blow this bitch up…"

"Wait, wha—"

"GO!" Manny shouts, springing up just as Jason turns.

I dive, snatch the dusty JanSport from the base of the altar, and bounce to my feet. The bag's heavy. Full. I clutch it to my chest and backpedal.

It's the drug. I tell myself. None of this is real.

But I know that's a lie.

Manny raises the jagged rock—bigger than a softball—and slams it into Jason's temple. His head jerks sideways. The skin splits, blood gushing down his cheek as he turns his glare on Manny.

Manny freezes.

I shuffle backward until iron bars jab my spine.

Jason pulls the knife from Manny's gut.

I breathe slowly through my nose. Swallow hard. Don't scream. Not yet. I'm hidden, tucked into this shadowed corner. It's my one chance to run—

SCREECH!

The gate moans as I pry it aside. "Aw fuck," I mutter, squeezing through the narrow opening.

I RUN. Fast. Wild. Faster than a fiend to a pipe. Jason saw me. I *know* he did. Beckett too—if that thing's even *real*.

First regret: that fucking gate.

Second: no flashlight.

I'm sprinting down a tunnel that's about to get so dark I'll forget what light even looks like. Worse—I didn't go back the way we came. Wrong tunnel. No clue where it leads.

"RAAAACHELLL!"

Jason's voice booms down the corridor—mocking, operatic. "Wanna bump? Or would a needle and a spoon suit ya better?" He sounds like he's *smiling*. "Don't make me come after you... I'll saw your fuckin' head off."

My heart thunders, sharp and hot. My side aches. My lungs feel like they're filled with ice—but I don't stop. I swing the backpack on, rings on my fingers catching on my jeans as I fumble for my phone. It slips through my fingers once, twice—I grunt, finally catching it with slick, shaky hands. I turn on the flashlight.

The weak beam slices through the dark. Barely enough. But enough.

Each step clatters behind me. Ahead of me. All around me. The echoes tell Jason where I am. But they also tell me—if he wants me, he'll have to hustle.

"Don't say I didn't warn ya!" he shouts from far behind, his words still laced with a smile.

I come to a fork in the road. The single hall splits off into three directions, a circular passage directly to my left, a real blink-and-you'll-miss-it path. There's the way forward or another circular entryway to my right, though it cuts more diagonally into the wall. Each way as dark as the last. I take the left. With any luck, he'll blink and miss it.

The tunnel narrows and running through its a bit like running through a fun house or—more specifically—one of those cylindrical spinny tunnels at county fairs. The ones where all the kids run through with ease, but once the shit-faced forty-something redneck tries it, he tumbles ass-over-head, spilling his overpriced light beer all over himself.

I hear the chunky clopping of Jason's boots as he charges up the corridor after me. His heavy steps echo and crisscross, sounding like a gang of steel-toed psychopaths running wild through the tunnels, screaming and hollering awful things. Could there be someone else down here, waiting for Jason's signal? No way he pulled all this off alone—these freaks always need friends. Maybe the Beckett-thing is real. Maybe after Jason kills me, it'll eat me, like it's planning to eat the others. But I'm hallucinating. I *know* I'm hallucinating that. Still, I know he has partners. They could be waiting down here in the dark. Every tunnel with eyes at the end, waiting to grab me—drag me down kicking and screaming into some hidden burrow. Running now feels like sprinting through a labyrinth of man-eating trapdoor spiders.

"How about one last fuck for old time's sake, before I cut ya down the middle?" He chuckles from the black behind me. "Or after—I'm not picky."

I keep running as fast as I can. My lungs feel like hot sandpaper. My heart's pounding in my throat, trying to escape. My foot slips, ankle twisting as my weight shifts to the ball. Thank fuck I catch myself before it gives. Last thing I need's a sprained ankle. I keep trudging forward, now aware the floor is rough and uneven. Suddenly a barrel chested bark echoes in my tunnel. My head turns in the darkness, expecting to see some gnarled, gnashing demon mutt leaping for my jugular. Instead, I see only shadows and the back of my hands catching myself from face-planting. The light goes when my phone smacks the rocks. As I look up from the ground, the tunnel is only blackness. Cold, salty, nothing.

Those heavy footfalls taper into four sets of feet: two, one...

"OOWWWWWW!" From that blackness, Jason howls like a wolf. The Hound of Heller is a man.

My fingers smack about the chunky poky rocks until I feel my phone. Flashlight broke. Fuck. I run forward, ignoring the fact that it's pitch black.

"I hear ya, bitch!"

A sob muscles itself out of my throat. I suck it back in, beat it down into my stomach with every ounce of my soul. I won't shed another tear for this motherfucker.

"You know, I always thought red was your color…"

I just need to find a place to hide. Somewhere. But he sounds so close I—SMACK. My head slams the low ceiling. Sharp, hot pain bursts. I feel the blood run into my hair. I move slower now, fingers tracing the uneven stone walls. The tunnel's narrowing. I stand tall—my head touches the top. I crouch and keep going. No stopping now.

"You always wore black, like you were goin' to a goddamn funeral. Guess you chose right today, HEH?" His voice echoes.

I breathe through my nose to stay as silent as possible. Air rushes through my teeth after I lose the battle with my swelling nose. I feel the sticky goop on my lips. Guess I bashed my nose on the floor after all.

"Don't worry, we'll add some red!"

I bash into a stony wall, the force knocking me back. My ass bone singing in searing cries. The metal housings inside the backpack jab my spine. I roll to my side. Still pitch black, but from the thickness, I *know* the blood in my mouth is dark. I get to a crouch, feel around. No—no—NO! A dead end. That can't be. No! My hand drifts forward—wait. A cavity in the rock. My shoulders can squeeze through. My hands go first. Knees in. I *will* fit.

I shrug off the backpack and push it ahead. Cram one knee forward and slide into the hole. My own rapid breath swirls past my ears. The space is shrinking. Jason won't fit— but what if I get stuck? What if my chest can't expand to breathe? What if I suffocate down here?

God please—my backpack drops out of reach and thumps to a stop. *There's space on the other side!* I push harder, squeezing into the micro tunnel.

"About as sharp as a marble, aren't you?" his voice slithers up from behind me. His face must be right at my feet. "You know those old houses—the ones with doors that go nowhere?"

I jerk my shoulders, inching through, sweatshirt snagging.

"Like doors that open to brick walls? Or staircases that go straight to the ceiling? I don't know where I've seen it before... somewhere." He clears his throat. "Anyway, they call it a False Door. Creative, huh? That's what this is, this little hole. It don't go anywhere. You're not goin' anywhere either..."

His laugh booms through the tunnel. I wriggle free from the crevice, reaching for solid ground. I find it. Pull my legs out and grab the backpack. Scoot away from the opening— his laugh fading behind. I unzip the pack, fingers finding the metal-encased explosives. I dig in my pocket for matches. Strike one. The chamber flickers orange. It's not tiny— maybe big enough for two people to stand. Across from me: a pile of bones under a tattered flannel and ragged jeans.

Another pile sits a few feet to my right—a black blouse and pleated skirt rotting with the bones. I shift as far from the opening as possible. Jason's breathy grunts reverberate.

The flame burns my thumb, and with a shake of my hand, the blackness is back. I'm going to die here. Jason's going to lodge himself in that hole like a rabid animal and block my way with his corpse. And I'm going to suffocate. Why did I choose left? I should've just kept straight!

"FUUCKK!" I cry out. I consider giving up. Maybe that's the best option. Just curl into a ball and let what happens happen. Another sob is able to wrestle its way out my clutches and so, out of my throat. I lay on my side, drawing my knees to my chest in the blackness. When my head touches the floor it's soft—like a blanket. I turn my cheek into the fabric. It smells like salt and rot. Like earth, not flesh. My fingers trace up the wall—there's heavy cloth stuck at the top. I pull.

The blanket tears. Sea air rushes in.

A dim light glows from the wall. There's a passage—set deep in the far corner, hidden. "Ohhhh-oh, oh fuck," I cry, scrambling to my feet. I grab the backpack, squeeze through the narrow gap—and emerge into a *large* tunnel on the other side. I can *see*.

"Bitch!" Jason roars from somewhere far behind.

I run toward the silver light—ocean light. The cold wind slams the musk out of my lungs. It lifts the weight off my chest. I hear the surf crash. A buoy clangs in the distance. A foghorn moans. The tunnel curves. My shoes skid in the loose stones as I race. I stop in my tracks, sweat dripping from the tip of my nose. Like a soft, ungodly, foul whisper, a chill strangles my spine and lingers at my lower back and behind my ears.

The Beckett-thing stands in the large crooked opening, blocking my way to the outside. To freedom. To living.

"You aren't *REAAAL!*" I scream at the thing. It grunts in response, steam-breath shooting out from the canvas fabric. "Get out of my way, you antlered FUCK!" I scream again. A fog lifts from my skull. "Or maybe I blow this whole fuckin' place sky-high," I say, brandishing the half-unzipped backpack full of explosives.

With an inhuman roar, the monster clatters to the ground, its bones disappearing into the past, the blood-stained tarp catching the wind and swirling out into the open air, lost in the sea below.

"There's no way out, *bitch!*" Jason howls from the dark behind me.

I look ahead—to the night sky. Then down. Sheer drop. Fifty feet, maybe more. Rocks below. No surviving that.

And Jason is coming.

I turn and sprint back down the tunnel, just far enough to find a straightaway. I drop the backpack. Uncoil the long fuse from inside. Stretch it taut. I don't know how long it'll burn. Just need a little time.

I fumble for my matches. Strike one. A weak, flickering flame. I touch it to the fuse.

Sparks hiss to life.

I run. Run toward the tunnel mouth. Toward the sky.

My phone is heavy in my hand as I dial the landline.

My chest tightens. I *have* to say goodbye.

A relief I didn't expect floods me when I hear my own

voice on the answering machine. And then—my throat locks up. Because I realize I'll never hear *his* voice again.

And this... this will be the last time he hears mine.

Beeeeep...

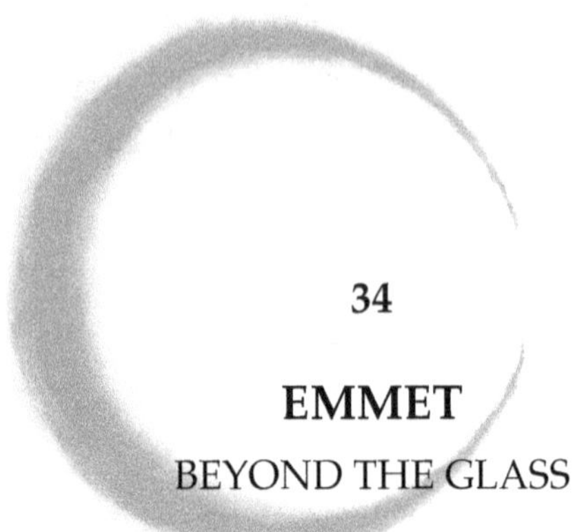

34

EMMET
BEYOND THE GLASS

THE FURTHER SOUTH I DRIVE, the easier I can breathe. Alissa sits shotgun, arms crossed. Head resting against the window, eyes puffy, red, and shimmering in the moonlight. She might think she's miserable now, but truth is, I'm saving her from misery. Just need to get her away from Heller—the place and the person. Might not be a perfect plan. More of a quick fix. But it's a call I can make, and if doing so ensures the safety of my kiddo? Well shit, who's not gonna make that call? I'm a father before I'm a cop. 'Spose sometimes I forget that.

"It's okay, girl," I assure her, placing a gentle hand atop her head. Don't ruffle her hair too much. I pull my hand away, thinking maybe she'll accuse me of treating her like the dog again. Damn, I miss that dog. Third dog that's run off or gone missing. I'm so goddamn unlikable even my pets run for the hills. I'm not the perfect father or husband, but I'm loyal. I give a shit, at least. Dammit, my kid doesn't deserve to pay for some dumb shit me and my friends did twenty-five goddamn years ago.

"I promise. It's all okay," I repeat.

Her eyes stare somewhere beyond the glass. "We've been driving for nearly five hours... and I gotta pee." She doesn't even acknowledge my reassurance. "I'd appreciate a rest stop." Her tone's cold. I don't like it, but I don't feel like I can say much right now.

"Sure, kid," I mutter, passing a sign for the next rest area. "Ten miles to go, can you make it?"

"Sure, I'll manage." Her head goes back to the window, fogging the glass as she sighs.

A few minutes later, I pull into the rest area—a sort of big roundabout off the highway. In the center sits a small brown brick structure with entrances on either side. A couple empty picnic benches sit to the left, a vacant grassy lot stretches to the right. Behind the building, a few Douglas-firs and a western hemlock guard the edge of the darkness. Down past them, beyond the black void, the Hodder River roars with invisible rapids. I clock an old Honda—dark blue—parked in the lot. Only other car out here. Probably just someone grabbing a few hours of shut-eye. Still. I grab Alissa's arm as she opens her door.

"Hold it a second," I say to her sharp eyes.

"I've been holding it, Dad." Her tone's got that sass again. Been that way for a few weeks now.

"Just do your old man a favor and let me make sure the coast is clear."

She doesn't answer with words—just a string of eye rolls and a grunt-sigh hybrid. If it translated to English, it'd probably be something like 'go fuck yourself, Sheriff Shitbag.' She closes the door, eyes fixed away from me.

I step out, close the door behind me. Tap on the hood.

Alissa knows that means lock the doors. I shine my flashlight toward the Honda. Nobody in the driver's seat. Can't help myself—I scan the back windows. Still nobody. I take a closer look. Doors are locked. Empty. Either it broke down and they got a lift, or someone's inside. Bathroom, maybe. Some loose gravel crunches under my boots as I turn toward the building.

"This is a little extra, even for you," Alissa calls from the car.

"I told you to stay in the goddamn car, 'Lissa."

"What're you gonna do, check every stall before I can pee?" She slams the cruiser's door and heads for the women's restroom. "We're like a hundred miles from Heller County and all its problems."

"I'm gonna do exactly that, girl. Hold your goddamn horses," I say, jogging across the lot to cut her off at the door. I twist the knob on the wall just inside—like a kitchen timer. The lights flicker on. Blinding fluorescent tubes hang from skinny chains off the grimy ceiling.

"Anybody in here?" I call, pushing one stall open after the other. "This is the Heller County Sheriff's Department—"

"Satisfied?" Alissa asks, already fed up.

"Hold on, hold on. I say, checking the last stall. Nobody. Even look inside the trash can in the corner of the bathroom. Some skinny little freak could scrunch himself down in there. Can't be too careful. "'Kay, I'm satisfied." I say as I step aside.

"Great," Alissa says shortly, before slamming the swinging stall door in my face. "Can't go with you standing out there." Alissa grumbles.

"Right, sorry," I say, exiting the bathroom. "Be right outside," I assure her as the door closes behind me.

I wait, eyes scanning the surrounding area. After a short minute, the whoosh of the toilet flushing roars from behind the door. I hear the clack of the stall door's latch. The steady stream of the sink, and the electronic hum of the paper towel dispenser. I poke my head in. "Alright kiddo, let's speed it up. Daddy's gotta take a leak."

Her face scrunches in the mirror as her reflection's eyes flick to me. "I'm not waiting for you in the men's room."

"Then get your ass in the cruiser. Let's move it."

"Fine." She tosses her scrunched up soggy paper towel in the trash. It hangs halfway on the lip, clinging to the black plastic. "Leave me the keys, please. I get no service out here. Maybe there's a radio station."

I walk her back to the cruiser, hand her the keys, open her door, shut it behind her. Tap the hood. Locks chunk.

The bathroom door squeals. I twist the little timer again. The lights buzz to life—one stays lit. The other fails, bathing the room in a sickly green-gray.

"Anybody in here?" I ask. My boot slips a little. I catch myself. The floor's flooded—not deep, but enough to coat the tiles. Slick as hell. Probably some asshole clogged a toilet and dipped. No answer. I make my way to the urinal, careful not to slip. A flash—a gut thought—of someone creeping up behind me while I'm pissing. I rethink the urinal. Too vulnerable. I take the second stall. First one's got no door and the bowl is overflowing with soggy, shit-covered paper. I latch the stall, don't bother with the belt or button—just unzip and go. A sharp chill rolls up my spine with the sudden relief. My piss echoes too loudly in the mostly empty room.

Then a sound. Soft. A hum. A tune. Familiar… but not quite. Probably Alissa. Found a radio station.

Hmmm-hm-hmmm-hm-hmmm-hmmm. A little louder this time. No, it's not from outside. It's coming from in here.

"Hello—"

The word locks in my throat as I realize I'm falling, something pulling my ankles from under the stall door. My chin smashes against the greasy toilet rim with a CRACK! I'm spitting white bloody pebbles as I'm pulled across the flooded bathroom floor. The back of my head smacks the bottom of the stall door, checking my chin to the floor. More blood, more teeth. The throbbing ache in my mouth comes after the shock of the cold water soaking my whole front. But the pain reminds me I'm in danger. I'm in a fight.

I grip my gun, yanking it from my hip as I roll over. The big black plastic trash can slams down on me before I can get off a shot. The gun sloshes across the bathroom floor. I swing my right leg into the shadowy legs of my attacker. He falls to the slimy tiles and I see the mask. I go for the gun, kicking off the stall to slide as far as I can. Black-gloved hands yank at my legs, pulling me back. He crawls up my legs, pouncing onto my torso. Black, misshapen eyes stare from a rotted soul. A knife glides into my ribs like I'm made of putty. I can't get Alissa's face out of my head. She's waiting. Counting on me.

"You leave my baby girl out of this! You hear me!" I shout through broken, blood-choked teeth.

"Aww. Don't worry, Daddy," the voice says—sounds like

Alissa, but *wrong*. "I'll be just. Fine." He laughs—a wet, chorus of demons.

He draws back the blade. That's when I really see it. Longer than my forearm. I'm gonna bleed out, no matter what. No one's getting here in time. I just need to stall long enough for Alissa to escape.

He places one hand over the other, cupping the knife's butt, ready to slam it down. And he does. I catch his wrist—but not fast enough. The blade dips—slashes my chin, maybe my cheek. Warm blood floods my collar. I shove back, but my strength's fading. The knife shakes above my face. My arms are jelly. My hands go numb.

Crunch.

The blade slides between my front teeth, tops and bottoms. What remains of them, at least. I keep my jaw clenched tight, pushing back with everything in me. But the cold edge slides down further, cracking and popping teeth out of place as it sinks deeper past my gums, gums that now split open and gush. I still clench my jaw, but the blade cuts further into the bone, popping open my mouth.

Chunk!

The blade sinks through the back of my throat, pinning my neck to the tiles beneath. My ears buzz and that buzzing turns to a high ringing. My body tries to gag with the knife lodged into my mouth. Feels like the muscles in the back of my throat flex around the blade, somehow sawing a larger wound. The bells in my ears sink to the bottom of a pool somewhere. I caugh as blood sucks into my airway.

Shink!

My head lifts with it as he pulls the knife out. Can't help but wonder what face I'm making. Can't really picture it. He stands up, seeming to study me. Blood, grime and water drips from the black vinyl draping over him. If it weren't for the mask, I'd say his expression was curious. Wondering how I'm still breathin' maybe. I crawl. It's the only thing I can do. I'm dying, but if I can warn Alissa...

He lets me crawl across the sopping floor, the blood from my wounds spilling into the pale green liquid. He seems almost intrigued. Curious how far I can make it before my body gives in. The water sloshes between my fingers and it burns. I glance my hands, and blood pours from both palms and across the fingers. I must've grabbed hold of the knife's blade at some point and didn't realize, maybe when he was pulling it out of my guts. He lets me crawl to the door. I squeeze my fingers under the door, between it and the jam. It opens a few inches as I slide further out, the headlights cut through the night.

Shunk!

The door slams on my fingers. The pain is blinding. I scream, a wet, bubbly mess of blood and noise. I look at my hands. They're pulp. Bone and flesh. Pink ribbons of what used to be fingers. Vision goes black around the edges. I try to hold on.

He drags me back.

The door swings open.

His boots splash water into my face.

When I close my mouth I swear I can feel air bubbling out the hole in the back of my neck.

He's going after Alissa.

The headlights glow behind him.

I reach with what's left of my hands. Wrap them around his boot.

He stops, looks down at me with his black eyes, but it's the third eye that has me. The one at the nose of my gun.

Tires squeal somewhere off in another place. Is that screaming too? Burnt rubber shoves its way past the blood clots in my nose.

Good girl.

35

DELSON
THE FOUNDERS' FIRE

I LIGHT a smoke on my way down the stairs, hack up the gunk from my lungs and send it flying into the front yard. People already have their dinky little grills out—charcoals burning—and I feel like I'm the last person out of bed at some backwoods family reunion. Some have their truck beds stacked with wood pallets, probably swiped from behind Safeway, or maybe the brewery. The Founders Fire festival has never seemed so significant or headline-worthy. But Blackroot has a sickness to burn out, and nowhere left to turn except tradition. But what good has tradition ever done anyone? Tradition's just an excuse to please a bunch of dead assholes who aren't around to answer for the state they left the world in. Fuck tradition.

I stop across the street from The Serpent. Several patrons fill the sidewalk lounge area—three small round wrought iron mesh tables and chairs. Horns blare and beep as I cross the road. I push through the door and slip past the small line at the register, cutting to the front.

Adele turns and sees me. The paper cup slips from her hands. Black coffee splashes at her feet.

"Delson!" She yanks a rag from her back pocket, drops it, then pushes the spill around with her shoe. The white cloth darkens quick. "I've been meaning to text, or—"

"Tell me you're not part of this."

Her eyes lock with mine. "I'm not. Delson, I'm so sorry."

"You really don't remember anything?" I press.

"Nothing. Whole days, just gone. I only know what the cops told me."

"You should be on a plane to anywhere else. Not here serving coffee to these small-town lifers." I hear grumbles behind me.

"I gotta make a living."

"At what cost?" I ask, but she just stares, eyes glossy. "Just be careful tonight," I say.

I stop at the pay phone near the gazebo, a few blocks from Town Hall. My fingers dig past the change and keys in my pocket, pull out the paper with the hospital's number. I pop in a couple quarters and dial carefully.

"Craven Creek Psychiatric Hospital." The voice buzzes from the other end, like some old-timey radio bleeding through this relic. I glance down at the chunk of black plastic in my hand, then tug on the metal cord as I speak.

"Morning... I'm just calling to check on my mother."

"You'll have to come in. We can't give out—"

I cut her off. "No—yeah, I get it. I just need to know if she's doing okay." I taste desperation on my tongue. "Like... did she hang herself with her sheets, or cut her wrists with a bedspring—"

"SIR, we cannot—"

"It's impossible for me to come in," I lie. "I'm out of town. Don't have money for a flight home." I pause. "Listen, I just wanna know if my mom's okay."

There's a long silence. Then a buzzy sigh. "Name, please?"

"Uh, mine or hers?" I ask, feeling stupid for needing clarification.

"The patient's, please, sir." She clicks her tongue. I give her my mother's name. The keyboard clatters like it was last used in the '90s. "She was discharged yesterday."

"Yesterday?" The plastic creaks in my tightening grip as I wonder where the hell my mom's been since yesterday.

"Yes, sir. Have a good day." The line clicks dead. A down-pitched dial tone moans in my ear.

I swallow that curveball and shove in a few more quarters. The old phone boops with each metallic click of the keys. It only rings once before he answers.

"Elias, listen to me," I say. "This is important. I gotta be quick. Leave your phone at home and meet me on the boardwalk." He tries to speak. "No. Just meet me." The whole chunky thing *CHINGS* as I slam the receiver down. I make one more quick call before heading to the boardwalk.

Farmer's market booths pock the roads—blocked off by orange cones—but end before the boardwalk. The crowd mostly hangs back. The fishy reek of the marina overpowers the scent of fresh produce. Gulls and pelicans swoop into the water. Seals bob up now and then.

"What's so important?" Elias calls from behind me. I turn.

"Delson!" Kenzie shouts, tearing away from her dad's hand and racing to me.

I scoop her up. Her smile warms the frigid hole in my chest.

"Where the HECK have you been?"

I set her down, kneel beside her. "You know I'd do anything for you, right, Kenzie-cakes?" She nods. "Good girl." I look at Elias. Stand. "You need to take Kenzie and your wife and leave town. Before tonight. Before the festival."

He lifts a hand. "I may not know exactly what's going on here but—"

"No. You have no idea. But if you've ever trusted me, trust me now."

"Delson, it's not that simple. It just isn't. And I'm not uprooting my family over something that... well, to be blunt, has nothing to do with us."

I bite my tongue. "This little girl is the most important thing in the world to me. You think they don't know that? You think they won't come for her just to get to me?"

He shakes his head. "What do you expect me to do?"

"Go home. Don't pack. Leave everything the way it is. Lights on. Fireplace going. Make it look like you're home. I'll call for a car. Leave yours in the driveway. Go to Hillcrest Airport. My friend will meet you. She has your tickets."

"Where are we going?" His arms cross.

"Doesn't matter. You won't be *here*. Please go." I kneel again beside Kenzie. "I love you."

"I love you too..." Her lower lip pouts as she clutches her father's hand. Her other hand grips the silver locket around her neck.

"I'll call you in the morning if I make it." I almost laugh.

"Dammit," he mutters. "Just come with us. If you're in that much danger—"

"It's not something I can run from," I say.

The dark, pungent muck beneath the boardwalk threatens to take my shoes if I go any farther, so I wait. Doesn't take long for Frankie to show.

"You bring it?" I get straight to it.

"First, tell me why you need it." Frankie tucks his thumbs under his backpack straps.

"You know why. Did you bring it or not?"

With a reluctant shrug, he drops the backpack, unzips it with a sigh. "You get caught with this, you didn't get it from me. Parole, remember?" He hands me the handgun.

"Don't worry." I check the clip. Loaded. Safety on.

He raises an eyebrow. "What, you don't trust me?"

"Just making sure it's loaded," I say.

"Rude as hell." He shuffles his feet, awkward. I wedge the gun into my waistband. "I put hollow points in the clip, so if it comes to it, you'll put a muthafucka down."

"A bullet's a bullet," I say.

"Hollow points expand and fragment. Multiple wound channels." He explains it anyway. I nod, letting him have it. "And Delson... no matter what... I love you, my guy. But I gotta be with Courtney at the hospital. Seeing as you're a cop magnet, I'm gonna dip, if that's okay. No offense."

"None taken." A quick hug.

Both cars still sit in the driveway. Elias' house looks exactly as I asked. Fireplace glowing. Scent of burning pine in the air. An unfinished lunch on the counter—PB&J with carrot sticks and hummus. Nathan, Rowan, and Luca arrive, all in black like me. Tonight, the shadows have allies. We do a full walkthrough. Every room, closet, nook. Place is empty. Takes a couple hours to set up the mini DV cams and sync the walkies. Each one perched in a corner. I check the tablet. One feed upstairs isn't working. The walkie buzzes.

"On it!" Nathan replies. "Tonight's the night."

"Bet," Luca says. "He's gonna pay for what he did to Eddie."

"For what they did to all of us," I say. "If anyone wants out, now's the time. No hard feelings."

"Tempting," Rowan says, rolling her eyes. "But I want to see this guy burn. Feels like I need to. Just to be sure." She scoffs. "We can't all have twenty-four-seven police protection."

"Alissa would be here if she could. She didn't have a choice." My tone's sharper than I mean.

"I'm just saying—well, isn't it a red flag that she disappears the night before it all goes down?" Rowan pushes.

"Shut up," I snap. Rowan's eyes widen, her head drops.

"Thanks for the vote of confidence," Alissa mutters behind us.

No telling how long she'd been standing there.

Rowan's eyes drop.

I turn. "What—how?"

She looks pale. Glassy-eyed. Black sweatshirt, black shirt, pants, shoes. "Took my dad's cruiser."

"Are you crazy?" I hug her. She doesn't hug back.

"We, uh, stopped at a rest area down south." Her voice is paper thin. "I, uh... I—" Her lips tremble, tears break. "I can't say for sure, but I'm pretty sure my dad's dead."

"What?" I ask, and everyone turns to her.

"Yeah. He was attacked in the bathroom. I didn't know what else to do. So I drove back before they could get me." Wide rivulets streak her cheeks.

Rowan plants a hand on her hip. "How'd you know where we are?"

My eyes narrow at Rowan. I look back to Alissa.

She stares at Rowan, like she can't believe the question. "I tried calling. Cordy's the only one who answered. She told me the plan." Her jaw clenches. Tears drip down her chin.

Nathan comes down the stairs. "Camera should work now—oh," he sees Alissa. "You decided to show after all."

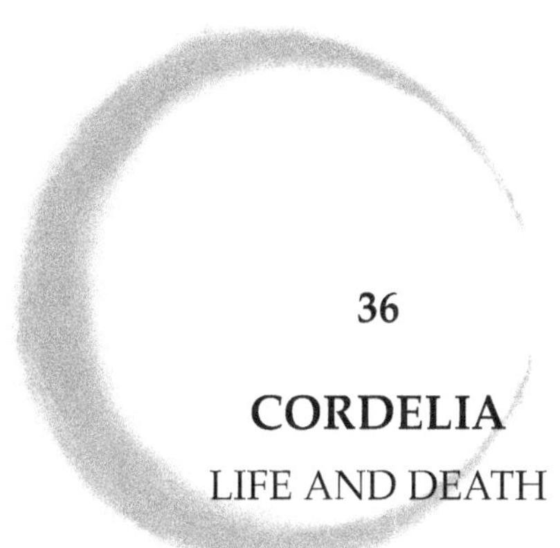

36

CORDELIA
LIFE AND DEATH

"Mom, I'm leaving!" I call upstairs.

"Where you goin', baby?" Her head tilts over the banister.

"Hillcrest," I say, holding the three plane tickets from Delson.

"What's in Hillcrest?"

"Hills. How wild is that?" I pause, waiting for her mom voice to strike. "I'm just doing someone a favor," I say, filling the silence.

"Not Delson, right?" Her voice drifts down.

"Why's that matter?" I shoot back. "I swear, y'all are tweaking."

"Come up here for a minute. I wanna show you something, baby."

"Can it wait?" She doesn't respond. I hear the sliding glass door open on the upstairs deck. "Mom?" I stomp up the stairs. "You're being reeeal sus right... now..." The white curtains billow toward me from the open sliding door, breathing icy air down the hall. The bleached-bone sky feels cold and suffocating, and I miss the LA sun like I miss childhood. I step onto the deck. "Mom?" I ask, looking up.

She's standing on the railing, back to the forest.

"What are you DOING?"

"Every attempt you make is more feeble than the last, baby girl. You think you're a survivor? You think he can save you? Give up."

"Mom!" I scream. "Please, p-please just get down!"

"I'm sorry you have to go through this." Her hair whips in the wind, black curls lashing across her eyes and mouth.

"Just get down!" I cry, stepping forward. Salty tears streak over my lips. "You hear me? Let her go! She doesn't have to die!" I scream into the wind.

A tender smile struggles to form on her snot-slick lips. She edges back on the railing.

"I love y—"

She steps backward.

A scream rips my throat raw as I lunge to the railing, reaching for her arms. But we don't even touch fingertips. The sound of her body hitting the ground—like a pumpkin smashed in a muddy field—robs me of breath. She lies crooked and still, three stories below. Her leg juts at a grotesque angle, white bone piercing through. I collapse.

That's when I see him.

The killer. The Blackroot Butcher. He stalks down the hall like a panther. His eyes—two dark asymmetrical voids—peer from beneath the sag of his hood. His mouth, twisted in a mask of agony, slack-jawed and lopsided. A sob bursts in my throat as I stagger to my feet. His leather face releases a cold, bubbling laugh. The plane tickets slip from my fingertips as the wind catches hold, ripping them away, sending them out somewhere over the forest.

My skin itches, wanting to jump from my bones. He's got me cornered like a rat. My heart tightens into a meaty ball as his boots clunk against the sliding-door frame. His knife lifts from the leather sheath on his hip, half hidden from the black poncho. The knife looks long enough to go through my gut and stick out the other side. A cold shudder tightens my muscles. I stumble back until I feel the wooden railing against my spine. I swing my leg over the railing, lift myself over, separating us by only small wood beams. My hands grip the broad handrail, feet wedged into two narrow gaps.

"Don't do this!" I cry.

He raises the knife. The blade flashes like silver bone in the pale sky. He slashes—and I drop.

The thin metal of my mom's van roof crumples beneath me. I can't breathe. I roll off the roof. My chest wheezes, airless. I crash to the ground, gasping. Rocks stab into my palms—no, glass. The van windows shattered. I gasp again. My lungs burn, but air comes. My muscles pinch from spine to calf as I try to stand, back locked tight.

"Ugh!" I groan.

I glance up at the deck. He's gone. I limp toward my car, keys in hand. The front door bursts open. He steps out, black vinyl flapping in the wind. I grit my teeth and run. My leg isn't broken, but something's pulled—maybe a pinched nerve. It makes the leg drag, but I beat him. I slam into the car, lock the doors, screaming. My hand shakes as if I've been plunged into ice, but the engine hums when I hit the button. As he reaches my door, I'm already flooring it. Tires spin and dirt flies.

"I did it!" I scream. "I fucking did it!" I sob as he watches in the distance, fading from my rearview mirror.

My heart plummets into my stomach like an iron ball as his face appears in the skinny mirror, sitting in the back seat! He grunts as a sharp, hot pain shoots into my lung. I realize the knife has gone through my seat and into my back, scraping bone, puncturing my lung. My mouth fills with hot liquid, and I'm too afraid to open it in case it's blood and not saliva. I swerve, my face bashing into the steering wheel, when I crash. White sparkles dance in my vision. Smoke stings my nose. Broken glass covers my lap. Tree bark shredded around me. The door opens and I fall out.

"Help meeee!" I scream, holding it as long as I can. "Please, somebody!" I inch forward, the mystery liquid pouring from my lips. Crawling in the dirt. The sound of my car door opening behind me freezes my spine. Boots crunch over broken twigs and glass. I don't want to die. I'm not ready.

"I'm scared!" I sob. "No—no-no. P-please don't do this. I don't wanna die. I don't wanna die!" I beg. I plead. Blood drips down my chin.

"Do you think there's something after?" he asks. The voices twist together—and for a moment, I swear I hear my mother's voice in the mess. "You think you'll see your mommy again?" This time, it *is* her voice. Clear. Gentle.

"I don't," the wicked voice says as the knife drives into my spine.

The pain collapses me. I grunt into the dirt, gasping, as the blade slides out and back in—smooth and easy. My arms curl to my chest. My vision shrinks. I won't accept this.

Please... wake up...

I WAKE, but only after believing I was lost forever in a cold, shadowy ocean. I still see the world through pinholes. It's quiet. I'm alone now. Dying alone. My fingers tremble. Numb as I pull my phone from my pocket, dirt sticking to the blood on my hands. It's hard to dial. I can't feel the phone.

"This is 911. Please state your emergency."

Darkness.

37

DELSON

FROM THE HOUSE OF HELLER

THE TOWN CELEBRATES as the cold dark of night snuffs out the last modicum of warmth. Orange flames rise from pyres of wood pallets, darkening the clouds as people raise glasses to celebrate the purging of evil from our town. Hope that some benevolent, intercepting hand will come down and abolish wickedness and perversion from our streets, our homes, and our lives. Sap the malevolent, nefarious, and ugly from here once and for all. Wasted cheers and misplaced faith. There is no divine hand. No intercepting good that stands above evil.

The house groans as I nudge the iron poker into the fireplace. The orange pulsing glow bounces off the hardwood floors and gleams off the banister leading up the stairs, where the crackle of burning wood shrinks into the dark. I leave the doors locked. Keep up the charade. Leave the primary bedroom lights on upstairs. I do a final radio check and receive confirmation from Nathan before switching to the other channel.

"It's time." My voice splinters out in a distorted choir from the walkie-talkies placed in all the high corners of the house. The foyer, my battleground. I take my place in the shadows. My heart clenches into a tight, meaty fist, slamming against the back of my sternum over and over. Unease trembles in my knees—for a moment. I shut it down. Swallowing gets hard. Breathing harder. Anticipation stabs like ice-tipped daggers in my gut. I wipe the sweat from my face. *Get yourself together.* I repeat it like scripture.

Chunk.

The front door's deadbolt chokes in the orange silence. My eyes snap to the tablet's feed. The large front door cracks open. Shoulders slouch, face hidden beneath a haggard mask tucked inside the shadow of a drawn black hood. The Butcher eases the door shut behind him—the fire's glow outlining every twitch of movement—casting a warped shadow across the wall. His head twitches on his shoulders like some prehistoric raptorial bird. His steps are cautious, almost diffident. He peeks through the arch into the living room. Then the kitchen. Darting around silently. The thud of his boots echoes like he's inside the walls. The closet I hide in feels more like a coffin. He stops dead in the foyer. His head tilts toward the stairs, toward the stream of light glowing from Elias and Kim's bedroom. One slow step at a time, he creeps upward.

I grip my walkie.

"I knew you'd come." My voice crackles through every corner of the house, ghosted in static.

His head snaps sideways. He freezes. Rotates in a circle.

"Knew you couldn't resist. The one thing that'd make me

break. The one thing that would take my purpose away. You sick fuck." I bite the inside of my cheek till I taste blood.

"**The role fits you well, Delson,**" the voices shrill out through the mask. Then he steps back. Slow. Intentional.

"What role would that be?"

"**Hunter...**" He stands in the foyer again.

"Tell me then, how's it feel to be hunted? To be trapped?" I seethe.

"**Trapped?**" he questions with an echo of sardonic maliciousness. "**You've only made it easier for us.**" His voices chuckle in the dark.

"Let's get something straight. You don't have me cornered. We aren't trapped. You are." I give the signal. Wait for Nathan with the bolt cutters on the second floor. The large crystal chandelier drops from the ceiling. Doesn't go as planned, but it smashes his shoulder on the way down. He falls to the floor. A mechanical grunt as he scrambles to his feet.

Luca bursts from the storage space under the stairs, a black figure, hood drawn up on his sweatshirt. Baseball bat collides with the masked man's ribs. Luca vanishes back into the shadows. The Killer's knife glimmers in the orange glow.

"How's it feel to be outnumbered?" I yell.

Rowan leaps from the kitchen archway—another black hood—crowbar raised high. She brings it down. The blow to his face knocks him back. He grips the bar to stay up.

"Must be hard to see in that thing..." I sneer, watching him adjust the grotesque mask.

Alissa appears from behind the bar, in the living room, a blade glinting orange in her hand. The kitchen knife plunges into his back—twice—before he knows she's there. He drops to his knees.

"Tell me..." My voice still crackles through the walkies as I step from the closet, slipping on a new face. "Does someone like you... ever feel *fear*?" The smell of old leather and dust seeps into my lungs. A strange power washes over me like cold, black water. I adjust Thomas Heller's mask, pull my hood up. Gun in my hand. The others join me in the foyer. The villain at our feet. "You will," I say, aiming the gun down at him.

"You want so badly, so deeply to be victorious." The voices hum out of the mask. **"You can't even see when you've been manipulated."**

"Just shoot him!" Luca insists. I steady the gun.

"Did you believe it would be this easy? Do you think wearing that mask gives you power?" the voices slow. **"Only a distraction."**

The resistance of the trigger pushes against my finger.

Phone vibrates in my pocket. "Bullshit!" I shout. "You're just buying yourself time." I spit at his feet.

"Time? *No*, I've got time. They don't."

"Who?"

"Answer your phone and find out."

I switch the gun to my left hand, keep him on the end of the barrel. Answer the phone. Screaming. Screaming for help. A woman's deep sobs. A little girl.

"Delson, don't let them hurt Kenzie!" Elias cries.

"I'm scared!" Kenzie wails.

"I swear to god, if you hurt them I'll *kill* you!" My hand shakes on the gun. "How do I know this is real? Not a recording? Not AI?"

"**It's real.**" My phone screen lights up—video call. "**They're waiting for you to come save them.**" His tone is casual. Cruel.

I answer. The camera's still—tripod mounted maybe. They sit in chairs. Bound. Elias bleeding from shoulder and lip. The video is dark, but I spot it—the big shop windows. The clocktower in the background. I grab a screenshot just before the feed cuts.

"You think this makes you vital? Essential?" My finger presses the trigger.

He lunges.

BAM!

The muzzle flash lights the room. I hit him center mass.

Not fast enough.

He tackles me. His knife stabs into my shoulder, halfway down the blade. Tissue. Bone. The heat of the blood runs over my chest, my neck. It pools in my shirt. The pain doesn't even register until he yanks it out. Then it's *white-hot.* Blinding. I see stars.

Blood sprays across my mask's mouth. Boots thunder past as he bolts across the foyer. Luca chases. I rise, stumbling, blood dripping. I aim. Fire three times.

All hits.

Still—he runs.

My hands won't stop shaking. *I missed again?* Luca swings the bat as the door opens. The bat cracks the frame as the figure ducks. An elbow crashes into Luca's mouth. The bat drops. Rolls down the porch steps. The knife slashes through the air—wild.

Luca grabs his arm, already bleeding.

The killer vanishes.

I RIP the mask from my face and race past Luca. Leap from the porch as Elias' car peels out of the driveway. I sprint down the street, screaming back for them to find the keys to the other car. Water splashes up my pant legs as I bomb down the shadowy sidewalk, smashing through puddles and knocking down trash cans. I throw off my hoodie. The fresh wound in my shoulder begins to burn and ache, feeling like my arm is being removed at the joint, stitch by stitch.

The town and the night are still. All but me, screaming down the road—bleeding, red-faced, manic. The streets have no eyes now. Nobody's watching. The bonfires on Opal Beach must be burning brightly tonight. The whole town gathered, celebrating. Burying our dark reality in some false sense of security. This town has done nothing for me. Turned its back on a child, left to fend for himself. Turned a blind eye to every bruise left by another strange man brought home by a drug-addicted mother. Said nothing about the ribs that peered out from the malnourished flesh of a small boy. No, this town has done nothing for me. To hell with it. To hell with the county. Burn it all to the ground. But Kenzie must be spared.

A horn honks behind headlights, tailing me. "Get in!" Alissa screams.

We blow through every stop sign and traffic light. As the clock tower comes into view, I open the passenger door. Rubber screeches against wet pavement as the car comes to a halt and I start on foot again. Glittering puddles reflect the pale yellow glow of the streetlights. The others trail behind me. The clock tower peers over the roofs of small businesses and shops. Watching over the madness from a distance.

"Start looking in windows!" I order. I examine the screengrab from the video call. Pore over the details. Consider the angle of the clock tower. Everyone spreads out. Luca checks Blackroot Books across the street. Nathan runs to the bail bonds place. Rowan peers through the windows of the Italian restaurant on the corner.

"Delson..." Alissa calls out. I realize it before she says another word. The angle of the clock tower. The large windows. The Serpent And The Rainbow. I race to her side, shine my phone light through the glass. The three of them sit tied to chairs. Kenzie is in full-blown hysteria. The others crowd beside us. I try the door. It's locked.

"Just break the windows!" Luca grunts, clutching his bloody arm. I hand the gun to Alissa. I grab the crowbar from Rowan and rear back, ready to shatter the glass—but I don't. "What are you doing?" Alissa's voice is cracked, desperate for resolution. I let the crowbar drop to my side. "Delson, talk to me." Her hands cradle my face.

"They're expecting me to do this," I say.

Luca grunts again. Eyes lift from his wound. "We got no time for this, bruh." Nathan rolls up his sleeves. "Let's just get them out, then we go after the guy."

I hesitate. "Don't think I can."

"Say less. I'll do it," Rowan growls, reaching for the crowbar. I yank it back. "If I'd just stopped and thought things through before, Edward wouldn't be dead." I grip the bar tighter. "There's another way in." I swing the crowbar into the window of the secondhand shop next door. The glass explodes. I knock away the remaining jagged shards. We funnel in through the gaping frame.

"What are we doing?" Alissa asks, stumbling through the dark, cluttered interior. Bookshelves and clothing racks crowd the room. Mannequins in dusty wedding dresses loom like ghosts. Surfboards and wetsuits line the back wall.

"This and The Serpent used to be one building. A bank," I say.

"So?" Luca pants.

"So I know a way through." I trail the shared wall, tapping the crowbar. *Bonk.* Hollow. After a few solid swings, drywall caves and the employee hallway in The Serpent appears. "Help!" I shout.

They tear at the opening, yanking away panels and splintered plaster until there's room for me to squeeze through.

"Delson, wait!" Alissa calls.

I creep down the back hallway, past the bathroom, and kneel at the corner. I shuffle behind the register. Kenzie's cries push my heart into my stomach. I notice their zip-tied wrists as Elias attempts to calm Kenzie down. There's a light ring from the blade as I pull it from the magnetic strip above the prep station. Crouched, I shuffle to Elias' side.

"Delson, it's a trap," he grunts.

"I know." I cut his wrists free, then his ankles. I move to Kenzie. She screams when she sees me. "Told you I'd never let anything happen to you." I kiss her forehead and free her.

Kim never stops crying—not until her ties are cut. She grabs Kenzie and bolts for the front door.

"NO!" I scream, spotting the tripwires glinting inches off the ground. Fine lines stretch across the floor, rigged to wooden contraptions on every side table. Mouse-trap-style devices, each fitted with red tubes. Kim's ankle snags one. The room erupts in white flashes and thunderous bursts. Kenzie hits the floor. Kim is battered back and forth—flesh and bone spray like butcher's pulp. Her body collapses in a wet heap of meat.

Gunpowder. Smoke. Kenzie's shrieks are heart-piercing. She keeps her eyes shut. I sweep her up and run. I unlock the door and squeeze her tight as I run for the sidewalk. Elias's scream will forever haunt me. He staggers through the door, joining me outside. He falls to his knees, vomiting in the gutter. I set Kenzie down. She clings to my leg as I rip her father from the ground.

"You need to get it together. Mackenzie can't see you like this." He lets out a sound I can only describe as unfiltered anguish. "Listen! Pull yourself together... she needs you."

"Daddy..." she whimpers. "Take the car. Go to the station," I tell him, placing her in his arms. Kenzie sobs into his chest as they run. "Delson!" Rowan screams from the wreckage behind us. "It's Alissa... She's gone!" Nathan stumbles through the door. "I swear she came in behind us..." Luca and Rowan follow him out.

The door to the secondhand shop creaks open. Alissa steps out, gun in hand, tears pouring from her blank, stunned eyes. "You can't save us." Her lips tremble. The barrel presses to her chest.

"NO!" I lunge. The gun fires as we hit the ground. Her head cracks against the doorframe. She goes still. The pistol clatters to the concrete. "Alissa, please... No!"

"Look out!" Nathan yells. He throws me from her body. The black figure in the doorway inserts a glimmering blade into Nathan's chest as easily as a rotten pumpkin. He wraps his arm around Nathan's neck and pulls him in. Three more to the chest in quick succession. Blood spurts as Nathan struggles, helpless, with his back to his killer. Airless screams mime on his bloody lips as his body drops.

Rowan screams. Luca yanks her away.

"C'mon, Delson!" he shouts, dragging me back.

The clock tower looms overhead as we run through the square. Rowan's screams echo down the hollow streets. Luca wheezes beside me. My vision flickers. I'm freezing. Bleeding out. A figure bursts from the alley. Slams Luca to the wall. His eyes plead. Rowan leaps to stop it. The Butcher drives his knife into Luca's chest, pinning him to the wall. A fist cracks into Rowan's face. She drops. The killer yanks the knife free. Luca slumps. Moaning. Drenched in red.

The killer's mask turns to me—blank black eyes, knife glistening.

"**I wouldn't run if I were you.**"

He points a gun at Rowan.

"**It's time you come to terms with this little... burden of ours.**"

I clench my fists. "Ours?"

A metallic click. "Tell me you knew it all along... felt it inside you." Rose's voice speaks from behind the mask. Takes a step toward me. Another metallic click. "Although," Eddie's voice now, "recent events have made me question whether we need you at all." Click. "**After that stunt back at the house... I'm not sure who I can trust!**" He rushes me, knife drawn back.

I duck into his body, plow my shoulder into his waist, and flip him over my back. I lose my footing and fall with him. We roll on the pavement. Both rise to our knees. I slam my fist into the mask. Sharp pain reverberates up my arm like ripples in water. As he falls back from the blow, I leap to my feet. With every savage swing of my leg, I pray I break ribs. Puncture a lung. Something! He rolls out of range, leaving the gun behind. I snatch it from the sidewalk. Follow him across the road as he runs, holding his ribs. He smashes through the double doors at the base of the clock tower.

I follow behind, chasing him to the top of the tower until there's nowhere left to run. He stands, his back facing the stone railing. A fall from here will kill.

I aim. The barrel barely a foot from his chest. I unload the weapon. Round after round. I fire until it clicks.

He stands still. Unharmed.

"What?" I stagger back.

"**Blanks.**" A short chuckle warbles from the mask.

Blanks? How? I don't understand. Doesn't make sense...

My heart goes cold with the realization. "Trueheart?"

He pulls off the hood. *Click.* "Hard being your friend, man. Like walking around with a target on your back." He drops the mask over the ledge. "Well, not this friend," Frankie sneers.

"Why?" My voice, just a hiccup.

"Why... Oh, I *knew* that was coming. I fuckin' *knew* it." He grins, blood leaking from his nose to his teeth. "Why why why—WHY!" He explodes, jabbing the bloody blade toward me. "Beckett Reid had a sister. I called her Mom. An she filled my head with prophecy, bloodlines, divine birthright. Tells me all about Beckett—my uncle *slash* father." He pauses. "Messed up, I know. Etcetera, etcetera. Left her fucked up in the head. I mean—WOW."

He seems reflective. "And after she blew her brains out, I

did some digging. Found you. Found your dad. "Wasn't hard to get my 'dad' to cozy up to your mom. Hell, that junkie bitch would've blown any asshole for a gram of meth. He spits. "The real kicker, though? My guy bails, and who swoops in to scoop up those sloppy seconds? *Rick*! My uncle. And I thought, no-fuckin'-shit, how could this be any more perfect? He was a loose end anyway. Had to die so I could truly take the mantle once all was said and done." He leans in, smiling. "That leaves me and you."

"Heavy is the head that wears the crown," I say.

"I can bear it," he snarls. "You and I—we could've been something great. *Horrific*, but great. Now I'm not so sure you deserve it."

"I don't want it. You can *have* it!"

"No no no," he whispers, stepping forward. "That's not how this ends. You gotta die."

"You're delusional."

"Determined," he corrects. "Like your pops. Gotta hand it to him. If anybody's determined to see this thing through, it's him. That's why he's the GOAT. But the way he talks about you—FUCK—it's like he thinks you're the second coming. Goddamn antichrist, our lord and savior, right?" He laughs to himself. "What, you surprised Daddy's a bad man after all?" Frankie spits; the snotty glob catches the wind and flies from the clock tower. "He's hardcore, man. Been in deep for years. Said he'd been waiting for me, knew I was coming and that he couldn't start until I joined the party. He's got some loose ends to deal with himself. I wonder if he's already killed your mom?"

I throw the handgun at his face, swooping in with a punch behind it. He turns his head as the gun strikes, flipping the knife upright in his hand. The blade flashes upward. I slam my arms down into the crook of his elbow, knocking the knife to the brick floor. I drive an elbow across his cheek. Lock my fingers behind his neck, yank him down. My knee shoots into his stomach. Again. His arms wedge between mine, swimming up until his hands clasp behind my neck and loosen my grip. He jerks my head down and buries a knee in my face. White flash. Blood floods my mouth. The tower tilts. The stone railing digs into my back as the sky spins above. Acid scorches my tongue, bitter and raw. Another hit. Another white-out. More stars. Again. I don't even know what's hitting me anymore.

"You wouldn't believe how easy it is to drug the people in this town," he pants. "They'll take anything. The Blackroot Society's alive and well—whether or not they know it. Blood is blood." He laughs. "You ever feel like you're being watched?" His grin twists.

"Not followers," I mumble, swollen lips sticky with blood.

"What's that?" he mocks, cupping a hand behind his ear. "Can't hear ya!"

"They aren't followers. They're drugged. It's power of suggestion."

"It's called obedience."

"It's called mind control."

"Yeah, well..." He presses a finger to his lips, shushing me like a lullaby.

A quick glance over the railing—Rowan still hasn't moved. Luca slouches against the herb shop wall, just as lifeless. A crumpled pile of clothes sits in the far corner of the tower. My eyes cut back to Frankie.

"Luca, don't!" I shout, eyes fixed behind him.

He whips around.

I tackle him to the floor. His face scrapes the brick. I flip him onto his back. Straddle him. Pin him down.

"Clever girl," he wheezes as I press down on his throat, grinding until my palm blisters.

My free hand balls into a fist. I slam it down into his face. Again. Again. Both fists now, one after the other. Harder. Wetter. Blood paints my knuckles and splashes across his already caved-in face. One hit for every victim. That's how it starts. One for every person affected.

Hard to see. Gets dark. Chest expands, pulling in deep the air I was neglecting my brain and muscles. I grab either side of Frankie's face. Nails dig into the already lumpy, slimy red flesh. Sparkles dot my sight again, screaming out some kind of primal howl of victory. Like tossing stones in a wood chipper, the gravelly roar flares from my throat. Vision spins. Lungs burn. My arms tremble with rage and blood loss.

"Don't move!" Jenna's voice cuts through the storm as she charges up the stairs, gun leveled.

I collapse onto my back. My chest heaves, filling with cold air.

"It's him." I gasp, a knife of breath slicing into my lungs as the knot in my throat snaps. My limbs go slack. My head floats, the pulse in my ears louder now than Jenna's voice.

She kneels beside Frankie, fingers to his ruined neck.

"He's alive." Her eyes shift to mine as I lie there, defense-less. "I'm gonna get you out, Delson. Stay with me, okay?" She fumbles for her phone.

I nod. Try to stay awake. I close my eyes. No! Not yet. Not now. I open them.

The hooded figure looms over Jenna. I try to speak her name, but all I manage is a broken breath. The orange brick crashes down on her head. She collapses over Frankie's body. A boot slams into her skull before she can move. She slumps to the railing, barely catching herself, chin dripping over the edge. Jenna lets herself slide down to the bricks, sitting now, dazed.

The phantom snatches her gun and fires every round into Jenna's chest. I watch in helpless horror as Jenna curls in on herself. He tosses the weapon over the side. Black holes for eyes watch me as he brings a boot down on Jenna's phone, snuffing out the tiny voice of the police dispatcher. The Butcher hovers over me as the needle punctures my neck. The liquid burns as the plunger is pressed down. I try to speak. No actual words form. Gloved hands inch for the mask. The figure comes into focus as the hood pulls back and the leather face falls.

I try to say her name. I close my eyes, only to reopen them and see her kneeling over me. *Alissa...*

"No, beautiful boy. It's not your turn to speak." She smiles crookedly as she tosses her long black gear. Removing her gloves, she shushes me. Her red hair goes wild as she unravels the braid. A small, dark red dribble leaks from her nose. "I know you must be confused... hurt, even. I'm sure you want to know why." She sniffs. "Well... so would I. But sometimes, things just are."

My body won't move. I don't know if it's blood loss, the drug, or shock.

"You're fucking psychotic." I spit, jaw clenched.

"Stand."

My body obeys her command. Against everything I want.

She smirks. "You actually bought all that Blackroot Society garbage?" She chuckles. "Such a bad look. Gotta give it to Frankie, though. He really believed all that mystical witchy crap. I mean—he's the real crazy one here, not me." She glances down, drives a savage kick into his mangled face. "I was hoping he'd just die back at the house."

"You're crazier than he is if you think you'll get away with this." I growl.

"You only speak when I tell you to." She growls. A quick smile. "I've already gotten away with this. The police have their culprit right here." She gestures to Frankie. "The witch hunt ends. Everybody's happy." She pauses. "Take this." She hands me her monstrous knife.

She undresses—down to her underwear—letting her snake skin shed and fly away from the tower to some alleyway down below. Her red hair twists and flaps in the gale, like undulating tentacles made of fire. Her skin grows rigid and bumpy as she shivers, slipping on the clothes left stuffed in one corner between two stone balusters. A light brown crewneck sweater and black leggings. She slips her boots back on before approaching me.

"Cut me." She points to her face, dragging a finger from the top of her left cheek down and across, over her lips to the start of her chin.

Blood runs from the shallow wound as I pull the knife away. My throat closes when I try to speak.

"Organized religion is a huge ick for me. And that's all the Society really is—religion. Your dad doesn't get that though, like every other small-minded self-absorbed radical..." She rolls her eyes. "Millennials, am I right?" She laughs. "If I have to kill him, I will."

She taps her chest. "This hunger… this gnawing, scratching, howling thing in me? It's still there. But for the first time… I feel full. Whole." She sighs. "All I had to do was convince Frankie I was Manson Family material. Easy."

She leans in. Kisses me.

The warm, coppery liquid runs over my lips and tongue, drips down my chin. She breaks away. Points to her shoulder.

"Here."

I drive the blade in. She screams as it scrapes bone.

"I hope you liked that!" She howls at Frankie's lifeless body. She stomps his face. "Give me the knife."

I give it.

She tosses it beside him. "Hit me."

I do.

Her head whips sideways from the slap. My hand stings.

"Again! Like you did Frankie!"

I attack.

Revulsion.

Malice.

Animosity.

Hate.

Knuckles split further as I sit atop her, bashing her head back and forth with each punch. Every strike only stretches her grin wider, teeth red and gritted through the blood.

"Enough." She gulps a sharp breath. "Get up." Her face is pulp—bloody and barely holding shape—but she staggers to her feet anyway. "Frankie couldn't make up his mind about you. I, however, couldn't be more sure." A laugh rumbles from her chest. "You got me all fucked up." She chuckles again. "Being with you was like reliving my first kill all over again... minus the barking and yipping." Her face glows with something sick. "I'm down bad. Like, bad bad. Sheesh, I might even love you."

Her face leans in. Swollen lips hover over mine.

"How fucked up is that?" she whispers, wearing a smile crooked and bloody.

A lament of sirens rise in the distance, growing louder with the wind. She breathes in slowly, wiping away any trace of panic with the back of her hand.

"I want you to help me downstairs," she says softly. "We'll collapse in the street together. Play it out." She takes my hand. "Forget my part in all this. It was Frankie—with your dad. They did everything. They admitted to it. The murders. The drugs. All of it."

We lie side by side on the cold street. Her fingers slip between mine.

"I'm just an innocent victim," she murmurs. "A girl who stole her dad's cop car to rescue the boy she loves. If it weren't for me, you'd be dead."

And just like that, the image comes together. Ugly pieces fitting snug. A perfect lie taking form.

BLUE and red lights flood the street, casting warped shadows up the sides of buildings. Alissa lies beside me—bloody, broken. Her hair, soaked and tangled.

It gets dark again. I don't remember coming down the tower. Voices echo. Radio static. Fire trucks scream. Lights flash, too bright and too loud. My head floats, the edges of my vision pulsing like a heartbeat. Yellow tape flaps in the breeze. Road flares burn at the edge of chaos. Cops form a wall, blocking cameras and questions.

Paramedics lift Luca onto a stretcher. He's unconscious, but alive.

Jenna Darkly sits upright in the back of an ambulance, shirt ripped open, revealing a kevlar vest, eyes never leaving me as someone tends to her wounds. They lift Frankie, strapped to a gurney, into the back of the ambulance. His stare is cold and patient and dark, so much unlike the eyes that belonged to my friend. The doors close, and he's taken away, police tailing.

Rowan screams as she wakes on the pavement.

"We got a live one!" an officer shouts as he runs to her. Other first responders dash to the officer's side. Rowan screams my name as she's lifted into the back of an ambulance.

"DELSON!" she screams again.

The EMTs slide something under me, and I feel myself rise. Glide. I turn my face from the flashing lights. My body, strapped down to the stretcher, leaves me feeling too restricted. Powerless. Alissa's hand grabs mine as she's wheeled past. A sickly weight slumps off me. The tightness in my chest eases for the first time in weeks as she watches me from the back of the ambulance. Her lip twitches into a sort of smile. The treachery seeps away like blood from a fresh wound, circling the shower drain.

Shadows slump. Cuts close. Scars form.

Still, something crawls at the edge of my thoughts—a low hum of dread. Foreboding. Maybe disbelief. Or maybe I'm just not ready to believe it's really over. Maybe none of us are.

"Over the course of a year," a reporter's voice echoes in the dark space behind my eyes, "the community of Blackroot has endured wave after wave of tragedy. Tonight, it came to a head during the Founders Fire festival, leaving six confirmed dead, several others in critical condition, and one man in custody. Local seventeen-year-old Delson Heller and his friends were reportedly the prime targets of the masked killer, who was allegedly inspired by the now-defunct cult known to locals as The Blackroot Society."

The voice continues.

"Tonight may be the first night in a long time that the residents of our small town will feel safe going to bed with the lights out."

EPILOGUE
WHEREVER THEY WAIT

"You sure you're ready?" Luca asks as we pull into the driveway.

"It's my house, I—" I pause, realigning the thought. "Listen, I'll tell your mom I appreciate everything, but it's time I move back in. I'm good, man."

We both flinch when a fist raps on Luca's window.

"You girls done with the yapfest or what?" Rowan smirks through the glass. "Check the fit, though. It's giving Winter-Fall... Is maroon my color?" She gives a little spin as we step out of Luca's car.

"It's definitely *your* color," I say to Alissa, right before our lips meet in a quick, soft kiss. Sweat beads along my brow. The muggy summer heat finally bears down.

Alissa smiles, her eyes peeking from behind the glossy forest-green tassel dangling from her burgundy cap. The scar tracing her cheek, across her lips, and down to her chin is now just a faint silver thread.

"Aww... barf," Rowan teases, grinning at us.

The four of us climb the porch steps, like we've done every Friday for the past six months. Somehow, this house has become our place. A place to talk about everything that happened. About everyone we lost. A place where we can unravel, no questions asked. No one demanding we be okay, because the truth is, none of us is okay.

Rowan squeezes past me and through the door, making her way down the hall to the kitchen. Alissa gently holds the fingers of my right hand as we cross into the living room. Luca tosses his gown over his body, his head rearing up through the burgundy fabric before popping through the top. His arms flail out, billowing the gown around him. He snaps the elastic of the cap around his head and the green tassel sways as he marches toward the kitchen.

Alissa glares at me expectantly, suppressing a smile.

"I left mine in the car," I smirk.

"Where the shot glasses at, Del?" Rowan yells from the kitchen.

I walk over to her and Luca, Alissa still holding my hand. Rowan's posted at the dish drainer where the shot glasses used to be.

"Cupboard to your left," I tell her.

"Since when?" she laughs, opening it to find the glasses.

The freezer lets out a sticky crackle as she yanks it open. She pulls out the bottle from last weekend—still half full of that fiery clear liquid. She slams the freezer shut with the hand gripping the bottle's neck and leads us back to the living room. Carefully, she pours four shots.

We each take one. Rowan fumbles with hers as her phone buzzes under her gown.

"Must be Cordy!" she says, digging it out.

"You weren't about to toast without me, were you?" Cordy grins from Rowan's screen, raising a crystal-clear shot of something top-shelf.

"How's the PT?" I ask.

"How's Seattle?" Rowan chimes in.

"It's good. I'm finally wheeling around on my own pretty well."

"Yeah babe, you're looking swole!" Luca beams.

"Oh, bet!" Cordy says, flexing her toned arms. "My dad's all pissed. I wheeled myself six blocks for a bagel and a protein shake without telling him yesterday. Now he's full-on helicopter mode." She pauses, her voice softening. "I miss you guys."

"We miss you too..." Rowan replies.

"Wish I was graduating with you all today."

"We do too, Cordy," I say.

"To us," Rowan says, lifting her glass.

"To us," we echo. All four shots go down in unison.

We slam our glasses down and head for the front door.

"Oh wait!" Rowan exclaims, handing Cordy's video call to Luca. "This is perfect." She reaches up to the cluttered shelf above the TV. She grabs a tall silver flask, and an old baseball rolls off with it, bouncing across the carpet. Something black and plastic clatters against the entertainment center.

"Who even has a landline anymore?" Rowan mutters, uncapping the flask.

I kneel down and pick up the clunky plastic phone. The small screen blinks: missed call. One voicemail. I freeze. The number stretches across the display, each digit clawing at me. My mom's number.

"You coming?" Alissa calls from the doorway. Rowan and Luca are already outside, still talking to Cordy.

"In just a minute…" I answer.

They step into the driveway. The June sun gleams off Rowan's car.

The phone beeps as I hit play.

"Hi, Delson. It's… it's Mom. I don't know if you'll ever hear this, but I don't have any other choice. I'm so sorry, sweetheart. I've let you down in so many ways. And now I'm standing here, thinking about you. I remember when you could fit in my arms. My little baby."

Her voice trembles. She sounds swollen, like she's crying through cotton.

"You were so small, so fragile… but you filled my heart with so much love. My baby boy. I promised myself I would always protect you. Always be there for you. Be a real mommy. But I broke that promise, didn't I? The drugs, the mistakes… they took everything from me. Including the chance to be the kind of mom you deserved."

She exhales, as if steadying herself.

"I'm scared, baby. Scared of what happens next. I wish I could turn back time—rewrite our story. Make it right. Make it happy. Make *you* happy. But I can't. All I can do now is tell you that I love you. That you're the light in my darkness. That you're the only hope I hold on to, even as everything else slips away. Please, if you can… forgive me. And know that wherever I go, I'll be watching over you and your sister. Loving you both with all that's left of me, out there. Somewhere. Goodbye, my beautiful boy. I'm so sorr—"

The message cuts off. Static hums in its place. And like that, she's gone.

My thumb hovers over the green button to replay the message. I *want* to relive that moment again and again.

Instead, I press down on the other and delete the voicemail. My vision blurs with hot, runny tears.

I slowly come to my feet, staring at the phone in my hand, wishing I could tell her I forgive her, that I miss her, and that wherever she is, I love her too. But I don't—because I'd want her to answer me back.

I place the phone back on its receiver.

I think of Edward. Of Rose. Of everything we survived.

A warm breeze drifts through the open door, brushing over my skin. It carries the scent of fresh-cut grass and cinnamon—something I might call *childhood* if it needed a name. And somewhere far away, a set of wind chimes gently sing. Some place beyond all this. Far away, where the ones we've lost wait for us.

Outside in the sun, standing in the front yard, my friends wait for me. Laughing. Smiling. But in every pair of eyes, I see it—a complex tangle of emotion. A kind of haunted anticipation. I don't know if it ever goes away. Maybe it never will.

So, no. The truth is, none of us are *okay*. Maybe someday we will be.

But for now, maybe not being okay... is okay.

ABOUT THE AUTHOR

Dylan DeGrave is a horror author from the misty redwoods of Northern California's Humboldt County, a place where the line between beauty and darkness sometimes blurs, and every shadow has a story.

Heller is Dylan's debut novel.

For more information and updates:
www.dylandegrave.com